A TALE OF DRUNKEN MONKEYS

Book 2 in the Hero of Thera series

ERIC NYLUND

A THOUSAND DRUNKEN MONKEYS

Copyright © 2019 by Eric Nylund. All rights reserved.

First print edition: January 2019

ISBN-10: 0-9862969-4-5

ISBN-13: 978-0-9862969-4-9

Cover: SelfPubBookCovers.com/SFcovers

No part of this book may be reproduced, scanned, or distributed in any printed or electronic form without permission, except in the case of brief quotations used in critical articles and reviews. Please do not encourage piracy of copyrighted material in violation of the author's rights. Thank you for respecting the hard work of this author.

This is a work of fiction. Names, characters, places, and incidents either are the product of the author's imagination or are used fictitiously, and any resemblances to locales, events, business establishments, or an actual person—living or dead—is entirely coincident.

DEDICATION

~To my family~

A small but merry band of adventurers are we.

ACKNOWLEDGEMENTS

First, many thanks to my family for, as usual, putting up with the time away from them and the required authorial grumblings that go into any novel.

More thanks to...

Syne, my alpha reader, for saving me from grave embarrassment, and for the neverending writer-to-writer life support.

My beta readers, Fred, Stuart, Jerry & Gina—for their eagle eyes. You have all earned the "Ranger Editor" achievement.

My gaming buddies for their camaraderie and the countless hours of mirth and inspiration.

And my readers for your encouragement and patience over the years.

AUTHOR'S NOTE

Hi. It's good to be with you again.

Two quick things.

First, following this note is a brief reminder of the people and events in the first novel as well as a "character sheet" for Hektor Saint-Savage. Some of you appreciate these things; however, if you're not one of them, or if you've just read *Hero of Thera*—please skip this prologue and start at Chapter 1.

Second, many of you have given, or have read *Hero of Thera* to your kids. I'm honored. Thank you. While that first book in the series had its fair share of violence, it was mostly directed toward monsters. That changes a bit in *A Thousand Drunken Monkeys* as there is more violence on a human scale. Think of this as PG-13 content, the Gaming (ESRB) equivalent of "T" or the (PEGI) equivalent of 12+.

In any event, welcome back to Thera!

Pull up a stool, let me buy you a Silvercrest Ale, and I'll tell you a story.

PROLOGUE

I play therefore I am.

Ego ludere ergo sum.

Yeah, I just mangled Descartes' "*I think therefore I am*," and possibly the Latin language. Sorry about that.

I am Hektor Saint-Savage, and I play a gypsy elf martial artist in the Game. I was formerly Hector Savage of Earth, Marine, ex-Death Row inmate, and life-long gamer.

What *is* this capital-G Game?

To explain, I have to go back to the beginning of... *everything*.

BANG! *Let there be light*!

Or whichever creation story you prefer; they all have a little bit of truth in them.

I'll just stick to the one I know. Shortly after the Big Bang, as the first protons and neutrons cooled from the surrounding gluon-quark soup, the proud architects of Creation patted themselves on the back—then started to argue, and finally fight over who would run the thing.

Only after these gods, demon princes, and other super-entities of power had almost obliterated the multiverse, did it dawn upon them that maybe they needed a *less destructive* way to settle this issue.

That way was the Game.

The easiest way to think of the Game is as the biggest version of role-playing RISK ever.

With three crucial differences.

First, to run their Game, the gods begat an impartial Game Master. This GM makes and enforces the rules, and within its limited domain is more powerful than the gods who created it.

Second, the Game primarily plays out in the Kingdom of Thera. It is a magical realm with gateways to many other worlds and realities—the crossroads of the multiverse, if you will.

And third, the gods don't play the Game themselves. They field clans of mortals to play (and die) for them. We players level up and complete quests to gain points. When one side gains a majority of the points in the Game, they win—everything.

Pretty straightforward, right?

Wrong.

In the twelve thousand years the Game has been running, no one side has ever come close to winning.

...Because it's *rigged* by the Game Master.

How can the GM be an impartial referee in the Game *and* cheat? Simple. Impartial just means treating everyone equally, which he is doing—by equally cheating against *all* the gods.

The Game Master does this because he believes if one side won it would be... well, it's hard to come up with a word that describes the genocide of most of the sentience in all Creation.

Imagine, for example, if some demon prince was victorious. They might transform all existence into their personal torture chamber. Even if a relatively benign entity won the Game, what do you think would happen to everyone ruled by the other gods?

Extinction on an unfathomable level—a quadrillion quadrillion souls snuffed.

No one (at least, no one sane) wants that.

I know this is a lot to digest, but contrary to what Einstein thought, the gods *do* indeed play with dice (metaphorically speaking).

How do *I* know all this?

Ah, good question.

I was originally recruited into the Game by some of those aforementioned demon princes (doing business as "The Lords of the Abyss"). Long story short: I escaped their diabolical clutches and went to work for the Game Master.

Now we're trying to keep the Game spinning along without a winner, and give people like you and me a chance to simply stay alive and figure things out for ourselves.

Okay, that's enough about the metaphysical details of the Game.

Let's get to the *juicy* details.

I play a "Spirit Warrior," the type of martial artist you might see in any good Hong Kong action flick—with a little chi-powered battle magic added for good measure. Cool, huh?

My current STATS and abilities are:

Hektor Saint-Savage
Spirit Warrior / LEVEL 4
Clan: Hero of Thera
Race: Gypsy Elf

BODY: 11
    STRENGTH: 3
    REFLEX: 8
    HEALTH: 120

MIND: 3
    INTELLECT: 0
    PERCEPTION: 3

SOUL: 6
    EGO: 3
    GHOST: 3
    MANA: 60

Spirit Warrior Passive Abilities
Fists of Steel (tier 3; *maximum*): Hit armored opponents without damaging yourself. Bonus damage increases with STRENGTH and REFLEX. May strike creatures that normally require silver, iron, or magical weapons to hit—or are incorporeal, out-of-phase, or dimensionally shifted.

Spirit Armor: Chi-created forcefield aura. Increased armor based on your SOUL stat and LEVEL.

Spiritual Mana: Gain a mana pool based on your SOUL stat.

Wire Work (tier 1): Partially defy gravity in the tradition of martial arts movies.

Spirit Warrior Active Abilities
Perfect Motion (tier 3; *maximum*): Zen-like trance in which combat and move speed increase by 100% for 10 minutes. Cost: 20 mana.

Spiritual Regeneration (tier 2): Regain health = (two points + ability tier) multiplied by your SOUL stat. Cost: 10 mana.

Non-Combat Skills
Bargaining (5/30): Know fair prices, seasonal variations, and may gain bonus information on items. Sell goods for more. Buy them for less.
Ride (Animal) (3/30): Use animals as a means of conveyance.

Languages
English (4/30): *North American* dialect.
Tradespeak (4/30): Common *Esperanto*-like dialect.
Elven (4/30): *Gypsy elf* dialect.
Elven, Dwarven, Hobbit, and *Gnomish* (1/30).

Jal'Tek (3/30): Synthetic language used by Theran royals, courtiers, and spies.

Racial and Character-Specific Skills & Abilities
Night vision equivalent to that of a cat's.
Immune to aging effects and spells.
Minor resistance to hostile magic.
Chance to detect dimensional portals within 100 feet.
Evolution (hands mutated by radioactive magic): +1 to REFLEX, ambidextrous, and an extra finger on each hand.
Charmed birthmark (4-leaf clover over heart): Effects unknown.

Achievements
The Hero's Scar (aka *The Fool's Star*): You have challenged a demigod-like entity and lived. This icon may be displayed on your player placard so others will recognize your exceptional toughness.

Taunting Tenor (achievement-acquired skill, no skill tier): If you overcome an opponent with your insults, they are *forced* to attack you for a period determined by the severity of those insults.

    I had just advanced from a third- to a fourth-level Spirit Warrior. Actually, I have enough experience points to make fourth level, but haven't yet officially committed to it. Once I do, I'll have the following points to improve my STATS, skills, and abilities (or buy new ones):

Stat Points: 4
Combat Skill Points: 3
Non-Combat Skill Points: 27
Unassigned Starting Languages: 3

I still have to figure out the best combination of skills and classes to maximize my survivability in Thera—only then, will I spend those points. I'd been rushed through the character creation process, and every time I'd leveled up since it has been on the run or under pressure. It was time to take a breath and do this right for once.

I also needed to invest the loot from my recent adventures on a serious gear upgrade, and then spend some time with fine company and a wide selection of well-deserved ales.

Before the party begins, however, it's probably best if I remind you what those "recent adventures" were and of the "fine company" I keep (a few of them are actually not-so-fine).

For my first quest in the Game, I had to stop a cultist from summoning some eldrich nightmare from the great beyond. This turned out to be part of a coordinated invasion of Thera, which my comrades and I ultimately thwarted by defeating an army of demons. I had a little help from a pair of evil artifact gauntlets, and almost lost my soul and sanity to the things in the process (but that's another story).

One other adventure worth mentioning was when I broke the death curse of some barbarian ghosts. Every night for the last ten years, they'd had to fight a cabal of evil wizard spirits, neither side ever winning. I helped the barbarians finally defeat the wizards and as a reward, their leader, Karkanal Kayestral, told me of a martial artist among his tribesmen who would teach me a technique or two.

Or, in Game terms, I got this pop-up alert:

NEW QUEST UNLOCKED
"A THOUSAND DRUNKEN MONKEYS"
Find the old martial artist among the
Far Field barbarian tribes.
Reward(s): Bonus experience and new bonus skill.
Suggested Party: N/A

Accept? YES / NO

When I get back to adventuring, that would go to the top of my to-do list.

Now, on to the "fine company" I mentioned.

First, there's Morgana Nox, a player working for the Tricksters LLC clan. A former biology teacher from an alternate version of my Earth, she's smart, beautiful, and a particularly resourceful multiclass druid-thief.

Next, there's Sir Pendric Ragnivald, a non-player knight who's sometimes fearless, sometimes timid, and also happens to be half Valkyrie. He was raised in Valhalla and trained by the greatest warriors in history. Alas, he decided he'd had enough "adventures" and left to wander alone for a time. He has... uh, personal issues to figure out.

Then, there's Elmac, the geriatric non-player dwarven barkeep. He was once the Grand General of all the Armies of High Hill, so he's a fearsome warrior despite his advanced years (and his equally fearsome thirst for large quantities of alcohol).

Although I've known them for only a few days—we've fought side-by-side, saved each other's lives—and I consider them the best friends I've ever had in either of my incarnations.

Now, unfortunately, we come to the *not*-so-fine company I keep.

Colonel Sabella Delacroix is an elven solar sorceress and the head of High Hill's secret police. She helped us defeat the demonic army, but she's more of a lukewarm acquaintance than a friend. She's snooty, terrifyingly powerful, and suspects that I had more to do with that demonic invasion than simply stopping it (and since the machinations of the gods, their players, and the Game Master were all tangled up in that event, she's not wrong).

Since, however, the Duke of High Hill officially recognized me as a "hero who saved the day," Colonel Delacroix can't *quite* justify tossing me into her dungeon and extracting my secrets. For now.

And at the bottom of this list (where he belongs) is my brother, William "the Bloody" Savage. He's a sixteenth-level anti-paladin player who works for the Lords of the Abyss, and was the guy leading that invading army of demons.

Every family has their black sheep; mine has a rabid dire wolf.

Bill is sitting in Colonel Delacroix's dungeon right now having a nice long discussion without a lawyer.

If this all seems like a lot for my first few days in Thera... I completely agree.

I figured I had three, maybe four, weeks of rest coming.

Regrettably, like Odysseus, Faust, and a host of other heroes who irritated the gods or demon princes—my luck tended toward the worst side of bad.

So, my plans to eat, drink, and be merry were about to take a detour to murder, mayhem, and heartbreak.

Well, so it goes.

CHAPTER 1

A quest! Nothing stirs the blood of a gamer like a gallop through fog-shrouded woods with an accompanying soundtrack of Wagner's *Ride of the Valkyries* or Metallica's *The Four Horsemen* (take your pick of the classics). Beyond yonder misty mountain we'll find a dragon's cavern filled with gold and a Princess or Prince desperate for their heroic rescue.

Unfortunately, the Game *I* play has no accompanying soundtrack.

Nor any eager-to-be-rescued princesses.

It's messier, too... as in how was I supposed to keep raw sewage off my new troll-skin boots?

Alas, I was *not* galloping toward glory, riches, and my one true love. Tonight, I was in Low District—still wondrous High Hill, but the worst part of town, basically a place where tourists like me ended up on HAVE YOU SEEN THIS PERSON? flyers.

I suspected every fantasy city had one of these places. When L. Frank Baum wrote of the Emerald City, I'd bet good silver that he omitted at least one alley filled with drunk munchkins pissing themselves. Stuff like that didn't sit well with readers who like their heroes sparkling—their damsels virginal—and a big fat happy in their endings.

There were no working gas street lamps here, but countless stars twinkled overhead along with two Theran moons, the marmalade-colored orb called Guda, and keeping her company was her brother, the porcelain sickle, Asago.

Keeping *me* company tonight was my pal, the geriatric, cantankerous, and definitely *un*-luminous dwarf, Elmac Arguson.

We stood under the eave of an abandoned butcher shop. A faded sign showed dotted lines crisscrossing an ironically smiling cow.

Notices had been tacked to one wall, most torn with just bits remaining, like:

We enchant weapons
Guaranteed to remain potent for days...

and

Were-boar seeks companion for business opportunity
and long-term relation...

and

Missing: black cat
Shadow teleporting, answers to "Amberflaxus"...

or this one freshly plastered:

WANTED

THE RED KNIGHT

Villainous brigand and his gang of cutthroats terrorize the countryside of Sendon, the alleys of High Hill, and the Duke's roads—committing murder, theft, and crimes too numerous and heinous to fully list herein.

REWARD

10,000 gold quins for the RED KNIGHT's death.

1,000 gold quins for information leading to his capture.

There was a sketch of this Red Knight in plate mail cobbled together from pieces and parts of various styles that made him look more Frankenstein's monster than Lancelot du Lac.

No quest alert popped.

Just as well. The money might have been nice, but I was helping a friend tonight, and then afterwards I had my own distractions to attend to that concerned more than mere coin.

"Wouldn't be staring too hard at that wall," Elmac muttered. His dwarven accent was a dead ringer for a Scottish brogue. "Timbers be so rotten, the whole mess could come down on our heads with one dirty look."

I grunted in agreement.

Elmac was correct about the state of the buildings in Low District: most were deserted, had windows broken, and two within sight had recently burned down.

"Didn't you say there was a building code in High Hill? Every structure has to be enchanted fireproof after the Southern Section burned?"

"Aye, but 'tis expensive, and I suspect no one would mind if all this" —he flared his pudgy fingers— "went *poof*."

We lurked in deep shadow ten paces from where we were *supposed* to be: the intersection of Street of Skulkers and Gut Slit Lane.

No way I was standing there, though.

Streams of effluent and excrement snaked over these "roads." Some puddles were so big I wondered if a horse might have drowned in those quagmire depths.

Have I mentioned the smells? Drifting upon the night air was a bouquet of shit, sickly sweet gangrene, and the lingering scent of burnt hair and roasted meat (toasted rat, perhaps?).

The skin at the nape of my neck crinkled to gooseflesh.

I was suddenly *much* more awake and did a quick tactical assessment.

Near the intersection were three alleyways, crammed with garbage, and capable of concealing a dozen enemies. Three rooftops offered excellent sightlines, the better to rain arrows down upon us unsuspecting fish in the proverbial barrel.

"Nice place for an ambush," I remarked.

"Nothing 'nice' 'bout Gut Slit Lane," Elmac said. "'Tis where you can find all sorts 'o illicit services, stolen goods, and dumped bodies."

"Speaking from personal experience?"

"Maybe." He shrugged. "But it be no secret that Gut Slit Lane has the honor of being the *least* desirable street, in the *least* desirable part 'o High Hill."

Elmac had a talent for speaking the obvious.

Ah yes, Elmac... what to tell you of him?

He was my friend, battle brother, and drinking companion. His left arm had been amputated at the shoulder, and the dwarf wore a magical prosthetic in its place that could punch through concrete walls.

Last week, we'd met and joined forces to save High Hill from an invading demon army. Stopping that evil horde, however, had not been Elmac's greatest battle. Forty years ago he had been the Grand General of the Armies of High Hill. With three thousand warriors under his command, he had faced a hundred *thousand* in the great War of Underhill.

Only seven heroes had returned from that epic battle. Elmac was one... but he had lost the love of his life, a son, and his two brothers.

For decades he'd coped with that loss by doing his best to drink himself into oblivion (which for a dwarf is saying something).

He was better now. I think. Going on that last quest had breathed some life back into the cantankerous little guy.

One important detail about Elmac: He owned a tavern called the Bloody Rooster. It was a dive, but it also had the best selection of ales in High Hill (of which I planned to sample his *entire* inventory).

Strike that. How could I forget? The *most* important detail about Elmac was *actually* this: He wasn't a player but nonetheless knew about the Game.

Huge security breach, I know. All my fault.

I had told him, though, because I had recruited him into my clan. That is, I *was* going to recruit him as soon as I reached fifth level and a new player slot opened in the clan.

Maybe helping Morgana tonight would get me enough experience.

I concentrated and summoned my game interface.

An alabaster-framed window popped into existence before me and tilted to an ergonomic angle for optimal reading. This was the augmented-reality user interface and my main link to the Game.

I tabbed to the Message Center where players conveyed notes to one another.

On-screen was the reason Elmac and I were here, my last message from Morgana:

>_Morgana Nox: My quest's gone pear-shaped

>_Morgana Nox: At Gut Slit & Skulkers

>_Morgana Nox: Hurry. Might need help

Morgana was a third-level druid, third-level thief player, and our mutual friend. Her distress call had pinged my inbox just as Elmac and I were lifting frosty Silvercrest Ales to our parched lips at the Bloody Rooster.

We had naturally dropped everything and heeded Fate's call to adventure.

Sure, there were reasons *not* to trust Morgana. She and I were, after all, on competing teams in the Game. Morgana had joined the Tricksters LLC clan—sponsored by gods like Loki, Coyote, or in her case, the Celtic nature spirit and giant rabbit, The Great Pooka—powerful practical joker deities never to be fully trusted.

Could this "rescue call" from Morgana be a practical joke?

I didn't think so. Morgana had risked her neck to save mine. She was also from Earth (although one in an alternate universe), and having a more-or-less common origin gave us a leg up in understanding one another. I might not trust her gods, but I *did* trust *her*.

Elmac and she were friends too. I suspected, though, he had a crush on her (somehow missing the age difference of about a hundred years between them). If that was the case, I predicted there was going to be a train wreck of a conversation between them soon—the "just friends" talk.

Or maybe I'd misread Elmac's intentions.

I returned to my interface and sent the following to Morgana:

>_Hektor Saint-Savage: We r here

>_Hektor Saint-Savage: Where r u?

An alert window instantly popped with:

ALERT!

Player has invoked PRIVACY.

Your message(s) will be stored in their mailbox.

That was my fifth attempt to contact her. And the fifth time I'd gotten this automated reply. At least it wasn't *"There is no active player, Morgana Nox"* ...which would have indicated she was dead.

So, good news, right?

Then how come with each passing moment, I felt less sure about this? Felt like it might not be only Morgana who'd need rescuing tonight?

As an experiment, I turned my interface to face the intersection. The light from the screen could illuminate the area and reveal some clue that Morgana had already been here.

No dice. The dark was still dark.

My augmented reality window apparently only existed in my brain. At least gazing into the lit screen hadn't ruined my night vision. As an elf, I could see like a cat. Elmac had no problem. Dwarves could see in total darkness.

For a second, I considered scrolling to the part of the interface on character classes. I'd started reading it yesterday... and there were *hundreds* of entries on new classes. If I was going to pick up a new class, become a so-called multiclass character, I'd need to do some serious studying.

It was but a momentary temptation. I wasn't here to read.

Where are you, Morgana?

I glanced around. Saw no one.

Elmac's hairy ears twitched. "Hmmm."

"What?"

"Shhhh... there be something, close."

I closed my eyes. Listened.

Gurgling water.

Two cats fighting (or, ahem, on a date).

A block away, drunken half laughter and yips. Werewolves having too much fun, I suspected.

And... ten paces around the corner, a faint "*sclorch*."

I nonchalantly poked my head out.

There was mud. Shadows. An angle of bat wing flashed by and melted back into the night.

I saw no one who might have made that *sclorch*.

Could the bat have been Morgana? As a thief *and* druid, she could sneak about and shift shape. I'd seen her transform into a panther, wolf, and she had also mentioned a mouse form as well. Why not a bat?

Another squelchy step. This time across the street.

"Ambush," I told Elmac.

By way of acknowledgement, he unslung his battle axe and gripped it tight with both meat and metal hands.

My hands balled into fists and I tensed.

This was bad ground to fight on. We were easily surrounded. Vulnerable from above. No cover.

But there *was* another option: across the intersection, a house. Its second floor was destroyed. The stone chimney rubble. But, apart from that, it wasn't *so* bad. The foundation was concrete and river rock. The remaining upright lumber could be silver-aged cedar (or at least not *completely* rotten). Maybe.

It did, however, provide cover... or possibly a spot where we might be cornered, but you know what they say about the availability of safe ports in storms? It'd do.

I nudged Elmac and nodded at the place. "Go. I've got your back."

Elmac sprinted across the street as quick as he could move his short legs.

I fired off my chi-powered buff, *Perfect Motion*, and it felt like electrified grease had been injected into my limbs.

Behind me: a trio of low whistles.

I spun—

—in time to see three steel blurs slice through the air at me as fast as a major-league fastball.

I was *faster*.

I caught the first inbound streak.

Ah, a dagger.

I slashed, deflecting the second blur speeding toward me—a shower of sparks—and then I sidestepped a third thrown blade.

I chucked the caught dagger back along its original trajectory.

And it impaled a shadow... that groaned, toppled over, and convulsed. This shaking figure wore a black jumpsuit and balaclava.

A poisoned blade. Of course. I'd have been disappointed if there wasn't *some* additional catch to this ambush.

The cut-rate ninja performed his death rattle and grew still.

It appeared that the poison they used was of the *lethal* variety.

The air filled with *whooshes* and *whistles* as thrown daggers, crossbow bolts, and shuriken came at me from every direction.

I twisted and bounded backward into a flip—landed, skidded, but caught my balance before doing a face plant in the mud.

Dark figures emerged to surround me.

I glanced across the street. No Elmac. He must be inside.

Good. I was done doing my impersonation of a bullseye.

I ran, zigging and zagging, to the building.

Projectiles splashed the mud at my feet and thunked into nearby walls.

I dove through a broken window and a shard of glass sliced my tunic. Too close.

Inside the building, I noted there were two other windows and one exit missing its door. Busted bottles, syringes, and unidentifiable sticky things littered the floor. The roof sagged.

And as predicted, Elmac was here too, with axe held high—*already* swinging. He halted his murderous strike before his blade made two *half*-monks out of me.

"They're" —I panted— "coming. Ten. Maybe a dozen."

Elmac pressed a slender gold flask into my hand. "Drink. Be quick."

"Come on, Elmac. No time for whiskey."

He glowered his impatience at my mud-splattered shirt.

I looked at whatever wasn't meeting Elmac's approval.

Blood seeped through my tunic. Must have been that glass.

I pulled back the fabric and saw a tiny cut across the ripples of my abdomen. Barely a shaving nick. The skin around the incision, however, *blistered*, *blackened*, and *peeled* as I watched. My tongue thickened. My throat swelled, and it was hard to even take a breath.

WARNING!!!
You have been poisoned with:
Sanguine Hellebore (*Helleborus album sanguis*).
Causes necrotizing blisters for additional damage.
Has a small, but cumulative, chance to auto-catalyze
and rapidly consume the entire body.

Ah, the just-late-enough-to-*not*-be useful game alert. I was beginning to think it only existed to rub my nose in this sort of stuff.

Elmac snatched his flask back, spun off the top, and shoved it at my mouth. "By all the gods' hangovers—'tis no whiskey. It be anti-venom from the Temple of the Three Sisters."

Thanks, Elmac. I guzzled it. The potion had the consistency of motor oil and tasted like habanero-flavored napalm.

I blinked away tears, but I *could* inhale again. The swelling and necrosis of the wound slowed and stopped. It still itched like hell though.

On the ruined second floor overhead were many padded steps. That had to be our new friends.

Elmac craned his neck. "Stupid to charge us all at once. They'll bunch up." He whispered a magical word to his axe and the blade crackled with blue fire and lightning flickers. A golden-toothed smile parted his gray beard.

My hands wavered with the mirage-heat of my *Fists of Steel* skill.

Stupid to charge us all at once? I thought they were doing pretty good so far.

Elmac's enthusiasm, however, was catching.

Adrenaline pounded through my blood. I was ready, even eager, to fight. I expected them to next rappel down and swing through the windows, heck even collapse the roof in on us.

Instead, though, outside a window, a body fell and hit the ground with that flat dead-body *thump*.

Elmac and I exchanged the same confused look. A *clumsy* ninja?

Before we could figure out why it had happened, the roof splintered and caved in.

Elmac and I dodged debris and ended up in opposite corners.

Eight hooded figures jumped down to join us.

Three of the wannabe assassins surrounded me, bouncing on the balls of their feet, weaving this way and that to throw off my defense.

Yes, these creeps outnumbered us four to one.

And yes, they were fast and had deadly envenomed weapons.

But their motions were crude, and as Elmac had predicted, they were bunching up so it'd be easy to step inside their reach— punch throats, dislocate elbows, and knee groins with impunity.

Sure, *I* could be killed any number of unpleasant ways... but I couldn't help grinning like Elmac (although I liked to think mine was more of a half-snarl of intimidation).

A millisecond pause.

Then everyone moved.

Two of the three on me lunged. One held back.

I twisted around a dagger thrust and closed—punched my attacker's throat, grabbed the voice box, and slammed him into the wall so hard, he went *through* and landed inert on the street.

I scissored a leg up—lashed down.

An instant neck snap on the thug who'd been angling for a backstab.

On the guy who had hesitated a few milliseconds, I let loose a series of rapid-fire punches that punctuated him, solar plexus to chin. He crumpled.

Meanwhile, with a mighty battle cry, Elmac severed the legs of the two he faced. He brought his axe about for another swing as two more filled the space where their comrades had stood. It looked like they were going to try for a grapple.

Usually it was a mistake to grapple a dwarf. It was *always* a mistake, however, when that dwarf was Elmac.

He embedded his massive axe in one of their thighs. Bright arterial blood gushed.

Elmac left his axe there, ducked, and came up with daggers in each hand—slashed knee and groin and left the other fellow gelded, screaming... and then silent on the floor.

A shadow blur streaked toward my throat.

I dodged two throwing stars—rolled toward this new attacker and open palmed his chest, splintering sternum and ribs. His heart punctured with a wet pop. The guy dropped at my feet.

I stopped.

Elmac and I were the only ones standing.

The odors of coppery blood, excrement, and bitter almond were thick in the air.

None of our attackers moved. Or even breathed. Not even the guy I'd slammed through the wall (who I thought might only be knocked out).

I nudged one with my boot and rolled him over. Foam bubbled through his black hood.

I'd read that some toxin was supposed to have an almond smell. Cyanide? Had they suicided rather than be captured?

Hmm. Maybe they weren't simple thugs after all.

Too bad they were dead. I would have liked to discuss *why* they were trying to shuffle us off this mortal coil.

"We best move on," Elmac said as he pulled free his axe.

I nodded. "I wonder why that first guy fell off the roof. Slipped?"

Elmac turned as if to offer his opinion, but halted, mouth open as he stared over my shoulder.

I turned.

From the ruined upstairs floor protruded a black snout, and from that... a rippling forked tongue.

A snake's head appeared. It was the size of a basketball.

I raised my hands, ready to take this monster out if it made a move toward me.

Elmac grabbed my arm and whispered, "Don't. That be a heartbeat cobra. I've got no anti-toxin for *that* beastie's venom."

I stepped back.

Look, I don't have a snake phobia, but this was Thera. Anything that could live here *had to be* deadly. And anything that made mighty Elmac pause—well, that went double.

The serpent's body flowed and dropped to the floor. It was a horrifying twenty feet long. Its scales were beautiful, though: black heart-shapes edged with crimson... that undulated in a mesmerizing fashion.

It reared up, hood flared—and lunged.

CHAPTER 2

The snake struck—

the dead man at my feet.

Only after it recoiled did I register how fast it was. Who would be quicker if we faced off? The serpent or me? Too close to call.

The bitten dead man writhed and cried out.

He'd been *faking*?

Convulsing, a small glass vial rolled from his grasp.

Inside swirled boiling purple vapor.

The man shuddered and ceased moving.

Dead for real this time?

I didn't dare check. The snake's unblinking gaze had now locked on me and Elmac.

We kept *very* still.

The snake tasted the air, then folded its hood; heart-shaped scales smoothed to a black bodysuit; fangs morphed into needle-pointed daggers held by hands and arms that split from the serpentine body. An emotionless reptilian face curled into a smile and the familiar features of...

"Morgana?" I asked.

You'd have thought I'd seen her shift shape enough to have been used to it, but it threw me every time. The metamorphosis caused distressing muscle tears, internal gurglings, and the snapping of bones.

Never seemed to bother her though.

She shook out a mane of luxuriant black hair that bounced into ringlets. Her flesh glistened like oiled bronze. Her eyes and ears tilted with a touch of something still wild.

"Don't be thick, mate," she said. "Who else?"

"Yeah, well... hi," I replied, swallowing my nausea.

Elmac gave her a courtly bow.

She returned a curtsey to the dwarf. "Good to see you blokes."

The two of them looked ridiculous exchanging social niceties among the corpses.

I moved from body to body, checking pulses, ready to lock wrist or shoulder joints to restrain any other fakers. None of them, however, would be answering our questions. All dead for real this time, three by suicide capsule.

"Cobra, eh?" Elmac said. "Good choice."

Morgana brightened. "Oi, a *heartbeat* cobra. Not just named for their scales, you know. You get bit, and you have one heartbeat before respiratory—"

I held up a hand. "Hang on. Are there more of these" —I waved at the permanently resting scattered about us— "out there?"

"Bunches," Morgana said, sobering. "Slinking all over the bloody place. I gave them the slip but then saw this lot moving your way. Thought I better lend a hand, or as the case may be, a fang."

"You couldn't have turned *off* your privacy and messaged us a warning?"

She pursed her lips. "Sorry about that. Got a game alert saying I'd detected an attempted magical scry to find my position. And then I *swore* I felt something looking over my shoulder, trying to read my interface. Crazy, yeah? I thought it best to run silent and dark."

Not so crazy. And definitely bad news.

Magical scrying usually meant a powerful spellcaster behind it. Even more troubling was Morgana's intuition of someone trying to read her interface—which should have been impossible. Others couldn't see your interface; the only exception I knew of was if you shared a quest with another player. I doubted Morgana had done such a thing...

Elmac gave one of the dead a kick. "And after that you ran into these *gentlemen*?"

"Spotted them around midnight," she said. "We played cat and mouse, shadows and daggers, for a bit, then I realized there were more than I had thought. Crawling all over Low District in packs, searching, or hunting, but I'm not sure for whom or what."

"Were they after you?" Elmac asked.

Morgana donned a "why, little old me?" expression. "I'm completely innocent." She tried a chuckle but it died in her throat.

Masking fear with bravado, Morgana? I thought that was my trick.

"We best check bodies for some clue to this mess," Elmac suggested.

I tried not to blush at my gaffe. Players, unless their lives were in immediate and dire peril (and sometimes even then), always searched their vanquished foes for treasure. I'd somehow let this basic game principle slip my mind.

I think I knew why.

It was a lot different simply *playing a game* than *being in* one. I wouldn't be re-spawning if I died. I got one life in Thera and that little fact had stuck in the back of my mind like a sliver of glass—distracting as hell.

"Of course search the bodies," I said as if I'd thought of this three minutes ago.

Morgana and Elmac set about riffling corpses.

I double-checked the one who'd faked his demise... and subsequently died what had looked like a swift but agonizing death from Morgana's bite.

I removed his ninja hood. The cloth was rough hemp and cheap black dye rubbed off.

He was human. Middle-aged. Smallpox scars. Ugly. A swollen blue tongue protruded between drawn lips. Eyes red with burst blood vessels stared back at me.

Note to self: *Stay on Morgana's good side.*

As I concentrated, his inventory window appeared, titled:

Assassin Squad Leader, LEVEL 2

Assassin? That tracked.

But then who was paying them? And why had they attacked *us*?

Well, this guy wouldn't be talking anytime soon.

He had three daggers and a folded square of parchment, which I transferred to my inventory.

I also grabbed the vial on the floor containing that weird purple gas. I made sure its cork stopper was snug and placed it with all the other stuff in my inventory.

A quick check of two others revealed them to be: "Assassin Initiate, LEVEL 1."

"Few daggers here," Elmac grumbled. "Be careful. They be covered in that poison."

"Same," Morgana said. Her eyes sparkled as she withdrew two throwing stars. "Oooh, I can use these." They vanished into her inventory.

I stood and did my best to brush off the filth and blood. "I think we've overstayed our welcome on Gut Slit Lane. Let's get to a safe place and talk. The Bloody Rooster?"

"Best idea tonight," Elmac said and smacked his lips. "We be needing a few proper drinks to grease the old mental wheels, eh? And I know a shortcut back."

"Put me down as a 'maybe' on the drinks," Morgana told him. "But yeah, let's get out of here."

"Let me check if the coast is clear," I said, grabbed one of the ninja hoods, and slipped it on.

I held my breath and looked outside.

No assassins.

For now.

That I could see.

I ducked back, gave my friends a "thumbs up," and removed the hood.

The hood might come in handy again, so I dropped it too into my inventory.

Elmac pushed past me and led us to an alley.

I had spotted it before. It was clogged with trash and buried by a collapsed wall. Impassable.

Or *almost* impassable... because I wasn't thinking like a dwarf.

Without missing a step, Elmac ducked, and then belly crawled under creaking timbers.

Morgana went next, easily wriggling into the unstable mess.

I took a deep breath and followed.

It was tight. Debris shifted as I squirmed and pushed through. Rats lingered just out of reach and red beady eyes locked onto me like I was dinner being delivered.

We went on like that—then out into fresh air—but quickly back through three more alleys, thankfully with less obstacles and fewer vermin.

We then emerged onto a much wider street.

I jumped at a dark figure next to me—and relaxed. Hello, my shadow.

A warm and welcoming illumination flickered from gas street lamps. Amber light reflected off the smooth cobbles that paved this avenue.

Halfway down the street, I spied the hanging sign for "Hiltmyer & Co., Trading Post Extraordinaire." It was a general store jam-packed full of gear for adventurers (I suspected they also fenced stolen goods). The place was run by a gnome conglomerate. I'd shopped there a few days ago and had liked the miniature merchant, Lordren Hiltmyer.

If Hiltmyer's was here, then this was Silver Avenue, and just around the corner had to be the Bloody Rooster.

Whew. It felt like sliding into home base. Safe. Almost.

We tried to act nonchalant but nonetheless broke into a jog the last half block. We slowed, caught our breath, then Elmac pushed aside the swinging door to his bar.

Like I said, the Bloody Rooster was a dive.

Inside was a long oak bar, two dozen tables, and a pair of granite hearths with crackling fires. The real attraction of this place, however, was the wall of liquor on the floor-to-ceiling shelves behind the bar—hundreds of bottles in every color, shape, and size—a patchwork of dark greens and ambers and garnet reds, dusty champagne magnums, two entire rows of assorted whiskies, and well, I could have stared at the stuff all night—not to mention the dozens of keg taps with gleaming silver dragon heads, castles, and maidens ready to be pulled and spill forth their frothy delights.

The Bloody Rooster was packed tonight with as odd an assortment of customers as there were varieties of drinks: elves in hooded cloaks, ruddy-faced dwarfs (of course), and also a small group of cat people (drinking White Russians), and one guy who I swore had vampire fangs (sipping what I hoped was red wine)... all who paused in their laughter, conversation, and guzzles, to turn and see who had come in at such a late hour.

Elmac gave his customers nods and waves as he strode to the bar.

His patrons relaxed, but still watched Morgana and me, wary, and hands rested on weapon hilts.

Marty "the Slasher," the half-orc, half-troll bartender was on duty. He had a heavy pouring arm and told outrageously lewd jokes that made everyone blush. Tattooed, pierced, covered with warts, he wore a grin that looked like he might burst into laughter or take a bite out of you. I liked him and always made sure to leave him a good tip.

Marty flashed me and Morgana a pointed-tooth smile, then listened as Elmac leaned in and whispered to him.

As they spoke I noted another "Red Knight WANTED" poster tacked to the wall. Duke Opinicus and Colonel Delacroix must really want that guy. Odd that I hadn't seen any of these posters last night... but then again, I'd been slightly under the influence.

Elmac surreptitiously passed an assassin's dagger to Marty.

Without looking, Marty made the weapon vanish under the bar while he wiped the counter with his free hand.

And as Elmac continued to whisper, Marty's grin faded.

Marty glanced at the entrance then ducked under the bar. He stood and passed a paper bag to Elmac.

Elmac grunted a response to Marty and left. He waved for Morgana and me to follow as he marched back to the storeroom.

I felt every eye in the place bore into the back of my skull.

As soon as we entered the storeroom, the talk and raucous laughter began once more in the bar.

Elmac opened a trapdoor and we descended into the tavern's cold storage. There, concealed behind an aging side of smoldering salamander beef, was a hidden passage and a staircase that led to a vault door.

This was Elmac's secure room.

He rented it to those who needed a place free of conventional or magical eavesdroppers—or like us, a secure place to talk without worrying about catching a poisoned dagger in the kidney.

Elmac spun combination dials and pushed open the foot-thick steel vault door.

Inside was a room seven paces across. The ceiling, floor, and walls were clad in sheets of hammered lead. There was a conference table covered with dirty dishes and mugs from the previous renter. To add a touch of class there was an X-rated painting of a dwarven bacchanalia, and overhead hung a chandelier that those of non-dwarven heights crashed into every time they stood.

Elmac closed the door, threw the wheel, and scrambled the locks.

Only then did I exhale and relax a notch.

I took one of the generously padded chairs that faced the door.

From the paper sack Marty had given him, Elmac withdrew a bottle.

Elmac thumbed the bottle's label, smoothing away grime, and read aloud, "*Elegy for a Fallen Star*. Not generally a fan 'o elven concoctions, but *this* brandy 'tis heavenly. Was saving it for a special occasion, which might as well be tonight." He took a swig.

His weathered face purpled. He sloshed the bottle at Morgana and me.

"Pass," I said (as much as I might have needed a good belt right now). Even sober, unraveling tonight's mysteries might not be so easy.

Morgana declined Elmac's drink as well. "Would you have a spot of tea?" she asked. "Even coffee'll do."

Elmac scoffed at us lightweights, but nodded at a silver thermos and stack of paper cups.

Morgana poured two cups and slid one to me.

The three of us took a moment to drink in silence.

You could have used Elmac's coffee as a decent paint stripper. It did, however, focus my scattered thoughts.

I'd start with the easy stuff.

"What were you were doing out tonight?" I asked Morgana.

"Bit of Thieves Guild business," she said. "Had a quest to steal a few personal letters and a necklace that'd embarrass a gentleman's lover, or lovers, I wasn't quite sure on that point. Then dozens of those slinkers popped out of nowhere. The ones on Gut Slit were one of three crews I spotted."

Elmac drummed his metal fingers on the table. "If they were Silent Syndicate there'd need to be a legal reason to sanction a hit—not to mention a good bit 'o motivation to pay for so many operatives."

"Silent Syndicate?" I asked.

"Assassins Guild," Morgana explained.

"Really? I can't believe Duke Opinicus and Colonel Delacroix would let *assassins* operate in the High Hill."

I always thought an organization of murderers was a ridiculous fantasy game trope. One good divination spell would ferret them out.

"*Let* them operate?" Elmac said and frowned at me. "The Duke helped *set it up*. How else can a society remove sociopaths and nepotism-lovers and other such disreputables from power?"

I was going to suggest a few *rational* examples, say like laws or voting—but come to think of it, laws hadn't worked out so well on Earth. I'd been framed for mass murder and almost executed before I escaped into the Game. And voting? Did anyone on my world believe that was a real thing anymore?

"Save the political chit-chat, gents," Morgana said, "and let's figure out why they're after me?"

Elmac flicked his fingers through his gray and silver beard and made it bristle (like I'd imagined a pissed-off badger would, fluffing his fur to look threatening). He then sighed and his gaze fell to his hands. "I think they be using you, Morgana… to get to me. I know some folk who'd like to see me very dead." He took another swig of elven brandy. "Not all my 'great deeds' as a former general… were, uh… so great."

I said nothing.

Not because this was the proper moment to quietly empathize with my friend.

No, I kept my trap shut because I knew very well these assassins could be after *me*.

CHAPTER 3

I gave it 50-50 odds that I was their target.

In my first few days in Thera I'd amassed a short and *terrifying* list of enemies.

There was my brother, the high-level anti-paladin (aka William the Bloody), but he was locked in the Duke's dungeons, so I doubted he could have arranged a hit. I'd received a few in-game messages from him—inquiries as to where I was and what I was doing. Obviously attempts to manipulate me.

When hell freezes over, Bill.

Then, there were the other player clans. If they knew there was a new clan in the Game, it'd be a smart move for them to pick off the competition while I was still low level.

Last, and the worst of the lot, the Lords of the Abyss. According to the Game's rules, these demonic princes couldn't target players... but being evil and agents of chaos, they had to be looking for a loophole around that rule.

I suddenly wasn't feeling so secure, even here.

"Are you sure this safe we're locked in is, uh, safe, Elmac?"

Morgana must have been thinking along the same lines because she added, "We're a tad backed into a corner."

"Reeelax," Elmac told us. "This room be lead-lined, airtight with an independent oxygen supply, and warded against magic, mental powers, dimensional ruptures... plus a few security features no one need know about."

"Don't suppose one of those features would be a loo?" Morgana asked with a smile (albeit a tad strained).

"Chamber pot's under there." Elmac indicated a crate in the corner. Nailed to it was a tree-shaped pine-scented freshener.

Morgana curled a lock of her dark hair about one finger. "Oh, that's okay then. I can wait." She pushed her coffee away.

I steered the conversation back to more life-or-death issues. "Let's take a look at the stuff off those assassins. Maybe we can figure out why this is happening."

I opened my inventory, tapped the icons of the parchment and vial of gas, dragged them over the table, and then released them.

The items appeared.

Elmac's eyes widened, but he'd seen such player inter-dimensional sleight of hand before, so he didn't freak out.

Morgana, however, gaped at Elmac.

She then looked to me with an expression that said, *Why isn't Elmac asking questions?*

"He knows about the Game," I told her. "I already signed him up to join my clan, which he's accepted... when that is, I hit fifth level."

Her mouth shut. Opened. Moved as if to speak, but there was no sound.

"He knows...?" She slowly nodded. "Yeah. A local with oodles of know-how about Thera? It's actually brilliant." She turned to the dwarf. "Have you picked a class? You know there's a Free Trial to get through. Completely insane, it is."

"We've covered the basics," I said. "Let's stay focused on the squad of killers that might be trying to kill one or all of us, yes?"

"Suppose 'twould be best." Elmac gave Morgana a quick wink. "Later though, I'd be delighted to hear *any* advice you be having."

Morgana shot back her own sly wink. "You're paying for the drinks. My advice isn't free."

"It be a date then."

I had to be misreading Elmac's... what... banter? The way he leaned toward her, though, seemed like flirting too. So maybe I had been right, and he *did* have a crush on her. This wasn't going to end well.

Elmac sat straighter and was suddenly serious. His finger stabbed the vial of gas—just before it rolled off the edge of the table.

I hadn't noticed it *was* moving.

In fact, a few seconds ago, the thing had been perfectly still.

Elmac kept his finger on it and lowered his gaze level with the container. He squinted. "Toxic gas, I'll wager. Or some vapor beastie locked inside. Had to have been a weapon 'o last resort."

I focused on the vial and its description window popped. Most of the words were redacted with black bars, except:

ALERT!
Description UNAVAILABLE
Item is magically CLOAKED

I relayed this to Morgana and Elmac.

Morgana knelt next to Elmac and squinted at the vial too.

Inside, purple smoke boiled, and I could see *something* deeper swimming around and around. Like a lion pacing in its cage.

"Cloaked?" she breathed. "Haven't seen that before." She undulated her fingers and whispered what I assumed were magical words, *"De occulta philosophia revelata."*

From the vial came a whispered reply—shrill and strident.

Morgana's eyes widened. She snorted and stood, hands on her hips. "Same to you," she told the thing in the vial. "'Beastie' is right. I cast a *Nature's Insight* spell on it... and well, never mind what it said. *Blimey*. A lady can't repeat *that*."

"Sounds like whatever's in there isn't happy about it." I plucked up the vial. "Let's save figuring out what it is for later. Like when we're *not* locked in an air-tight room?" It went back into my inventory. "Maybe we'll have more luck with the note?"

I dragged the square of parchment out of my inventory.

"Morgana?" I asked. "Mind checking for traps? If those assassins had suicide capsules, who knows what kind of toxic powder or other surprises could be inside."

"Right." She produced a leather bundle and unrolled it. Within were dental picks, tiny pry bars, wires, and other assorted tools for the fine trade of burglary. She lifted a fold of the parchment and inserted a wire probe. She then withdrew it and smelled the tip.

I hadn't noticed before how long and slender her fingers were, the kind you'd see on a violin player. Or a safecracker.

A few more pokes and prods and she announced, "No traps or poisons detected." She pushed the paper square to me. "*Should* be safe to open."

This was a classic thief maneuver: check for traps but then let someone *else* open the thing.

I unfolded the paper and braced.

No puff of toxic powder. No explosion.

The paper was, surprise—a note. The writing on it, however, looked like Sumerian cuneiform executed by a preschooler. There were several lines of the erratic script followed by a list with thirteen entries.

Elmac peered at it. "That be Sabbah, the Silent Syndicate's secret code."

"So you were right," Morgana whispered. "It *was* the Assassins Guild."

"Don't worry," I told them, "I can handle this Sabbah-code stuff."

Elmac stared at me. In a cold flat tone, he asked, "And how do *you* be knowing Sabbah?"

"I don't, but being a player has its advantages. I've got three freebie starting languages still unassigned. That's how I learned Jal'Tek the other day in the Duke's court."

"Right," Morgana said, "but you can't—"

"Just a sec," I told her and tabbed over to the SKILLS & ABILITIES section of my interface.

She rolled her eyes. "Suit yourself." She tilted her chair back and propped her boots on the table.

I perused the list of available languages. *Sabbah* was right there between *Saba-Leippya (nature spirit of rice paddies)* and *Sac (one-legged primordial dwarf)*.

Sabbah, however, was grayed out and un-selectable.

I turned to Morgana and made a "well?" gesture.

"Ready to listen now, are you?" She pretended to buff her chipped and split fingernails.

I waited.

Thirty seconds.

"Well then," she said, sitting up. "Sabbah is an assassin *only* skill, you twonk."

I scoffed and tried to check the un-selectable skill.

A tiny pop-up declared:

This is an ASSASSIN-class only skill.

There *was* a way around this. I could multiclass as an Assassin/Spirit Warrior. Heck, there was a specialization path for my class called "Master of Death" that would probably work great with assassin skills.

But not really an option for me.

Despite Elmac's earlier claim that assassins were an integral part of civilized society—I had no intention of becoming a cold-blooded killer. I preferred my killing to be justified, self-defense, noble even, if I could swing it. After all, I was a "Hero of Thera" not a "Justified *Murderer* of Thera."

Also, when I'd added skills before, memories had been spliced into my brain to account for the update to my character. I could now recall, for example, being lost in the mountains, half dead, then rescued by the monks at the Domicile of the Sleeping Dragon.

This *was* a real memory. Just not mine.

It was no big deal, as long as I kept straight which memories belonged to Hector with a "c," and which belonged to Hektor with a "k."

The *long-term* effects of these implanted recollections, however, might get... tricky.

Case in point: my brother. Sure, he'd been evil (maybe insane) *before* he'd come to Thera and become an anti-paladin. I bet, though, the backstory of his character's villainous origin hadn't helped Bill's moral compass point in the right direction.

"Hey—hello? Hektor?" Elmac waved a hand in front of my face.

"Sorry. Thinking about something else." I blinked. "Is there any way to decipher the note *without* being an assassin?"

Elmac turned the parchment around. "Seen enough 'o this stuff over the years. Sometimes you get lucky if you guess a few symbols right." He tugged at his beard as his gaze darted over the odd code. "Colonel Delacroix is better at this, but asking her would add, uh, political complications."

Delacroix was a powerful solar sorceress and head of the city's secret police. She was smarter than the three of us put together. She and I, however, weren't exactly friends. She suspected me of some illicit involvement with the demonic invasion last week. In fact, she'd wanted to debrief (interrogate) me about it.

"Hang on," Morgana said. "You *really* believe these low-level assassins were dumb enough to carry a coded message? Just waiting for their enemies to snatch it and get a handy clue?"

It *did* seem a little convenient.

"A plot coupon?" I wondered out loud.

"Or a deliberate plant of *mis*-information," she replied.

"Plot coupon? What be that?" Elmac asked.

"Sorry," I said. "It's a game term. They're the crumbs in a trail of breadcrumbs. Like you track down a wandering hermit who then sends you to an enchanted frog, and once you dispel the frog's curse, he gives you a secret map, that then leads you to the sleeping princess you were looking for all along."

"Lazy storytelling, if you ask me," Morgana said.

Elmac grabbed a pencil, licked the end, and scribbled notes on a pad of paper. "Be it one of these coupons, the Great Scarlet Herring herself, or a genuine clue, might as well see what my old noggin can do with it."

Morgana stared at me, her eyes narrowed, and she pursed her lips. "Crikey. You haven't leveled up yet?"

"I'm still calculating my optimal progression path. Hey—wait. How do *you* know I haven't leveled up?"

"Your player tag." She waved over my head to the name, clan affiliation, and level placard that only other players could see. "'Hero of Thera,'" she read. "'Hektor Saint-Savage.' But the 'Spirit Warrior/4th level' part's dull. It goes all sterling silver when you *commit* and actually assign points."

"Look," I told her, a defensive tone sharpening my voice, "I'm trying to do this right, not like my first three levels when I'd been forced to make snap decisions."

That came out a bit more cutting than I'd meant. Morgana had touched a sore spot, though.

"Sorry," I said without meeting her eyes.

"It's okay, mate. But use your loaf." She scooted closer. "Better skills and more health might have come in handy tonight, yeah?"

"Yeah…"

This was the problem with being a borderline obsessive-compulsive min-maxing player. We were always holding out for that *perfect* combination of stats, skills, and class abilities. I thought it made me a good player… but yes, I acknowledge now it was also pretty dumb to sit on a pile of unspent points.

Elmac cleared his throat and jabbed his paper with a stubby pencil. "If you be interested, I got three on this list—the easy guesses. The rest'll take more brain sweat than I got. Maybe after I get a few more drinks in me…"

He turned the page for Morgana and me to read.

In precise block lettering next to the indecipherable Sabbah, Elmac had written:

> Padre John Adam-Smith
> Dame Rose Beckonsail
> Niblen Chatters

"This supposed to be a hit list?" Morgana whispered.

"Doesn't make any sense if 'tis," Elmac replied. "Padre John is a lovable old priest with the Three Sisters. Dame Beckonsail be the most honored sky captain in the Duke's gryphon cavalry. And Niblen? A court scribe, if I remember right."

"Is there a connection between them?" I asked.

Elmac shrugged.

A new interface window materialized from the shadows and I jolted with surprise.

"What?" Elmac said, his hand reaching for his axe.

"Next quest," Morgana said, her irises constricting to cat slits as she examined the text.

I read it out loud so Elmac could follow.

NEW QUEST UNLOCKED:
"*SOMETHING ROTTEN IN THE DUCHY OF SENDON*"
The Silent Syndicate has sanctioned innocent people for elimination. Investigate and get out of High Hill before you too are *murdered*.
Rewards: Tier-IV (or better) treasure, political secrets.
Suggested Level: You and anyone else you can convince to help.

Accept? YES / NO

Did I detect sarcasm in the "Suggested Level"? Or a hint that this quest might be over our pay grade?

Morgana reached toward her interface. "Plot coupon or not, looks like it's our next step."

"Wait," I said. "Don't accept."

She fixed me with a stare. "That's what we're supposed to do, innit?"

"Exactly," I told her. "But two things have seriously bugged me since we got here. First, what type of game is the Game?"

She shook her head.

"I mean, is it a bunch of linear plot threads we're obliged to follow? Or more sandboxy?"

"I understood the words you be using, lad," Elmac muttered and crossed his arms, "but not what they all mean together. A sandbox?"

"So to speak," Morgana replied. "A sandbox world is one where players are free to explore and find their own way through the game."

"The other extreme is a linear, predetermined world," I told him. "Players are led from quest to quest. Right now I could make a case for either possibility in *the* Game. It sure seems like we're making our own choices, but considering how neatly my first few quests lined up…" I shrugged. "I could've been herded down a particular path and not even known it."

The Game Master had told me he'd set it up so I'd collect the two evil artifact gloves he wanted out of the Game (that were still rattling around in my inventory, by the way). How much more was due to his influence?

"It be the standard free will versus determinism debate," Elmac said, stroking his beard.

Morgana arched an eyebrow. "You know your Plato?"

"And 'bout the 'animal' and 'rational' parts of our nature, aye," he said.

Morgana turned back to me. "That's all toss, Hektor. Assassins are trying to off these innocent people all the same. That Padre whats-his-nose, and Dame Lady whoever. We've got to save them if we can."

"I'm not saying we don't. But if this quest turns out to be as hard as stopping a demonic invasion, there may be *smarter* ways to do it."

She slowly shook her head and examined me. "Yeah? Like what?"

"Okay, say the Game is a sandbox type. Couldn't we knock out a few easier quests, level up—*then* come back and do the assassin quest *better* prepared for it? In fact, I have the perfect little quest that'll get us out of town for a few days."

She stared off into space. "Assuming that everyone the assassins are after don't have their throats slit in the meantime... and if quests don't scale with our level... yeah, that *could be* better."

Elmac opened his mouth to ask.

"Scaling," I told him, "means the higher level you are, the harder the quests get. I don't think they do."

"What makes you say that?" Morgana asked.

"Well, that's the other thing that's been bugging me. We've accepted quests that no low level had any business attempting. Fighting off an army of demons? A shadow demigod? I think it's on us to determine what quests are a fair challenge and which are suicide—regardless what the 'Suggested Level' says in the quest description."

I could see the wheels turning in Morgana's head. She still didn't look convinced.

"One more thing..." I said. "I *really* hate quests with assassins. They have nasty twists like—*hey, surprise, your dearest friend is actually a killer disguised as your pal.*"

"That's barmy," Morgana said and went on in an increasingly strained tone. "And so is believing all those murderers will just forget about us while we flounce about because of some game mechanic like us not accepting the quest."

"Either way it's a risk worth taking. Think about it: the quest text said 'get out of High Hill before you too are *murdered.*' Sounds like if we stay here under the current circumstances, it goes bad for us. On the other hand, if we level up and *then* take the quest, maybe, just maybe, we have a chance of actually helping those people."

"I don't know," she whispered. "We're gambling with people's lives..."

We were silent a moment as we considered the weight of that statement.

"Shouldn't we let Colonel Delacroix in on this?" Morgana asked. "She seems the type to take charge and do something about it."

"Aye, she is," Elmac muttered. "If it be a legal sanction, though, there be little she can do." He paused, glanced up, and then nodded in agreement to whatever he was thinking. "Still, I'd bet my last bottle of *Casa Del Oro Ladrillo* sipping tequila that she'd make the Syndicate wait while she double-checked the bureaucratic details, and meanwhile see to it that those folk 'bout to be murdered got far, far away."

"Good idea," I said. "We'll send her a note—*then* hightail it."

I took a moment to bask in the satisfaction of a plan well formed.

Morgana glowered and ruined my moment as she said, "Sure, all makes bloody perfect sense. Just one thing. Given what happened earlier tonight, how do we get out of High Hill with a legion of assassins—quest accepted or not—*already* hunting us?"

CHAPTER 4

"So…" I said, "we should go while it's still dark, shouldn't we?"

This air-tight vault felt more like a shrinking coffin every second.

"Easy, lad," Elmac said. "We best wait a wee bit."

I took a deep breath and forced my heart to slow.

I'd have to be dumb to not hear Elmac out. This was his home turf. His tactical analysis on this subject, sober or not, was light-years better than mine.

So, I grabbed his bottle of *Fallen Star* brandy and took a swig.

It was molten gold going down and left my vision a blurry glow. I exhaled vapors of honey-tinged smoke, swayed… and now had more control of the fight-or-flight instinct building inside me.

"I'm listening."

"If we go now in the middle 'o the night," Elmac went on, "Morgana can be using her skills and shifting her form to slink away, but you and I'll be standing out like dung trolls at the Royal Equinox Cotillion. Wait 'til morning, though, when the market opens and all the Heartland melons be rolling in, then the streets'll be jammed with folk wanting to get the pick of the season."

"And you two will be lost in the crowds," Morgana said, tapping her lower lip.

I shrugged. "Guess that makes sense."

"Good." Elmac made a "gimme" gesture for his brandy, so I passed it to him. "While we wait" —he took a pull from the bottle— "ahhh. I'll give that note another crack."

Morgana closed her eyes. "I'll just meditate and refill my mana then." She opened one eye and fixed me with a cat-about-to-pounce stare. "Suppose we *all* got *constructive* things to be about."

I got her meaning: *Level your character, idiot.*

So, ignoring my premonition of ninjas surrounding the Bloody Rooster while us sitting ducks just, well, sat here—I opened my game interface.

Really, what was so hard about leveling up? Besides me making up my mind?

It boiled down to three options.

First, I could level up as a plain Spirit Warrior and improve my existing base skills—attractive, as I knew, more or less, what I'd get.

My second option: graduate to a *specialized* Spirit Warrior sub-class. The catch was when I picked up such a specialization, I'd stop progressing as an ordinary Spirit Warrior and could *never* again improve my basic combat skills.

The worst thing about that? The full details of these specialized classes would only be revealed *after I* picked one.

This seemed to be a design feature of progression in the Game: *Surprises*. Free skills popped up, unannounced class branches appeared, and I bet a few unpleasant gotchas were in there as well.

If I was in an established clan, I could have *asked* for help. Older clans must keep records of past character choices to guide their new members.

Not a trivial advantage... but one I'd have to get by without.

My final progression option was to add an entirely new class, become a so-called multiclass character—Wizard/Spirit Warrior, Thief/Spirit Warrior, and so on. If I worked it right, that extra class would give me skill and stat synergies to potentially leapfrog my effective power.

The catch?

There were *hundreds* of classes to choose from—too many for my perfectionist brain to wrap itself around in a few hours, or even days.

I looked up from the interface.

Elmac had stuck his face so close to the assassin's note, his nose actually touched the words.

I wondered if he needed glasses.

Morgana sat cross-legged, deep in a trance. I caught flashes of her aura, gold and green astral energies that undulated like a star's corona.

But, back to my own problems.

There had to be a compromise between my obsessive-compulsive perfectionist tendencies and what would be "good enough" to survive the next encounter. I'd start by roughing out a few choices for my three options. Then, in a pinch, at least I'd just have *those* to pick from, not dozens, or hundreds of unsettled possibilities.

I sketched crude spreadsheets on the back of napkins and squeezed every molecule of logic from my gray matter.

After two hours, this is where I landed.

If I decided to improve my straight-up Spirit Warrior—I'd drop points into my PERCEPTION and REFLEX stats to increase mana and health. I'd also boost my *Spiritual Regeneration* to its maximum tier.

These were good, simple gains. No gambles.

Next were my specialized Spirit Warrior options. Their descriptions were *a bit* lacking.

First was:

Time Walker
Spirit Warrior who hones their chi to decrease reaction time and expand mental processes and senses. Masters make their bodies impervious to harm (for a time), travel astrally, become clairvoyant, and are said to be able to stop time.

Wow... Amazing stuff. I was intrigued by slowing, or even stopping, time (even if those powers manifested only at high levels). It was more spellcaster than fighter, though. If I needed magic, I might be better off multiclassing with a dedicated wizard type. Hmm.

Next was:

Spirit Speaker
Spirit Warrior who summons ancestors for counsel and battle. At higher levels, may call spirits with unique and powerful abilities. A master Spirit Speaker may summon several such spirits at the same time.

Okay, essentially a "pet" class. It was nice because if you needed a cleric, thief, or fighter—just call your great-great uncle.

Whose ancestors would I be summoning though? Hector Savage's from Earth? Or Hektor Saint-Savage, gypsy elf?

What wouldn't I give to see my mother and father again?

But at what cost? Summoning the dead often came with a price tag... and whatever it was, it wasn't mentioned in the text.

I chewed my lip as I perused the third specialization:

Path of the Dragon
The most difficult Spirit Warrior path. Quests, unraveling Zen koans, and other trials unlock advanced chi and combat skills. Such Spirit Warriors can eventually transform into a custom-created dragon avatar.

WARNING: Failed quests or questionable morals may cause the player to *fail* on this path and block ALL further progress as a Spirit Warrior.

What could be cooler than shapeshifting into a dragon? But along with that grand reward came a commensurate risk: a halt to your advancement in the class. Forever. Yikes. I'd have to think long and hard before I picked this one.

The last specialization option was:

Master of Death
Spirit Warriors dedicated to creating and mastering exotic weapons—such as the *Inferno Chain*, *Flying Guillotine Hat*, *Möbius Blades*, *I.L. Sword*, and the *Meteor Hammer* to name a few. Masters of Death learn secret techniques with these instruments to stun, paralyze, or instantly kill.

This was a fighter on steroids. The plethora of weird, lethal weapons made the kung fu movie junkie in me drool with anticipation.

Still, the Path of the Dragon spoke to me. Maybe it was the challenge.

I smoothed over my forearm. Golden scales gleamed and the tattooed reptile seemed to frolic among inked clouds and stars on my skin. I'd showed up in Thera with this. It gave me an odd sense of pride.

A clue from the Game Master which option I should pick? Maybe.

Not all dragons were good though. I'd once glimpsed the terrifying Nightmare Dragon who wanted nothing less than the destruction of all Creation. Evil beyond evil.

Add to that the risk of failing some quest and torpedoing my Spirit Warrior progression? No thanks.

So, when I did specialize, my top pick was Master of Death.

I imagined whipping a razor-edged chain sword in a huge arc, slicing and dicing my enemies into sashimi… and oh, Flying Guillotine hats! I smiled.

A trickle of perspiration snaked down my side. Must be from my intense concentration and the pressure to make the right choice.

I ignored this and considered the last potential path: the multiclass route.

I'd skimmed the class descriptions in the game interface before, but had only gotten a fraction of the way through. Still, I'd found a dozen solid possibilities. Two, though, had seemed like an especially good fit.

First was:

Battle Psychic
Warriors who use mental abilities to enchant themselves and their weapons. They are feared for lightning-quick strikes and an uncanny knack to predict their enemy's next move. At higher levels, entire combats play out in their mind *prior to* battle that allows them to know the likely outcome and pick the most efficacious strategy.

EGO was a Battle Psychic's primary stat. Any investment in EGO would increase my SOUL stat, which in turn, would boost some Spirit Warrior abilities and my pool of SOUL-based mana.

The downside?

Battle Psychic was *a lot* like a Spirit Warrior. "Enchant themselves" sounded like my *Perfect Motion* buff. Would those abilities stack? Or would I only be able to use one at any given time?

The other potential class was this:

Mage of the Line (aka Line Mage, Hand Mage)
Spellcasters who tap into primordial mana ley lines to create magic. Because a Mage of the Line must reach *in between* dimensions to touch mana ley lines, high PERCEPTION and REFLEX stats are critical. Mana pool is based on their REFLEX stat.

NOTE: Mage of the Line is NOT available as a starting class.

This sounded good, too. I could increase my REFLEX to benefit both my Spirit Warrior class and this one.

But there *could* be a drawback if their mana pool was based on REFLEX. Were there consequences if you *depleted* that pool? Would you become clumsy?

And why the prohibition against taking this class to start?

So many details were missing from the descriptions. Normal games lavished players with data about their classes and associated perks. Part of the challenge of *this* particular game, however, was figuring that stuff out on your own.

If, however, someone pressed a gun to my head (not that guns worked in Thera, but you get the idea), and made me pick one new class between the two candidates I'd found so far, I'd take Mage of the Line.

So, I had my three choices—improve my standard Spirit Warrior, go for the Master of Death specialization, or became a Spirit Warrior/Mage of the Line multiclass character.

I paused because, despite the pressure, I was having a *blast* figuring this out. I loved making the best character I could—and in this case, it was doubly satisfying as I was making the best version of *me* in Thera.

I'd been here many times before, hanging out with friends (in chat rooms or sitting at an actual table with dice and miniatures). We'd talk strategies for leveling up, what our next quest might be, discuss the best gear and how to get it—you know, playing games.

True, now I was surrounded by *real* death and danger, but damn if I wasn't having fun doing it anyway.

…even if the lack of information was frustrating.

Ah, Morgana might be able to help me.

I could ask her if she'd be willing to message her clan with a question or three on my behalf.

Although, maybe not. It wouldn't be fair to make her choose between our friendship and her dedication to the Great Pooka and her Trickster clan (technically a clan I was supposed to be competing with).

All moot. She was already occupied.

She and Elmac had scooted close—shoulder to shoulder, both grinning—as she read him descriptions of the character stats from her game interface.

She glanced my way.

I shot her back an annoyed look, a combination of—*Are you trying to recruit the guy I just signed up?*—and *Not cool to string the old guy along* sentiments.

She must have gotten part of that because her smile faltered and she mouthed, "*Later.*"

"So the BODY stat number," Elmac asked her, "that's STRENGTH plus...?"

"REFLEX," she said.

"What are you guys up to?" I asked.

"Oh... just be asking Morgana 'bout the basics 'o the Game," Elmac said, looking as if he just now recalled I was in the room. "Getting ideas how to be building my character."

"Don't worry, oh mighty Hero of Thera," she told me. "I already pressed Elmac for details on your mysterious clan. He very nicely told me to shove off and 'mind me own business.'"

They shared a sly glance, thick with meaning.

"But I must say," Morgana went on, "a lady *does* fancy a bloke with a few secrets."

Elmac blushed.

"So," Morgana continued, "different character classes prioritize different stats."

"You might want to stick to a basic fighter type," I said, trying to get involved. "You'd have a head start knowing so much about combat already."

Elmac considered—then his smile faded and he sniffed.

I caught an odor as well, that *I'm burning dinner* scent.

And it *was* warm in here. Definitely *not* my imagination or simple brain sweat.

"Best check the oxygen supply," Elmac said. "Sometimes the valves stick and the air gets a wee stale."

He jumped up, went to the far corner, and pressed three bolt heads on the lead-covered wall.

A concealed panel sprung open.

Elmac, however, turned away from the panel to face the vault door… and froze.

"What is it?" I got up.

Morgana stood as well.

All three of us approached the vault door.

I moved a hand over the surface, close but not touching.

The foot-thick slab of steel radiated heat like a stove.

"Someone's taken a bleeding blowtorch to it," Morgana whispered.

"Don't think so," Elmac whispered back. "A torch'd heat one spot. The whole door be broiling."

"I think," I told them, dreading to speak the obvious, "the Bloody Rooster is on fire."

CHAPTER 5

Just to make sure, I touched the door.

My fingertips sizzled. Dumb.

I jerked my hand away and stuffed the offended digits into my mouth. Even with my *Spirit Armor*, they'd been blistered.

Elmac set his metal hand on the surface. "'Tis almost six hundred degrees Kelvin," he told me. "Just 'bout hot enough to melt lead."

Morgana rubbed the back of her neck. "Better cast a few *Endure Flames* spells then."

"If the Rooster be burning" —Elmac's lips puckered into a scowl— "it'll ruin me four hundred and thirty-seven bottles of very fine, very expensive liquor in the storeroom too."

I wasn't sure what rattled me more... that we were going to parboil in this metal box, or that Elmac's treasured stock of booze might blow up and save us from a slow death.

I'd already escaped *one* burning building this week. One full of ghost wizards to boot. There had to be a way to wriggle out of this too.

At the moment, though, I could only think of two lousy options.

First, we could wait it out and hope Morgana had enough mana to keep us alive with her *Endure Flames* spell. The heat this vault could absorb, however, might take *days* to radiate away. And there was the other issue of a small lake's worth of flammable liquid a dozen feet over our heads.

So, that left the other option.

"Morgana, cast your *Endure Flames*," I said. "Then we'll open the door and make a run for it."

I imagined the stairs on fire, choked with smoke-filled air… maybe the whole building would collapse on us.

Morgana frowned, but not having a better idea, slowly nodded in agreement. She cast *Endure Flames* on herself and pressed her ear against the vault door.

Elmac cleared his throat. "That plan, quite frankly, sucks. 'Tis most unlikely the Rooster be *accidentally* burning."

"The Syndicate then?" Morgana asked.

Elmac nodded. "And they'll just be waiting for us to come out." He made a throat-slitting gesture.

I glared at him. "You have a better plan?"

Elmac smirked.

"What," I demanded, "do *you* know that *we* don't, you cantankerous badger?"

"*Shhh*," Morgana said. She had produced a stethoscope from somewhere and held its diaphragm to the vault door. "Think I hear some of the buggers out there." She wheeled on Elmac. "How can you be so *bloody* calm?"

"There be an old dwarf saying," he whispered. "Never enter a cave with but *one* exit."

Morgana pulled away from the door. "There's another way out?"

"Of course," he said.

I turned and looked but there was no sign of a handy escape hatch.

"Just wait, lad," Elmac told me *sotto voce*. "We *want* them to think we be stuck in here." He pounded the vault door with his metal fist. "HELP!" he screamed. "This blasted door be jammed!" He faked a cough. "Suffocating..." He pounded thrice more, each knock weaker than the last. "Not... much... longer... agguhhhhh."

"I thought this place was soundproofed?" I said.

"'Tis," Elmac replied. "But any fool would be hearing *that* banging."

He may have been acting, but I sure felt like there was no oxygen left in the room. Every breath I took seemed like I was sucking it through a straw.

Morgana slapped an *Endure Flames* spell on me and Elmac. The air instantly cooled and freshened.

"Thanks," I said with an exhale. "Wait—what about all that whiskey, that highly combustible whiskey, upstairs?"

"Oh." Elmac's features turned to stone. "That be a tragedy, but don't worry 'bout that lot exploding. The heat'll ruin it all, but the bottles be enchanted to absorb no heat past the flashpoint 'o ethanol. City ordinance."

It might have been nice if he'd mentioned that earlier.

"So where is this other exit?" I asked him.

"Hang on." Morgana scrutinized the room. "Give me fifteen ticks to see if I can find it." Her eyes narrowed and she tapped her teeth together.

I looked as well. Lead sheeting covered every surface and had been riveted firmly in place. How long until the stuff started to melt? I crossed to the side opposite the blazing hot door and ran my hands over the welded seams and rivet heads. Apart from the panel that popped open for the air controls, nothing else stood out.

"Wish I'd used the ladies room upstairs," Morgana muttered under her breath.

We locked eyes and both turned to the crate in the corner: the chamber pot, the one spot no one in their right mind would linger long over... or bother to search for a hidden passage.

Morgana and I hustled over there and I picked up the crate.

As promised, there was a clay chamber pot (spattered and stained), a pitcher of water, and miracles of miracles—a roll of real toilet paper.

I slid these items to one side with my boot.

Underneath, four hairline seams made a square in the floor.

I pushed, pulled on the floor—nothing.

Morgana knelt, squinted, and touched a rivet head a bit shinier than the others.

A *click*.

She poked around the edges with a pick, nodded to me, and handed me a pry bar from her kit.

I levered the square.

It came free and revealed a hole plunging into darkness.

Elmac left the vault door. "Time to go." He pushed past me and stepped into the hole. "This'll be a one-way trip, so grab anything you want to be seeing again."

There was a hint of sadness in his voice. He wasn't talking about coming back to this vault. Elmac meant we wouldn't be coming back to the Bloody Rooster. Ever.

I searched for something to say that might console my friend.

But there was no time for fancy words. We had to move.

I swept *everything* off the table into my inventory (even the thermos of coffee and paper cups). Why not?

When I turned back, Elmac was gone.

Morgana was already halfway down the hole.

"Replace the lid when you follow." She pointed at the chamber pot, pitcher, and toilet paper. "That lot too. And make sure the air freshener is on the crate. Basic rule of concealment: the little details matter."

Right. Morgana was the expert after all.

The temperature jumped like someone had flipped a switch. There was no way her *Endure Flames* spell had expired already, so something else had to have caused it.

A spot glowing dull red appeared on the black metal vault door. The air about it smoked and wavered. As I watched, that spot brightened to the color of a sunrise streaming through amber.

Someone was trying to burn through.

I had to *not* be here.

I got into the hole and clambered down four rungs of a ladder bolted to the tunnel wall.

Upon the square plate, I arranged the chamber pot, pitcher, and toilet paper. I then placed the crate (air freshener and all) atop the thing. Balancing the precarious package, I lifted it over my head and took three very careful steps down the ladder.

The crate started to slide off.

I got it level before disaster struck. Whew.

How funny would that be? On top of everything else tonight, me dumping a load of crap on myself. Hilarious.

Two more steps down... easy does it... and I got the plate set overhead, nice and snug.

The seams magically heated and welded solid.

No kidding this was a one-way trip.

Below, a light winked on.

I descended another twenty rungs and jumped the last few feet.

"No!" Morgana whispered.

She grabbed my arm and pulled me to the ledge she and Elmac were on... a ledge that ran alongside a ten-foot wide channel.

Not quite all of me, though.

Before I could fully arrest my momentum, one boot dunked into raw sewage. The stuff trickled in and soaked my sock.

CHAPTER 6

Sometimes the universe just has it in for you.

Or maybe my luck tonight was literally excremental.

Oh well.

I shook my foot. No dice. I'd be mucking around in this stuff until I could take off my boot and sock and take a boiling-hot bath.

"I'd hoped to never be using that trapdoor," Elmac said, looking up, his eyes crinkling in pain. With a heavy sigh, he turned back to the passage and held up a silver coin with an illumination enchantment (the magical equivalent of a tactical flashlight).

Dwarves could see in total darkness, so Elmac must have had this on his person to accommodate us lesser, non-dwarven creatures.

He unsheathed a dagger and marched down the tunnel.

Morgana followed.

I took the rear guard position.

High Hill's sewer was just what I expected: a channel containing assorted floating bits, ledges on either side, curved walls of ancient brick, slick stalactites of dripping algae… oh, and a world-class *stench* that made Low District in comparison smell like the mythical Avenue of Endless Blossoms in Thera's capital, Maraval.

"Keep your eyes peeled," Elmac whispered. "There be poop elementals on the prowl, mucus men, and lermix that'll suck every drop 'o blood out of you. Least this be better than the lower levels. Uhg." He shuddered. "Oh, and try to not be making any *more* noise." He stared pointedly at my *smucky*-sounding boot.

"You think," I whispered back, "the assassins will follow us? Fighting here might get tricky."

"They ought to be busy enough burning me bar," Elmac muttered darkly. "But just in case, we'll be quick, cross to River Street—then up and out."

We slogged along and I noted symbols on the walls—some scratched into the brick and blackened with mold; a few patches of phosphorescing slime molds too organized to be random; and three recently chalked arcane glyphs.

There were also tiny directional arrows, hobo symbols, sloppy graffiti (in dark elf?), and an odd pictograph of an anthropomorphized fungus man with a throng of stick figures kneeling in worship at his feet... his stem? He pointed to the passage on my left.

"Psst," I hissed and nodded at this.

Morgana took a glance, then shot me an annoyed look for sightseeing instead of watching for danger.

Elmac leaned back. "That be the Mushroom King. We avoid him at all costs."

Okay, a cryptic and threatening answer. But perversely, now all I wanted to do was go that way. I bet if I did, a quest alert would pop.

I didn't. Instead, I made a note of it in my game journal for later investigation.

Around the next corner, the light-emitting slime molds vanished and the glow from Elmac's fist was our only illumination.

I had to get one of those coins. Useful little things. Assuming I ever got on her good side, I wondered if Colonel Delacroix might enchant one for me?

"Either of you seen Delacroix?" I asked, so low I wasn't sure my companions heard me.

"She went to Brötmandel Chasms," Elmac said at a similar volume. "Checking that Abyssal gate be truly shut. Took one 'o the Duke's cavalry gryphons to fly there last morning, so she should be back by now."

That explained why she hadn't dragged me in yesterday for a debriefing (her polite word for "interrogation").

Had Elmac said "cavalry gryphon?" Hmm. He'd mentioned that Dame Rose Beckonsail, who was on the Syndicate's hit list, was a captain of such a unit. A coincidence?

But wow—*gryphon* cavalry! And I thought Pendric on his titan warhorse, Bell Ringer, had been bad news. With apologies to my brother and sister warriors in the 101st Airborne, gryphon cavalry gave a new twist to the motto: *"Death from above."*

"Those assassins on Gut Slit Lane," Morgana said. "Sure was lots of them, poisoned weapons and all. But don't you think it was, I dunno, *easy?*"

"Might be something to that," I said. "Their leader was only second level, the rest, first."

"Maybe they were *meant* to herd us along to the Rooster?" Elmac suggested.

"We'd have been sitting ducks in any *normal* vault," Morgana said.

Elmac raised his free hand. His other closed about the enchanted coin.

We plunged into total darkness.

Nice that Elmac could see in such conditions, but my elven eyes were useless. I kept still, lest I slip off the ledge, and take a few involuntary laps.

A small hand touched my arm. Morgana.

We locked grips. Her skin was warm and calloused. Fingers long and strong.

A guy could get used to holding such a hand...

Ahead was a splash.

My wistful thoughts washed away.

Ten paces ahead, a gout of flame lit the intersection—just an instant.

Burned into my retinas was the image of five assassins poised flash-frozen: two chest-deep in the channel muck, two on the ledge, and one clung to the arched ceiling like a gecko. The guy on the ceiling had held a tube belching the fire.

This next part is hard to describe. I got just a glimpse.

Something *else* was in the intersection. It was the size of a car, gelatinous, with tentacles wrapped about the assassins on the ledge.

I think one more assassin was *inside* the thing's body.

Whatever I thought I had seen in that instant, I could now only hear it surge and thrash in the dark.

Water was displaced by these motions. Lots.

Churning. Slopping closer.

A wave crashed over the ledge, up to my hips. It had to have *covered* poor Elmac. I gripped the wall with one hand, Morgana with the other.

Disgusting.

But she and I thankfully had remained on the ledge.

Suddenly there was light and wavering lines on the curved tunnel walls. Elmac was in the drink, treading water, and sputtering through a soaked beard. He must have dropped his light coin.

The gelatinous monster in the intersection turned toward us.

Three assassins were now trapped inside the thing, their features stretched in tortured anguish, flesh and bone dissolving. Their blood tinged the creature pink.

And, since our luck apparently *could* get worse, it did.

Down other passages leading to the intersection... two more teams of assassins came slinking. Ten, maybe fifteen of them.

The idea of half swimming, half choking, in this sewage muck, grappling with a giant amoeba, *and* dodging a few poisoned darts? Well, discretion seemed better at the moment, not valor.

I would have given anything for a good old-fashioned M67 "baseball" frag grenade.

But maybe I had something that might work just as well. A "weapon 'o last resort", Elmac had called it.

Morgana reached down just as Elmac got back to the ledge.

"Underwater," I told them in English. "Swim. Straight ahead. As fast as you can!"

Morgana looked at me, then to the monster and assassins closing.

She trusted me, took a deep breath, and jumped.

Elmac was already gone.

I opened my inventory, grabbed the vial the assassin on Gut Slit Lane had tried to open in his final moments—and I chucked it.

How did I know the vapor creature inside would provide distraction enough for us to get away? Or for that matter, how did I know it wouldn't attack *us*?

I didn't.

But if you're about to be killed by one monster, did it make a difference if you were killed by *two* monsters?

Odds were it was going to do *something*... and I'd take whatever came.

The vial shattered on a wall.

A purple cloud rapidly expanded and filled the intersection. It reminded me of the genie emerging from his bottle in the classic 1940 movie, *The Thief of Bagdad*. This, however, was no djinn offering me three wishes. These vapors reddened to the color of rubies and flickers of static sparked inside like heat lightning.

It stretched and curled about the amoeba as if in an embrace.

The two creatures coiled and thrashed trying to envelop each other.

I stood and stared, fascinated. Terrified.

The amoeba relented and retreated up a wall.

The cloud retreated as well, concentrated its gases into a needle-like lance—pierced the monster gelatin over and over, disintegrating where it touched.

The gigantic single cell shuddered and spilled thick gel from its wounds. Where that stuff touched the wall, bricks smoked.

The assassins that *had* been coming, turned and fled.

Lucky for me I was still gaping at the scene because even as the sentient cloud of death sucked the amoeba dry, the retreating assassins in their haste made *splashing* sounds. Very *loud* splashing sounds.

When I looked back, the amoeba was gone and the cloud sent tendrils down the passage after the assassins... searching.

It stretched thin enough to reveal its inner workings: a thousand pinpoints of light boiled. Bioluminescent insects? Molecular acid? Antimatter? I had no intention of finding out.

Misty tentacles caught the closest assassins and made short work of the ninja-clad appetizers, leaving dried husks and skeletons... and then nothing.

Gone in a single heartbeat.

The cloud rippled as if it liked what it had tasted.

A dozen new vaporous tendrils probed the tunnels, up and down, right and left.

One snaked straight toward me—fast.

That snapped me out of my stupor.

I closed my eyes, ducked underwater, hoping the noxious smell and/or taste of raw sewage masked my presence—and then swam straight ahead for all I was worth.

I didn't dare open my eyes, so I went blind, heart pounding as *things* touched me, some squishy, others curling, feeling with tiny suckers.

There was a caress on my thigh. It burned like a hundred fire ants.

I awkwardly kicked, made contact, kicked again, and something peeled off.

I focused on paddling, getting as *far* away from the intersection, as *fast* as I could.

When dots swam on my eyelids and my chest was about to burst, I forced myself to keep going for five more strokes—then surfaced, wiped my face clear of muck, spat, and took the longest inhalation of my life.

I was in the dark (figuratively and literally). No sparks. No flashes of fire. Just inky black.

So where was Elmac? Morgana?

Then the smell (and taste) of my little dip registered.

I suppressed my gagging, which would have made far too much noise.

I waited for three heartbeats, straining to hear splashes or feel incoming waves.

Nothing.

So I moved toward the side of the tunnel, or at least what I thought was the side... slowly, very slowly, so as to not cause even a ripple.

"Here..."

I almost missed her voice, the racket of my pounding heart almost drowning it out.

Ah, Morgana.

I almost answered her but held my tongue. No need to make more noise. If she was calling to me, it was a pretty good bet that *she* could see me in this total blackout. There had to be a druid spell for that.

I bumped against the ledge and carefully pulled myself up.

"Slow and steady, mate," she whispered, took my hand, and placed it on her shoulder. "Other hand on the wall and follow, yeah?"

So, we went like that for a while.

I was dazed, but nonetheless had the presence of mind to fire off a few *Spiritual Regenerations*. I had a feeling I was about to get an in-game alert telling me that my leg was infected with "instantaneous gangrene" or something of equivalent lethality.

My leg healed... and distressingly filled in chunks of flesh that had been missing.

There wasn't as much as a flicker of light, not even one bit of phosphorescing mold. Maybe that was a good thing; otherwise, I'd have slowed us down, every two seconds looking over my shoulder to see if the cloud was coming after me. I shivered.

If our assassin buddies had managed to open that vial, things would have turned out *very* differently on Gut Slit Lane.

Now that I thought about it, capturing and compressing such a high-level monster into that container must have taken a lot of magic and cost a fortune. Who would give a second-level *flunky* such a powerful weapon?

Someone rich. Someone desperate to remove us from their calculations.

Morgana halted.

A faint glimmer ahead, no more than an anemic firefly from a clenched metal fist.

Elmac must have had a spare magical light coin.

My eyes adjusted.

He had halted at a dead-end.

Elmac patted the wall. He stuck his face against the bricks for the closest look he could get, back and forth, practically dragging his large nose over them.

"Ah, gotcha," he whispered, pushed one brick, and then rotated it a quarter turn.

I felt a *thud*.

Elmac then used several protruding bricks (that had not been protruding a moment ago) as handholds, climbed up—and vanished.

Morgana and I moved closer.

A bobble of illumination and a dwarf-shaped shadow ascended through a hole in the ceiling.

Morgana leaned close and, lips pressed to my ear, murmured, "This where we're *supposed* to be?"

Under other circumstances, a beautiful woman's lips touching my skin... well, it would have been a lovely distraction. All things considered though? I was just glad to have a *person* touch me.

"Your guess is as good as mine, but please, ladies first." I made a gallant gesture for her to go ahead.

She went. I followed.

As soon as I'd cleared the tunnel's ceiling, the secret passage to the sewer shut.

"Glad to be out of *there*," Morgana said. "Monsters, dysentery, and crikey, can't even imagine how much my old human joints would've ached in that damp."

I could sympathize. I had a tiny piece of shrapnel near my spine. That is, Hector Savage of Earth had. Every time it rained, it felt like an icepick twisting in my back.

Morgana might have had a similar injury.

We climbed forty feet, then halted because Elmac's butt blocked the way.

He scratched at the roof overhead.

A pull ring came free. He gave it a tug and there was a faint *ping*.

Hey—I knew that ping. It sounded just like the hotel front desk bell on the counter of Hiltmyer & Co, Trading Post Extraordinaire.

So we *had* made it across River Street.

There was a *click*.

Elmac pushed the trapdoor open and pulled himself through.

So did we.

Elmac fully opened his fist and light flooded the room.

If you could call it that.

Apart from a patch of stone under our feet, there wasn't anything here. Literally. Outside Elmac's circle of illumination was flat darkness. My eyes couldn't, or wouldn't, focus on anything out there.

I reached out.

Elmac grabbed my sleeve. "Don't. Seriously lad, no."

"What kind of rabbit hole did you just take us through?" Morgana asked.

As if in response, the strange dark parted like a curtain and a dozen gnomes stepped through... each holding a tiny crossbow (most of them aimed at me).

CHAPTER 7

The leader of this miniature gang was a dead ringer for a garden gnome statue with red hat, coat, and curly-toed boots. I knew him, Lordren Hiltmyer, proprietor of Hiltmyer & Co., Trading Post Extraordinaire.

My casual acquaintance with the guy, however, only went so far...

Guns, bows, Shakespeare's slings and arrows of outrageous fortune, broken bottles, and shivs filed from prison-issue toothbrushes—*any* of these pointed my way put me in a foul mood. That went triple tonight.

I stepped forward to grab one of those toy crossbows, stuff it right up—

"Halt," Lordren commanded in his helium squeaky voice. "You have three words to explain yourselves, then we open fire."

Elmac cleared his throat. "Don't. Be. An. Ass."

Technically four words.

I didn't point this out as they seemed to be the *right* words.

"Oh dear." Lordren blinked, obviously recognizing Elmac's voice, but not the sight of the bedraggled dwarf dripping before him. "I am *so* sorry." He waved his hands at his cohorts and they lowered their weapons.

Lordren removed his hat and bowed to Morgana. "Deepest apologies, Madam Nox. I did not know who or *what* to expect when the backdoor bell rang."

"No harm, no foul," Morgana said.

Lordren gave a microscopic nod my way. "Master Saint-Savage..."

He then gave Elmac a bear hug.

"Now—just—that be—" Elmac protested, but gave up, and patted the little guy consolingly on the back.

"We saw the fire." Lordren's voice cracked and he squeezed Elmac tighter. "We tried to—I thought you might be..."

"Aye, well, I be fine." He pushed Lordren back.

"Sorry to interrupt," I said, interrupting, "but where are we?" I waved about at the infinite darkness surrounding us.

"This is a void cube," Lordren told me. "It is where Hiltmyer and Company secures its most *interesting* items. Come, follow me, and please stay on the path at all times."

Black flagstones paved a corridor four paces across under my boots—then there was a nothing so devoid of... of anything, dust, light, even a sense that there was "space" there, it was painful to look at for long.

Lordren's gang parted what seemed like black curtains, let their boss through, and waved for us to follow.

We did, everyone scrunching near Lordren as he walked into pitch blackness. The stone path appeared only a moment before his foot touched down—remained for mere seconds after.

"Void cube?" Morgana asked. "What's that then?"

I detected a bit of professional safecracker curiosity in her tone.

"Very old magic," Lordren answered. "Shaped by the Titans from a shard of the primordial void. It is the quintessence of not being. To touch it is to be *un*-created."

I tried not to think about this *un-creating* nothing as I marched forward, and concentrated on putting one foot as straight as possible in front of the other.

Ahead was a sliver of light. We entered and—emerged in Hiltmyer & Co, Trading Post Extraordinaire.

I exhaled and turned.

The rest of the gnome firing squad marched through what appeared to be an ordinary closet door.

The door shut on its own.

It didn't have a lock. Or a doorknob.

I made a note to never break into Lordren's shop or even wander off unescorted.

The shop was the type you ran across in any fantasy game: jam-packed with everything a would-be adventurer might need. One's eyes tended to wander… pickaxes, packs, rope, and so much more. Think of it as a cross between a sporting goods store, antique shop, and a hoarder's attic, then squeeze it all into a long, narrow building almost too cramped to navigate the aisles, and you had the idea.

The thing that caught my attention, though, was the front window.

The blinds were down, but the slats cracked open enough so light streamed through, glowing orange, and reminding me of the wires of a space heater.

A light that had to be coming from Elmac's bar. Burning.

Elmac was halfway across the store before I realized it. Morgana and I trotted after him.

We looked between the slats.

It felt like a blade of ice had been shoved into my gut.

The Bloody Rooster was gone.

All that remained were smoldering timbers thrust up like the ribs of a giant burnt offering. The center had caved in and formed a pit glowing like molten steel.

The basement must have collapsed.

I swallowed. It stuck in my throat.

If there hadn't been an escape hatch in his vault, it would have been a long time before anyone would have even found Elmac's safe under all that, let alone figured out a way to open it.

It would have been a torturous end.

"This is *my* fault." Morgana's voice tightened and she clutched a silver chain about her throat. "It was just a bloody quest for the Thieves Guild. I'm so sorry, Elmac."

"No lass. Don't." He turned to her, eyes glistening with unshed tears. "'Tis not your doing. There be more to this than one of your quests."

I agreed. It could have been someone after me. Or Elmac. Or none of us. We were operating in the dark.

I strained my eyes searching the street for *something* that might offer a clue.

There was easy access to River Street from a number of alleyways. Any pyromaniac could have snuck in and out undetected. No help there.

The intensity and speed at which this fire had reduced Elmac's beloved bar to a pile of ash was impressive. It was as if someone had used white phosphorus or a fireball. The buildings around Elmac's, however, some so close they'd practically touched the bar, were *unscathed*. Not even scorch marks.

I pointed this out to my companions.

"'Tis what I told you before," Elmac replied. "There be building codes. After the southern section of town burned down, every structure has to be enchanted to resist fire—if not made *entirely* fireproof. I had the best money could buy. Would have taken strong magical fire or an unholy flame to overpower it."

"So this was started by a wizard?" Morgana asked.

"Aye, maybe."

Strong magic like the stuff that had compressed a monster cloud of death into a tiny vial?

Again, there was only one group I knew who had that kind of juice, an equal propensity for overwhelming vengeance and violence, *and* come to think of it access to all things unholy: The Lords of the Abyss.

So what about the rule prohibiting them from targeting players?

I felt like I was missing something obvious.

I inhaled deeply and took in the scent of burnt oak blended with a hundred different single malt whiskeys and other assorted vaporized liquors, savoring the last of what might have been many pleasant memories that we'd never again have in the Bloody Rooster.

A breath shuddered out of Elmac. "Me bar..."

I set a hand on his shoulder.

Elmac dropped his head.

It was a cruel myth that old soldiers preferred to lick their wounds alone. They needed comforting more than most.

Behind us, Lordren politely coughed. I turned and saw all the gnomes stood pointy hats in hands, gazes downcast, some quietly crying, all respectfully waiting.

"What can we do, Elmac?" Lordren asked.

Elmac shook his head (and clandestinely wiped his face). He looked up and faced Lordren, eyes bloodshot and wild. "Did you see Marty? And the rest 'o the customers? Did they get out?"

"Some," Lordren whispered. "They were taken to the Temple of the Three Sisters. I am not sure exactly whom... or how many survived."

Elmac went rigid, and not I suspected, from grief.

I looked outside once more.

There was a silhouetted crowd gawking from a safe distance.

As my vision adjusted I made out a few dozen people, and over the heads of some, wisps of smoke seemed to linger. My eyes were inexplicably drawn to the stuff.

It slowly came into focus. Silver letters.

I took an involuntary step back.

There were other *players* out there.

I squinted, but no matter how hard I tried, I couldn't *quite* make out the words.

"Still got that spyglass?" I asked Morgana.

"Crikey, why didn't I think of that?" She blinked, her gaze darting back and forth, and a brass spyglass appeared in her hand. She extended the thing and looked.

So far, I'd met only three players in the game.

In the "nice" column was Morgana, true-blue pal, dangerous, mysterious, always there for me.

The two in the "naughty" column were Fhullrokotop, cleric of the Elder Lovecraftian gods and certifiably insane—and my brother, the anti-paladin working for the Lords of the Abyss. Both of them practically clichés of evil.

So, these new players were what? Friend? Foe?

Morgana passed her spyglass to me.

I held my breath and peered into the eyepiece.

The first player was hard to miss. She was a wood elf who wore a three-sided pirate's hat bedecked with ostrich plumes, a ruffled red shirt crisscrossed with bandoliers, black leggings, and a wide leather belt holding a hand crossbow, rapier, and assorted pouches. It looked as if Douglas Fairbanks Junior and Errol Flynn had tried to, and done a poor job of, copying *her* flamboyant style.

Her player tag read:

Cassie Longstrider
Ranger (Swashbuckler) / LEVEL 12
Wonder Women

I whispered this to Elmac.

"Regular customer," he told me. "'Twasn't there when we walked in. A bit, er, rowdy when she's had too much. Grand tipper, though."

"Wonder Women?" Morgana looked into the distance, searching her memories (or checking her interface). "Yeah, the likes of Athena, Hera, valkyries. If Joan of Arc was in the Game, that's the clan she'd be in, if that is, she wasn't already a Catholic saint."

I continued my search and spotted another player—this one climbing *out* of the molten pit. He wore a chainmail hauberk that fit him like a second metal skin. It glowed red-hot but rapidly cooled to dull silver. Completing this heat-proof ensemble was a helmet with curved horns and a metal club big enough to flatten a horse.

I read his tag for the others.

Grimhalt
Cleric (Zealot) / LEVEL 9
The Wild Hunt

Morgana growled, "Ran into that one before."

When I'd met Morgana in the Free Trial, she'd told me that one of these Wild Hunt people had hassled her. Couldn't have been this guy because he was too high level to engage in PvP combat with a first- or second-level character.

Although, if Morgana hadn't known about this rule at the time, he could have chased her into that zombie-infested forest... where the unliving would have torn her to pieces for him.

So, one more on the naughty list.

"He's psychotic, that one," Morgana said.

"Agreed," Elmac muttered. "The Wild Hunt has gods that—"

I held up my hand. "I know about the Wild Hunt."

I hadn't meant to be so rude and cut Elmac off, but just then I spotted another player, and *couldn't* focus on anything else.

This guy wore gray robes whose silky fabric shimmered with subtle twinkling reds and greens... nebulae and stars that were *not* merely embroidered; rather, this looked like the real thing, a window into the cosmos.

I didn't think he was human.

His features were angles and planes devoid of a single curve. It was like Picasso had chiseled a face from blue-gray slate—the color of a drowned corpse. Yet he was also somehow unearthly handsome. Creepy too, because crowning his bald head was a ring of seven-penny nails driven halfway into his skull, reminiscent of Pinhead in Clive Barker's 1987 nightmarish flick, *Hellraiser*.

Almost in a trance, I read his placard for Elmac's benefit.

Harlix Hadri
Wizard (Researcher) / LEVEL 12
Sapientia Aeterna

"Sapientia Aeterna?" I said. "My Latin's rusty. That's what... 'Smart Forever'?"

"Eternal Wisdom," Elmac corrected.

"Heard of *them*," Morgana said, tapping her lower lip, not sounding happy. "Think from one of my guildmates. Just a tick. I'll send a quick message." She typed on an invisible keyboard.

I watched this Harlix wave over a city guard.

The guard jumped, started to salute, but halted the gesture mid-way.

Looked like the wizard had pull with the city's officials, but wasn't one of them.

I set the spyglass down, tabbed to the notes section of my interface, and wrote down everything I'd just learned. Unlike Morgana's clan, mine had no database on players, clans, and game abilities. This was as good a start as any.

When I had it all copied, I grabbed the spyglass and continued to search. There were plenty of guards and onlookers, but no more floating title placards.

I didn't see the one person I *thought* would be here: Colonel Delacroix. If anyone could get to the bottom of why these assassins were after us, it'd be High Hill's Chief of the not-so-secret secret police. Where was she?

I forgot all about Delacroix as another person caught my eye.

She wore a veil and white dress with gold spirals along the arms. In the firelight, it looked drenched in blood.

She turned *from* the smoking ruins and looked across River Street.

If I hadn't known better, I'd have said she gazed directly *at me*.

The light was all wrong, though. I was in deep shadow behind slitted blinds, and the flame-lit glare off the store's window would have further obscured my presence. For all intents and purposes, I should have been invisible from her vantage.

Behind her veil, I thought I caught a glimpse of ghostly indigo blue eyes, like smoldering coals.

She then turned back toward the remains of the Bloody Rooster.

"Here we go," Morgana said. "Got a reply."

I stepped back and lowered the spyglass.

She paused to scan the message. "Eternal Wisdom... blokes are a pack of wizards and higher IQ types... dedicated to gathering knowledge and secrets." Her features slackened. "Membership includes liches, elder god devotees, and evil genius types."

Lovely. Smart *and* evil. One of my least favorite combinations (right up there with ignorant and loud-mouthed).

"Wait," I said, "that doesn't mean this Harlix guy is *necessarily* evil. His wizard specialization is 'Researcher.' That has to be, what, like a librarian?"

"Hang on," Morgana whispered, scrolling ahead.

"Yeah..." she told me. "No. Says 'Researcher' is more like an 'Inquisitor.' They're known to extract knowledge from items, history from places, and secrets from people—and are none too particular on the condition they leave the things that information gets extracted from... as in erased, destroyed, or dead."

Regardless of rules against high-level players annihilating lower-level ones—I had a strong preference to stay far away from these three. At least until we knew what they were up to.

"I vote we stick to our plan," I said to Elmac and Morgana. "Send a message to Delacroix, then a tactical retreat, knock out an easy quest, and level up a bit. In the process, we might give these assassins the slip."

"I can go along with that for now," Morgana whispered.

Elmac said nothing and stared out the window, dark eyes unblinking.

"Elmac?"

He shook his head. I wasn't sure if that meant he didn't like my plan, or if he just wanted me to shut my trap.

Morgana moved to his side, hesitated, then put an arm around his shoulders. "You can rebuild. We'll help. The important thing is you're alive, mate."

The tension melted from Elmac. He slowly, reluctantly I think, withdrew from her. "Aye, lass. Thank you. We *could* rebuild, but I think this be a sign that I move on."

"So," I asked, "are we sticking to the plan?"

"We stick to the plan." There was steel in his voice. "Get word to the Colonel, 'o course, and then a tactical retreat. But when you be making fifth level, Hektor, I get in the game, no delay... so I can be arranging a bit 'o dwarven vengeance."

Elmac faced Lordren. "And if we be doing that, Master Trader, we be needing your *five-star* service. So, best wake the entire staff."

CHAPTER 8

What exactly *was* five-star service?

In short (no pun intended), it was every player's shopping *dream.*

Elmac had barely drawn a breath after his request when Lordren turned to the squad of attending gnomes and clapped his hands.

They jumped into action—screwed the blinds fully shut and lowered steel shutters over the windows and doors to further secure the shop. Orbs of cut crystal flickered with light and transformed dingy to brilliant.

Another legion of gnomes appeared from nowhere—swept, dusted, mopped, polished—and vanished again. Before I blinked, there were more crews: running back and forth; opening trapdoors; pulling back curtains to reveal alcoves, changing rooms, misty magic mirrors, and a small kitchen with coffee percolating. They straightened shelves; removed common items and set out new clockwork gadgets, cases of gemstones, rows of boots, and racks of robes, jackets, and cloaks of exotic leathers, furs, and silk;

sunflowers were set in Ming vases, incense lit... and much more that I caught only blurs and half-glimpses—impossible things that *had to have been* my imagination.

Three elder gnomes in matching silver-pinstriped suits approached us. These gentlemen eyed us up and down, shared a glance, and nodded to one another.

I was about to introduce myself when they undulated their hands and chanted three mystical words: *"Emundabit, percula, heilen."*

Fist-sized cumulonimbus thunderheads condensed about me.

I resisted the impulse to backflip away from this uninvited and potentially harmful spell. I was perhaps a bit on a hair-trigger tonight after all that had happened.

Elmac calmly stood there, raised arms over his head, and slowly turned in his personal cloud formation.

If it was okay with Elmac, I guess I could play along too.

The clouds gently steamed my clothes, faded stains, straightened wrinkles, and the smell—oh nice, no more *eau de outhouse,* but that refreshing off-the-clothesline scent that reminded me of summer. The rips and tears I'd recently acquired mended as well.

I looked, smelled, and felt as if I'd just stepped out of a shower, toweled off, and been professionally pressed.

Before I could thank these wizard cleaners, they reported to Lordren, whispering in hushed tones.

"Lordren's staff be taking good care of you two," Elmac told Morgana and me.

"Us two?" Morgana asked. "What about you? And what's this five-star service costing? Not that I'm complaining. Entirely."

"Costs nothing," Elmac said. "Lordren owes me a few favors."

Good thing. If my prior dealing with Lordren was any indication of his business chops, Elmac's purse would have been considerably lightened.

And also good because we could all use a little five-star treatment. You know, live a little. We might, after all, be dead before the sun rose.

"Thanks, Elmac," I said. "Just one more thing. With assassins potentially skulking just outside... well, I'd hate to bring trouble to Lordren's doorstep."

Elmac managed a halfhearted grin (the best he could muster under the circumstances). "No one has ever, *ever* broken into this shop," he said. "And I doubt any ever will."

He stepped closer and in a low murmur told us, "Now, make sure you be tipping your personal assistant. *Generously.* They get a wee touchy if the transactional-social niceties be forgotten." He paused, frowned, and then added, "You be needing a little gold for that, Hektor?"

Lordren politely looked away, pretending to not be listening.

"I've got it covered."

"Good. I'll just be a few minutes. Maybe an hour. Or two."

Without further explanation, Elmac and Lordren marched to a back office I was pretty sure hadn't been there when we'd entered.

I got a weird feeling watching those two—like they'd fought and drank and mourned lost comrades together.

I imagined them younger in a party of adventurers. Why not? Lordren was about the same age as Elmac. Heck, the gnome might have been one of the fabled seven heroes to have survived the epic Battle of Underhill. I knew one had been Elmac, another Pendric's father, and sure, I could see Lordren as the party's thief. Might as well add the immortal solar sorceress supreme, Colonel Delacroix, to round them out.

Or it could have just been me connecting dots that weren't really there.

At kneecap level, there was a tiny cough and the squeaky clearing of a throat.

Two gnomes stood before Morgana and me.

These had to be our aforementioned "personal assistants."

The gnome in front of Morgana was a gentleman wearing a hunter-green three-button vest and lime-colored slacks. A banker's visor shaded his eyes, so the only part of his face I could see was his courteous smile. He held a human-sized silver pocket watch that barely fit in his hand.

My personal assistant was a lady gnome in a black blazer and pinstriped pencil skirt. Her hair was pink and bobbed in some ultra-fashionable asymmetrical cut, and her nails French manicured to perfection. She would have looked at home in any Fantasy Fortune 500 boardroom.

"Begging your pardon, Mister Saint-Savage," she said with a minute curtsey. "We have a comfortable spot for you over here."

She motioned at a set of curtains and they parted. Beyond was a tiny parlor with a writing desk, chaise lounge, a tray of cookies, and a steaming cup of what I prayed to all the gods was coffee.

Morgana's assistant was already showing her the way to her "comfortable spot."

"You going to be ok?" I asked her.

"Think so." Her forehead crinkled. "Just a bit turned around by everything happening so bloody fast—but yeah, let's tool up and do some shopping."

"Good luck."

"Luck to you too, mate."

I let my personal assistant lead me into the parlor behind curtain number one.

She pulled the curtains closed.

I sat on the chaise lounge. Its leather was red and butter soft.

Okay—shopping is an essential part of gaming. You *had to* upgrade your gear or get crushed as you inevitably encountered higher-level monsters. One way to upgrade was by looting the villains and monsters you defeated. The usefulness of that stuff, however, depended on a random number generator coughing up the goods—that, let's face it, most of the time didn't come through. This led to the second way to get good gear: selling the useless stuff and buying what you wanted, usually at an *outrageous* exchange rate.

I slid onto the floor so I'd be face to face with…

"I'm sorry, I didn't catch your name."

"My apologies, sir." She tilted her chin up. "I am Lillian Carat-Bringer, Concierge of the Order of the Silver Spoon, Adept of Fitting, Acolyte of Bargains, and senior apprentice accountant here at Hiltmyer & Co."

"A pleasure to meet you, Miss Carat-Bringer."

She pulled out a notepad and gold fountain pen and waited.

"Uh," I said, lowering my voice, "this is my first time using 'five-star service.' What precisely are we supposed to do?"

"Of course, sir. I am here to help find whatever you need, at the best prices, and provide you a level of comfort, luxury, and service that you will find nowhere else in High Hill—*only* for Mr. Hiltmyer's *most* important customers."

Why did I suddenly have an itch mid-way down my spine, as if someone was about to stick the mercantile equivalent of a dagger there?

"If you could tell me what you wish to see," she said, "and the parameters of your budget, we can get started."

Ah. Here was the catch. The old "*What a coincidence! Your total today just happens to equal all your money*" gambit.

This service, free or not, or paid by Elmac or not, might end up costing me a lot.

I couldn't blame Miss Carat-Bringer. Sure, she was *my* personal assistant, but she *did* work for Lordren.

She poured me a cup of coffee.

I took a sip and exhaled with satisfaction. The brew was strong, smoky, and smooth.

It'd be way too easy to get comfortable. I needed to stay sharp.

Whatever the cost, the correct strategy was still to spend a lot *right now*. I was drowning in an ocean of danger, so walking out of here with anything less than the best I could afford would be flat-out stupid. How often have you seen a buddy too cheap to buy the magic armor that could have stopped the one point of damage that killed him?

With a wink, I opened my game interface and added five points to my *Bargaining* skill, bringing it to a total of ten.

I recalled how my father had taught me how to sell our caravan's goods, make a profit, and *always* leave the customer happy. This was the usual memory re-wiring to amend my character's backstory. This time, I hardly noticed it... barely a tickle in my mind. Good. Progress over the ice-pick-through-brain sensation I'd had before.

And, I now knew how to handle my personal assistant.

"Excuse me a sec." I turned away from Miss Carat-Bringer and summoned my inventory. From it, I pulled out a bag of inferno diamonds that Elmac had liberated from the hellfire demon we'd killed two days ago.

I turned back and poured the diamonds into my open palm.

Each was the size of a cherry pit and they gleamed and glittered as if I held a constellation of tiny orange suns.

Unlike when I'd handled these before (and I think because of my higher *Bargaining* skill) a large description window popped:

Inferno Diamonds (perfectly matched set of seven)
(Tier-VII non-magical gemstones, very rare)
DESCRIPTION: These flawless Zed-Shift 4 (fancy vivid) colored diamonds are facetted with *chaos cuts*—that is, each facet on a stone is a different angle and size than others. This is an exclusive technique known only to a select few demonkind. Inferno gems are imbued with a spark of hellfire, making them appear as if they are burning.

SPECIAL ABILITIES: Cannot be consumed by fire. This set is in pristine condition, and as such is suitable for enchantment.

VALUE: For a single diamond: 15,000-20,000 gold quins.

NOTE: There is a large variance in price depending on fashion trends and if these gems are sold individually or as a complete matched set. For the matched set: 230,000 gold quins would be a fair market price under current conditions.

TIP: Trade for equivalent value items *without* selling for cash first.

A kingly sum. Then again, it was my share of the loot for defeating a full demonic invasion, so I considered it fair compensation.

Lillian Carat-Bringer's eyes went wider than I thought possible.

"These are what I'll be spending today."

Apparently, gnome eyes *could* open wider.

"And this" —I set a finger on one diamond— "will be your tip. Uh, kind of."

Lillian arched an eyebrow and suspicion tightened her features. Her demeanor quickly cooled back to professional courtesy (with just a crinkle of concern remaining about her lips). "And how is that, sir?"

"You must know the matched set is worth much more than if I were to sell the individual gemstones."

She nodded in such a way that neither confirmed or denied this key fact.

"So, I will sell the entire lot to Lordren as a set, and your tip will be one-seventh of those proceeds. In other words, the full potential value of one diamond. I'd guess in the neighborhood of 32,000 quins."

"*Most* generous…" she whispered trance-like, gazing at the small fortune held in my open hand.

I snapped my hand shut. "With a caveat."

She blinked and looked once more at me.

I slowly opened my fist and the inferno diamonds cast reflected shards of amber light upon her eyes.

"This is your *maximum* tip," I explained. "Overly inflated prices, less than standard quality items… anything that detracts from my shopping experience and your tip will proportionally decrease."

I hated to act like a jerk, but with my increased *Bargaining* skill, I knew this was a viable tactic. Greed was a great motivator.

After a moment's consideration, she said, "I completely understand, sir. And if you don't mind me saying, a very cunning move."

I couldn't tell if she was impressed, irritated, or incentivized. Maybe all three. But I was pretty sure I now had a personal assistant who would walk over flaming broken glass for me.

Lillian snapped to attention, pen poised to take notes. "Where would you like to start?"

In so many words I explained that I was a martial artist looking for excellent quality, mid-level enchanted gear. It was no use window shopping for high-level stuff that I could neither use or afford.

From my previous shopping at this place, I knew the prices for quality gear was high. And for quality *magical* gear? Those prices could scale exponentially. I might be able to afford only a few choice pieces.

She nodded, scribbling copious notes, flipping pages.

"Oh, I'll need a few light coins. Or at least something to help me see in total darkness. Maybe throw in a few healing items too? And some anti-toxin potions if you have them."

"Anything else?" she asked.

Hang on. I still hadn't leveled up. My choice of how I proceeded could radically change my shopping list.

So, what would it be? Level up my core Spirit Warrior abilities? That path had the least risk. Choose a monk specialization subclass? Riskier, because while I'd gain new abilities, I'd close off options in the core class. Or—the option with the most unknowns, but maybe the most gains—go the multiclass route.

It seemed like the optimal time to pick another class. I'd be able to augment my new (and comparatively feeble) first-level class abilities with enchanted gear.

All right then, Battle Psychic or Mage of the Line?

(Yes, I'd previously made up my mind on this, but it'd be smart to review my reasons before I committed to such a life-altering choice).

Battle Psychic still felt like a bit of a mismatch for Spirit Warrior. I had a decent EGO stat, but my zero INTELLECT stat might be a handicap. And truth be told, I already felt overwhelmed in the thinking department. Something more "hands-on" sounded better.

So, Mage of the Line it was.

"Also a few simple... beginner wizard-type accessories?" I told Miss Carat-Bringer. "Wands, rings, and the like. Nothing too complicated. Nothing too expensive, either. I just dabble in the arcane arts."

More scribbling. "Yes, sir. I must, however, temper your expectations. Such novice arcane spell casting items are always in great demand. Our supplies may be limited."

"Understood."

I navigated through my interface and re-read the Mage of the Line class description.

Mage of the Line (aka Line Mage, Hand Mage)
Spellcasters who tap into primordial mana ley lines to create magic. Because a Mage of the Line must reach *in between* dimensions to touch mana ley lines, high PERCEPTION and REFLEX stats are critical. Mana pool is based on their REFLEX stat.

As usual, not many details, but making major decisions based on little to no data was part of the Game (just like real life).

I had a hunch, though, that a Mage of the Line with their high REFLEX requirement might have some stage magician in their DNA. *Pick a card, any card!* Cool.

"And maybe a few...?" I struggled to find the right words. "Props that, you know, sleight of hand stuff? Trick cards, vanishing coins? Doesn't even have to be real magic, although that would be nice too."

She set her notepad down, her complexion paled, then she shook her head as if to clear some unpleasant memory. "I believe we *might* have a few items like that in stock. Not many customers for such things... these days." Her gaze darted back to the inferno diamonds.

"Great. Let's see what you have, and we'll take it from there."

"I shall return in a few moments." Miss Carat-Bringer slipped out through the curtains.

I poured more coffee. Nibbled a lavender-infused chocolate chip cookie. Delicious.

My finger moved over the interface.

Select MAGE OF THE LINE as a second character class?
YES / NO

How about a "MAYBE?"

I was just about to tap YES when this popped:

=TUTORIAL (continued)=
Cost of Adding a New Class
You are about to add MAGE OF THE LINE as a second class. It must, however, be "purchased" for the experience points required to advance from the first to the second level of that class.
The cost to add MAGE OF THE LINE
is 3000 experience points.
Do you wish to spend the experience points? YES / NO

I almost spit out my coffee.

Now I understood why this couldn't be a starting class. The buy-in cost was ridiculous. 3000 points? That was almost the amount for me to advance from third- to fourth-level Spirit Warrior.

Either it was a blatant *ripoff* or maybe it cost more because it was an *elite class*. More bang per level, but also more experience to progress. Well, I wasn't rethinking my decision now. I'd risk it.

I tapped YES.

WARNING:
MAGE OF THE LINE is a RESTRICTED and SECRET class.
Are you *sure* you want to select this class? YES / NO

I froze.

The Game had never given me a warning like this.

It had to be because of the extra experience cost. Being an immortal elf, however, I wasn't worried. I'd have plenty of time to rack up the points.

In fact, I felt pretty good about this choice.

I hit YES.

A red-hot bar of adamantine punched through the back of my skull—splintered out my forehead—and sent my *useless* gray matter splattering onto the floor.

CHAPTER 9

Sorry. Not literally. The theatrical melodrama is a gypsy elf thing... almost as annoying as my human predilection for old movies.

It only *felt like* my skull had been bashed in and brain pulped.

Here's what really happened.

Waves of agony came, crescendoed, faded, and I came to.

Cold air brushed my face. Pine boughs rustled. In the distance, eagles screeched. I managed to crack open my eyes and found myself standing on a rock, a forest at my back, and I beheld a vista of glacier-covered mountains.

I laughed, pretending I was an Olympian god surveying his domain. "Fear me, mortals," I proclaimed to the eagles circling the valley below. "Bow down before Hektor the Mighty!"

This might have impressed someone, if there had been anyone within earshot, and if my thirteen-year-old, about-to-hit-puberty voice hadn't just cracked.

We gypsy elves are a more practical lot than our snooty high elf cousins, maturing a lot faster than they deemed appropriate. Screw 'em.

I was out of breath from the hike, but the view was worth it. On one side of this pass were the Hillgloom Dales, and on the other stretched the vast Burning Plains... and farther, just a speck of murky green, the lush oasis city-state of Jaljala.

Never a prettier sight had I seen among the seventeen worlds, fifty continents, or the hundred and thirteen cities our caravan had visited in my short life.

We'd toiled for three days up the twisting trails of the accursed Mendrinic Mountains and along the way broke five wheels and seriously annoyed every donkey pulling the wagons. Dad had pushed everyone, wanting to cross over the pass before nightfall.

Jaljala awaited!—filled with acres of shaded bazaars, daydream opal merchants, and if you believed the legends, wizards who could summon genies.

And oh, I believed. I wanted more than anything to see a real genie.

I knew magic too. Not a lot.

But I *would* one day.

That was the real reason I'd come up here: to practice.

Dad had ordered our troupe to make camp some two hundred feet below. There was a little spring, good shelter, rabbits to hunt. Tomorrow it was going to be a knee-crunching crawl down the mountains. With a wink, he'd ordered me to gather firewood.

I'd understood perfectly.

I chucked a rock.

It sailed over the eagles and vanished into the clouds below my perch.

A twig snapped.

I wheeled and drew my dagger.

It was Dad.

Finally. I was beginning to wonder.

Balaster Saint, even for an elf, looked, well, not old... but weathered. His tanned skin was covered with a map of worry and laugh lines, each hard-earned from miles on the road. I could only hope to be as handsome when I was six hundred and four. His long black hair had a streak of silver down the center. My stepmother called him her "skunk" (although no one else would have ever dared say that to his face).

He'd seen it all. Done it all. And everyone in the Saint-Savage Caravan respected him—if not for his fair and even leadership, then because we always turned a profit.

I loved him and would count myself lucky to one day be half the merchant he was.

"I stepped on that twig on purpose," he said and flashed his perfect smile.

"I know."

"Did anyone see you come up here?"

I shook my head.

"Are you *sure*?"

I rolled my eyes.

He crossed to me in five great strides, yanked me off the rock, and shook me by the shoulders—not too hard, but hard enough to make my teeth *clack.*

"This is no game, Hektor!" He released me and straightened my tunic. "I am sorry."

I wasn't a crybaby. Dad had shaken me plenty of times. No big deal. But that's as far as he ever went—that, and his withering stare that even made our donkeys flinch.

This time was different, though, like he wasn't so much mad at me as he was mad at himself. I wasn't sure why.

"No one saw me sneak up here," I whispered. "Just you. I'm *sure*."

His features clouded, and he stared at something a thousand leagues distant.

"It's just at the Laughing Basilisk Inn last week," he said, "when we performed *Hamlet*... I think someone realized I did a small pass, not mere sleight of hand. Maybe." He sighed. "My vanity, alas. *You* must do better and keep our secrets secret, eh?"

I'd seen it, but such a tiny thing, it was hardly worth mentioning.

Dad had wowed that audience when he'd pulled poor Yorick's skull from thin air. They'd loved the trick as much as his soliloquy.

I never understood why Dad insisted—no, *demanded*—that we keep the hand magic an absolute secret, even from my stepmom, and especially from my many brothers, sisters, and cousins.

Every time we practiced, he made me swear an oath, as his father had made him, and so on back seven generations.

His hazel gaze turned to me and his smile returned. "Are you ready for a lesson?"

"I've been ready for the last six weeks!"

I loved our lessons. It was something just between Dad and me and none of my other siblings or half-siblings. When we were together like this, I felt special—not because of the magic, but because I knew *I* was special to Dad.

I raised my hand and recited: "I swear by the three wandering gods, and may the shadow places of the earth swallow me up if ever I reveal the magic of the hand to any other... uh, and may all my teeth rot out—"

Dad held up a hand. "That's good enough. Today we'll practice the small pass."

He waved his hand and a dull copper coin appeared from nowhere... which, in fact, it hadn't. I could tell this was ordinary sleight of hand or "close" magic as we called it in the trade. Just trickery and misdirection, a warm-up for the *real* thing.

Dad took the copper coin and held it between his index finger and thumb. He inhaled and held his breath. His eyes narrowed to slits of concentration. He squeezed.

The coin vanished.

"Check your pockets."

I did, and even though I knew what I'd find, I still laughed with delight as I found the coin there.

"Perfect technique." I made to give it back.

"No, that's yours now. For good luck."

I turned the slightly warmed coin over and over. On one side was the profile of a majestic bearded king; on the other side were two ears of durum wheat.

"Now, it's your turn. Just like we practiced."

My blood cooled. Suddenly my fingers were leaden.

"You know how, Hektor. Go ahead."

I shook out my arms, flexed my fingers, and held the coin like Dad had.

What he'd done that last time was *not* sleight of hand. Heck, anyone could have done *that*.

No, he'd moved the coin from one spot to another—a "small pass" from here to there—traversing the space between *without* moving through it.

"Look deeper," he breathed, "past the illusions of the surface world."

I focused… and trembled.

I *knew* how to do this. I'd practiced (although always with Dad's help). This was in my blood: the seventh offspring of the seventh offspring from a line of Hand Mages that stretched back to antiquity.

So many things could go wrong, though. A fraction of an inch off… and it wouldn't just be the coin to make a small pass, but my fingertips.

And then there were Dad's many warnings that if I lost focus, I could "break the world." He wouldn't explain what that meant… but Balaster Saint wasn't the type to exaggerate (outside the confines of a barter, that is).

I concentrated. My vision tunneled, my heartbeat thundered… stopped, and power surged through my blood.

The mountains, trees, even the sun blurred; colors faded as I pierced the surface of this world—and plunged beneath, through… beyond.

The underlying structure of the universe then came into focus: the ley lines.

They crisscrossed my field of vision—brilliant gold, smoldering crimson, pulsing emerald green, and colors in-between that I knew were there but my eyes slid *around* unable to comprehend—all stretched between the very atoms to the outer-most reaches of reality.

No beginning. No end. They just were.

They sang to me, groaning like glacier ice straining, countless voices in a choir of antediluvian tones that were more than would fit in my tiny mind.

Dad had told me they brought magic into the world, and that they'd been here long before anything else.

The lines blurred and slipped away.

No. Idiot! I couldn't let my thoughts wander.

I squinted and bit my lip until I tasted blood.

The lines returned.

My astral form reached for a nearby silky gold filament. Dad had taught me the gold ones were the most basic of the lines, the ones that determined the "space" of things. I didn't quite get what he meant by that, but I knew what they *did*: each of these threads wove a cloth, or map if you will, of *where* things were in the world. Manipulate a line; you could change where a thing was.

As my hand neared, the line of shimmering sunshine moved toward me as if it were a piece of lodestone and I iron. We met and it felt like when you made that perfect catch of a tossed ball—that satisfying "smack" in your palm.

I smelled ancient stone freshly cracked and tasted metal and sparks in my mouth.

I took a moment and let the cascade of sensations fade.

I then drew the line closer and made a tiny loop of it. I ever-so-carefully brought that loop to the coin, and like a ghost, I pushed it *through* the solid disc held in my fingers, so the loop protruded on the other side of the coin.

With a gentle tug, I pulled the loop farther out and then encircled it about the copper. I then pulled the loop tight and the ley line caught something "solid" about the coin's circumference.

Okay. That was one of the harder parts to a small pass. I'd had to practice making the thread ethereal, and then *not*, a hundred times before I'd gotten it right.

For the next part, I ran up the golden ley line, gathered a second loop, and pulled that to a spot between me and my dad.

Then slowly... very, *very* slowly I pulled the first loop around the coin tighter.

This action made both the first loop *and* the coin within shrink.

At the same time, a brilliant point appeared inside the second loop that hung in the air between Dad and me. This point grew larger and dimmed to a mere glimmer until it was a circle of dull copper.

Meanwhile, the coin in the first loop between my fingers continued to shrink, smaller, smaller, until it vanished.

The original copper coin then existed—translocated, but *without* being moved through the space between—where no coin had been a moment ago.

Before I lost my nerve, I released my focus.

The ley lines vanished.

My thumb and index finger snapped shut on thin air.

The coin suspended between Dad and me—fell.

I caught it.

"Excellent!" Dad whispered and his eyes sparkled with delight. "Just take it slow. There's no need to go so fast just yet. Perfect the technique. Then we can move from the gold lines to—"

Eagles screeched, lots of them, almost as if they were commenting on my performance... only the sound continued and echoed off the cliff faces.

Dad paled. He turned toward camp and shielded his eyes.

I squinted and saw our camp and many-colored wagons—patches of checkers and stripes and paisley silk—cooking fires smoldering... but wait, one wagon was on fire! Another burst into flames, exploded, and people tumbled out on fire as well.

Not eagles—*my people* were screaming.

"What's—"

"Shh, Hektor." He pulled me behind the rock I'd stood upon. "Someone *did* see me at the Laughing Basilisk." The delight I'd seen in his eyes a moment ago was gone, replaced with something I'd never seen in Balaster Saint's gaze: Fear.

I wriggled from his grasp and peered over the rock.

There were soldiers. Had they been following us? Why? Crossbowmen among their ranks fired. Many of my brothers and sisters fell.

Rage boiled my blood. I would *kill* these murderers!

I reached for my dagger.

This time Dad practically yanked me off my feet onto the ground next to him.

"You don't understand," he whispered. "They will kill us all to make sure every trace of our bloodline is erased."

Tears blurred my vision as I stared at him—not tears of pain, tears of outrage. Why was he talking when we needed to get down there?

Another explosion—and more cries of agony and desperate pleading, that were then cut short.

Tears streamed down his cheeks now as well. "By all the wandering gods, why did I risk it?" He held out his hands and examined them as if the answers were writ upon his palms. "For a bit more applause? A few silver coins? Vanity!"

I shook him by the shoulders. "We have to help them! We've fought bandits before…"

"No!" His gaze locked onto mine. "These are *no* bandits. They are royal marksmen and wizards—hunters of the practitioners of our secret art. They will show no mercy. We must run… No." A bit of the man I knew then seemed to return. "*You* must run, Hektor. They saw only me."

Before I could say another word, he tapped the center of my forehead with his fingertip.

There was an electrical *crack* and I felt a weave of ley lines wrap about my mind.

I couldn't move, think.

"I bind what you know, my beautiful son," he whispered as he blinked away his tears. "Even if they find you later, torture you, probe your thoughts with magic and psi… they will never find our secrets. But the magic will always be there, waiting for the right time to be remembered."

I...

I... blinked and sat up from where I'd been napping on a bed of pine needles.

The sun had shifted. In fact, it had set, and the western sky was fading.

Dad was gone.

Had this been a nightmare? Serve me right for coming up here and taking a nap.

Wait. Why was I here?

I searched my thoughts. Ah, yes, firewood.

My hand was closed in a fist. I opened it and found an odd copper coin.

An unfamiliar voice came far down the slope. "He was up here. Canvass the region. Shoot anything that moves."

These are no bandits. They are royal marksmen and wizards—hunters of the practitioners of our secret art. You must run, Hektor.

Boots scrambled over rocks just a dozen paces from me.

I remembered—just flashes: Dad. Fire. Death.

Death was coming for me.

Undiluted panic spiked my heart and it beat jackrabbit fast.

I couldn't help myself. Even if I had wanted to fight, or hide—none of that mattered because my legs were already pumping and propelling me forward.

I was in a full sprint before I understood I was not in full control of myself.

...Dad.

Crossbow bolts whistled past me; one nicked my ear.

I didn't look back and made for the tree line, plunged into the forest—kept running until every muscle screamed, my lungs burned—and somehow found the strength to keep going until long after dark.

This world's silver moon hung before me, just enough light for my elven eyes to pick out faint game trails... then a man-made path that angled higher up the Mendrinic Mountains.

I finally fell over, unable to move another inch, every muscle cramping, done.

And yet, I was still under the compulsion to escape. So I crawled until even that was too much.

The moon-lit world dimmed and went black.

The last thing I felt was my hand clenched tight about my dad's final gift to me: the copper coin.

CHAPTER 10

"Mister Saint-Savage? Hello? Are you all right?"

I blinked. No more mountains or fire. Or blood.

Instead, a rather concerned Miss Lillian Carat-Bringer peered at me. Behind her, I noticed a green pushcart holding cloth bundles, boxes, and small treasure chests.

"I'm great," I said. "It's just... been a long night."

She set a tiny hand on my arm. "I know," she whispered. "You're worried about the people who were in the Bloody Rooster. Me too. I—I know what it's like to lose friends."

I swallowed the lump in my throat. "Thanks."

What the hell had just happened?

Obviously, a huge chunk of recollections had been crammed into my mind to account for my new class.

But this was very different than previous times.

It *had* happened. Perhaps it was the memory of some other Hektor Saint-Savage in a far-flung parallel universe—but it was real for *me* now too.

God, I was grieving for my parents all over again.

Definitely not cool, Game Master.

I wanted to curl into a ball and rock back and forth. The pain of losing him, them, was so fresh.

An interface window hovered before me, and a shimmer of light played over its alabaster frame as if to say, *Hey, don't forget me!*

Congratulations on selecting a new class
MAGE OF THE LINE
You must pick two beginning abilities.
Choose wisely, for these will not be offered again.
Future spell/skill branches will be opened
(or sealed) based on these choices.

A line of icons appeared and seemed to vibrate in anticipation of being selected.

With a thought, I closed the window.

No way. Later. Much later.

Like after I'd a chance to recover from the hammering of my hypothalamus.

Damn, I missed them all so much. My older brothers, sisters, my many cousins, even my stepmother... gods, and no please, please not Dad too.

I gazed into the cup cradled in my trembling hand.

"Say, you wouldn't happen to have, you know, something stronger than coffee?"

"Of course, sir. Might I suggest a fine cognac?"

"Perfect. Thanks, and please bring the whole bottle."

"I'll just be a moment." She curtseyed and vanished through the curtains.

This was seriously messed up. Why couldn't I shake the pain of that memory?

What had Hector's brother Bill told me? *"Over here you start becoming the character, start forgetting you're a player."*

Now I know what he meant.

Maybe that was part of the reason Bill was such a bastard. If I played an anti-paladin, I might be just as evil. On the other hand, what kind of psycho picks the anti-paladin class in the first place?

Miss Carat-Bringer returned and presented a mahogany box to me.

Inside was a brandy snifter and three bottles.

One bottle was a slender flask with a stopper of hollow green glass blown into the shape of a tree. In a spider-fine white script, the label read: *Hardy Le Printemps*.

The next was a fat canteen-shaped hunk of crystal, and etched upon it was: *Rémy Martin Louis XIII Grande Champagne Très Vieille Age Inconnu*.

The last was a half-melted bottle. I could barely read the dusty label: *1762 Gautier Cognac de Âme*. Ah, we had a winner.

"You have exquisite taste, sir," she breathed, looking longingly at the bottle. "Rather than spring water, they use dragon tears. Very difficult to obtain."

(Actually, I'd just picked the least pretentious-looking one).

She unstoppered the bottle and made to pour a few fingers into the brandy snifter.

"May I?" I asked and reached halfway for the bottle.

She handed it to me.

I poured two generous glugs into my coffee.

Miss Carat-Bringer's mouth dropped open (just for a moment), then she shut it.

Combining such a rare cognac with coffee had to be an act of mixological sacrilege. Yes, I am a barbarian, so what? I sipped.

The liquor slid into my thoughts—smoke and whispers from lost loves and the fading light of a perfect sunset.

I let out a sigh. "That'll do."

After another cup, and then another, I'd recovered enough to look over the goods Lillian had brought me.

First, the weapons.

There were a dozen swords of various breeds, a punch dagger, a pair of axes that were on fire, some glowing sickles, assorted polearms (pulled from extra-dimensional cases), billy clubs, staves, throwing stars, darts, even a six-foot-long blowgun.

"If you are interested in the history of a particular piece," she said, "its documented magical powers, or its estimated value, please ask."

I nodded but thought it best to first look over the items' description via the game interface.

I focused on the whole lot.

All their description windows appeared at once, overlapping each other.

Carefully considering every choice here would take too long. I waved away the windows.

There had to be a faster way.

Okay, what did I *really* need? A weapon that could attack at range, and one for close combat. Bonus for something I could conceal. That eliminated the polearms (extra-dimensional cases or not, their hafts *still* protrude four feet), and other larger items, and as much as I liked the novelty of the thing, the blowgun too.

Ah, *this* looked promising: a set of brass knuckles, only more knuckle, less brass because they were *actual* bones, blackened and fused.

CESTUS (RIGHT HAND)
Malinbus, Fist of the Devil God-King
(Tier-VI magical weapon, unique, one of a set of two)
DESCRIPTION: Crafted by the blind monks of Dolodroom Tower in the seventh ring of Hell. Made from the knucklebones of a now-forgotten demigod. It has the color and weight of lead. Fully articulated as to not impede manipulation skills or inhibit "soft" or open-handed martial art techniques.
SPECIAL ABILITIES: +1 to wielder's STRENGTH and REFLEX. Adds moderate damage to every (right-handed) strike. Upon command, once per day the fist may cause an *explosion* on contact—pulverizing a cubic yard of stone, or cubic foot of iron—causing any target MAJOR damage with a significantly increased chance of a CRITICAL HIT.
REQUIREMENTS: Keyed for martial artist classes only.
VALUE: If someone would sell this for mere coin, it would fetch an equivalent of at least 50,000 quins.

HISTORICAL NOTE: Once worn by Ratree Aslan, aka the Mistress of the *Seven Sinister Strikes*, who expunged all traces of evil from this item.

NOTE: When donned, the wielder must activate the Fist of the Devil God-King with a mental command. It will then sink into and bond to the hand bones. The wielder's entire hand will appear slightly enlarged, the knuckles more so. Once bonded, this item may then only be removed by surgery or amputation.

Seriously nice. The mega-damage blasting effect was spectacular.

I also appreciated the amount of helpful information in the description. That might have been from my improved *Bargaining* skill.

The only thing... the price.

I'd seen this kind of economic effect before in games.

Money started to lose its value when compared to mid- and higher-tier magical items. Who wanted to trade a +5 Holy Vorpal Sword for forty million coppers? Instead, magic gear tended to get bartered for *other* magic or rare items. Except for the highest-level magical stuff. To obtain that, you usually had to fulfill some nearly impossible quest.

"May I try them on?" I asked. "*Without* activating them, of course."

She made a little "go ahead" gesture, and gave that smile every car salesman had when you asked if you could just sit inside to "see how it feels."

I slipped them on.

My fist felt like it had been dipped in molten lead, but that weighty sensation quickly faded.

It morphed shape, knuckle bones rearranging to accommodate my smaller elven hand and even my sixth finger.

I made to smack my right fist into the left, but stopped, deciding that would be an amazingly stupid thing to do.

I removed them and set them aside.

They'd take a serious bite from my budget, and I still needed something with reach. A definite possibility, though.

Ah—I then spied a twelve-foot length of chain. Attached to one end were a handle and straight blade. Halfway along the blade's length, another curved blade sprouted (imagine an elongated lowercase "r"). On the other end, was a knobby weight the size of my fist.

This was a *kyoketsu-shoge*, the traditional weapon of ninjas in my beloved Hong Kong action flicks.

It was versatile because you could throw the blade, or use the chain to block, entangle, trip, rip a weapon from an opponent's grasp, and of course, strangle.

Masters of this weapon could whip the chain around their limbs or neck to seriously increase its velocity. Anyone else attempting such maneuvers would end up smacking themselves in the face.

In my other life, I never would have touched one of these things. You needed years of training.

But... Hektor Saint-Savage *had* such training.

The description popped:

KYOKETSU-SHOGE (ninja chain) with MORNING STAR ATTACHMENT (EXOTIC, FLEXIBLE weapon class)
***Shé liàn*, The Living Serpent Chain**
(Tier-V magical weapon, very rare)
DESCRIPTION: Comprised of a silver-mithril alloy blade, living xi-mercury links, and a blackened tungsten weight. Crafted by the now-extinct Mecha-medusae of the Island of Ea. Only four such weapons are known to exist. This one is the "Taipan" among the set (named for the snake's speed, not its deadly venom).
SPECIAL ABILITIES: Enchanted to moderately increase hit probabilities and damage. The chain is alive and responds to simple mental commands, able to slightly alter its link shape, tensile properties, color, and may stretch to a length of eighteen feet.
REQUIREMENTS: Keyed for martial artists only AND the weapon must accept you as its master.
VALUE: If sold for mere coin, consider 75,000 quins a steal.

I could think of so many uses for this. A definite must-have. Damn the price to hell.

"Go ahead," Lillian urged me.

I grasped the leather-wrapped handle of the blade.

The chain tensed. Tiny razor-sharp blades *"chincked"* out of the links—like a cat extending its claws.

This must be part of the "weapon must accept you" requirement.

I sensed a connection between us now... like a phone call where the other person was silent, waiting for me to start the conversation.

I thought: *Hello? Look, I don't have a lot of time, so I'll just level with you. I've got a ton of questing to get done, a thousand fights, and more blood and pain than I really care to think about. If you're not up for it, well, better to know right now and we can go our separate ways.*

The chain relaxed and the tiny blades in its links retracted.

Hmm. That didn't feel like a rejection, not quite acceptance, either.

I'm Hektor Saint-Savage, Spirit Warrior, and I guess, part-time Mage of the Line. I'm trying to reshape the very nature of Creation—give the little guys a chance to determine their own fates. I can't guarantee I'll come out the other end of this thing alive, but I'm going to try. Are you game?

The chain lay there inert.

I guess it had made up its mind.

I set the blade down. Too bad. I'd liked it.

The thing then, however, gave me a mental "ping" with an encoded thought: it relished the long odds of my task, and more importantly, that I was trying *anyway*.

The chain wrapped about my wrist.

For a heart-stopping second, I thought it might sprout razors once more and constrict.

Thankfully not. Just a tiny squeeze.

I did my best Rick Blaine in *Casablanca* and thought: *Shé liàn, I think this is the beginning of a beautiful friendship.*

I coiled the chain, and set it next to the demon bone knuckles.

There was a knock on the wall.

Morgana poked through the curtains. "Oi, Elmac said" —and she continued in a poor imitation of his dwarven brogue— "tell Hektor that we be moving out in an hour. So that slowpoke better finish." She smiled at her impression, but the expression dried up as she saw the look on my face. "Everything good here?"

"I'll explain later." I frowned. "Wait. *One* hour?"

She nodded. "Was pretty firm about it too. Look, I've got to wrap a few things up myself. See you in a tick then?"

Elmac must have his reasons, but I had vowed to burn through my cash tonight, or rather this morning, and that's what I was going to do... just a little faster than I'd figured.

In short order, I sorted through a dozen rings, a silk tunic with embroidered dragons, and ten more candidate weapons. Nothing fell into the "must have" category.

Miss Carat-Bringer then presented me with a tray of starter mage items: assorted wands, charms, and the like. All too pricey for what they did, but she *had* warned me this stuff was in high demand.

"Any stage magician accouterments?"

Her ever-present smile faded.

She pulled a lead box off the pushcart and let it thud onto the floor. Without flourish or preamble, she shoved it my way.

Had I committed a cultural faux pas with respect to... sleight of hand magicians? That didn't make sense. I'd have to ask Elmac.

Inside the box, I found packs of playing cards, one with five suits and an extra face card, the "Court Magician." There were also plenty of technical props like breaking steel rings and three-cups and balls, but none of those clicked with me.

Except... I then spied something jammed in one corner of the box, buried in dust and something sticky (chewing gum?).

Blackwell's Band
(Tier-III magical ring, very rare)
DESCRIPTION: Made of seven braided crystalline filaments (each a different, but dull, rainbow color). It remains cool to the touch even when worn.
SPECIAL ABILITIES: In the aether, the wearer of this ring triples the range at which they may manipulate ley lines.
REQUIREMENTS: Must be able to enter the aether and manipulate ley lines.
VALUE: Unknown as so few can use, or understand, this item to properly appraise it. Based on material value alone, the ring will likely fetch 1,000 gold quins.

Huh. This could be extremely useful. That note about so few being able to understand its use had to account for its bargain-basement price.

If it worked as indicated, it'd be a steal. Nice.

Next, I examined a rack of stoppered test tubes, vials, and tiny bottles.

Finally healing potions! I set aside all six doses they had. I took a few bandages enchanted to cure infection and disease. No more lich rot for me, thank you very much. I also grabbed the two vials of *"Karl's Guaranteed De-toxinifier"* in stock to counter poisoned weapons.

I was short on time, so I briefly scanned their descriptions just to make sure they were what they said they were.

I then got a few pairs of clean socks, underwear, loose pants, tunics and t-shirts, a waxed canvas jacket, a new wool cloak... and why not? An assortment of silk sashes of assorted colors. Yeah, amateur fashionista here, but no self-respecting gypsy elf would pass a chance to upgrade their wardrobe.

"Anything else?"

"I hesitate to show this to you, sir." Miss Carat-Bringer pursed her lips and with both hands held out a thin ivory box.

I took it. Inside was a strip of silver-white silk.

"But you *did* ask for something to bolster your sensory acuity. You will find no item of higher quality."

I felt magic roiling off this thing.

I concentrated, but no item description popped.

Really? I redoubled my mental efforts.

From the center of the band, an eye winked open; its gaze darted back and forth, and then fixed upon me.

I almost dropped the box.

Azramath's Headband of Grim and Fateful Insights
(Tier-VII magical armor, unique)
DESCRIPTION: Crafted by the insane archmagus, Azramath the Trembling, this headband is woven from the silk of glass moths only found on the slopes of active volcanoes.
SPECIAL ABILITIES: Grants a defense bonus against gaze-type weapons. Allows the wearer to see the infrared and ultraviolet portions of the visible spectrum. Thrice per day, it can reveal magic auras. Once per day, the eye can reveal the *absolute truth*.
REQUIREMENTS: EGO 4 or greater.
VALUE: May be traded for an equivalency of 45,000 quins worth of similarly tiered items.

NOTE: Seeing the absolute truth may cause the wearer to go blind, be driven insane, fall into a suicidal depression, or experience other deleterious effects.

Nice. I'd never have night vision problems if I had this. Expensive, though. I wasn't sure about that "absolute truth" thing, but I didn't *have to* use that ability. Hmm. I'd have to boost my EGO to meet the requirement. I had yet to assign stat points for my new level, so that was possible.

Running short on time, Miss Carat-Bringer and I then rolled up our sleeves and haggled.

When she whipped out a slide rule, however, and proceeded to show me the items' depreciation schedules over the next century to demonstrate their actual increasing worth vis-a-vis my initial investment, I caved.

Her *Bargaining* skill had to be at least double mine.

It was okay. I got all the non-magic gear I wanted, the healing items, the demon bone knuckles, *Shé liàn*, the headband, and Blackwell's ring.

And, after I figured in Miss Carat-Bringer's tip, I had a whopping seven hundred gold quins left over.

I'd burned through a *fortune*. On the other hand, hey, seven hundred gold? A week ago, I would have considered *that* a fortune.

Well, easy come, easy go.

"You are amazingly adept, sir, at identifying and assessing an item's value," Miss Carat-Bringer said. "If you ever find yourself in need of employment..."

"Lordren asked me to join your crew last time I shopped here. I don't know, maybe after I get a few things straightened out in my personal life."

Like saving the multiverse from a bunch of power-hungry deities. I wondered if Hiltmyer & Co. offered medical and a pension?

Still sitting, I bowed to Lillian Carat-Bringer. "You have more than earned your gratuity. Thank you. Thank you, very much."

She beamed. "You are more than welcome, Mister Saint-Savage. Please ask for me by name next time you visit. I'll just leave this." She nudged the bottle of cognac in my direction. "Compliments of the house. Master Lordren insists. I shall get your change." She packed up the cart, minus my new items, and trundled off.

I tied a green sash about my waist.

I then went to pick up the kyoketsu-shoge, but before I could, *Shé liàn* snaked up my body and burrowed under the sash—neatly out of sight. A ninja weapon indeed.

I slipped on *Blackwell's Band*, but nothing immediate happened.

The knucklebones and headband could wait.

I opened my inventory to safely store it all...

And froze.

In the lower-right corner slot was a dull 1912 S Wheat Lincoln penny.

It was the coin my dad had given me the night he'd traded his life for mine.

I took it out, held it, and cried.

CHAPTER 11

I was in the dark. Again. Covered in excrement. Once more.

Kind of the theme of my life for the last twenty-four hours.

Oh, and I was in a coffin.

You see, Elmac had a new, *better* idea to sneak us out of High Hill under the noses of the Silent Syndicate.

His "genius" plan had four parts.

The first part took advantage of the fact that today was trash day for Lordren. Along with the junk deemed unsalable by his appraisers, Lordren's janitorial staff also had to dispose of the street sweepings they'd collected this week in front of Hiltmyer & Co. This morning it would all be hauled by wagon to High Hill's dump.

Part two entailed Lordren's engineers taking three rat-chewed coffins, drilling air holes in them, and then fitting those holes with air filters.

(No one had asked why Lordren had three coffins lying around in his office, but there had to be a story to it).

For part three, our band of adventurers suppressed their inner claustrophobic (except Elmac, who didn't seem to have one), and we crammed into the aforementioned death boxes... which were then nailed shut.

And finally, the coffins and their not-so-dead corpses were laid to rest in a wagon and all the junk and street sweepings got shoveled on top of them.

Did I mention how *many* horses traversed River Street in front of Lordren's shop in any given week? And the quantity of their... leavings?

So, a few thousand bumps over High Hill's cobblestoned avenues later, we rolled onto an even rougher rutted track, indicating that we'd cleared the city gates.

About an hour after that, I heard whispers between Elmac and Morgana's caskets. They were so faint, though, I had to press my ear to the side of my coffin to make out any words.

I didn't get it all, but enough to get the gist that Morgana was asking why there was no aluminum (pronounced "al-you-min-i-uhm" in her British accent) and metals like titanium in Thera. Elmac gave the same explanation he'd given me that chemistry worked ever-so-slightly differently in Thera. No gunpowder, for example, and high-carbon steels and exotic metals degraded faster than pig iron left out in the rain.

They then started exchanging life stories.

It sounded personal... and not meant for eavesdroppers in adjacent coffins.

So, I stopped lurking.

I had my own fish to fry.

Namely, I had to finish leveling up.

I concentrated and my interface appeared, thankfully in focus even though there were only two inches between my nose and the coffin's lid.

Congratulations on selecting a new class
MAGE OF THE LINE
You must pick two beginning abilities.
Choose wisely, for these will not be offered again.
Future spell/skill branches will be opened
(or sealed) based on these choices.

Ah. The standard "pick a path and don't look back" character design philosophy I'd seen before... only not with a new first-level character. When I'd played a fighter in the Free Trial, and for my Spirit Warrior, I'd picked which skills I wanted at the start, yes, but I had the option to get the rest of them later.

A lot more rode on my initial choices for *this* class.

I read the few first abilities:

Small Pass (Physical): **Teleport an object less than five pounds.**
Range: 10 yards.
Cost: 10 mana.
NOTE: Attempts to move one object inside another *significantly* decreases the chance of success and may have dire effects on the object *and* spellcaster.

Small Pass (Light): **Alter the color and pattern of light to produce visual effects or reproduce images.**
Maximum volume: One cubic yard.
Range: 10 yards.
Cost: 10 mana.

Small Pass (Mental): **Project your thoughts into the mind of another. Limited to short messages and/or non-complex sensory transmissions. Such thoughts may be *forced* upon another, producing a variety of possible effects.**
Range: 1 mile.
Cost: 10 mana.

These last two were illusionist and psychic-type powers. As handy as those might be, I'd stick with the physical version of *Small Pass*. Sure, there was that caution about teleporting one object into another (an obvious no-no), but the physical version of *Small Pass* was the last thing my dad taught me…

No. Not going there.

Back into your box, oh unwanted implanted memories.

Yeah. Not so easy. I took a few moments to try to sort through it all, but it was too much pain to process. And it was so damnably fresh in my mind… well, because it had been seared into my neurons only a few hours ago.

A new tiny window appeared:

MAGE OF THE LINE SPECIAL CLASS FEATURE
Unlike other spells that require gestures, foci, or some ritual—none are required for Mage of the Line abilities as the manipulation of ley lines occurs in the AETHER, a dimension outside normal space-time. Mage of the Line abilities, therefore, appear in the normal world to be cast *almost instantaneously* and there are no corresponding spell cooldowns.

This explained why Balaster Saint had been so lightning fast when he'd demonstrated his abilities to me. My attempts had always seemed *so* slow in comparison because I was in the aether. From Dad's perspective in normal space-time, I would have looked just as quick.

Okay. That cleared that up.

On a more practical note—wow! This feature was a m*ajor* bonus.

In the aether I could spam as many spells as I wanted in the middle of combat, taking no relative time to do it. The only limitation seemed to be my available mana.

Actually, this was a little gross. What was the catch?

I was sure I'd find out soon enough.

I moved on to the last three abilities to choose from:

Energy Redirection: Energies directed at the Mage of the Line may be harmlessly channeled into the aether. Range: 10 yards.

Mana Cost: 1 mana per point of energy deflected, maximum 10 points.

Energy Tap: Tap local ley lines and project energy into the normal world (cone of fire, electrical discharge, sonic boom, etc.). Type of energy is dependent on the particular ley line tapped.
NOTE: Discharged energies usually do not harm the caster.
Range: 10 yards.
Cost: Fixed at 20 mana to channel 10 points of energy.

Life Energy Drain: Use dormant ley lines to siphon the life force from a living creature into you.
Range: 10 yards.
Cost: 1 health drained/healed per 3 mana expended, up to maximum of one-third the target's total health or 10 points health drained (whichever is greater).

Energy Tap was a basic bread-and-butter attack ability. More versatile than a normal beginner mage spell, however, because you could choose the damage type. Cool.

Life Energy Drain was this class's starting healing ability. Necromancy? Evil? I wasn't sure. In any case, I'd just boosted my *Spiritual Regeneration*, so the chi-ability's healing-to-mana ratio was much more effective than this.

Energy Redirection was nice, but as a Spirit Warrior, I already had a decent chance to dodge such dangers.

So, I crossed *Energy Redirection* and *Life Energy Drain* off the list, which left *Energy Tap* and the physical version of *Small Pass* as my two abilities.

I hoped I'd be able to combine *Energy Tap* with my martial art skills.

Fists of Fire! *Lightning Kick*! *Freezing Death Touch*!

I better not get carried away. I still didn't understand all the ins and outs of the ley lines and the aether.

I think I now got why you selected your two starter abilities before you really understood this class. It was like picking a class specialization path first. Depending on your choices, this class became a mentalist type, illusionist, necromancer, or in my case, battle mage—all with correspondingly different progression paths.

But that begged the question: Why do it that way?

I finalized my choices and new text appeared.

MAGE OF THE LINE SKILLS & ABILITIES

Passive Skills:

Reflexive Mana: Gain a mana pool based on your REFLEX stat. This manifests as the ability to reach into the aether and manipulate the slippery psycho-physical ley lines. If this mana pool ever drops to zero, your REFLEX stat also drops to ZERO until this mana pool *entirely* regenerates.

Obscura Totata: Your player title placard is altered to conceal this class.

Active Skills:

Visualize Aether: Project your astral presence into the aether to see and manipulate ley lines. Since you are attuned to the true underlying nature of reality, you gain a one-time bonus of +1 to your PERCEPTION.

Range: Visualization range varies from region to region in the aether. Ley line manipulation range is the same as your normal physical reach.

Cost: Varies slightly from region to region in the aether, but approximately 1 mana per second of subjective time spent in the aether.

WARNING: If you exhaust your reflexive mana in the aether, your astral presence will be severed from your physical body. This is fatal.

Basic Spells:

You have selected *Small Pass (Physical)* and *Energy Tap* as your beginning spell-like abilities. At higher levels, more options and higher tiers of these basic abilities may be unlocked.

(Tap and hold spell names if you wish to review details here.)

Skills:

Sleight of Hand (5/30): Perform feats of legerdemain and prestidigitation—card tricks, making coins vanish, three-card monte, etc. This is a physical skill, not a magical one.

As you have selected a new secondary class, you receive: THREE STAT points and SEVEN non-combat skill points to distribute as you see fit.

A few surprises here. The bonus PERCEPTION was appreciated. And as expected, a mana pool based on my already high REFLEX was great, but the downside of depleting that pool was serious. I'd have to watch that—*especially* while I was in the aether. Also, I hadn't expected my range of manipulating ley lines to be the same as my physical reach. I was glad I'd picked up *Blackwell's Band* since it tripled that.

But what was up with this *Obscura Totata* skill? It had to have something to do with the Mage of the Line being a "secret" class.

And hey! Sleight of hand. I'd always wanted to do card tricks. I had a hunch that with a little practice and ingenuity I'd find a few combat applications for that skill too. Thrown playing cards perhaps?

As far as the extra stat, combat, and non-combat skill points?

If I'd leveled up as a Spirit Warrior, I'd have had four stat points. I'd gotten three here with a freebie +1 to PERCEPTION, so that was a wash. The combat skill points I would have gotten as a Spirit Warrior were gone—but considering I'd just received an entirely new set of abilities, that was more than a fair trade. The non-combat skill point increase had remained the same.

Not too shabby.

Congratulations!
ACHIEVEMENT UNLOCKED!
"Black Swan"
You are the first Player in over a hundred years to be a MAGE OF THE LINE.
You are indeed a rare breed.

An icon of a silhouetted swan with spread wings appeared and faded.

Good?

Why, though, was I the only player in over a century to pick this class? Maybe since the Game had a bazillion classes, this "rare" achievement wasn't really so rare after all.

Over the next few hours, I ran through all the ways I might assign my points.

I ended up adding a point to REFLEX, EGO, and STRENGTH.

My REFLEX was already high, and I'd want it even higher as so many of my martial arts abilities and now my Mage of the Line mana depended on it.

I needed the extra point in EGO to use the headband. This also boosted my spiritual mana, so that was good.

Why bother with STRENGTH? I'd get more health, it would add damage to my strikes, boost my carrying capacity, and well, this wasn't strictly a min-max strategy, but I wanted to look a bit more buff too.

So, along with the PERCEPTION bump for being a Mage of the Line, and the +1 STRENGTH and REFLEX bonuses from the demon bone knuckles, I had:

BODY: 15
- **STRENGTH: 5**
- **REFLEX: 10**
- **HEALTH: 160**
- **MANA (Reflexive): 100**

MIND: 4
- **INTELLECT: 0**
- **PERCEPTION: 4**

SOUL: 7
- **EGO: 4**
- **GHOST: 3**
- **MANA (Spiritual): 70**

I felt faster, stronger—just better! (although one of these days I was going to have to give myself a point of INTELLECT).

And new non-combat skills? I'd wait. I'd had enough memory cutting and pasting for one day.

Besides, just then the wagon came to a halt.

There were scrapes and shuffles overhead as debris was cleared, and then the lid of my coffin was crowbarred open.

Two gnome drivers peered down, both holding their noses and waving me to get out.

It was good to finally breathe fresh—whoa! The smell was like a punch in the face (followed by a roundhouse kick).

I got over the side of the wagon and puked...

right next to Morgana who was doing the same.

"Oh, shoulda warned you." Elmac knelt next to us. "Sorry 'bout that."

I purged the scrambled egg breakfast Lordren had served us along with coffee and rare cognac. After my stomach had given up its last and my eyes were done watering, Elmac herded us away from the stench.

There was no sign of High Hill's wall. There were open meadows and fields of corn that stretched to the horizon. I turned and saw the overwhelming smell was not coming from the stuff in Lordren's wagon, but from a five-hundred-foot tall mountain of trash and decomposing organic material.

"'Taint pretty," Elmac said, "but Father always told me to be judging a civilization by the quality of its waste disposal engineering. He said 'A city covered in shit, be shit.'"

He dusted off his hands. "Now, let's go see 'bout supper."

CHAPTER 12

We moved a half mile—*upwind*.

It was late. The rays of Thera's golden sun reached toward the horizon, so Elmac found a spot within a stand of willows to set up camp. From his massive pack (which was as large as himself and stuffed to the bursting point), he pulled out a cantaloupe-sized stone, spoke a word to it, and set it on the ground. The stone glowed red hot.

How had I ever gotten by without magic?

He then found three sandwiches wrapped in wax paper and doled them out. Between slabs of a French baguette was a half rasher of crisp bacon, lettuce, and tomatoes.

You'd have thought after my earlier gastrointestinal distress, food would have been the last thing on my mind. Wrong. I was *ravenous* and tore through the thing in ninety seconds.

Elmac handed me a second sandwich (Morgana too) and set a stovetop espresso maker on the heat stone.

"So... Elmac," Morgana said around mouthfuls. "Go back to what you were saying before. That entire mountain is a loo?"

"Aye, 'twas built centuries ago," Elmac explained. "The pit dug, pipes laid—all fine dwarven engineering, mind you."

"That makes no sense," I said.

I turned around to study the "mountain" of trash situated in a crater. It was surrounded by a wide moat of sewage that poured in through dozens of ten-foot wide pipes. Really *gross*.

You've undoubtedly caught a whiff of an ordinary latrine, but consider adding the smells of troll dung, dragon poop, and other mythological creature waste by-products. Without going into details—the odor I'd gotten a sniff of earlier was of equal mythic stature.

"That thing is almost overflowing," I said. "If it was dug 'centuries ago,' it would have filled up a hundred times over."

"Actually," Elmac told me, "it 'bout fills every week."

Morgana and I exchanged a perplexed look.

"Someone carts it all off then?" she asked.

"Not exactly," he said and squinted at the sun as it inched toward the edge of the world. "'Tis best you be seeing it yourself. Let's take a look, eh?"

Morgana shrugged, as did I, and we three walked to the edge of our little grove.

After a moment, the sun kissed the earth and its rays painted the eastern sky with pink and orange.

The ground trembled.

The titanic pile of refuse shifted and avalanches of trash tumbled down its slopes. My ears popped, willow branches rustled, and the air filled with a near sub-sonic sucking sound.

The moat boiled. Plumes of steam geysered about the edges. Parts of the pile caught fire and spiraled into cyclones of flame.

The moat then drained away, and the entire pile of putrefying poop started to sink, picking up speed as it went... to *where* exactly?

In the span of four heartbeats, it was gone. All of it.

Amber light flickered within the pit, faded, and went dark.

"That was..." I started but honestly didn't even have a guess.

"A volcano?" Morgana offered.

"No," Elmac said. "The pit be dug over a cyclical gate to some hell dimension. There be two reasons for that. First, the whole mountain be a plug so no beasties get through to Thera. Second, the other side has a lower atmospheric pressure. When the gate opens" —he made a fist, stuck his thumb in the bottom, then quickly pulled it out to demonstrate— "*whoosh*! The whole kit and caboodle be pushed through and dumps a mile over the ground on the other side."

"Holy sh—" Morgana whispered.

The citizens of High Hill just might have found the most audacious (and perhaps most practical) use for a trans-dimensional gate ever.

Somewhere in the many hells, it was raining trash and crap upon the heads of whatever demons were plotting no good. Poetic justice if you ask me. Although... I wondered if perhaps this was a contributing factor as to why demons were so hostile toward mortals.

I loved Thera. Where else in the multiverse could flushing a toilet be a spectacle of epic proportions?

Moreover, this felt like a metaphor that my luck had finally come to a turning point.

We'd almost been similarly sucked into that assassination quest. While I knew there was outstanding business to stop said assassins from murdering innocent people, and some payback for the Bloody Rooster, we *had* extracted ourselves from a very sticky situation.

And now? Level up, get Elmac in the Game, and be able to think without worrying about getting stabbed in the back. Hopefully, by the time we returned to High Hill, Colonel Delacroix would have gotten Elmac's message and come up with a way to help.

It was a tricky balance. We weren't powerful enough to take on the Silent Syndicate, but every day we were away gaining levels and abilities... people might die.

I didn't like it, but it seemed the *least*-bad strategy.

On the philosophical side of this, we were now forging our own path instead of being led by the Game, or Game Master. Not a trivial point. How was I going to free all of Creation from the machinations of the gods, if I couldn't even free myself? Practice what you preach, brother.

Elmac passed me a dented flask. "Nip?" he asked.

I took it, braced, and sipped. I was pleasantly surprised to taste a smooth and chilled-just-above-freezing vodka martini.

I handed it to Morgana, who took one, two, three slugs.

She returned the flask to Elmac. "Brilliant."

The show over, we wandered back to camp and settled about the glowing heat stone.

Morgana lay on her side before the warmth like a cat in front of a radiator.

She had new gear too. Her old leather armor had been upgraded to a full matched suit, complete with hood and little ears. This was *not* the cute lingerie outfit that probably just popped into your head… none of that breast-popping corset or bare midriff stuff.

The armor was matte black leather with subtle blackened mithril exoskeletal articulations at the knees, elbows, and one shoulder. There were a half dozen sheaths on the thighs, two crisscrossing the back, and a few on the forearms—all to hold an arsenal of darts, throwing stars, daggers, and short swords. Fine scales of black metal covered the vulnerable areas. The boots were made of a thick pebbled hide that could have come from some gigantic Gila monster.

Morgana didn't make a sound moving in it, either.

I was curious, so I asked if it was enchanted.

She brought a finger to her lips then whispered, "A lady has to have her secrets. You'll see soon enough."

"Can't wait," I remarked a tad acidly.

Her gaze darted over my head. "What's with your placard?"

I shot her a quizzical look. "I can't see it. What do you mean?"

"Well, you leveled up" —she snorted— "congrats. But it doesn't say *what* you leveled up to. Third-level Spirit Warrior… and then there's an 'M' …but the rest gets cut off like someone used too big a font."

That must be my new *Obscura Totata* skill in action.

I shrugged. "Guy's got to have his secrets."

Two could play that game.

Her lips pursed. "The bloody Black Swan achievement, too? You have all the luck, you do. That thing is supposed to be *beyond* rare."

I took a mock bow to hide my growing concern.

With so much unknown about my new class, I didn't think it wise to flaunt this particular achievement anymore. It would only lead to questions I couldn't answer.

I went into my interface and de-selected the icon from my player placard.

"So you leveled up?" Elmac asked me. "How much more till you be fifth? I be itching to start. Got a few ideas for my character... and then a few necks to break for what happened to the Rooster."

How was I going to explain to Elmac that a new first-level character would have no chance against a society of assassins? I'd already told him that while he'd be reincarnated into a new body, he might lose some of the abilities he had in this life. I wasn't sure that had sunk in yet. We'd have to get him to *at least* third level, or better fourth... or fifth, so he'd stand a decent chance of surviving.

On the other hand, in the Free Trial Morgana and I had prevented an elder god from entering Thera. Who was I to say what could and couldn't be done? Of course, we'd also come within a hair's breadth of being sacrificed to said elder god.

"Soon," I told Elmac. "I'm close."

The experience from defeating Bill and his army of demons had nearly pushed me up *two* levels... if I hadn't made a detour along the way with my new Mage of the Line class and its surprising buy-in cost.

"One more good battle should do it," I said.

And speaking of leveling up, I just now noticed Morgana's player placard.

Morgana Nox
DRUID (Mischief Maker) LEVEL 4 / THIEF LEVEL 3
League of Tricksters, LLC

Nice. A total of *seven* levels. And, I bet, well on her way to *eighth*.

There was a slight twist of jealousy in my gut. I guess I still had a hangup about coming in second place from all those years playing with my brother.

But Morgana *wasn't* Bill, and I refused to feel anything but happiness for her. Besides, she'd had a three-week head start on me in the Game.

What was a little competition between friends?

Is that what we were? Friends?

I hadn't considered anything more. Don't get me wrong, Morgana was gorgeous, smart, funny… but I didn't want to mess up our adventuring group by adding romantic and cross-clan complications. And, more importantly, I'd never gotten a hint that she was interested.

This might be a problem for Elmac, though. The old dwarf had a crush on her and had it bad. I'd better have a talk with him before he embarrassed himself and got his ego steamrolled.

"You'll be getting that battle soon enough," Elmac told me, snapping me back from my thoughts. He poured three espressos into tin cups and passed them out. "The path to the *Ojawbi* Far Fields, where the Far Field barbarians be, from the Far Fields of *Thera*—uh, that all be a tad confusing with the two places having near the same names... but that often be the case with these adjacent worlds—well, that path has a gate guardian."

"Tell me that guardian is *not* a hellfire demon," Morgana said.

"Worse," he whispered. "Years ago I escorted a caravan through and lost them all to a giant seven-headed horse that breathed clouds of venomous insects. 'Twas a Chaos Knight."

I paused mid-sip of espresso. "This knight of chaos rides the horse?"

I recalled how murderously effective my comrade, Sir Pendric Ragnivald, had been on his terrifying steed, Bell Ringer, and shuddered.

"No," Elmac said. "The seven-headed horse *was* the Champion for the Lords 'o Chaos. She takes a new shape every time you see her. Sometimes a wee butterfly, other times an undead dragon, or like when I saw her, that nightmare mutation."

So we might have to face something like a plutonium golem? But hey, defeating it *would* put me over the top to the next level... even if it was posthumously.

"We'll figure it out," Morgana said. "We always have. But I'm knackered. Someone take first watch, yeah?"

"I've gotcha covered," Elmac said. He rummaged through his pack, found a tiny pillow and offered it to Morgana. I kid you not— he'd brought a silk pillow with him.

She brightened and took it. "Thanks, mate. Much appreciated."

"Sweet dreams, lass."

"Hang on," I said. "It entirely slipped my mind with…"

I'd almost said *"what with all the fire and blood we'd waded through in the last twelve hours,"* but caught myself. Elmac didn't need to be reminded of that.

"…with everything going on," I amended. "The side quest we're on? Here—"

I shared out the Drunken Monkey quest to Morgana and took a moment to re-read it myself.

"A THOUSAND DRUNKEN MONKEYS"
Find the old martial artist among the
Far Field barbarian tribes.
Reward(s): Bonus experience and new bonus skill.
Suggested Party: N/A

It seemed perfectly straightforward.

Morgana scanned it and accepted. "Drunken monkeys and barbarians, huh? Pencil me in. Sounds like a riot."

She then yawned, stretched, and midway turned into a black panther. The cat circled around once, lay with the pillow tucked between her front paws, and kneaded it (in the process puncturing Elmac's pillow many times with her claws). She conked out, purring.

"As soon as you're in the Game," I told Elmac, "I'll be able to share it out to you too."

He nodded, found his clay pipe, stuffed the bowl, and lit up.

It was getting dark. As an elf, I could see a bit by the glow of the heat rock... but I thought I might be able to do much better. It was as good a time as any to try *Azramath's Headband of Grim and Fateful Insights*.

I slipped it over my brow—and it was like someone had flipped on stadium lighting and cranked the color setting up to ultra-vivid.

Very nice. No buyer's remorse here.

Elmac meanwhile puffed merrily away on his pipe.

"I was wondering something..."

One of his bushy eyebrows arched.

"At Lordren's I was talking to my personal assistant, and something called a 'Mage of the Line' came up. She changed the subject quick. Is it a taboo subject in Thera?"

That wasn't a lie. It *had* come up. I'd just never articulated the subject, you know, in actual words.

I *did* want to tell Elmac the whole story, but my gypsy elf family had been slaughtered because of the mere suspicion that my father was a Mage of the Line. I had to play this close to the vest until I understood why.

Elmac snorted smoke. "By Odin's balls, lad, why were you talking 'bout *them*?"

"Just discussing magic items? I don't know."

Elmac glared at me, relaxed, and took another puff. "Well, don't know much. Just that there be no more."

"They left Thera?"

"Oh, aye, they left—right into the ground. 'Twas centuries before my time, but if I recall, there was, and believe there still be, a royal sanction on the whole lot."

It took all my Spirit Warrior discipline not to go white with shock.

What the hell had I done?

Oh sure, *now* the "secret and restricted" class thing made perfect sense... because Mage of the Line was an *outlawed, kill on sight* class—in a world, mind you, where assassination was legal.

I whispered, "What did they do to deserve that?"

"Best ask Delacroix," Elmac said. "She was around to help hunt the last of 'em down."

Right. Colonel Delacroix, who had blasted an army of shadows to ashes with her nuclear-power magical eye beams. The solar sorceress who didn't trust or like me. She'd be the last person I asked.

Elmac gazed at the stars just making their evening entrance. "I'll take first watch. Don't worry, nothing'll get by me. Get some rest."

He fished out the assassin's coded note, a pencil stub, and started scribbling. His gaze was laser-intense.

I wrapped my wool cloak about my shoulders and tried to sleep. It took a long time for me to drift off... and when I did, there were only nightmares of being trapped in Elmac's vault, and Delacroix melting the door to get to me.

CHAPTER 13

The next morning, we hiked through farmlands, meadows, and then across fields of tall wild grass punctuated by the occasional honey mesquite and meandering creek.

"Watch your step," Elmac said. "Not quite the season for 'em, but the place sometimes be crawling with virescene vipers. Three-headed beasties. Venom dissolves the flesh off your bones."

Ah, just another casual stroll through Thera. I was mildly surprised the grass here wasn't carnivorous or floating on seas of quicksand.

Elmac led us along game trails, changing from one to another seemingly at random. He looked confident, but I swear we headed west half the day, and then back east until late afternoon.

"So, we're looking for... what did you call it this morning?" Morgana asked. "A trans-dimensional causeway?"

"Aye," Elmac replied.

"Uh, for us slackers who were still asleep two hours before sunrise?" I said. "Trans-dimensional causeway? That's just a gateway to another world, right?"

"There be all sort 'o gates," Elmac told me. "Temporal. Truncated. One way. Helical. But this one has an *in-between spot* from here to there." He waved his hands about as if that made his explanation more comprehensible.

"And that's where this Chaos Knight will be?" I asked.

Elmac nodded. "Try not to be worrying, lad. There be plenty 'o time before we be dealing with her. Relax and enjoy the scenery."

Relax, he says. Just watch out for flesh-dissolving three-headed serpents of death.

And yet, that's exactly what he and Morgana did. They got a little ahead of me, chatting, and Morgana occasionally tried to tickle him with a stalk of long grass.

Was I the only adult here?

"Hey," I said, interrupting their fun, "didn't Pendric say that there were no more Far Field barbarians? How can that be when the first step in our Drunken Monkey quest is to find them?"

"I think," Elmac said, pausing to brush pollen from his beard, "what Pendric meant is that there be no more 'o them traveling to Thera. 'Bout ten years ago the drunken louts stopped coming to the Fall Festival to drink the town dry and—"

"—find worthy brides," I finished for him. "I know. The barbarian ghost who gave me the quest, Karkanal, told me as much."

"Oh, they be looking for worthy husbands too, mind you," Elmac said. "The Far Field folk use group marriages, chains, and uh, looser, more polygamous arrangements." He blushed.

"*Really?*" Morgana said with a lurid grin. "You ever try anything like that?"

Elmac sputtered and blushed a shade deeper.

"So, you're suggesting this gate guardian has prevented the Far Field barbarians from coming to Thera?" I asked, trying to steer us back to the relevant topic. "It—she can shift shape. What other powers does she have?"

"Killjoy..." Morgana muttered.

I wondered if Morgana was embracing her Trickster side a bit too much? I'd have to have a private chat about her leading Elmac along. If it was a joke, it wasn't funny.

"I think that depends on the form she be taking," Elmac answered me. "Few survive long enough to be making a study 'o the eight Champions of Chaos."

Elmac scrutinized several game trails that branched out before us, picked the leftmost and kept going. "The funny thing about gate guardians, especially for them camping the in-between places, is that they not always be there. More often than not, this particular gate be left unguarded." He halted, considered, then added, "Guess I ought to have mentioned that."

I liked Elmac. A lot. After you've been through battles together, such comrades became like your brothers and sisters... and like siblings, you also occasionally felt the urge to strangle them.

I let it go.

We walked on and Morgana regaled us with stories of her namesake, the greatest hero-queen in the history of Britannia, Morgana le fey.

Hero-queen? I didn't interrupt to ask. Different Earth, obviously different legends.

"...Then Princess Morgana had to go to war with her half-brother and his thug wizard henchman, Merlin the Bastard, to take her throne back," she told us, waving her hands about to demonstrate their combats. "She and her lover, Lance du lac, fought all the buggers off at Avalon, signed a peace treaty with the fairy folk, and put an end to that nonsense about searching for a holy grail. When all her foes lay dead at her feet, she and Lance founded the Round Table of noble women and men—and that eventually became our modern Parliament. Right straight head on *that* woman, I tell you."

She went on like this for a time—spinning tales of court romances, betrayals, and a few more wars for good measure. Morgana le fey and Lance du lac ended up having a passel of young princesses and princes that were the progenitors of Britannia's modern royals.

Seemed like a better deal than my Arthurian legends.

The sun set and two of Thera's moons—the cracked and ever-erratic Joslue, and his sister, the unblemished golden and glowing Mimolette—stepped upon the starry dance floor to waltz. (In case your wondering, Thera supposedly has thirteen moons. I've only ever seen twelve myself. I suspected the thirteen never-seen satellite is a myth).

Elmac halted and whispered. "It be just ahead."

A tiny footbridge spanned a creek.

"All that bloody build up for *this*?" Morgana asked.

Elmac shrugged out of his pack.

"Looks ordinary on *this* side," he said, "but just over be the in-between spot I told you 'bout. It be a tiny island in the middle 'o interstellar space. And if the Chaos Knight be there, she won't be letting us pass 'cause 'o our good looks." He gave us a dead serious look. "Best be prepared."

That, I agreed with. I unwound *Shé liàn* from the sash about my waist. The ninja chain tensed and flexed as it readied for combat.

I also tapped the demon bone knuckles in my inventory and they appeared on my right hand.

Might as well bond with it now.

I gave the thing the mental go ahead and hoped it didn't hurt too much.

It heated and grew so heavy I could barely keep my hand raised.

The blackened bones seeped into my skin... burning hotter as they went deeper—not so much pain, but that on the edge of torture/pleasure thing you got from a professional massage.

Then it was gone.

I flexed the hand. My double-knuckles popped and cracked as it all settled into place. My fist *was* a little bigger, especially the knuckles, but nothing anyone would notice with a casual glance.

Morgana's eyes were wide and she gave me an appreciative nod.

She then pulled up and cinched tight the hood of her battle suit. As she did so, her edges blurred and it was hard to see her (even with my headband on). Impressive.

Elmac unslung his battle axe and whispered the magic words that made the blade come alive with crackles of lightning.

"You be ready?" he asked.

Morgana and I nodded.

Elmac led the way; I followed. Morgana? She was suddenly nowhere to be seen. Well, she was a trickster thief, after all. No real surprise there. I'm sure she had our backs.

As I stepped over the crest of the footbridge, it felt as if I passed through a door. The temperature dropped a few degrees. My ears popped.

The other side of the little bridge suddenly ended in another place.

It was an island floating in outer space.

The thing was fifty feet across, covered with a mossy lawn and dotted with a few worn river stones. A tiny spring fed a stream that snaked across the island—and fell off the edge, becoming a glittering tail of ice crystals in the star-filled void.

Important safety tip: Stay *on* the island.

On the opposite side was another footbridge like the one we had just crossed.

Sitting on a rock in the center of the island was what I assumed was the Chaos Knight.

It had taken the form of... a fairy?

He was a foot tall and wore a black trench coat, black tee shirt, black leather pants, and tiny mud-encrusted platform Doc Martens boots. Rose-colored sunglasses covered anime-sized eyes that were ringed with melting mascara. He could have just stepped off the stage of a heavy metal concert.

The little guy tossed aside the *Sandman* comic book he'd been reading. His dragonfly wings ruffled, and he leapt to the ground.

Elmac whispered, "Be looking a wee bit *different* than last time."

With arms akimbo, the fairy declared, "Halt, unworthy travelers! Return whence you came or dare to win passage by a test of wits or force of arms!"

CHAPTER 14

"Uh, no offense," I said, "but you *are* the Chaos Knight guarding this gate, aren't you?"

The fairy looked around as if he was unsure I was addressing him, then blinked, and said, "Of course not, cretin. Do *I* look like the Grand Imperial Champion of Disorder and Slayer of the Seven Sovereign Justices of Elysium, Her Greatness, Dominota Koroleva?"

He huffed. "But I see how *you* might make that mistake. My power can overwhelm simple-minded riffraff such as yourself. Rest assured, however, I am more than capable of dispatching your likes." He rolled his neck, cleared his throat. "However, if you wish to wait for her Ladyship, she is presently on her coffee break and will be back in... in... uh, later. I'm not sure precisely when. Time can get a bit tricky in the in-between."

My mouth opened to reply, but honestly, the little guy had me stumped. Was he for real?

"What will it be then?" he asked and tapped his boot. "Wait for the Grand Imperial Champion to kill you? Try your luck with me by honorable combat, or" —he chuckled— "trial by *riddle*? Or take the most prudent option, depart and live to tell the tale of how you cheated fate this day."

He glanced to his discarded comic book as if all he really wanted was to get back to his reading.

Suddenly by my side, Morgana said to the fairy, "One moment please, good sir."

She then huddled with me and Elmac.

"This guy is full of it," I whispered. "I say just dropkick the runt into outer space."

Elmac paled and Morgana shook her head.

"Don't," she whispered. "Fairy magic is right tricky. You go and kick him and that starts his test by 'honorable' combat. He wouldn't have offered that without something up his sleeves."

"And riddles..." Elmac shivered. "I'd rather fight another hellfire demon than try a *fairy* riddle. They not be known for losing."

"Quite right," the fairy said.

The creep had better hearing than I realized. I looked up.

A stupid grin was plastered across his sharp features.

His gaze locked on Morgana, and he sobered and bowed. "My pardon, lady. I didn't see until just now that you are a distant cousin to the fey. Please accept my apologies and profound wishes for your continued good health."

"Cousin?" I murmured.

"Later—" she hissed.

Morgana gave him an awkward curtsey. "Good day to you too, cousin. Suppose there's no letting me and my mates just..." She nodded to the far bridge.

"Alas, no," he said with a sigh. "This is a Union gig, and..." He spread his hands as if that explained it all.

At least I finally knew why Morgana's features had always struck me as more sharp and wild than a normal elf. She had a few pixies infesting her family tree. I bet it gave a boost to her shapeshifting powers. But I wondered if her choice during character creation had been mere pragmatism, or had she been emulating her namesake, Morgana le fey?

"Just so we be knowing the rules," Elmac said. "We win, we pass. But if we lose?"

"Ah, indeed," the fairy replied. "*When* you lose, I will claim one of you as my slave, for say" —he tapped his pointed chin— "one year. I need a new roadie for my band. Our last one lost his hearing, eyes... uh, and a few other parts."

Cobra scales rippled over Morgana's throat. "*Not* bloody likely."

The fairy vigorously shook his head. "No. No. Not you, cousin." His gaze turned to me. "Him."

"I don't think so."

Elmac set a hand on my arm. "Let's just be leaving. There may be another way 'round to Far Fields. Longer. Different... risks." In a ghost of a whisper, he added, "But no *fairy* magic."

Morgana nodded her agreement.

"Hang on a second," I said.

I wanted to think this through.

The fairy was trying to rattle me.

And it was working.

I took a deep breath and set aside my growing urge to stomp him flat.

Morgana was right. It was too obvious a choice to fight him. That had to be a trap.

I also agreed with Elmac. I was okay at riddles, but my zero INTELLECT wasn't going to cut it with such a supernatural creature.

A window popped open:

QUEST ALERT!
A THOUSAND DRUNKEN MONKEYS — *BONUS* SEGMENT
("ONE LITTLE COMPLICATION")
Defeat the fairy in a contest of arms or wits.
Reward(s): Bonus experience and a special reward (dependent on outcome).
Suggested Party: You're on your own.

WARNING: Failure may result in enslavement.

Accept? YES / NO

Morgana cocked her head. "That confirms we're on the right path, yeah?"

Elmac, not being able to see it, glanced about, confused.

I read it to him in English.

"But it be a '*bonus* segment'," Elmac whispered back in English. "So, *optional?*"

"Well?" the fairy demanded. He looked annoyed, probably because he didn't speak my native language.

"Put a cork in it," I told him.

He glowered and started pacing.

I was thinking about this all wrong, thinking like Hektor (with a k), gypsy elf and resident fantasy character—not like Hector (with a c), who had a college degree in computer science, with a minor in physics... and a brand of magic all his own.

"This so-called trial by riddle," I said, "would it be possible for *me* to ask *you* a riddle?"

The little guy tilted his head, then burst into laughter so hard he fell over, holding his sides, which slowed to hiccups as he got back to his feet.

"*You* riddle *me*? What would be the point? I've heard them all."

"Hektor," Elmac said, "what be you doing?"

"I've got this."

Sure, I know, famous last words.

What *was* this magic I had? Well, the funny thing about all those physics and computer science classes I'd taken, they'd all had *math* prerequisites.

Not that anything fancy was required here. Good old-fashioned algebra ought to do the trick.

"You know, mate, it's your butt on the line," Morgana whispered.

I waved away her concern.

"Do you agree?" I asked the fairy. "Or perhaps it's too *large* of a challenge for you."

I felt my *Taunting Tenor* skill warm to a simmer.

The fairy's face turned a lovely shade of lilac. He puffed out his chest. "I accept your challenge, foolish elf. Riddle away."

"Ah. One moment," I said. "I demand reciprocal conditions. In addition to letting us pass, if I win, you become *my* slave for a year."

The fairy pulled his sunglasses down a bit and peered at me over the rims. "Sure. Whaaaatever." He cracked his tiny knuckles.

"Very well then." I cleared my throat, draped *Shé liàn* over my shoulder, then pretended to consider long and hard, and finally with a thespian flourish said, "What is the sum of plus one and negative one, divided by the sum of negative one and plus one?"

The fairy blinked. "What?"

I repeated myself. Slower.

"That's not a riddle," he declared and crossed his arms over his chest.

"Are you sure?"

He frowned, brightened, and from his back pocket fished out a tiny book.

I squinted and saw the gilt title: The *Fey Un-Practical Guide to Trickery, 213th edition.*

He riffled through gossamer-thin pages, found what he was looking for, and mumbled aloud: "'A riddle is defined as a question or declaration that requires imagination, intuition, and/or intellect to deduce or guess its answer or meaning.'" He gave me a smug smile.

"Then," I replied, "I believe I just gave you a question that requires 'imagination, intuition, and/or intellect to deduce or guess its answer.'"

The little guy's smile held but a trickle of sweat appeared at his temple.

"I'll give you thirty minutes. Why, any fourteen-year-old on my world would have the answer in seconds."

If said fourteen-year-old had been paying attention in algebra class.

"Or perhaps," I said, "an even *shorter* period of time."

He trembled with rage at my taunt.

I felt a bit like a bully egging him on, mainly because it was too easy, but since my own skin was at stake here—too bad.

He gathered himself and stood straighter, perhaps a full thirteen inches. "This will be trivial."

He reached behind the rock he'd been sitting on, retrieved a satchel, pulled out a scroll and quill, and started scribbling.

"Let's see... One and negative one, that's zero. Minus one and one—how silly, that is also zero. What a dumb riddle. So, zero divided by zero is simply...."

His face went slack.

"Oh..." Morgana said.

A former high school biology teacher, Morgana had to have substituted in for a few math classes, so she got it.

Elmac murmured to me, "But anything divided by itself be—"

"Shh," I told him. "No helping. Not even a *teensy-weensy* bit."

At this, the fairy snapped the tip of his quill, spattering ink everywhere. He growled and reached into his satchel for a spare.

"Yes, zero divided by zero is one," he said to himself.

"Is that your answer?" I asked.

He looked up, hesitated. "Uh, no—wait. Something's not right." He bent over his scroll once more and scratched away. "Ah! Yes. Of course, so easy. Why, anything multiplied by zero *is* zero. Child's play... Or, no. Anything *divided* by zero is infinite."

"Is *that* your answer?"

He glanced back and forth among the three results he'd jotted down.

This was the crux of the riddle, but he didn't realize the answer was staring right back at him.

His eyes bulged and he pulled out tufts of his black hair, which I noted was only dyed jet black. He had lime-green roots.

And so it went for a time...

The fairy filled five scrolls with increasingly complicated equations. "No—that can't be right. Ah! No... What?!" He finally stomped about in a circle, kicking the scrolls, booting his satchel, and spilling the inkwell.

"Aghhh!"

"Is *that* your answer?"

He wheeled to face me, panting and puffing, teeth grinding. "No! This-this *riddle* is *wrong*. What madness is this?!"

I decided to finish him before he figured it out.

"Tut tut," I said. "No need to have such a *short* fuse, my man. Perhaps you require a *little* more time?"

He froze and, although I thought it not possible, his apoplectic lilac shade deepened to eggplant.

"My apologies, good sir, I had no intention of *diminishing* your status as a self-proclaimed riddle master. Oh, pardon my faux pas. I meant to say there is no need to be a *baby* about this. Ah, again pardon my insensitivity. By way of apology could I offer you a beverage to calm your agitated state? My companion here could provide you a pint... or maybe more appropriately, a *half pint*?"

"Gah!" He drew a slim gold dagger from his belt. "DIE, interloper!"

"Oh no, you don't." Elmac said. "You agreed, fairy—a trial by wits. And wits it'll be or you be forfeiting the contest."

At this, the fairy tossed his dagger aside, threw himself on the grass, and wailed.

Morgana shook her head. "Must you torture the little blighter?"

"Oh, absolutely," I said.

He sobbed and pulled out handfuls of grass and stuffed them into his mouth.

Had I driven him over the edge? I almost stepped forward to tell him it was okay—that the riddle was a simple trick.

Fortunately, the good intentions that might have been my undoing were stopped.

There was a thumping sound like cinderblocks dropped onto a hardwood floor.

Morgana, Elmac, and I turned to the right.

A new bridge appeared with what could only be the Chaos Knight back from her coffee break standing on the threshold.

"Blimey," Morgana whispered. "That's not..."

"Aye. Has to be," Elmac told her.

Yeah, we were pretty much screwed.

CHAPTER 15

The Chaos Knight had taken the form of... well, the closest match was the multi-armed statue of the goddess, Kali, in the 1973 movie, *The Golden Voyage of Sinbad* (with stop-motion effects by the legendary Ray Harryhausen). If you missed that flick or never had it on your version of Earth, let me explain.

The guardian in the movie was a ten-foot tall, six-armed clay golem who resembled the Hindu goddess.

This one, however, had *twelve* arms, towered *twenty* feet, and was made of metal (steel, if I was not mistaken*)*—and oh, she had *three* faces evenly spaced about her head to give her a full three-hundred-sixty-degree field of view.

If I were a Chaos Knight who could morph into any form? I might have picked the same thing. *Total* overkill.

The fairy kicked his notes under his satchel, stood at attention, and announced, "All tremble before the terribleness of the Grand Imperial Champion of Disorder and Slayer of the Seven Sovereign Justices of Elysium, Her Greatness, Dominota Koroleva!"

And like he needed to, he added, "Oh Imperial Great One, kill these intruders!"

She stepped onto the island (and I swear I felt the entire landmass tilt).

The bridge behind her vanished.

I noted the bridge we'd used to get here was now gone too. Lovely.

So... no running.

I didn't think I'd be taunting my way out of this one, either.

And frankly, I didn't see us defeating such a combat machine.

I concentrated and transitioned into the aether—literally taking a time-out to think.

The island in-between worlds slipped away and my astral body resolved... elsewhere.

I marveled at the beauty.

Lines ran this way and that from every direction... and simultaneously came from *no* direction. They vibrated with harmonics and shimmering spectrums, with laughter, cannon booms, howling hurricane, whispers; wind and rain, wasp stings, and kisses brushed my face as sensation passed through me; memories came and went too, mine, others, fragments of thoughts from long-dead gods, and *things* my mind refused to comprehend lest it be crushed—all mingled with my astral soul in a glorious choir that sang the hymn of the multiverse.

Before I lost myself in the cacophony of synesthesia—I pushed it away to a mental arm's length.

Whoa. The toe in the water I'd dipped into the aether as a child was *nothing* like this.

I carefully focused *only* on the ley lines and the rest faded.

There was the usual web of golden threads that represented location, a few nearby smoldering crimson strands, glacier blues, and brilliant filaments of lightning against star-filled space.

I also could see the ghostly outlines of Elmac, Morgana, and the Chaos Knight. All frozen.

This wasn't a true time stop. My physical body was immobile as well. Only my mind and the things in the aether that I could influence moved.

I noted I had a new green indicator bar under the gold one for my spiritual mana and the red one showing my current health. This had to be my reflexive mana bar. A green pip winked out, reminding me that I was paying for this subjective "free" time.

There was the slightest tingle in my fingertips ... or rather, my astral body's fingertips. That had to be a side effect of burning through my reflex-based mana. Not entirely unexpected, but nonetheless disconcerting.

Well, down to business then. First thing, first.

I powered my *Perfect Motion* buff.

Next, I reached for a nearby line of glistening gold. It made contact with my outstretched astral hand with a satisfying clicking-into-place sensation. This particular ley line, however, then started to vibrate. I had to hold it tight to keep it from slipping away.

I took another length of the thing and looped it about *Shé liàn*—and as a test, I used my *Small Pass* ability.

The handle of the ninja chain appeared in my hand.

That was *so* cool.

But that maneuver had used ten points of reflexive mana. With the mana burned to remain in the aether so far, this left me with 88/100... and the tingling in my fingertips now felt like pins and needles.

I better stay on task—so next up, a tactical analysis.

I took a good long look over the Chaos Knight. The casting of the statue's steel was top-notch. Even the tiny shrunken heads on her necklace had fine details like open screaming mouths and tiny tears running down their burnished cheeks.

I got the sense the statue wasn't a hollow casting, either. If she was a *solid* mass of steel, she'd weigh at least six tons.

It was going to be tough to make a dent in her, let alone do any real damage. Maybe if we soaked her in water she'd rust? ...Given a few days.

Okay, forget fighting the armored tank with swords and fists.

I noticed a few more pips had gone dark in my reflexive mana bar.

How about the terrain? Any help there?

A few rocks, grass, one small stream. No escape routes—unless I wanted to take a flying leap into outer space.

Ah! Could we push her off this rock?

A quick thumbnail calculation, and... there was no way. The physics didn't add up unless Elmac had a bulldozer or thirty-foot-long crowbar crammed in his pack.

Where was my friend Pendric and his titan horse Bell Ringer when I needed a suicidal charge and a hundred thousand newtons of force?

I glanced at my mana bar. Two more pips had vanished.

Hanging out in the aether was amazingly useful. I'd cast my buff, readied my weapon, and sized up our enemy, *without* having to worry about being immediately slain in the process. It could, however, become a trap. If I ran out of mana here, my astral form would permanently detach from my physical body, i.e. death.

And one more green pip winked out to punctuate this point.

I'd done all I could here. We'd have to engage this thing to get more data.

I phased back to normal space-time.

The Chaos Knight stepped toward us. The ground trembled.

The fairy cheered. "Slash them to ribbons!"

Slash? With her fists?

The statue of Kali made a grasping motion with one hand. A ten-foot-long scimitar appeared there—and in rapid succession, her eleven other hands did the same, and the air rang out with the collective sword "*shiiiiiings.*"

Bad news. Not only the slashing part, but she now had tremendous reach.

...in addition to impenetrable armor.

...and vastly superior strength and mass.

"Ideas?" I asked.

Elmac and Morgana stared open-mouthed at the thing. No help there.

"Use ranged weapons," I said. "Don't close. Keep moving. Spread out."

That broke their state of shock.

Elmac sprinted right; Morgana went left.

I held the center position and yelled, "Hey, you rusty pile of scrap metal. Over here. I've got a can of oil for you, Squeaky."

The knight's three pairs of eyes tracked us, and then she maneuvered to a tactically advantageous position in the middle of the island.

My taunt had apparently bounced off her metal skin.

The fairy fluttered onto her shoulder. "That one," he snarled and pointed at me. "Kill him first."

One of her gazes narrowed at me.

The skin along my spine went cold and crinkled with a primal terror response.

She lumbered toward me, each step leaving ten-inch impressions in the loam.

"But take your time," the fairy added. "Make him *suffer*."

What a nasty little piece of—

I darted right, faster than she could follow. Thank you, *Perfect Motion*.

Morgana and Elmac maintained their relative equidistant positions. Morgana threw a dagger at her; Elmac shot a hand crossbow—and both attacks pinged harmlessly off the metal.

The statue's head swiveled as she moved to keep visual contact on us.

"How long can we play at this?" Morgana called out in English.

I had a feeling not as long as Her Greatness, Dominota Koroleva could. We mere mortals would eventually run out of mana and stamina and pass out. If she truly was a magically animated construct, she'd *never* tire.

"If we be doing something," Elmac replied, also in English, "best do it while we be strong."

I didn't like Elmac's suggestion, but he *was* right.

"Agreed," I said. "Let's go in on three."

Elmac dropped his hand crossbow but kept a one-handed grip on his battle axe. An iron ring on his free hand popped into a buckler, popped once more to become a medium-sized shield, then a third time to the equivalent of a curved tower shield of dwarven proportions. It was crafted from a single gigantic scale that might have dropped off the World Serpent. Enameled upon it was a coat of arms: war hammers crossed and a fire-breathing dragon twined between them.

Nice. Good for you, my friend.

"One," I yelled.

Not to be outdone, bumps appeared on Morgana's leather armor, roughened, darkened—and became smoking black stones as she shapeshifted into... *what?*

Her head melded into her neck and disappeared in a broadening torso. Raw topaz eyes winked open. Her back thickened and elongated into a heavy tail, and where it dragged along the ground, the grass ignited.

Was she transforming into some sort of earth elemental?

I blinked. Yes.

Foot-long quartz crystals grew from Morgana's spine. Her hands absorbed into her arms and became chiseled basalt. Her legs swelled to stout stone hindquarters, and in the seams of her rocky form, glowing magma flared and dripped lava.

This was a *huge* leap from her previous panther and wolf shapes. How was she doing it? However she was—*Brava, Morgana. Brava.*

"Two!"

I estimated Morgana's new earth form to be half the mass of the statue. Could she go toe-to-toe with it?

"NOW!"

We rushed the Chaos Knight.

CHAPTER 16

The Chaos Knight halted.

Four scimitars angled toward each of her inbound targets.

I stopped short of her bladed reach and tossed the weighted end of *Shé liàn*.

She easily parried the chain.

That, however, caused the weight to whip around, and the chain to wind about the hilt of her scimitar.

I dug in my heels and yanked.

To my astonishment, I ripped the sword from her grasp.

The curved blade sailed end over end and *thunked* into the sod.

With a gesture, though, a new scimitar appeared in her hand.

At the same time, she sliced at Elmac.

He took it on his shield and was bowled over.

Elmac landed, rolled with the curve of his shield, and was up on his feet. Pretty nimble for an old guy.

Morgana closed a lot faster than I thought she'd be able to in that stone form. Her near-molten body flowed with an odd grace through the earth. She drew back her chiseled arms and punched.

Two scimitars deflected her strikes and sent a shower of sparks off the basalt.

The Chaos Knight's other two blades struck true.

With a rumbling roar, Morgana reeled back, lava gushing from the slashes.

One hand went to my chest as if I'd taken those hits too. There had to be tremendous force behind those blows to cut rock like that.

If the Chaos Knight had stabbed, instead of slashed, Morgana could have been shish-kebabbed, and drawn in for an easy kill.

"Break off!" I called.

We backed up to equidistant positions.

After a moment's hesitation, the statue once more began its unrelenting march toward me.

Just what I wanted.

I had to take the pressure off Morgana... who was moving slower.

The deep gashes in her chest cooled and sealed. Druid healing spell, no doubt. But she'd tapped her finite mana supply to do it.

Elmac stopped and glared at the Chaos Knight over the edge of his shield. The look in his black eyes was the same one I'd seen when he'd watched the Bloody Rooster burn.

"Elmac," I called out. "Listen to—"

He yelled, "I'll not die dancing 'round this island like some coward."

He was *raging* mad—not just about the fight, but because the woman he liked had been seriously wounded... and he hadn't been there to help her.

I got it, and maybe I'd have come to the same heroically stupid conclusion he had.

Elmac *charged* straight at the thing.

The statue swiveled, pointed *all* twelve scimitars at him, and closed.

She slashed and stabbed at Elmac before Morgana or I could rush in.

He turtled behind his shield.

Most of her strikes scraped and screeched off the gigantic reptilian scale; three, however, neatly carved off chunks the size of dinner plates.

I wasn't sure what held Elmac's shield together anymore other than dwarven craftsmanship, pure determination, and a hefty enchantment.

Elmac stayed on his feet this time, but he backed up—actually more was *forced* back by the sheer power of her continuous rapid-fire impacts. He was strong and skilled, but he simply didn't have the mass to mount an effective defense.

He was getting close to the edge of the island... closer to the void of interstellar space. Whatever magic kept a breathable atmosphere around this rock probably didn't extend too far.

Morgana and I advanced and tried to slip around either side of the knight, but her reach was too great, and two blades swiveled to block each of us, more than enough to keep me fencing back and forth.

I nonetheless *tried* to get inside her reach—and got sliced open shoulder to groin.

I lost fifty-eight of my one-hundred sixty health in one go. *Ouch!*

I staggered back and had just enough time to fire off a *Spiritual Regeneration* before I had to dodge and parry more incoming strikes. That repaired about half the damage; enough to keep my guts from spilling out.

Morgana closed, pinning three of the statue's arms to its body. Morgana's chiseled limbs then flared with orange heat. Where she held the statue, the steel grew red hot. A scimitar slumped and melted.

The Chaos Knight pulled an arm free, combined grips for a two-handed strike—and slashed partway *through* Morgana's body.

Morgana pushed back, and I saw that she had barely avoided being cleft in twain. Her rocky form dissolved into the ground.

Dead?

No.

Please no.

I prayed that she had just taken cover in the earth.

The Chaos Knight's melted blade, however, did *not* magically re-appear in her hand.

That was *something*.

Meanwhile, Elmac had run out of maneuvering room.

He balanced right on the edge of the island. The only thing he could do now was take the beating, and he did—getting pounded into the ground... which was beginning to crack around his boots.

What was left of his shield finally fell apart.

But it wasn't only his shield that broke—something *inside* Elmac must have snapped too at the sight of Morgana's grievous wound.

Battle axe in one hand, a short sword in the other, he screamed and threw himself at the knight. Weaving steel back-and-forth—he parried her scimitars and battered her arms, chest, and knees, scoring two-inch deep grooves in her metal skin. It was the most impressive display of close blade work I'd ever seen.

He held his own...

for a few seconds.

Six scimitars then struck true and he gushed blood from as many mortal wounds.

I tried once more to get to him but met a wall of flashing blades.

Elmac's skin was paper white (where he wasn't drenched in blood). He was forced to play defense, and just by the skin of his teeth did he parry the incoming barrage of sweeps, stabs, and slashes.

I didn't understand how he was still standing. Let alone still fighting.

From the corner of my eye, I caught a few stones and a furrow roiling through the ground... between the statue's legs... then there was a small eruption under Elmac's feet. A stone tip reached up and touched him. A few of his most critical wounds stopped bleeding. The cracking bit of island under his feet seemed to heal as well.

I offered my silent thanks to the trickster gods and their healing spells.

The Chaos Knight's attacks, however, never slowed.

Morgana pushed up through the ground and fought by Elmac's side. Lava wept from her previous wound—more so, as she battled and tore it open.

The knight mercilessly pounded them, scoring hit after hit... while easily keeping me at bay.

They were going to die.

And I was helpless to save them.

Almost unthinkingly, I entered the aether.

The battle paused, startling me.

Then I understood and I relaxed.

A tick of reflexive mana vanished... but my depleting mana was buying me a minute or so to think. It was a bargain by any standard.

Once the Chaos Knight had finished Elmac and Morgana, she'd come for me. I felt like a loathsome coward for even *thinking* that. I'd rather have been on the other side of this thing, fighting, however futilely, with my friends.

Focus, Hektor.

Okay. What was going to happen when I dropped out of the aether?

I'd have about two seconds before she murdered my friends.

What could *I* do about it?

...Nothing. I couldn't fight this thing. I couldn't help my friends get away! I couldn't get away!

I stopped... counted to three... and tried to stop my runaway thoughts.

Panic. It's more common in battle than you'd think. You just had to know how to tap the brakes.

Let's try this again. What could I do?

I wasn't sure, but I could start by running down the list of my abilities and items.

How about a *Small Pass*? Move—or rather *remove*—this thing's head from its neck?

That would be great. I didn't think, though, a first-level ability was going to instant kill the Grand Imperial Champion of Disorder.

I had *Shé liàn*. I'd used it to disarm the knight before. But one less blade that'd be replaced after a heartbeat got me nowhere.

My headband? Would seeing the *absolute truth* of the Chaos Knight reveal some weakness? Even if it did, it'd take too much time. And although I could use the ability here in the aether while things were on hold, it was probably a very bad idea to view even one true glimpse of *this* primordial dimension.

My demon bone knuckledusters? They had that power to blast through a cubic foot of iron. That *might* take out one of her legs—unbalance her, so we could push her off the island.

A few problems with that scenario, though.

I'd have to get to a leg *without* getting sliced, diced, and flayed. At best a long shot.

Say hypothetically I managed that. Even one footed, she'd be able to brace herself with two or three arms, and crablike, proceed to slay us with only a minor delay.

Also, she'd still weigh nearly six tons. The three of us simply didn't have the leverage to move that much mass.

A glance at my reflexive mana: 74/100.

The blasting power of the demon bone knuckles had seemed so promising.

Had I missed something? I opened my interface and re-read its description.

SPECIAL ABILITIES: +1 to wielder's STRENGTH and REFLEX. Adds moderate damage to every (right-handed) strike. Upon command, once per day the fist may cause an *explosion* on contact—pulverizing a cubic yard of stone, or cubic foot of iron...

Wait. *Pulverize* a cubic yard of stone? How much *earth* pulverizing power did that translate to? Three cubic feet? Ten?

And how much volume of stone and earth and dirt comprising this island would one have to blast in order to make the Chaos Knight fall off... into all that lovely empty space?

Let's see, depending on the angle of the underside of this island, well, there was no way to tell.

But blowing up the island—which wasn't going to fight back—seemed like a heck of a better option than trying to defeat an invulnerable opponent.

Elmac and Morgana would have to get out of the way, and fast—but their capabilities were *not* the weak link in this plan. That would be the host of my assumptions about the island's composition, the displaced volume required to topple the Chaos Knight, and the power of the demon bone knuckles... that I'd never tested.

So, a shot in the dark.

I could up those odds. Slightly. Maybe.

I grabbed a blazing ley line the color of a tangerine, and smelled hot copper and felt my hand and arm sunburn as I coiled it about my fist.

A little extra fire damage for good measure *and* points for style.

Yeah... I felt pretty good about this.

Oh, not my odds. Come on, let's be real.

But what else are you supposed to do when life handed you impossible—correction—*nearly* impossible odds?

Why, smile, and step up. *Semper Fi.*

I entered normal space-time.

My fist was a blazing bonfire.

I cocked my arm back and screamed, "Jump—left—NOW!"

Elmac stood still, dazed.

Morgana grabbed and shielded him, and her rock form sped through the ground at an astonishing rate.

Not fast enough, though.

Six scimitars crisscrossed her back.

I jumped as close as I could get to the Chaos Knight.

My arm rocketed down to meet the ground.

I triggered the power of my knuckle dusters.

The air around my fist ignited white hot, a blazing furnace of power.

Five sword points closed upon me—a classic pincushion maneuver.

I laughed.

And my fist *exploded*.

CHAPTER 17

The earth rippled as if I'd punched gelatin.

Shockwaves flashed through my bones and the air.

My flaming fist liquefied stones and dirt—that in an instant expanded, cooled, and shattered into a cloud of sparkling particles.

I was immune from the effects of my own abilities and gear. A couple of ricocheting stones, however, dinged my chi armor, but only a few points of damage got through.

And the best news? I hadn't been stabbed to death by the Chaos Knight, because I'd pulverized a sizable chunk of the island's edge. Everything standing there had been blasted out into the void, which included the Chaos Knight... and me.

I tumbled in freefall—among dirt, rocks, and with all twelve arms writhing as she tried to regain *some* control, the six-ton steel statue of Kali.

As I'd thought, just beyond the island's perimeter the gravity and magically-contained atmosphere *stopped* and the vacuum of interstellar space *started*.

Oh man, it was beyond plunged-into-ice-water cold.

I would have shivered, but my body was too busy swelling, trying to burst from the difference in pressure.

My health bar plummeted, leaving a trail of blue-white pixels that either faded to black, popped like balloons, or appeared to be gasping—a neat graphical representation for the freezing, depressurization, and asphyxiation damage.

I remembered reading that a person without a spacesuit might last fifteen seconds in hard vacuum.

Right now, I had a bit less than half of my health.

I spammed *Spiritual Regeneration* twice and got back to one hundred thirty-one points, then watched my precious red pips vanish as fast as my thundering pulse.

I wasn't dead. Not yet. But soon.

I spun out of control—everything a blur of stars and space and rocks.

I extended my arms to slow my rotational velocity, and I saw a new twist to my imminent death as the Chaos Knight rotated back into view.

She grabbed for me with all her arms.

All it did, though, was make her tumble.

I kept as still as I could.

I was just out of her reach, and she seemed to be moving a *little* faster than me, getting more distant by inches every second.

I continued my turn, back toward the island.

I was only ten feet away.

It might as well have been ten *miles*, though, because there was nothing to push against to change my direction. I considered and dismissed attempting to push off the knight. Even if I managed such a thing without her crushing me first—I couldn't get to her in the first place.

I could only drift... farther from the island with each heartbeat.

As a matter of scientific curiosity, I noted a sizable piece of it was missing. I'd guess about the volume of a mid-sized sedan, but it was hard to tell as my trajectory had propelled me "under" the surface of the landmass. Beneath was a curious inverted mountain, like an iceberg, I suppose.

Since I couldn't see topside, there was no way to tell what had happened to Morgana and Elmac, either. I chose to believe my comrades were safe and sound and singing my praises. Perhaps Elmac was even now raising a flask in my honor.

...I was getting punchy.

I continued to spin once more away from the island.

There was blackness—stars—and one very angry-looking Chaos Knight trying her best to swim closer.

I gave her a little wave.

A pleasure to make your acquaintance, mademoiselle. Let's go to hell together, shall we?

As if to prepare for combat, I unthinkingly gripped and re-gripped *Shé liàn* and broke the rime of ice that'd glued my sweaty palm to its leather-wrapped handle.

Wait. I *did* have a way to get back.

If I tossed the ninja chain and caught a rock on the island, I could reel myself in.

Odd, the stars had dimmed. The darkness between them had swelled. A dizzy, but not unpleasant, sensation suffused through my body. It was actually kind of comforting.

In no particular hurry, and for no particular reason, I glanced at my health bar.

Sixty-five points.

I snapped to, fully alert!

I fired off two *Spiritual Regenerations* and healed back to a hundred and five points.

A trickle of warmth flowed into my body, which all too quickly started to drain away.

I'd nearly blacked out. This was going to be close.

I should fold in my arms and speed my rotation to face the island faster. No, wait. Now that I thought about it, I'd been lucky before when I'd decelerated my spin. Any extra motion could send me gyrating in an unpredictable fashion, and then who knew when, or *if*, I'd see the island in time again to take my shot.

So I turned.

Slowly.

Very, very slowly.

And then the island came back in my sights. It was definitely farther away.

No more time to think. I aimed, prayed, and tossed *Shé liàn*.

The bladed end flew true, chain unfurling behind... and I rotated out of view.

With extreme care I passed the weighted end from one hand to another, so the chain wouldn't tangle about me. I'd need every inch of its reach.

The toss, though, along with my other motions started me tumbling, head over heels, but thankfully nothing too fast to make a difference one way or the other.

I waited. My pulse thundered in my ears.

Catch, I urged the semi-living weapon. *You got this.*

The island came back.

The blade was still on target.

My toss, however, had increased my *backward* velocity (thanks for nothing, Sir Isaac Newton and your, *For every action, there is an equal and opposite reaction*). Along with pushing me back, since I held one end of the chain, I was also shortening *its* effective range.

I used my last *Spiritual Regeneration* and then my mana tank was dry.

I had a bit over half my health. That wouldn't last long.

One more half rotation... and I saw that little extra push had shoved me *closer* to the Chaos Knight.

She smiled as her hands clutched in anticipation of catching me.

Back around once more.

Shé liàn's blade was going to hit exactly where I had aimed, a nice knobby stone.

The chain, however, pulled up short by three feet.

Stretch!

I sensed it had already elongated as far as it could, but *Shé liàn* tried anyway to go farther. I felt the effort make the metal ping and groan with stress.

If it snapped, I'd be just as dead as if I'd missed.

My momentum the other way continued to pull the blade back.

Dread chilled my already hypothermic core.

That was it.

Nice try, Marine. Close. Two out of three points for effort. Sorry, still KIA.

A bloody dwarven face peeked over the edge of the island, eyes widened, and Elmac then disappeared back to solid ground.

He returned a moment later and pushed—what was that... a tree branch?—over the edge and clambered down its length. He had his battle axe held between clenched gold teeth.

That wasn't a branch; it was the spined tail of Morgana's new form.

Elmac got to the end, let go with one hand, took his axe and used it to try and reach *Shé liàn's* blade.

He stretched.

As did *Shé liàn*.

I felt a link pop (but saw just *one* side of the link had broken). The chain precariously held together.

The two blades caught... but the ninja chain still had my momentum pulling it away, so it slid up the curve of Elmac's axe.

Elmac twisted the haft.

Shé liàn caught. Held.

I jerked to a stop.

My heart hammered so hard I thought it would explode (which wasn't so far-fetched, considering the difference in pressure inside versus outside my chest).

Elmac grabbed *Shé liàn* and gave the chain a yank.

I flew forward.

Elmac climbed up the tail and then was once more beyond my view.

Thank you, my friends!

But no one tried to reel me in, and neither Elmac or Morgana so much as glanced over the edge to check on me.

What was going on up there?

The chain went slack and floated uselessly between me and the only breathable atmosphere for light-years.

My new forward momentum, however, kept me moving toward salvation.

I would make it... *if* I could hold out a few more seconds.

I checked my health: twenty-nine points.

I stopped thinking about my life or death. There was nothing I could do about it. It came down to the "cold equations" of my momentum and position.

Instead, I found myself perversely curious enough to risk a glance back.

The Grand Imperial Champion of Disorder, Her Greatness, Dominota Koroleva, was thirty feet distant, growing darker as she drifted away from the island in-between worlds.

She'd given up trying to grab me... now just tumbling, a few hands reflexively stretching toward the land.

If she could have shifted shape to a form capable of getting back, she most certainly would have by now. In a few hours, the island would be a speck to her, lost among all the other specks in infinite space.

She was doomed to coast forever, alone, in the dark and cold.

I felt sorry for her.

Not that I regretted my actions. I just wished I could have given her a cleaner end.

I turned my head back.

I flew up and over the edge of the island.

Gravity took hold.

I fell to the ground.

And inhaled.

It tasted as sweet and warm as my first kiss (Elisabeth Warden, 6th-grade, in the library if you wanted to know).

I clawed at my eyes to clear the ice that had frozen them open and squeezed my bruised lids shut until the tears returned.

"Thanks—you—two," I panted. "I was—"

I opened my eyes and saw then why my friends hadn't bothered to reel me in.

A corpse-pale Elmac lay face down on the grass.

Morgana, or rather a pile of rock and hardening lava, sprawled next to him. She then reverted to her human form, and blood pumped freely from her many wounds... mingling with Elmac's.

I hadn't thought I'd ever feel any colder than I had been in outer space. I was wrong.

I crawled to them and checked pulses.

Gone. No... there, but very weak. Fading.

Elmac had dozens of nasty cuts with chunks of his armor *and* flesh missing. Morgana had wicked slashes on her back and that one on her front had practically gutted her.

How had they stayed conscious long enough to save *me*?

I wouldn't be able to return the favor.

Hang on. I had healing potions!

I opened my inventory, got all six vials I'd purchased at Lordren's, and poured the contents into their mouths—three into Morgana's—three into Elmac's.

They didn't stir.

I focused on the empty vial in my shaking hand.

Mother Henpeck's All-Purpose Vitamin Extract Formula (berry flavor)
(Tier-IV alchemical, rare)
DESCRIPTION: This healing potion is considered one of the best and most economical among adventurers wanting "life insurance." Taste and smell vary by batch and expiration date, but it is *never* even close to "berry."
SPECIAL ABILITIES: Heals any physical damage short of severed limbs or complete disembowelments and the like. Mends bones, repairs organs, reverses some forms of brain damage, even temporarily relieves the imbiber of common acne and dandruff. Absolutely guaranteed to heal 10% of one's maximum health or double your money back (provided potion is not regurgitated).
WARNING: A maximum of five doses per month may be safely used without causing irreversible liver damage.
Value: 1,000 golden quins.

No indication of how long it took to work. Figured.

It wasn't like most other games where you could chug gallons of healing potions in the middle of combat and instantly mend without missing a beat or needing a bio break.

But then, thank all the gods, Morgana's bones pulled back together, her flesh and viscera knit, and her chalk-white pallor pinked.

And Elmac? I wasn't sure there was any blood left in him. His flesh was more hamburger than dwarf. Nonetheless, bits started to come back together as well.

His eyes fluttered open and he took a breath.

"Gah!" He sat up and spat out blood clots, then reached for his weapon... groaned and fell back onto the grass.

"We won," I said.

"Aye. Kind of figured that out for myself." He gingerly pushed on his ribs and they snapped into place.

Morgana stirred. "Feels like my insides been bloody replumbed," she whispered. "Ugh. What'd you give us?"

"Mother Henpeck's healing potions."

"I *hate* those things," Elmac rasped. "Lordren dinna have any Green Field's spearmint-flavored—ach, nevermind. We'll be tasting rancid fish for 'bout a week." He cast about on the ground around him. "Where be my flasks?"

His gear lay scattered across the grass. I found a stoppered bottle shaped like a mermaid and grabbed it.

"Here." I set it in his hand.

He pulled the cork and smoke wafted out. He took a nip. "Ahh. Better. A bit."

Elmac dragged himself to Morgana and gingerly passed her the bottle. He took in her face like seeing her alive was all the healing he'd ever need.

Morgana didn't notice (or if she did, she didn't let on).

She took a sip, then another. "Good," she whispered. Morgana glanced at me and her nose wrinkled. "Oi. *You* look like hell."

I had four points of health left.

"That doesn't matter," I told her. "For a moment, I thought you two were..."

I couldn't say the words.

Me dying? I'd come to terms with that in San Quentin. Every day I was talking, walking, and breathing was all gravy as far as I was concerned.

Them dying? I don't know what I would have done—maybe quit, and just chucked the whole Game out the window. Maybe not. I was just glad that today wasn't the day I had to figure that out.

I then noticed the bridges, or rather the *lack* of them. The one back to Thera was still gone. So was the one the Chaos Knight had used to make her entrance.

Elmac saw too.

"But we defeated the guardian," he said. "That shoulda brought them back."

"What if we had to kill her to win?" Morgana squinted at the stars, fished her spyglass out, and searched the night.

"Oh, that be just dandy," Elmac muttered. "We be running out 'o food, and more important, liquor, before too long."

Leave it to Elmac to make sure we had the important things covered.

"Hang on," I said. "Where's that fairy?"

There was no sign of the little punk.

Elmac searched under his pack.

Morgana cached her spyglass, sniffed, then nudged me and nodded at a rock.

I strolled along the perimeter of the island... then snuck a look that way.

Nothing was there, at least nothing normal eyes might see, but thanks to *Azramath's Headband of Grim and Fateful Insights*, I discerned in the ultraviolet part of the spectrum a crouching fairy-shaped outline.

I meandered that way, never looking directly at the rock—then kicked him.

The fairy landed five feet away, bounced, and became visible. "Ow!"

"Let me slice him up a piece at a time," Elmac said, getting to his feet with a grunt.

"Don't be cruel," Morgana told him. "If you're going to kill him, just slit his throat and be done with it. No, wait." She turned to me. "Weren't you two gents in the middle of a riddle?"

"Indeed we were." A smile flickered over my lips. "Well, fairy? Your time's more than up. What's your answer?"

He cast about as if help might be forthcoming, or he'd find some sudden inspiration among the stars. "Uh, let me see... zero divided by zero. Is it zero?"

I savored the moment. Sweet, sweet victory.

"No," I said. "You actually had the answer before. Zero, one, *and* infinity. All and none of them."

He looked like he'd been hit with the flat of Elmac's axe.

"Since there are three different arguments one can make based on the method and assumption one uses," I explained, "and three correspondingly different answers obtained by using those arguments, then that particular mathematical equation is technically undefined."

"*Undefined?*" he whispered, then declared louder, "why—why that's a trick question!"

"As many riddles are," I said. "Any self-proclaimed 'riddle master' should have known that."

He opened his mouth to protest, but quickly regained his composure. "Well played, wandering elf. You have bested me fair and square. You are free to go about your way."

With a wave of his hand, the bridges to Thera and the Ojawbi Far Fields reappeared.

"'Bout time," Elmac said. "Let's get off this ruddy rock while we can."

"Not so fast," I said to the fairy. "We had reciprocal conditions. You lost, so as I recall, you have to be my servant for a year."

He froze in his tiny tracks. "I don't recall..."

"Oh yes," Morgana added. "Those *were* the terms."

"But," the fairy blubbered and fat tears streamed down his cheeks, "I have a family to support. Sixteen mouths to feed. A balloon payment due on my mushroom cottage. My band is set to start their tour. I just can't—"

I shook my head. "A deal's a deal."

His crocodile tears vanished. He frowned and took a very deep breath. "Very well, *master*." He said this last word as if he'd been force-fed Mother Henpeck's liver-dissolving healing potion and was barely holding it down. "How might I serve you?"

"Very good, uh, what's your name?"

"Oswald. Oswald Ottercakes."

"Well, Ozzie, you can start by gathering up Elmac's gear and neatly put it back in his pack. Then, you'll carry it for him."

"Carry it?" Oswald sputtered. "But I'm—it's—"

"Tut-tut," I told him. "No excuses. Be quick about it."

Morgana smirked and gave me a wink.

Elmac nodded his approval.

I waited and watched, most satisfied with my clever and cruel revenge.

QUEST ALERT!
"A THOUSAND DRUNKEN MONKEYS"—BONUS SEGMENT
("ONE LITTLE COMPLICATION")
COMPLETED
You have bested the fairy at his own game.
Reward: Passage is granted to the Ojawbi Far Fields.
Bonus: As you have also nullified the gate guardian, this causeway to and from Thera is now free and open for all travelers, and extra experience points are awarded.

Bouquets of virtual fireworks popped about me.

Congratulations!
You are LEVEL FIVE
You have the experience to reach the next level in your Spirit Warrior class.
You have stat points to assign.

You have skill points to assign.

There are new skills available to buy.

CHAPTER 18

We stepped off the footbridge from the island in-between
—and into the Ojawbi Far Fields.

It was a savannah reminiscent of my Earth's Kenya a century before my time—tall wild grasses and rivers, clusters of thorn-covered trees, and patches of lavender. Herds of gazelle, zebra, and wildebeests (their colors more Dr. Seuss than camouflage) grazed and warily watched us as we tromped along.

The sun was orange and larger than Thera's. It was wondrously hot on my skin (which, after swimming in the frigid vacuum of outer space, was a real plus).

Behind us the well-worn footbridge that spanned worlds was half overgrown with grass and vines, I suppose because none ever travel but half its length before vanishing. Such great magic concealed in such an ordinary-looking thing...

Did magic work the same in this realm as in Thera? Specifically, were there ley lines for me to use?

I peered into the aether.

A wave of force and sensation swept away my astral form like a bit of flotsam. Ley lines thundered and churned about me—rainbows of elemental forces with their overlapping heat and cold and static and gurgling water and odor of freshly turned soil; there were darker ultraviolet threads that shot through me like shards of glass and filled me with revulsion and a desperate desire to curl into a ball and cease to exist; there were also pinks that pulsed with a million heartbeats and I remembered my mothers, elf and human, and longed for the lost homes I'd never see again; still other lines were multidimensional, inexplicable jumbles that screamed through my mind and the merest glimpse of those pushed my sanity to the shattering point.

I surfaced from this torrent—a split second—just long enough to regain my wits to step back into normal space-time.

The silence... the sudden lack of sensation and color and memory... it was almost as disorienting.

I breathed in, out, three times to quell my racing heart and banished the afterimage impressions that no human mind, no matter how well trained, was meant to comprehend.

That had been *extremely* dumb.

I'd phased right into a trunk line of energies powering a gateway between worlds, strong enough to blast my astral form to subatomic particles if I'd stayed longer.

I glanced at Elmac and Morgana.

They hadn't even noticed my brush with mental annihilation and death.

Why should they have? From their perspective, no time had passed and nothing had happened.

Okay. Well, at least I knew there *were* ley lines if I needed them. I'd chalk the experience off to "lesson learned," and take extreme care the next time I was near galactic-spanning magical constructs.

Back to the business at hand; namely, how to find Karkanal's barbarian tribe?

No obvious clue awaited us. I supposed that's why it was called a "quest" rather than a guided tour, right?

I asked my comrades if they had suggestions.

By way of a reply, Morgana halted, cast a minor healing spell on me, and then cast another spell that called a pink hummingbird.

It alighted on her finger and twittered.

She whistled back.

The bird continued with a string of non-stop peeps.

She translated for us: "He says he's seen 'herds' of humans recently, but not sure of where or which direction." With a flick, she sent the still-chirping bird on its way. "All I could coax out of him. That one has a brain the size of a grape seed."

"If we go east for a day or two," Elmac said, "there be a wee trading outpost most of the Far Field folk come to. 'Least there was a few years ago. Ought to be still standing. Someone there's bound to know where Karkanal's people be."

"Sounds good," I said.

Morgana nodded.

And so we walked.

"Morgana," I said. "How'd you get that new elemental shape?"

She inhaled deeply and coughed. "Didn't *get* it. Had a one-shot item, gift from the Druids of the Grove of Thirteen Ancients. They think I'm a bloody hero." She snorted. "Figured I'd better use it back there."

"Good call."

We let our next words linger unspoken. *Or we might have all died.*

I let Morgana and Elmac get a little ahead of me. I needed time and space to myself to figure things out.

Elmac's pack kept pace, teetering through the grass after him. There was an occasional grunt and a choice curse from Oswald as he carried the burden.

I didn't feel a bit sorry for him.

A quarter mile in the distance I spotted a herd of buffalo. Azramath's headband allowed me to see far more detail than I normally could. These were *not* like the version of bison that had once roamed my world. These shaggy creatures sported a ten-foot rack of horns, and I had to take a moment to make sure I was seeing this right: a third horn in the middle of their forehead. The adults were the size of... of... well, think the same mass of an elephant, but longer, and much more muscle.

Good thing they were herbivores.

Buffalo *were* exclusively plant eaters, weren't they? Morgana didn't seem worried, and the creatures only glanced our way once and then ignored us.

We'll just leave you guys alone and you leave us alone and everyone will be cool.

Overhead soared white eagles; a flock of silver sparrows; and closer to us earth-bound folk, more hummingbirds, rainbow clouds of shimmering, chittering, fluttering motion all about us—that then vanished in a flash of iridescence.

A slight breeze made the grass a wavering sea of green, hypnotic and soul soothing.

I exhaled.

This too was magic of a sort.

Enough sightseeing. There were chores to do, or depending how you looked at it, presents to unwrap.

I had to level up.

If the Chaos Knight was any indication of the dangers we'd face in the future, I'd need every mana and health point I could get my hands on, and as soon as possible.

Besides, I'd promised Elmac to get him into the Game when I had the experience points for fifth level.

I accessed my interface. So, how *was* I going to level up?

I faced the same choices as last time: level up my core classes, pick a class specialization, or select my third and final character class.

I'd start with the easy choices.

I couldn't improve my Mage of the Line class because I didn't have the experience points. It looked like it cost more than twice as much as Spirit Warrior to advance.

Also an easy decision: I *wasn't* adding a third class any time soon.

I'd barely recovered from yesterday's sudden "recollection" of all those suppressed memories about my dad and I secretly being Mages of the Line.

As often as not, I now found myself thinking I *was* Hektor, gypsy elf and Shakespeare devotee... not Hector, a human soul simply stuffed into an elf body playing the Game.

I had to figure this alternate personality thing out or risk losing myself.

To a lesser degree, the same rationale applied to picking my Spirit Warrior specialization. I couldn't imagine how, for example, my backstory would be re-written to account for becoming a Master of Death. Learning how to create and wield those exotic weapons? That sounded like years of training... years of new memories.

Nope. My brain was taking it easy today.

This left me with boosting my Spirit Warrior class to plain-old fourth level. I'd improve my foundational skills, and there'd be no need to fiddle with my neurons.

This wasn't min-maxing, per se... or was it?

Preserving the recollections of Hector the gamer had one huge advantage (besides me staying me): I'd keep treating the Game *as* a game, jigger its systems to my advantage, and draw upon the experiences of the many characters I'd played in previous games.

Yes. That was definitely the way to go.

Okay, so advancing from third to fourth-level Spirit Warrior I got 5 stat points, 3 combat skill points, and a bunch of non-combat skill points that, added to my previous unspent non-combat skill points, totaled a whopping 36.

I'd wait on the non-combat skills until I could take a few days to read through the hundreds of non-combat skill descriptions. Maybe I'd pick up a crafting skill.

First, we had to get through this and the assassin quests. So it was probably more prudent to bank those points for any skills I might need on the fly.

I started with stat points.

I dropped two into REFLEX, and one into EGO and GHOST. I still wasn't exactly sure what the GHOST stat did, but best to hedge my bets. EGO and GHOST both boosted my SOUL stat, which in turn, upped my spiritual mana—that seemed to always be in short supply.

The last point I put in PERCEPTION. Noticing the little details had saved my skin more than once. I'd like to be able to keep doing that.

Next, combat skills.

I'd previously maxed out my *Perfect Motion* and *Fists of Steel* skills to their highest tiers. My *Spiritual Regeneration* could be bumped from second to third tier (also the maximum for that skill) and that would improve the ability's mana-to-healing ratio. A no-brainer, especially as upping it cost a single point.

There was only one other combat skill to purchase, *Chi Disruption*. It let me burn mana to do more melee damage. It cost a skill point to purchase at tier one, but *two* more points to take it to the next tier.

I wasn't enthused about *Chi Disruption*. At first tier, I didn't get a lot of bang for the buck i.e. damage for spent mana. Since I never seemed to have enough spiritual mana to go around, it was a less than optimal choice.

Also, if I bought it, I'd have one combat skill point left over.

I checked if I could use that point on my Mage of the Line abilities, but there was no option to increase the tiers of those yet.

I decided to test something.

I maxed out my *Spiritual Regeneration* but held off spending those last combat skill points.

Why? Well, when I'd advanced from first to second level, the Spirit Warrior specialization paths had unlocked.

When I'd leveled up to third, I'd been given a freebie skill—*Wire Work*, which let me run up walls, sprint over the tops of bamboo stalks, and other similarly improbable acrobatics feats like I was in a Hong Kong action flick.

Could *another* surprise be waiting? Perhaps something I might need combat skill points to buy?

If I was wrong, I didn't think I'd lose the points. Just like I hadn't lost any of the non-combat skill points I'd banked.

I rubbed my face, considered, and what the heck—hit the LEVEL UP button.

Nothing.

And then... more nothing happened.

Well, you couldn't be right all the time.

I took two steps to catch up with Morgana and Elmac.

A glowing amber frame popped up and blocked my path.

ALERT!

You have maximized the Spirit Warrior base abilities: *Fists of Steel*, *Spiritual Regeneration*, and *Perfect Motion*. This fulfills the requirements for Game Progression Tier 1 (GPT-1). Through your dedication and study of the Spirit Warrior fundamentals, you have become an acknowledged MASTER of the art. You may now develop a new MASTER TECHNIQUE derived from one of these base abilities.

Congratulations, Master Saint-Savage.

CHAPTER 19

I smiled. This was *so* cool. I was a *Master*.

This "mastery" mechanic gave characters who didn't immediately specialize a way to compete with those who did. As a bonus, the aforementioned new skill supposedly came from a recent inspiration, which I hoped meant *no* new backstory memories.

The Game, however, hadn't forgotten to throw me a curveball.

Progression Tiers? What were those?

More text appeared in the window:

Select one MASTER TECHNIQUE from the following:

Master of the Fist of Ghost Steel
Fists of Steel **has made your hands diamond-hard mystical weapons. You may now phase through matter to various degrees and bypass an opponent's physical and magical defenses, thereby greatly increasing your potential damage.**

First Disciple of the Red Ribbon
(aka Master of Death's Dance)
Your mastery of *Perfect Motion* has honed your body into a kinetic maelstrom able to simultaneously attack and defend. Dramatically increases your defense, attack potentials, move speed, and grace.

High Adept of the Sun Soul
Your expertise with *Spiritual Regeneration* now cures a variety of conditions (disease, paralysis etc.). Furthermore, you may also empathically heal others.

NOTE: Only you will know your chosen MASTER TECHNIQUE. While other Spirit Warriors in the Game may develop similar abilities from time to time, the technique you select will forever be unique and solely yours.

A unique ability all mine?

I felt... honored.

Still, an honor or not, I had to choose *one*. Best to think of them like any other skills in the Game and reduce my options to the basics.

It boiled down to being better at offense, defense, or healing. Simple enough.

Okay, I'd pass on *Fist of Ghost Steel*. Increased damage was always welcome, but if it only worked with my fists, I'd have to get close to an opponent to use it. I wasn't quite ready to pigeonhole my fighting style yet. After all, a ranged weapon had saved my life in the last fight.

Death's Dance? I was a huge fan of *not* getting hit. Could I have dodged the Chaos Knight's attacks if I'd had this? A better defense might stop damage from occurring in the first place, rather than burning mana later to heal it. Hmm. This was a definite "maybe."

And finally, *High Adept of the Sun Soul*. Very tempting. It had been unbearable to watch Morgana and Elmac bleed out. If it hadn't been for those healing potions...

I smoothed a finger over the back of my right hand, feeling the ridges under my skin from the demon bone knuckles.

"...give them great meals of beef and iron and steel, they will eat like wolves and fight like devils."

That was Shakespeare's wisdom on the matter. Warriors must be warriors, even in the face of certain defeat.

I bet Henry V, though, never had to level up.

If I'd built my character to prioritize my SOUL over BODY stat, *High Adept of the Sun Soul* would be a slam-dunk choice. But I'd crafted my character to be far more "warrior" than "spiritual" spellcaster. I'd also picked a second class that depended on a high REFLEX stat, so choosing the High Adept mastery would only split my progression priorities.

As much as I wanted to be a better healer, I felt that boosting my defense and speed was the better call.

So why couldn't I shake the image of my friends dying?

I pushed that scene aside, and instead imagined performing an outrageous series of acrobatics that culminated with a spinning kick to one of the Chaos Knight's faces—so hard, she teetered on the edge of the island and then fell to her doom.

Yeah. That.

First Disciple of the Red Ribbon (aka Master of Death's Dance) it was.

Congratulations, First Disciple!
You have made an enlightenment-like breakthrough in kinesthesia, the awareness of the position and movement of your body by your senses and proprioceptors in muscles and joints. Your balance, grace, and precision are unparalleled among mortals.

This does not, however, mean that you *always* hit or are *always* missed in combat. There is a modest increase in your attack and defensive potentials, and you are merely considered the best within a "normal" range for a martial artist of your level.

Ah... so, in reality, this was nothing more than a minor bonus and a very fancy title. Not as great as I'd first thought, but hey, I wasn't turning my nose up at a freebie.

Then this appeared:

You may, however, now improve your base motion-related skills past all others who are not a Master of the defensive basics.

Furthermore, as the one and only Master of Death's Dance, you may be able to later unlock new skills and abilities not available to *any* other player.

Okay... more cool.

If I was understanding this right, it kind of *was* a big deal. I could improve my base motion skills to *supernatural* levels. And developing skills and abilities that no other player had? My own private progression path?

I got the chills.

Abilities available for immediate upgrade:

Wire Work **(tier 2) Further enhance this passive ability to perform even greater acrobatic feats such as running up walls, springing off the blade of an enemy's strike, leaping twenty feet into tree branches, and other maneuvers limited by your imagination and only sometimes the force of gravity. Cost to Improve: 2 combat skill points.**

Perfect Motion **(tier 4): A burst of supercharged adrenaline that boosts your** *Perfect Motion* **ability for one minute, further** *doubling* **the number of your attacks and speed.**
NOTE: Within five minutes of using this ability you must rest for an hour or risk permanent damage to your health.
Cost: 50 mana to use tier 4 boost.
Cost to Improve: 4 combat skill points.

As promised, I could now improve my motion-based skills past what would otherwise be their maximum tiers.

I was so glad I'd hung onto those two combat skill points. It gave me the option to either improve *Wire Work* now or bank the points and get the *Perfect Motion* upgrade next level. This assumed I'd get three combat skill points like I had for advancing the last two levels in Spirit Warrior.

By the numbers, the improved *Perfect Motion* was hands down the better combat skill.

But who was I kidding? I'd known the instant I'd read their descriptions which one I'd pick.

I selected *Wire Work* tier 2.

I loved *Wire Work* at the first skill tier. What was better than approximating the stunts of my favorite martial art stars? *Absolutely* nothing.

I felt a shift in my thoughts. It wasn't a new memory, rather a sharpening of my old ones. I'd watched hundreds of acrobatic feats and spellbinding fight sequences in the movies. Now, however, I saw them as human Hector *and* gypsy elf Hektor. Together we analyzed and understood how *we* could pull off the same stunts—even embellish and improve them.

I offered my silent respect to Masters Chan, Lee, Li, Liu, and the Brothers Shaw.

I closed my interface windows and centered myself.

Awesome.

I had never felt so good in either of my lives. Besides my new martial art skills, I had keener eyes and ears, and a whopping 180 health. I bet if I had wanted to I could have plucked a dust mote out of the air.

Along with my new gear and their boosts to my stats, and new Mage of the Line abilities, it was like I was a new character.

My power had taken a quantum leap.

That's what fulfilling the requirements of Game Progress Tier 1 must have been all about. Did that mean, though, the opponents I'd face from here on out would be similarly more powerful?

That thought splashed cold water all over my happy. Well, one would have to be a fool to frown on such good fortune.

I looked around. The scenery was different.

I must have spent hours with my face stuck in interface windows.

Elmac and Morgana had halted on a sandspit in the middle of a stream. A school of cobalt-striped trout flashed by and one jumped up—glistened a moment in the sun—and then *plunked* back into cool waters.

Elmac settled into a tiny folding director's chair (that he must have had crammed into his pack), and then suggested to Oswald that he set up the heating stone, ready a pot of tea, and catch a few fish to broil up for lunch.

Oswald muttered darkly and complied.

Morgana nodded over my head and smiled. "See you leveled yourself up. Brilliant! But crikey! You're practically glowing, mate. What *is* that effect? Tier 2 smugness?"

"That's the aura of my awesomeness," I remarked, ignoring the sarcasm. "It indicates I'm on a higher plane than you lesser beings." (And yeah, I did feel a little smug).

She snorted.

"So you be fifth level?" Elmac's bushy brows arched. He took a puff on his pipe, slitted his eyes, and exhaled. "That means I can get into the Game now?"

He offered me the pipe but I declined. Last time I'd smoked that druid weed, my head had spun for hours.

"I think so. Let me check."

I thought about how to add a new member to my clan and turned back to my interface.

The faithful game tutorial did not disappoint.

=TUTORIAL (continued)=
Clans—Basic Functions

As the highest-level player in your clan (at, or greater than, fifth level), you are hereby designated its LEADER. You may now access the CLAN MENU via the *clasped hands* icon. From there you may use your clan vault, summon clan members once per month to meetings, set up clan communication channels, and add new clan members.

I tapped the icon of clasped hands (that before had been greyed out and unselectable). A new window framed with polished black walnut appeared. Everything was there—including a field to enter a name, and next to it an ADD MEMBER button.

=TUTORIAL (continued)=

Clans—Adding Members

New clan members may be added once the highest-level player reaches successive increments of fifth level. New members must be within sight, must accept the invitation and terms of the EULA, and pass the requisite Free Trial.

NOTE: Once added, members *cannot* be removed until their permanent and final death. So choose wisely.

I read this aloud (in English so Oswald wouldn't have access to sensitive game information), and then felt the new responsibilities and consequences of being "clan leader" settle on my shoulders like a cloak of lead.

"Aye," Elmac said. "It be like Morgana told me."

"I briefed him on the limited starting options," she added, her features pinching tight, "and how the Free Trial is a bloody grinder, and death is just as permanent in the Game as it is outside of it."

I was glad Morgana had covered the basics, so I could move onto my next—just as important—point.

I glanced over at Oswald, who seemed to be busy trying to catch a fish with a tiny net—unsuccessfully I might add, as he flopped face first into the drink.

"Look," I leaned closer and whispered to Elmac, "are you *sure* you want to do this? There's no one I'd rather have in the Game and in my clan, but there's a bunch of baggage that goes along with it: gods, politics, other players" —I smiled apologetically at Morgana— "who I can tell you from first-hand experience, aren't as friendly as Miss Nox here."

"*Ms.* Nox," she corrected me.

"Sorry."

Elmac set his pipe down. "Thanks for that, Hektor, but I think I know what I be doing. For a broken-down old soldier like me, this be a ray of light in a very dark world. To be getting to adventure again, and young..." His eyes brimmed with tears. He quickly wiped them away. "Lad, I can't tell you what that be meaning to me."

"Okay," I said. "So... now?"

"No reason to be waiting," Elmac told me. "You and Morgana have a bit 'o walk ahead. I'll get my character made and breeze through the Free Trial in a few hours." He said this like it was a foregone conclusion. "I'll select High Hill as my starting area, leg it back to the Far Field gate, and catch up to you in a day or two."

"The Free Trial may not be as easy as you think," I said.

He patted my arm. "Don't you be worrying 'bout that. I've got a plan." He touched the side of his large nose. "Just be on the lookout for the most handsome devil you ever laid eyes on in two days. That'll be me."

I hoped he knew what he was doing.

I nodded. "Give me your full name to enter."

"Right." He stood, straightened, cleared his throat. "Elmac Hendrix Arguson. And a fine name it be."

I typed it in and reached for the ADD MEMBER button.

"Oh, wait," he said. "I'm a ruddy idiot. Shouldna smoked too much. I nearly forgot. I'll be needing one small favor."

"Sure, anything."

Elmac shucked off his armor shirt and greaves—and by all the gods he was one hairy little cuss. He then dropped his battle axe, short swords, leather gladiator belt, even pulled off his boots. He then did the last thing I expected: He unlaced his magical prosthetic arm and it dropped to the ground with a *whuump*.

This left him standing only in tartan boxers.

"Oh, a few other things." He reached into his pack and pulled out a large duffel. He gestured to the pile in front of him. "I'll be needing you to put that in your inventory for safekeeping 'till I get back."

I stared at the stuff. His armor, weapons—yeah that made sense. The equipment would give him a huge boost at first level.

But his prosthetic arm? What was he going to do? Hack his new one off? No. Obviously, it had to be worth a fortune so he was going to sell it.

I glanced in the duffle. There were a half dozen books in languages I didn't recognize. A short staff. A bolt of silk. A few boxes (all locked). And a small buttpack containing a bunch of junk: thimbles, chicken feathers, seeds, dung balls.

What the heck?

"I *think* I have the carrying capacity," I said, honestly too bewildered to ask why he wanted me to schlep it all around. "Or wait." I hefted the duffle—which couldn't be an ounce less than thirty pounds—and dropped it into the clan vault.

It vanished. The bag and all of its contents then reappeared in the inventory window with plenty of room left over, and best of all, no impact on *my* carry capacity.

"Yeah," I told him, "this won't be a problem." I transferred the rest of his belongings.

This clan vault would come in handy. I could load it up with whatever gear we might need later and it wouldn't slow me down.

Elmac dusted off his one hand and held it out toward Morgana.

She took it—and folded him into a hug, rocking him back and forth, squeezing, as if this might be a permanent goodbye.

"Be safe," she whispered.

"Your concern be touching, a true treasure, lass, but don't you be worrying 'bout me." He stepped back from her and thumped his bare chest. "Tough as mithril."

He held his hand out to me and we clasped forearms.

"You be my brother by bloodshed and battle, Hektor Saint-Savage. I shall not forget the grand favor you be doing me today."

"Just come back in one piece, old dwarf. That'll be enough."

"Well then." He sniffed. "Enough with the cheerful goodbyes. I be ready."

I took a long look at him, then tapped the ADD MEMBER button.

Elmac took a step back, startled by what had to be his game interface appearing before him for the first time.

He squinted. "Ughhh, this license agreement. You should've told me. I might have hired a demonologist to summon me a lawyer."

"Just scroll ahead and hit ACCEPT," I told him. "It's what we all do."

Elmac nodded but nonetheless spent several minutes trying to read the EULA, moving his mouth to sound out the especially tangled gobblygook legalese, and then he finally gave up and tapped the air.

He vanished.

And that was the last we ever saw of Elmac Hendrix Arguson.

CHAPTER 20

Me, Morgana, and Oswald broke camp and marched in silence for a while.

As a gesture of—I don't know, good faith, guilt?—I took Elmac's half-emptied pack and let Oswald rest atop it.

He passed out, and for a tiny guy, his snores were impressive.

I think my magnanimous gesture had more to do with Elmac's departure than anything else.

I was worried.

I bet Morgana was, too.

She and I had barely survived our Free Trial. It had been a serious skin-of-teeth scenario. Sure, Elmac knew the ins and outs of Thera, but he'd be by himself and no longer a grizzled fighting machine. And since the Free Trial had limited starting character options, he'd be in an unfamiliar *human* body. He wasn't going to be happy about that.

"You okay?" I asked Morgana.

"Yeah," she said and shrugged, indicating that she wasn't.

The wind stilled; the grasses ceased their endless waving. Even the Far Fields seemed to be holding its collective breath waiting for Elmac to return. Or not.

"You know Elmac has a massive crush on you, right?"

Morgana halted. Stiffened. Exhaled. "I do," she said more icily than I'd expected.

"I just don't want his heart broken."

She chuckled. "And what makes you think that's going to happen?"

I turned to her, puzzled.

This is as good a time as any to admit that I'm not the multiverse's greatest ladies' man. I've had a few romances, brief encounters—Marines passing on the battlefield kind of thing, but all few and far between.

I wondered if there was a game skill that might help me out in that department?

I'd check later. I had to straighten this out first.

I could think of only two things Morgana might be driving at.

First, and I was 95% sure this had to be it, she probably thought Elmac's interest was harmless and would eventually go away.

But she hadn't seen him mooning over her like I had.

The other, remote possibility was that *she* was interested in him. But that was... It couldn't be.

"Even if—" I started. "I mean *when* Elmac comes back, let's say he has a new body. I guess that'd be... but there's still a massive age difference, isn't there? He's what? A hundred and fifty? Two hundred?"

Morgana faced me, hands now on her hips, lips pursed, and a wow-you-really-need-to-shut-your-gob look on her face.

"You know," I said and held up my hands, "I just overstepped, didn't I? Let's forget I said anything, okay?"

She sighed. "Oh Hektor, you are *so* young."

"What does *that* mean?"

"It means there's less difference between Elmac and I than you think."

"Uh... what?"

My brain then finally caught up to my mouth.

I'd just assumed Morgana was young because her character looked barely legal to order a drink. She'd told me she'd been a high school teacher before the Game, so naturally, I pictured this perky, slightly nerdy, hot, twenty-something brunette.

But there was no reason to think any of that was true.

Her expression cooled from anger to something closer to pity as she stared me down. "Elmac and I have" —she paused in her whisper and closed her eyes— "have both buried people we love."

I could tell saying this caused her great pain... pain I'd caused her to dredge up.

"I'm sorry, Morgana. I'm an idiot."

She opened her eyes. "Yes, you bloody well are, Hektor. That's part of your boyish charm. But you need to know this so we can understand each other. I survived eighty-nine years before I died in an ice crevice in London and got recruited by the Great Pooka. Eighty-nine years... No one should live so long to see the deaths of their four children." She gazed far away, then came back. "My seven baby grandchildren too. Each of them took a little piece of me when they left." Her eyes were unwavering and filled with sorrow the depths of which I could not imagine. "Those last decades were *very* long, *very* cold, *very* lonely years, mate."

I had to look away.

We both stood silent for a moment.

She stepped closer, lifted my chin, and *made me* look at her. "Don't worry about Elmac and me. We're both well past our salad days, we are. Besides, I fancy the little badger."

"Yeah…" I said so soft that I barely heard myself.

Morgana clapped me on the shoulder. "Come on then. Let's get moving. Can't chitchat all afternoon."

And just like that, I knew she'd forgiven me for sticking both feet into my big mouth—which is one of the many reasons I admired her and counted myself lucky to have such a friend.

Now that I thought about it, it was a good thing I'd run into Morgana instead of anyone else in the Free Trial. I doubted another person would have given a guy allied with the evil Lords of the Abyss a chance. S*he* certainly hadn't made any assumptions about *me*.

And then this unlikely and very much unwanted thought struck: Had I misjudged my brother as well? I'd never gotten the full story of what had happened to him.

I opened my interface, tabbed to the Message Center, and scanned the messages he'd sent me: more queries about where I was—what I was doing—and to please, please write him back.

I couldn't deal with this now. Unpacking *more* emotional baggage this afternoon was not on my schedule. Besides, the guy had tried to *kill* me. I didn't need to make any assumptions about *that*.

I'd sleep on what to do about Bill.

For a day or two.

Maybe a week.

We kept trudging through the tall grass.

I was too much of a coward to try more small talk with Morgana, so instead, I poked through Elmac's gear in the clan inventory.

The first and most obvious curiosity was his battle axe. I'd seen the massive weapon cleave hellfire demons, split shadow monsters, and sunder assassins in twain.

Its description popped:

Dadoldow Kar ("Dreadful Cleave" in ancient High Dwarven). Double-Bladed Battle Axe (Two-Handed Axe Weapon Class) (Tier-VII magical weapon, unique)
DESCRIPTION: Forged for the hero, Bajarne'spiter Jarlson, by an elemental spirit-god. It is cast as a single piece of foamed mithril-omnium alloy impregnated with mana-infused *ovum philosophorum* and the ground hearts of lightning elementals. This imparts the blade with a pearlescence and seemingly infinite depth.
SPECIAL ABILITIES: Enchanted to significantly increase attack and damage potentials. The weapon is magically conductive and upon command will either alight with flame or become electrically charged up to three minutes per day—or

it can use both powers and be flaming *and* electrically charged for one minute per day. The wielder is granted limited immunity to fire- and electrical-based attacks. Once per day it may be thrown (without penalty) and will return to its master's hand (range dependent upon wielder's STRENGTH).
REQUIREMENTS: Keyed for dwarves only. Minimum 16 STRENGTH.
PRICE: Unlikely this one-of-a-kind weapon would ever be sold for mere coin, but if it was, expect the bidding to start at 500,000 golden quins.

No wonder Elmac wanted to keep this. A first-level warrior with this monster of a weapon would be the equivalent of... I wasn't sure.

But wait. Could he even use it at first level? With a required minimum STRENGTH of 16, I didn't see how. If he put all ten beginning stat points to STRENGTH, he'd still be shy six. If he assigned all his points from leveling to STRENGTH, that would take... I counted—two more points at second level, three more at third—he'd have to be fourth level.

And that's if he put *all* his points into STRENGTH.

Sure, he'd have a hundred-seventy health, but no REFLEX, so a lousy defense, and a zero PERCEPTION, which wasn't a good idea either.

Maybe his enchanted prosthetic metal arm boosted STRENGTH.

I focused on it.

> **ALERT!**
> **You be a dwarf?**
> **Do you be knowing the password glyph?**
> **No? In that case, this item be enchanted to block skill-based, magical, divine, and psychic information-gathering techniques.**

The window rudely snapped shut.

Hmm. Okay, my friend. Keep your secrets for now.

One more thing, though. Even if the arm had a STRENGTH enchantment... well, it was made for a person *missing an arm*. Was Elmac planning to amputate the arm of his new character? That seemed a *tad* extreme, even for him.

Or it could be like I'd thought earlier. He was simply going to sell or trade this all for gear he could use. That had to be it.

What else was here to rummage through?

Ah. I'd almost forgotten: the note I'd lifted off that assassin leader; the one partially decrypted from *Sabbah*, the secret language of the Silent Syndicate. Elmac had figured out three names on their hit list:

Padre John Adam-Smith
Dame Rose Beckonsail
Niblen Chatters

For the next two hours, I tried to puzzle out the code using the notes he'd printed in the margins. Cryptography had never been my thing, though, so no dice.

I considered waking Oswald to see if the self-proclaimed fey riddle master might be able to untangle it... but this idea fell into the category of "not smart." Maybe as a last resort, I'd trust him with state secrets.

Perhaps there was a non-combat skill I might buy?

Or better yet, this was the perfect time to test *Azramath's Headband of Grim and Fateful Insights*. It had the power to see "the absolute truth." That had to include decoding stuff like this.

But there was that warning: "*Seeing the absolute truth may cause the wearer to go blind, be driven insane, fall into a suicidal depression, or experience other deleterious effects.*"

If I looked *only* at the parchment, though, then that ought to limit those side effects. I mean, what could be so dangerous about a piece of paper?

So I held the note, locked my gaze onto it, and willed the headband's inner eye to open.

Every symbol snapped into sharp focus—no, "focus" wasn't even close. I could see the individual fibers of the vellum. It had been made from the skin of an unborn female calf. Her mother had been called Betsy Blue, and the farmer had slaughtered them both on the Day of Gratitude, in the month of Harvestfest, in the year of the Silver Gryphon. It had been an unseasonably warm morning, specifically 72°F. The farmer didn't want to do this, but he needed the money to pay off a loan to cover his gambling debts. Dice. A game called "smackers." His wife didn't know and—

Whoa. Stop. *Way* too much information.

The data stream flooding my mind, however, didn't slow; in fact, it accelerated.

The ink was ferrous sulfate and oak gall dissolved in vinegar with three drops of gum arabic and one-half drop of *magnus impermate* to stabilize the mix. The note was penned by the blind master assassin, Gashton Grex, using the *Wretched Hand* calligraphy style, and he had intended it for first lieutenant Yamina Sussara, aka the Serene Knife, aka The Whispering Blade, aka The Shadow Lotus, aka The Bearer of the Final Kiss...

Gods, *stop*!

I was *drowning* in information.

I forced my mind to pull away, tried to close my eyes (but even that didn't help), and was about to rip the headband from my head... when the rush of data eased a notch.

As it did, the symbols rearranged into simple Tradespeak.

> *Yamina,*
> *As prescribed by shadow and blade, herein are thine orders, not to be circumvented by blood nor bane nor broken heart: terminate these unfortunate walking dead with extreme prejudice. With regards to the last six, use Summa protocols, and even then additional precautions may be warranted.*
> *Good hunting.*

Then came the list of names, now also in clear Tradespeak. Many were unknown to me, but one, smack in the middle of the pack, I *did* know: *Duke Reginald Opinicus*.

I was no expert in the politics of Theran royalty, but it was a safe bet that whoever would, or could, order a hit on the ruler of High Hill and the Duchy of Sendon had serious political cover. Otherwise, the rest of the royals would do everything in their power to make a very public, very messy example of them for any others considering such an ill-advised action.

So, who had the clout to order a *Duke's* death? Another royal? Could this be the opening move of a coup to seize the Duchy?

This was much bigger than we'd thought.

Leaving High Hill, for that matter Thera, had been a stroke of amazing fortune. We had stumbled onto something way over our heads. Odd, though, that this note had been on a *second-level* assassin.

That curiosity I immediately forgot, though, because my gaze landed on the last six names on the hit list. I knew them. Unfortunately, very well.

Sister Rada Borovkova
Colonel Sabella Delacroix
General (retired) Elmac Arguson
Captain (?) Pendric Ragnivald
Hektor Saint-Savage
Morgana Nox

I re-read the names. My heart beat faster.

Of course, I'd been almost certain me, Morgana, and/or Elmac would be on the list. After all, the Syndicate had already tried to kill us a few times.

Still, seeing our names made it seem somehow more "official"...and final.

What about the others?

Sister Rada was the blind old priestess who'd given me a little prophecy to chew over before we'd gone off to stop Bill's invasion (that before I saw her again, I'd lose someone I loved). She was likely a powerful ally of the Duke, so that would make her a target as well.

Colonel Delacroix, of course, taking her out made sense. If you were after Duke Opinicus, perhaps the biggest obstacle would be the Chief of the Duchy's secret police.

But Pendric? Why him? Yes, he'd been a Captain Knight in service to the Duke, but he'd abandoned his post to go wandering after our last adventure. He shouldn't be a threat to anything but a well-stocked bar. He was also half Valkyrie, trained by the most fearsome fighters in Valhalla, which made him possibly the best swordsman in Thera. Why mess with *that* if you could at all avoid it?

The headband's magic faded.

I blinked, opened a blank window, and jotted down the names and instructions just in the nick of time... as the information faded from my mind.

The assassin's note was once more indecipherable.

My eyes and optic nerves felt like they'd been flayed.

I staggered.

Morgana shot me a quizzical look. "What?"

"Just used some magic to decipher the assassin's note," I whispered.

I copied and pasted what I'd written down and messaged it to her.

Oswald awoke. "What did I miss?" He yawned. "Is the gypsy elf buried yet?"

He took in Morgana, smiled, then spotted me, and his expression soured. "Oh, a thousand pardons, *master*, but I had a *terrible* nightmare. You were torn apart by venomous centipedes and eaten alive." He sounded wistful.

Maybe I should cancel his one-year servitude. Petty revenge was a fine thing, but not if I was going to get my throat slit one night.

Morgana finished reading. Her face went slack, and she breathed, "Wow..."

"Delacroix," I said. "We didn't see her outside the Bloody Rooster. You think they got her?"

Morgana shook her head. "Not likely. When that one goes, I expect there'll be a crater left behind."

Maybe, but suddenly I was more worried than I ought to be for someone who was as likely to throw me in a dungeon as buy me a beer.

"So they *were* after us," Morgana murmured. "Blimey—the Duke too. Who's this Sister Rada bird?"

"Priestess of the Three Sisters. Practically a saint, as far as I'm concerned."

Morgana's gaze darted to the left. She nodded that way. "Only one thing to do now."

I turned and saw, silhouetted in the afternoon haze, a distant fortress. This was the "wee trading outpost" Elmac had mentioned?

"I'm sorry? What one thing?"

She patted her abdomen. "Can't think on an empty stomach, mate. Come on. Let's grab dinner and a few pints."

My stomach rumbled its opinion on the matter. "Best idea of the week," I replied (especially as those pints of ale now danced in my vision).

We double timed it and when we got within a hundred yards of the structure, I saw more details: a wall, a guard tower, and a central three-story inn roofed with slate tile.

ALERT!
The Wayfar Waypoint Inn is NEUTRAL GROUND.
All non-consensual PvP combat is suspended
inside the property's walls.

Morgana grinned. "Make that dinner, a few ales, *and* a good night's rest, yeah?"

I smiled back and nodded... but got the sinking feeling that none of those things were in our immediate future.

CHAPTER 21

I'd pictured the Far Field trading outpost as a few tents, campfires, and friendly aboriginals. This thing, however, could have been lifted from the 1948 John Wayne flick, *Fort Apache*. Three acres were surrounded by a twelve-foot tall adobe and pine-log wall. Past the open gate squatted a three-story tower with iron shutters over the windows.

I hadn't seen any particular dangers on our hike. Maybe just being *close* to Thera warranted such defensive measures?

Guards atop the tower waved and welcomed us in a variety of languages and Tradespeak.

"*Bonsoir*," I called back.

"*Bienvenue bon monsieur*," replied a woman with a crossbow slung over her shoulder.

This place might not be so bad after all.

I then spotted two dozen severed hands nailed to the open gate. I'd seen such displays before in Lordren's shop. Warnings to would-be thieves.

"What is it with this medieval justice?" I muttered to Morgana. "Haven't these people ever heard of misdemeanors?"

"Barking effective, though," she said.

"You'd think people would get the idea and not risk it."

"You ever starve, Hektor?" she asked.

"Yeah. I have. And I get your point."

A few days without food and you'd risk anything to feed yourself or the ones you love.

Overlaying this grisly, but otherwise warm, welcome, appeared:

ALERT!
The wall opposite the gate of the Wayfar Waypoint Inn compound marks the effective boundary of the Game.

=TUTORIAL (continued)=
Game Boundary
Past the Game's boundary, many interface functions, game rules, alert systems, and other features cease to work. Experience points and achievements earned beyond the boundary will be awarded upon reentry.

"There has to be more to *that*," I whispered and had that disturbing feeling you got when you stood near a cliff and peered over the edge—like you were about to fall off; like you perversely *wanted* to fall off.

Morgana frowned. "Best be careful while we wait for Elmac to catch up, yeah?"

Past the tower sat a three-story house in the center of the compound with two large flagstone chimneys, split-log walls, a few windows (but only on the upper levels), and a slate tiled roof. Around back I noted a stable.

I caught the scent of flame-broiled meat... and could that be the aroma of caramelized sugar and apple strudel?

I wiped the drool from the corner of my mouth. "I completely agree."

One good thing about the Game: true, every step might be your last—but I'd never been so well-fed or had such a dazzling array of drink options in my life. It made the extreme and constant danger almost worth it.

Two guards in full plate mail stood on either side of the inn's front door. They nodded at us. One opened the door, gesturing us inside. The other pointed to a sign over the entrance that, in a variety of languages and pictograms, basically said:

NO FIGHTING OR WE KILL YOU

Fine by me.

We entered a mudroom, carefully wiped the grime off our boots, then rounded a corner—and ran smack into a wall of sound.

So many voices: All yelling—arguing—shouts—laughs—cries of outrage and grunts in a babble of multiple languages; I caught Tradespeak, a smattering of French, Farsi, Elvish, Mandarin, and clickings and clackings, trills and whistles.

After my ears adjusted (or rather, were deafened enough so the rest of my senses could catch up), I took in the place.

The ground floor was split in half. On one side were rows of long tables with people on either side haggling over goods. The other side was crowded with tables and booths where people feasted upon platefuls of food and quaffed tankards of ale.

The folks at the trading tables shook fists at one another, shoved piles of coins and jewels and treasure maps back and forth; there were moldering books, swords, shields, crystal balls, racks of potion bottles, and I swear—even a pile of live snakes!

All these people couldn't be just from the Ojawbi Far Fields. Some were indeed barbarians similar to Karkanal's tribe—Viking types—minus, however, the distinctive threads of pure gold artfully woven into their braids and beards like Karkanal's people had sported. There were also muscular gladiators wearing armor bits and at least thirty pounds of gold bracelets apiece; tall green women crisscrossed in ropes of jade beads; two towering cyclopes, brandishing furs by the fistful; anthropomorphized bears in top hats selling animals that squeaked and squealed within cages; there were even a few elven types (but to my disappointment, not one gypsy). There were more, but they all jostled and blurred before my eyes in flashes of silk, leather bondage gear, and priestly robes.

I also spotted what had to be standard issue for every fantasy inn, a bulletin board with calls to adventure and help needed notices... along with the same RED KNIGHT WANTED poster I'd seen yesterday in Low District and the Bloody Rooster.

The best part, though? The smells!

The air was luxuriant with a metallic tang, sandalwood smoke, musk, perfumes—and cinnamon and cayenne and cardamom and saffron and a thousand other spices that I have never inhaled before or since.

Add to that the cornucopia of scents wafting from the kitchen: cornbread, butter, vanilla, toffee, chocolate, seared salmon, lemon... and so much, so concentrated, I could have been nourished just breathing.

A tap on my shoulder.

I turned and was pleasantly surprised to see a lovely young lady, who under ordinary circumstances, I would've never missed even in a crowded room.

She was my height, caramel skin with hair to match, and eyes the color of luminescent tropical waters. Her long-sleeved peasant dress was clean white linen. She was half elf, half... hmm, something that highlighted her cheeks and brow with tiny golden scales. Mermaid? Or perhaps sea elf?

She looked us over. "Table for two?" she yelled in Tradespeak over the noise. "Or do you need to register a merchant license?"

"Table for three!" Oswald piped up.

She flashed the fairy a heart-melting smile. "Oh pardon me, sir." She stepped to the hostess station and asked, "Booth or table? And you will be paying in...?"

"Booth," Morgana answered. "We'll pay in golden quins."

"Very good, ma'am."

She led us to a booth in the corner (even found a booster seat along the way for Oswald).

As soon as we sat, the noise fell away. It was either some magic or some very well-planned acoustical engineering. I couldn't tell.

Our hostess handed Morgana and me menus, rummaged about in her apron pocket and found one the size of a pack of playing cards for Oswald.

The menu was more of a book, fifty pages of fish, fowl, vegan, and meat entrees, pastries and pasta, even sushi and insect dishes. The last twenty pages were devoted to specialty cocktails and this little tidbit at the end: *Ask about our fine selection of fermented drinks!*

"My name is Sadie," she told us.

I found her voice alluring without being flirty, smart without coming off as aloof.

"If it's your first time here," she went on, "it's payment up front, but with a money back guarantee." Again that smile. "Unless you have any questions, I'll just give you a moment then."

She flounced off.

Morgana cleared her throat. "Let's eat, yeah? Then we can talk strategy."

I nodded and buried my nose in the menu.

You could drop some *serious* cash in this place. Here was one of the offerings:

> Emperor Sushi Platter
> Fresh seasonal varieties from the Highland Lakes of the Ojawbi Highlands and (as available) from adjacent realities. Today's selection is *Saizen*-grade *Otoro (fat belly tuna)*; Kraken roe (three); Sea Hydra goujonettes,

Cambrian Protozoa compote, Jörmungandr filet, giant squid (abyssal variety) tentacles with noir ink au jus, and pickled *Perleidus*—served with wild imperial ginger shavings and fresh *nara-do* wasabi combined with sky herring blue-green photophores. Presented on minced butter lettuce and chopped three-fin seaweed.
Serves 6.
Please allow two hours preparation time.
40,000 golden quins.

This is what game designers called a "money sink," made to separate players from any hard-earned coin they may have so foolishly accumulated. Then again, the Game was not just *a* game. This food was real. The experience of tasting such delicacies *might* just be worth it.

If I had liked raw fish.

Then there was:

Wayfar Hamburger
One pound of ground Kobe sirloin (weighed after broiling), covered with thick slices of aged Heartland extra-sharp cheddar, applewood-smoked slabs of honeyed bacon, and served on a freshly baked poppy seed bun. All extras included. *Try our special secret sauce!*
Comes with a heaping portion of triple-spiced wedge-cut fries and a small salad.

No need to look further. It had been decades since I'd had a non-soy protein hamburger.

I guess I'm just a simple guy with simple tastes.

Oh and lest we forget, of course, a tankard of Silvercrest Ale. Maybe two.

The ale, however, made me think of Elmac, the burnt Bloody Rooster, and I felt like a slimeball that I was about to enjoy a fine meal while he was risking his body and soul in the Free Trial.

"He'll be okay," Morgana said as if she had read my thoughts. "He's tougher than dragon gristle, that one."

I grunted an acknowledgment as I noted that despite Morgana's words, there were also glimmers of worry and doubt in her eyes.

Elmac was indeed tough, but there were still any number of game mechanics, tests, and tricks he could trip over.

And there was nothing I could do about it now. Except stew.

Sadie returned and took our orders. She nodded as if she approved of my pick of the comparatively simple hamburger.

Morgana asked for a *lasagne di carnevale* and a glass of the house Chianti.

Oswald ordered a slice of New York cheesecake (human-sized portion) and a root beer float.

Sadie tallied it all up and presented the bill: 500 quins (with a 20% gratuity already added).

Whoa. *Outrageously* expensive. I could live for a month in High Hill, and live *well*, on such a princely sum. If the normal patrons of this place, however, were rich merchants and adventurers (perhaps even traveling from other worlds) then maybe the price is what the traffic bore.

What the heck. I *was* curious if the menu's description would live up to my expectations of "best hamburger ever."

I was happy to pay for Morgana, too. I owed her, well, for a lot of things—chiefly her putting up with me.

I opened my inventory and scraped out most of my remaining coin. I paused, however, seeing the old wheat penny still in the corner.

If you could see me now, Dad, I wonder, would you be proud?

I let the moment of maudlin reminiscence go, and paid.

"If there's anything else you need," Sadie told us, "just flag me down."

A customer at another table waved at Sadie and she left.

The fairy looked at me, narrowed his eyes, and sneered, "Thanks for the lunch, *Master*."

"Let's drop the 'master' stuff," I said. "It was funny once, but the whole slave thing is not my style. I'm your employer, and if you help me out now and then, I'll take time off for good behavior. Deal?"

The sarcasm melted from Oswald's features. "That's... actually decent of you. For a gypsy elf."

"Just call me Hektor, okay?"

An elderly human in a white chef's coat then wheeled a cart to our booth. He pulled the silver covers off the plates with grand flourishes. The portions were ogre-sized. Our food was piping hot and a cloud of steamy scents curled about the table. We unthinkingly leaned closer.

Don't ask me how they'd slapped this all together in a matter of minutes. Gastromancy?

The three of us did our best imitation of a wolf pack devouring their kill for the next half hour.

The meat in my Wayfar Hamburger was charred just right on the outside, juicy medium rare inside; the bacon was smokey and thick and crisp; the cheese molten, extra sharp; the poppy seed bun still steaming and toasted to perfection; and the secret sauce had a touch of jalapeño that somehow brought all the tastes together in what I can only describe as "divine." So yeah, for the record, that *was* the best hamburger I'd ever had—before or since. Oh, and it paired well with my Silvercrest Ale.

We leaned back, stuffed.

Sadie returned. "Anyone for dessert?" she asked.

Ah, I'd been hoping for this.

Among my many failings, I must admit to one more: a sweet tooth. I was about to ask Sadie if there was a dessert menu (a slice of apple pie and a cup of coffee would hit the spot), but the words never got past my lips.

Instead, I fixed upon the three people tromping down the stairs from the second floor. Actually, it wasn't the people so much that gripped my attention... as it was the placards floating over their heads:

Cassie Longstrider
Ranger (Swashbuckler) / LEVEL 12
Wonder Women

Harlix Hadri
Wizard (Researcher) / LEVEL 12
Sapientia Aeterna

and

Grimhalt
Cleric (Zealot) / LEVEL 9
The Wild Hunt

These were the same three players we'd seen outside the Bloody Rooster as it burned to the ground.

The Grimhalt guy halted on the stairs and scanned the room.

His gaze locked onto us—and he made a beeline for our table.

CHAPTER 22

Grimhalt shoved patrons and waitstaff out of his way as he barreled toward us.

Sadie glanced up. "I'll just give you a moment to think dessert over," she said and quickly made her exit.

Two troll bouncers moved toward the Wild Hunt cleric.

Harlix intercepted the trolls, spoke a few words, and the bouncers smiled and laughed and forgot all about what they were doing.

Cassie nonchalantly moved to one side of the room, her left hand concealed behind her back.

Morgana hadn't even looked, but she nonetheless silently drew two daggers and kept them under the table.

Oswald had vanished.

Grimhalt grabbed a chair and dropped it at our booth. He slammed one booted foot on the seat and leaned over us.

"Well, well," he said, leering at Morgana. "A trickster. A pretty one. Too bad I have orders to string your kind up."

I was about to jump to my feet and snap this joker's neck, but an in-game message popped:

>_Morgana Nox: WAIT

>_Morgana Nox: We r safe here

>_Morgana Nox: His clan & mine = KOS

KOS was gamer speak for "Kill On Sight."

But okay, if Morgana knew more about what was going on, I'd follow her lead.

Or try to.

This close I saw burn scars covered Grimhalt's face and his left eye was partially melted shut. The injuries looked old, or maybe they'd been magically healed... badly. The gigantic mace at his side must have weighed forty pounds. He smelled of sweat and machine oil. He wore plate boots and greaves, but it was his chainmail hauberk that caught my eye. The pattern... well, I couldn't see one. There were sections that crazed along in a serpentine-like weave, but every ring was a different size, and in spots, so many linked together it was practically a solid mass. He shifted and I glimpsed flickers of ghostly fire among the rings as if the mail had been drenched in kerosene and set alight.

He must have a heck of a STRENGTH to fight in that gear.

Morgana's more informed opinion on the situation notwithstanding, I just couldn't help myself. I wasn't going to let his threat to her go unchallenged.

After all, I had a special skill for such occasions.

"Hey buddy," I said in a surprisingly casual tone. "Why don't you chase more appropriate quarry with your Wild Hunt pals? Maybe a hobbled rat would be more your speed. No... I'm thinking a crippled stink bug. Or if that's too much of a challenge, perhaps catch a few worms?"

Morgana kicked me hard under the table.

Grimhalt paled, turned to me, then glanced over my head.

"Spirit warrior?" He laughed. "Fourth level? Today *is* my lucky day."

He hefted his obscenely over-sized mace.

Perhaps taunting the zealot of the Wild Hunt was not my smartest opening maneuver. But jerks like Grimhalt *always* got under my skin.

Every multiplayer game had them.

Call them idiots, griefers, or whichever *noms de guerre* you like—they all fulfilled the same role: make life as hard as possible for everyone else. They ruined quests, flooded chat channels with unimaginative obscenities, camped corpses, kicked puppies, and drowned kittens.

You just wanted to kill them over and over until they logged out.

Three things, however, stopped me from answering his aggression with aggression of my own.

First, was Morgana's warning (that I probably should have heeded a few seconds ago).

Second, the Wayfar Waypoint Inn had a policy of non-violence on the premises. I had no desire to be permanently uninvited from this place.

Besides, this was neutral ground. The Game wouldn't permit non-consensual PvP combat.

And I wasn't consenting.

Third, Grimhalt had *four* levels on me, which made the odds very much tilted in his favor.

Corollary to that last point: yes, he was a flaming asshat, but he was a *living* flaming asshat... so he had to be a pretty good player to have survived with such manners in Thera.

I was about to shift into the aether, scout the magical terrain, and buy time to think, when Harlix Hadri and Cassie Longstrider caught up to their companion.

The ring of nails pounded into Harlix's bald slate-blue head freaked me out. It just looked *wrong*. Was it a curse or had he done it to himself?

My instincts screamed that this guy was more dangerous than a dozen Grimhalts.

Cassie was a wood elf—long curls of dark brown hair, slightly slanted green eyes, high cheekbones, and delicately pointed ears. All standard-issue sylvan. But she had that "Look all you want, sailor, but hassle me and I will hand you your own head" aura that was pure Special Forces.

Neither, however, looked like they were spoiling for a fight.

Harlix drew Grimhalt closer. "Don't start," he told him in a whisper that could have sliced glass. "Look closer. He has a truncated, second player class in his placard. That means a *secret* and *restricted* class, you imbecile."

Grimhalt squinted over my head and sneered as he saw it.

So my secret class wasn't so secret. At least they couldn't read what it was.

Cassie looked Morgana over and gave her a nod. Of recognition? Wasn't sure. Cassie made a gesture to Harlix, and he made another back to her.

Sign language? Clever.

Cassie pulled Grimhalt back five paces.

"Please forgive my temporary but necessary associates," Harlix said, his tone softening.

"Fine," I said. "All is forgiven, as long as you keep him on a short leash... and pick up after him." I voiced this loud enough so Grimhalt heard.

It got no response from him, but Cassie laughed.

These three made a decent party: a tank cleric, spellcaster for damage at range, and a swashbuckler ranger who could likely fill whatever role was required in any given situation. They were lean and mean.

Harlix went on, "The Game is hard enough without purposely seeking trouble, don't you agree?"

I gave a noncommittal shrug.

"In any event, if you could just answer a few questions, we will be on our way."

Morgana said, "We'd be happy to help and part company peaceful-like." She made a cutting motion by her lap that only I could see.

Harlix withdrew a folded parchment from his starry robe and handed it to Morgana.

She glanced it over, shook her head, and passed it to me.

WANTED
THE RED KNIGHT

Villainous brigand and his gang of vile cutthroats terrorize the Duchy of Sendon—committing murder, theft, and many other crimes most heinous.

REWARD

25,000 gold quins for the RED KNIGHT's death.

3,000 gold quins for information leading to his capture.

It was the same poster I'd come across in High Hill and here at the inn—or almost the same. The reward had been significantly increased. This loser must be on a tear.

The sketch of the Red Knight had also been improved with a few more details. His red full plate mail was chunky, ugly as sin, battered, and well, there was no other word to describe it but "evil." The helmet had tiny slanted eye slits and breathing holes in a fanged-mouth pattern. A bit dramatic, but effective in a terror-inducing way.

In fact, it was something my anti-paladin brother might wear… if that is, he wasn't safely being tortured in Duke Opinicus's dungeon.

I wondered if these three had been looking for this Red Knight the evening the Bloody Rooster burned. Did they think he'd set it? That implied a possible connection between the knight and the Silent Syndicate.

Without knowing what these three were really fishing for, I wasn't going to offer my opinions.

"Sorry," I told Harlix. "Believe me, if I'd seen this guy I'd tell you. Not so much a fan of jerks running around and ruining my day." I glanced at Grimhalt.

A brush of static stirred the tiny hairs on my arm.

Magic? From Harlix?

Harlix nodded and his odd face revealed no readable emotions. "Again, my apologies. If our paths cross again, I hope they are under more congenial circumstances. If you do see this knight, however, please send me a message. I will reward any assistance."

I smiled and did the smart thing: kept my mouth shut.

A first time for everything.

The wizard returned to Grimhalt and Cassie.

They exchanged more sign language.

Grimhalt nodded, looked once more at my placard, and the three then departed.

I noticed how quiet the room was.

The entire place had been watching our exchange. Now that the show was over, though, they went back to their eating, drinking, and bartering.

My hands shook.

There are few things in any game more dangerous than another player. I'm not sure what would have happened if Harlix hadn't been here to smooth things over.

"Morgana, what's the deal?"

She glanced about to see if anyone was still eavesdropping. "The Wild Hunt," she whispered. "Well, you said you knew that lot."

I nodded.

I *sort of* remembered something about them from a freshman English class. They were hunters…? Chasing a White Stag questing beast thing? That wasn't right, but close enough.

"Us tricksters," Morgana continued, "sure we cause a good bit of mayhem, and yeah, sometimes it gets a tad violent, but it's all in the name of fun and setting things right. Most of the time. Those Hunt wankers, though, *like* to kill."

"Yeah, he's a certified creep all right," I said. "Why do you think Grimhalt is with those other two?"

"That Harlix bloke said he was a 'necessary and temporary associate.' Could mean anything."

Oswald fluttered back and sat on the edge of the table. He looked ready to throw up.

"You're so lucky," the fairy muttered. "The Wild Hunt—*uuugh*." His wings shuttered. "I—I'm going outside for a smoke."

"You have cigarettes?" I asked.

"A few…"

"Can I bum one?"

He frowned. "One."

"You smoke?" Morgana asked with that *high school teacher giving you detention* tone.

"Not usually," I said, "but I just burned a few pints of adrenaline and had to sit here doing it." By way of explanation, I held up a trembling hand.

"Right. I'll come with you. Don't really feel like dessert anymore."

We went outside. The sun was two handspans above the horizon and pinking the sky there.

Oswald handed me a cigarette the size of a broken pencil lead.

"What am I supposed to do with *this*?"

He snapped his fingers and it grew to a proper size. Oswald then offered one to Morgana.

"Oh, what the hell," she said.

We got a light from a guard and we smoked like a bunch of juvenile delinquents.

I felt better.

Then *this* ruined it all:

>_Grimhalt: Did NOT appreciate comment re: me hunting WORMS

>_Grimhalt: Let's dual

>_Grimhalt: Can be nonlethal if u want

>_Grimhalt: I'll handicap 4 levels

He'd misspelled "duel."

And great, now he had my name and could spam me all day with more poorly worded threats. There had to be a way to block unwanted messages.

"Just out of curiosity," I asked Morgana, "when someone offers a handicap in a duel of so many levels, I assume the game drops their skills, abilities, and gear by a proportional amount?"

She crossed her arms over her chest. "Tell me you're not that thick."

"He sent me a challenge. I'm not going to take him up on it. Just tell me."

She let out a tremendous sigh of smoke. "I'm no expert, but as I understand it, a handicap's like you said. Not sure how the game compensates. Could be the opponent who picks what gets lowered."

"And just for informational purposes," I went on, "what do I get if I win a non-lethal PvP duel? I mean, besides the pleasure of beating this clown's honor to a pulp?"

She rolled her eyes. "You can set any terms beforehand. Forfeit an item or some gold. But blimey, Hektor, let's just tuck in, have a few drinks, and wait for Elmac. We have enough trouble chasing after us."

"You're right. As usual. I'll buy the—"

>_Grimhalt: Chicken?

>_Grimhalt: Then I'll sweeten the deal

>_Grimhalt: One little non-lethal dual and

>_Grimhalt: I WON'T follow u and your girlfriend

>_Grimhalt: and pick you off one at a time

My face reddened and I ground my teeth.

>_Hektor Saint-Savage: What—are you like 13 years old?

My apologies to young players for that comment. I have known many thirteen-year-olds to be noble warriors or worthy and honorable adversaries. I only meant that Grimhalt was being unwise and immature—both for picking such a dumb, testosterone-dripping name, and because he'd stupidly announced his intentions to do me and my friend harm.

There came no immediate reply to my message.

Could Grimhalt have been recruited by the Wild Hunt at the age of thirteen? That would explain a lot.

Morgana's pupils turned to cat slits. "Hektor? What *are* you doing?"

"Now he's threatening to follow us if I don't agree to his dumb duel."

I left out the part about him "picking us off."

"Wait. You said we could set *any* terms?" I asked.

"That's what I've heard."

Then there was a way to get Grimhalt off our backs. Permanently.

A four-level handicap should, in theory, make it an even fight. Although, I didn't think it *would be* even because Grimhalt would never figure out I was a Mage of the Line. His type more often employed a strategy of *ready—fire—aim*. I'd have a few surprises for him.

"Don't," Morgana said. "Whatever wonky scheme you're hatching, I got a feeling Grimhalt's going to cheat his way around it."

"Yeah. Hang on."

I typed:

>_Hektor Saint-Savage: I have one victory condition

>_Hektor Saint-Savage: I win, you NEVER threaten

>_Hektor Saint-Savage: or do harm to me or my friends.

>_Hektor Saint-Savage: EVER.

Still, no reply came from him.

"I think I just called his bluff."

>_Grimhalt: LOL

>_Grimhalt: K. Deal

>_Grimhalt: Meet at east wall so no sun in our eyes. 5 minutes.

>_Grimhalt: Hammer out details there

"...Or not," I muttered to Morgana. "I guess it's on."
She pursed her lips. "You are a *complete* prat."

CHAPTER 23

I leaned against the wall of the compound and stretched my hamstrings.

Grimhalt stood a dozen paces away and warmed up by swinging that sledgehammer mace of his around like it was a four-pound aluminum bat.

Oswald fluttered among the gathering crowd and took bets. He had three-to-one odds *against* me. I wasn't sure if he was a little traitor or had plans to cash in big when I won.

I had to admit, though, Grimhalt *did* look impressive... while I didn't. I had no obvious weapons or armor or flashy magic. If I hadn't known better, I'd have put my money on Grimhalt too.

Morgana leaned against the wall next to me, trying to look nonchalant. Her hand, however, rested on the handle of one of her many sheathed daggers, fingers tapping. "You seriously doing this?"

"It's nonlethal combat," I said.

"You so sure about that? Never heard of these Wild Hunt types dueling." She glanced at Grimhalt, then back to me. "And you've had what? Two Silvercrest Ales at thirty proof apiece? Your blood's up, mate. I get it. Been there myself. But you're not in the best place to make good decisions, yeah?"

Her confidence in my lack of cognitive ability was so reassuring. Didn't mean she was wrong, though.

"Let's wait for Elmac," she whispered. "He's got to know more about the Wild Hunt."

That made sense. Also Elmac, as a newly-minted first level, would be safe. Grimhalt couldn't touch him because of the Game rule that prevented PvP combat between players more than five levels apart.

"Look," I told her. "Why *not* try this? Worst case, I lose and we're back to where we are now. Or Grimhalt might be satisfied with his win and wander back to Harlix and Cassie. But if I win, then he's off our backs for good."

"You make a few good points," she said. "*Something* stinks about this, though, and I don't like it one little bit." Her hand stilled upon her dagger; she drew it from its sheath a fraction of an inch to loosen it for a quick draw. "But if you're set on doing this, I'll have your back. Like always. Just *you* watch your back too."

"I will," I told her. "And thanks. As always."

She gave me a pat on the shoulder. "Now go rip the bastard's bloody head off."

I nodded and walked over to Grimhalt.

"Yeah, about this fight."

"Not having second thoughts...?" Grimhalt got distracted by a trio of veiled elf ladies among the spectators. He stood taller and turned his head so they saw only the unburned side of his face.

"No, but I wanted to check that you're good with my terms: leaving us alone if I win."

"You're not going to win," he said without looking my way. "But sure, why not?" He scratched his head. "Let's add a side bet, though, a hundred quins? I'll be thirsty after this and'll need a few drinks before I head out."

"Fine by me."

I wondered if Grimhalt had a magic item that gave him such supernatural overconfidence? What an idiot. This guy had no idea he was dealing with the person who'd defeated the Grand Imperial Champion of Disorder, Her Greatness, Dominota Koroleva.

I better not get *too* confident, either. Morgana's instincts were usually right.

"Let me see." Grimhalt looked like he was ticking off boxes in his interface. "Four-level handicap. Winner declared when the other guy's at half health. Non-lethal damage. A hundred quins. Me never hassling you guys if you beat me." He grinned like this was a joke. "Oh, one more thing. No spells before combat. You okay with that?"

"Hmm." I pretended to think this over.

No spells prior to combat gave *me* a huge advantage. As soon as we started, I'd slip into the aether and fire off a *Perfect Motion* and tap all the ley lines I wanted. Grimhalt would never know what hit him.

"I *guess* we can do that."

"Great!" He cracked his knuckles. "Let's get started. I've got to catch up to Harlix and Cassie before it gets too dark."

He sounded like a kid who had to get home before dinner or he'd catch hell. He also acted like he had this in the bag.

Had I missed something? I didn't *think* so…

I double-checked and accepted our terms, set a seven-second countdown, and shut my interface.

ALERT!
You are dueling Grimhalt, Cleric of the Wild Hunt.
Both contestants have accepted the terms of the duel.
Good luck!

We moved six paces apart.

The crowd shuffled in closer.

Grimhalt swung his mace in a wide circle with a hurricane-like *whoosh*.

Everyone backed off.

I concentrated—my perceptions tunneled, and I emerged in the vast null space-time of the aether. I noted a few sparking ley lines that probably represented electrical forces. Most of the lines within my mental reach, though, were turquoise and fumed with spectral fog. I caught a whiff of peppermint and felt pinpricking gooseflesh crawl over my astral body.

Elemental cold. I could use that.

When I'd first seen Grimhalt he'd climbed out of a red-hot bonfire of a pit. That chain armor of his with its ghostly flames likely imparted fire resistance. That tracked with the extensive scarring on his face. The guy must have been seriously burned before and wouldn't want to go through that again.

Cold, however, I doubted he'd be prepared for.

I stepped back into normal space-time, trying hard to keep my poker face.

As promised, no spells before combat.

BEGIN THE DUEL? YES / NO

I nodded at YES.

The crowd shouted encouragements and taunts.

START COMBAT IN...
7...

We shuffled a step closer to one another.

Grimhalt donned his horned helmet.

I halted at the edge of his reach with that mace. Perfect.

6...

I'd rush him—get inside his effective swing radius—land a few punches, maybe a kick—then dance out before he could react.

5...

Could I halve his health before he even got in a shot?

4...

On the other hand, rushing him *was* the obvious move. How would he try and counter that?

3...

Did it matter? I'd be in the aether and spin up my *Perfect Motion* buff before this lummox could blink.

2...

Wait a second, was he *laughing* inside his helmet?

1...

Obviously trying to psyche me out.

GO!

I entered the aether.

Grimhalt froze mid-lunge—mace already raised over his head.

I was impressed. This guy was *fast*.

I powered up my *Perfect Motion* buff, grabbed a double fistful of the icy blue ley lines, and wrapped loops about each hand.

The cold burned my fingers, hands, and shocked my heart with needles of pain. I remembered practicing barefoot in the snow outside the Domicile of the Sleeping Dragon and how young Hector Savage of Earth caught a snowball in the face, sidearmed by his maniacal brother.

More induced memories and synesthesia. Neat. But distracting.

I focused.

So far, so good. I still had plenty of spiritual mana but was down by a third of my reflexive mana. I might have overdone it a bit using *two Energy Taps*.

Still, I shouldn't worry too much. This was going to be over fast.

I shifted back to normal space-time—coiled to spring.

Grimhalt was right in front of me. He swung—

And I...

There was a blank spot in my memory—

then I watched the sky reddening as the sun lowered toward the horizon—

and, hey, a few puffy clouds were spinning overhead.

I was... floating?

And tumbling through the air.

Then it hit me... *he'd hit me*!

First.

Before I'd even moved.

Not just hit me, either. He'd been an All-Star slugger, and I'd done my best impression of a slow-pitch softball.

I sailed *over* the wall.

Pain announced its arrival loud and clear, only slightly muted by my rapidly diminishing shock.

My ribcage had collapsed and bone shards punctured... I wasn't sure, a bunch of soft bits inside.

I fired off two *Spiritual Regeneration*s.

My insides melded together, just as painful as their separation, but my health bar surged to full, after coming perilously close to the halfway mark.

And I hadn't even got in a *single* hit.

How had he done it? I mean the physics of his swing were obvious, but how was he so darned fast?

Wire Work righted me like a cat and I floated toward the ground.

WARNING!
YOU ARE ABOUT TO CROSS THE GAME BOUNDARY
Past the Game's boundary, many interface functions, game rules, alert systems, and other features cease to work. Experience points and achievements earned beyond the boundary will be awarded upon reentry.

And *then* I finally understood how deep the hot water was in this end of the pool.

Earlier, I'd seen the alert about the Game's boundary being the far wall of the Waypoint Inn's compound, but never connected the dots to Grimhalt's request to fight next to it.

The Game still existed beyond the boundary; I was still gypsy elf Hektor, Spirit Warrior and Mage of the Line. Many rules wouldn't be in effect, though... like the ones covering duels and PvP combat.

I inwardly screamed in rage at my naiveté.

Grimhalt had had this all worked out. He'd somehow known he'd get in that home-run shot and launch me outside the Game... where he'd then be free to *kill* me.

I tucked, hit the grass, and rolled.

I was thirty feet outside the compound's wall.

And damn, the guy had already run out the front gate, rocketed around, and sprinted toward me, each of his strides eating up *yards* of terrain.

I braced, not to attack, but to *dodge*.

Whatever speed magic he had, I had to assume he'd hit me *again* before I could return the favor. I couldn't afford to take another blow like the first.

He was on me—and swung his blur of a mace.

I rolled to one side.

He left a crater where I had been.

I kicked the back of his leg.

He went down on one knee.

I followed up with a punch to the back of his head.

Crackling ice covered his helmet. Nice side effect from the channeled elemental cold.

I hit him twice more so hard he rocked back and forth like a speed bag. The demon bone knuckles under my skin added weight and *umph* enough to dent the metal of his horned helm.

He swept his mace out blind in a great arc.

I had to back off or be flattened.

He got up and tore off his ice-covered helmet.

My fists continued to fume like they'd been dipped in liquid nitrogen, so the ley lines I'd attached must still be pumping out cold. I'd felt, however, after my first two punches, more mana had drained to pay for the extra damage on that third strike of mine. I better be careful. My reflexive mana was down to 57/120.

I darted inside his reach—chopped his wrist, hoping he'd drop his weapon.

The metal of his gauntlet groaned from the stress of the extreme cold. Grimhalt grunted with pain. Bits of the armor pinged and broke as he forced his hand to clench his mace tighter.

He drew the weapon back. He was too choked up to strike at full power, but he *was* going to get in *a* swing.

I stepped into the aether.

I had to figure out what was happening.

I wished I could *move* in the aether, but hey right now, I was just grateful I *could* hit the pause button and think for a few relative seconds.

His inbound mace was going to connect, and choked grip or not, it would hurt.

My options were to try to dodge, block, or take my chances and counter-attack.

Could I do enough damage to significantly slow him down with more cold? Unlikely.

That left dodge or block.

Dodge gave me the best chance to survive, but it'd place me outside the range where I was most effective.

Block? Ha. No—I wasn't quite ready to re-enter orbit, thank you.

Or maybe it didn't have to turn out that way.

I had more options right in front of me.

I grabbed a sparking line of electricity—wincing as it nipped my skin. My hair stood on end. My teeth buzzed and my tongue curled as if I'd licked a nine-volt battery.

If I blocked Grimhalt's attack holding *this*, the resulting discharge might effectively taser him in all that nice conductive metal armor.

With all the jumping into and out of the aether, however, those blasts of cold and prepping this shot of electricity—I'd burned through almost all my reflexive mana: down to 8/120.

I didn't dare spend any more time here.

I stepped back into the fight.

His mace was a smear of grey—the strike more punch than a swing at this distance.

I barely got my hand into position to block.

Mere millimeters from my outstretched fingers, lightning flashed from me—to his mace—his armor.

Between us, a double thunderclap split the world apart.

I flew backward, tumbled to a stop, and miraculously got to my feet.

My hand had snapped at the wrist. Between the delicate and shattered metacarpal bones it felt as if a thousand volts still ricocheted.

I fired off a *Spiritual Regeneration* and flicked my hand as I did so to give the bones a chance to heal right. *That* hurt.

A dozen feet from where I stood, Grimhalt was knocked on his ass.

He lay there, smoldering, tiny sparks arcing over his chain armor.

But... he shook it off and got up.

Back to square one.

"I'll give it to you," he panted. "You put up a fight. A decent one. I'll carve it on your grave marker."

He hit me.

I didn't even *see* him do it.

Later, I'd piece together it had been an overhand stroke. It had to have been a critical hit to my left leg as he shattered both tibia and fibula, pulped the muscle—and I went down.

But not out.

The injured leg was unresponsive, but I managed a kick with the other, nailed him in the stomach.

He staggered back two steps.

My health was down to a quarter. While Grimhalt was off balance I had time to use two *Spiritual Regenerations*—not enough to fully fix my leg, but enough to keep me from slipping into shock.

Now, my spiritual mana was dangerously low.

And I was out of options.

Like a strong man at a ring-the-bell carnival attraction, he raised his monster mace for a coup de grâce—brought it down at supersonic speed.

I tried to roll away but knew I wasn't going to be fast enough.

There was a *thud*.

Dirt and sod pelted me.

He'd missed? How?

I blinked.

Someone stood between me and Grimhalt.

Morgana? ...No.

It was a dwarf brandishing a short wooden staff.

Another *player*, whose placard read:

Melmak Argenté-Wolfram

Wizard / LEVEL 1

Heroes of Thera

Melmak? Heroes of Thera?

Elmac?

As impossible as it seemed (because Grimhalt and his mace had to outweigh Elmac many times over), he'd deflected that strike.

"Now lad," Elmac told Grimhalt, "that'll be enough of *that*."

CHAPTER 24

Grimhalt stared down at Elmac—then at his own mace.

Confusion melted his murderous grin as he tried to understand why my brains weren't splattered all over his weapon.

I was wondering the same thing.

He grunted, raised the mace, and brought it down once more.

I was so stunned to be alive I could only watch as Elmac brought his staff in line with the strike and again deflected it.

Thud!

Stones and dirt rained down.

Elmac had made it look easy.

The new Elmac, or excuse me, Melmak Argenté-Wolfram was a dwarf with wavy flame-red hair shot with gold, a bushy beard of the same colors, and a wicked slash of a smile (all teeth intact). I'd guess he was in his late twenties in equivalent human years. He was four feet tall, on the slim side of the standard dwarven stout, and possessed an air of meditative calm that was kind of irritating given my life-and-death circumstances.

And he had only *one* arm. The right.

Where his left arm *should have been*, the sleeve of his simple hemp robe was pinned.

Either he'd lost it on his journey here from High Hill or… he'd cut it off?

No way. Even Elmac wasn't *that* hardcore, no matter how awesome that magical prosthetic arm of his was.

Hang on… a first-level, one-armed wizard, wielding a simple staff was a match for a ninth-level cleric wielding an enchanted mace of death?

I clearly had taken too many blows to the head.

As Grimhalt and I were trying to figure this out, Elmac poked the cleric in the gut, his knee, and smashed his boot.

Grimhalt jerked in pain.

How were Elmac's strikes getting through that heavy chain armor?

Whatever he was doing, and however he was doing it, he was just getting started.

He rapped Grimhalt's gauntlet, spun the staff, and nailed his thumb.

Grimhalt dropped his mace and knelt to retrieve the weapon.

Before he could, Elmac walloped him over the head.

I started to rise.

"Stay down," Elmac said without looking at me. "You be safer that way."

I stayed. Who was I to argue with the dwarven equivalent of a Jedi master?

Grimhalt shook his head to clear the bell ringing he'd taken and flexed his gauntlet with a ring-popping crunch. A new mace of a greenish metal appeared in his hand. It was half the size of the previous and glowed with a blue haze of magic. A backup weapon, no doubt, from his inventory.

Elmac, however, was on him—whack—*whack*—*WHACK*.

Grimhalt flinched with each blow, and in turn, did his best to flatten his diminutive opponent.

The little guy deflected and effortlessly stepped out of the way of each attack—and while he was doing it his smile grew and he casually landed another half dozen blows.

Grimhalt chanted mystical words as he took three steps back.

Elmac mirrored every one of Grimhalt's steps with two of his own. He jabbed the cleric in his solar plexus, short-circuiting his spell.

"*Furantur etyes vita—ooouphff!*

I gave up trying to figure out *how* Elmac was doing this and just enjoyed the show.

Elmac poked away—finding every exposed square millimeter in Grimhalt's defense—then unceremoniously tripped the mighty cleric.

The dwarf stood over him and beat him like a rug.

In the nearby grass a shadow slinked closer. A black panther soundlessly emerged and padded toward me.

"I think he's got this," I told Morgana.

Elmac kept pounding the now balled-up Grimhalt until the dwarven wizard was slick with sweat. "Had your fill 'o fighting, lad?" Elmac asked him.

There came no answer.

"Guess so then."

Morgana was human again. She set her hands on my mangled leg and yanked to straighten the bones.

The pain was a scalpel slash along my leg. I clenched so hard, it stifled my scream.

Healing magic poured through her fingertips.

"Much appreciated," I whispered with a trembling exhale.

Without a word to me, Morgana ran to Elmac.

She hugged him so fiercely, they almost fell over. She then planted kisses on both cheeks, and one on the lips... lingering... long... deep.

Elmac reluctantly, *very* reluctantly, disengaged. "I've never tasted anything sweeter, lass." He wiped away her tears. "No need for those. 'Twas never in any danger with the Free Trial nor this—" He kicked dirt onto Grimhalt.

"Hey, don't take this the wrong way," I said, "but you *are* El—"

Elmac shook his head and nodded toward the Inn.

The crowd who'd gathered to see Grimhalt and I beat each other senseless had come around the long way through the front gate and headed this way.

Elmac stepped to Grimhalt's mace. He touched it and it vanished (presumably into his inventory). "That be one *heavy* weapon," he said and waddled back to the cleric.

Elmac slapped Grimhalt. Hard. "We're done, you dolt. Let's finish this so I can get on with some proper drinking."

Yes, this was Elmac all right.

Grimhalt un-balled from his protective fetal position. He bled from his nose and ears. He shook his head and blinked. "Who—? *What* are you?"

"I be the first-level, one-armed, dwarven wizard who just beat the living snot out 'o you." He tapped the side of Grimhalt's head with his staff. "If you'd like to avoid more 'o the same, you'll sit there, nod and smile at the nice people, then I'll be telling you exactly what to do next."

"I'm not taking orders from a gimp dwar—"

Elmac prodded his staff into Grimhalt's groin.

And then once more for good measure.

And... a third time, because it's what the twerp deserved.

Grimhalt replied, "—"

"Any more questions 'bout who be in charge?"

"No," Grimhalt squeaked.

The crowd gathered about us.

Oswald buzzed over Grimhalt and circled me. He stopped, hovering, and took off his rose-colored sunglasses. "So? Who won?"

"It be a tie," Elmac declared. "Right?" He looked knowingly at me.

"A complete draw, folks," I said. "Sorry. Better luck next time."

Grimhalt wisely said nothing and nodded.

A disappointed "aww" rippled through the spectators and then they pushed about Oswald for a refund of their wagers.

"Wait, everyone," Oswald sputtered. "There's going to be a rematch, right? Right?"

"No rematch," Morgana said, raising her hands. "Show's over, folks. Thanks for watching." Under her breath, she added, "*Bloodthirsty pack of dingos...*"

As the crowd wandered back to the inn, I whispered to Elmac, "You're going to have to explain how you just did what you did."

"I will," he said and nodded at Grimhalt, "but we best deal with this sack of rabid squirrels first."

Grimhalt glanced around then demanded like a petulant child, "Where's my mace?"

"That mace'll be one of the things we be talking about," Elmac told him. "You just sit tight right there or I be breaking your kneecaps."

Grimhalt looked Elmac up and down, considered, *re*considered, and then did as he was told.

"Now we discuss the terms of your surrender," Elmac said. "All gentlemen-like."

"And lady-like," Morgana added.

"Surrender?!" Grimhalt turned to me and his hands clenched. "I'd rather *die* than surrender to the likes of *him*."

"Hektor," Elmac said, "would you mind digging a hole for this fellow? It be in poor taste to make a man dig his own grave."

I wasn't sure if Elmac was serious or not (and at this point, I really didn't care).

"Did you want one big hole?" Morgana asked and drew her daggers, "or a bunch of little ones for the pieces?"

"...Perhaps," Grimhalt muttered, "I was hasty. Let's hear these terms."

"Smart lad." Elmac leaned closer to him. "First thing: you're going to be forfeiting that mace of yours."

"Never!" He tried to stand.

Elmac smacked his shin. I heard bone crack.

Grimhalt clutched his leg and rocked back and forth.

"Now, if we kill you," Elmac continued in an even tone, "we be taking all your gear anyway." He cocked his head, and it looked like he thought this might be the better option.

Elmac sat on his haunches and went on in a conspiratorial whisper, "As I be understanding it when a worshiper 'o the Wild Hunt dies in some ignominious manner, their souls become one 'o the Hunt's undead hounds. Rumor has it the Hunt be eating those poor beasties from time to time. And after the meal... they bring 'em back for another go."

Grimhalt paled. He swallowed.

"So then," Elmac said, "death and doggy afterlife? Or you be giving up the mace?"

Grimhalt replied with a strangled sound, "Fine. What else?"

"You never lay a finger on any Hero of Thera or Trickster for the rest of your days, either instigating an attack or being the means of others attacking us—'cept, I suppose in the case of *us* attacking *you*. That be only fair."

I wanted to ask Elmac why he thought this guy would honor *any* deal not backed by the Game's rules. They both looked dead serious, though, so there had to be more to this than mere words.

Grimhalt twitched, which might have been a microscopic nod of agreement.

"In exchange," Elmac told him, "you get to walk away, and we never be telling that you were beaten by a first-level wizard."

He chewed this over for three heartbeats. "Yeah..." He concentrated until it looked like something was about to snap inside his thick skull. "Just one thing," he told Elmac. "If you get the chance, you should melt that damned mace down and drop what's left in the ocean."

Elmac's eyebrows raised. "I'll consider it. But no promises."

That was a strange request. It was as if Grimhalt wanted his mace back—and wanted it gone—at the same time.

I glanced over to Morgana, but she shrugged, just as baffled.

Elmac coughed up a wad of spit into his palm and offered it to Grimhalt. He did the same and clasped the dwarf's outstretched hand.

In a ceremonial tone, Elmac said, "And so you do swear by the unwavering and unending fury 'o the generals 'o the Wild Hunt in all their incarnations, may they trample your soul should you go back on your word."

"I do so swear," Grimhalt said in a low whisper.

The temperature dropped twenty degrees, the air stilled, and from every direction came the bays of distant dogs, galloping hooves, and cries in an ancient tongue that made my blood run cold.

Then it was all gone.

A breeze kicked up and the crickets resumed their dusk symphony.

An oath to one's gods apparently was taken seriously in this universe. Good to know.

Grimhalt gave Elmac a half smile. "Maybe a rematch one day, dwarf?"

"Maybe," Elmac mused. "But *not* today."

Grimhalt shot one last glance my way.

The look on his face? Something between rage and icy calculation.

I had no doubt he was already thinking of ways to try and wriggle out of that oath he'd sworn.

I also had no doubt that one day I'd see Grimhalt again.

He got up, turned, and limped back to the inn.

"We're just letting him go?" I asked Elmac.

"If I could've gotten away with it," he muttered, "I'd have done it with my first strike. The Wild Hunt gods have, though, what's called an 'Adamant Pact 'o Vengeance.' Off one of them, the rest come after you. A messy business. All in all, I think we made out okay."

"Fine. Let's table that then for the moment," I said. "What happened to *you*? How'd you beat him?"

"Oi," Morgana interrupted. "First things first."

She went to Elmac, and for a moment I thought she was going to plant another kiss on him. Instead, she crossed her arms and glowered—then uncrossed her arms and gently touched his cheek, his one arm, the shoulder by the amputation—as if she couldn't decide whether to be angry, concerned, frustrated, or relieved.

Morgana took a breath and composed herself. "How'd you get through the Free Trial so quick? *And* get back here, in what? Less than six hours? And your arm..." Her features pinched with sympathetic pain. "We'll figure a way to regrow that."

"We'll get to all that," Elmac told her and held up his one hand. "More important, on my way here I ran 'cross a squad that *looked* like city guard, but weren't. Asked 'bout three travelers who just left the city."

"Silent Syndicate?" Morgana asked.

"Didn't stick 'round to find out," he said.

"Three travelers?" I said and cupped my chin, thinking. "Could have been looking for us, or after Grimhalt and his two pals for all we know. We should find a way to cover our tracks, though, just in case. Hmm."

I looked around. "Oswald? Where are you?"

There was a rustle and the fairy stepped out of the grass. He hitched up his leather pants, obviously having had just taken care of business.

"I have a task uniquely suited for you."

"Oh?" His voice was thick with wariness.

"Fairies can make illusions, yes?"

He puffed out his chest. "I am a *full* adept at the art of phantasmancy."

"So you could, say, produce three figures that look like El—uh, my new dwarven friend here, the Lady Morgana, and me?"

He snapped his fingers. *Poof*!

We stood facing decent copies of ourselves. My double, however, had a lazy eye, and I was sure this wasn't from Oswald's lack of skill.

"Uh, perfect. I guess. Okay, Oswald, I want you to keep these illusions up and head south. Make sure anyone you see gets a good look at our copies."

"As you wish." Oswald gave me a short bow and made it somehow look condescending.

"Keep hiking south for, give it, three weeks. After that, I'll consider your debt paid in full."

Oswald froze and stared at nothing as if he was playing back my words to make sure he'd heard them right. "Really?"

"Yeah. Good luck. Live long and prosper."

He jumped, clicked his boot heels, and remained in the air, fluttering his dragonfly wings. "Yippie! See you around, suckers." He bowed to Morgana, nodded at Elmac, and then flew over and offered me his tiny hand.

I extended a finger and we shook.

Friends? Not really.

But maybe not enemies anymore.

He waved once more, then he and our doppelgängers started their trek south.

Morgana rubbed her jaw. "That was your call," she said, "but the little blighter might have come in handy later."

"The whole master-slave thing—just not me."

"Fair enough," she said.

I sank to the ground and massaged my recently broken and mended leg.

Magical healing had always looked easy and painless in video games. Don't get me wrong, it *was* nothing short of a miracle, but it was *not* painless. Or perfect.

I ran my fingers over tiny achy misalignments in the bones, bumps, and gristle in previously smooth muscles. My ribs had been mended as well, but they popped every time I inhaled.

I wondered if there was a decent chiropractor in High Hill?

"Well..." I stood. "We better get walking too."

"Walk?" Elmac scoffed.

With his one hand, he made a series of sharp, quick gestures that could have been the sleight of hand skill. Along with these motions, however, he chanted, *"Venit Servi Animalibus."*

Elmac then stood on his tippy toes to see over the tall grass. "Aye, just wait for it."

I heard, then felt it, before I spotted them: Six of those super-sized buffalo I'd seen before thundered our way.

"What are..." I remarked, but then my brain stopped trying to make words, and shifted priorities to figuring how fast I'd have to move to avoid being trampled by the monsters.

Elmac chuckled and faced the stampede.

The beasts slowed and halted before him with a chorus of snorts.

He reached up to the biggest one.

She sniffed and bowed her gigantic woolly head.

Elmac scratched behind her ears.

"I be a wizard now, lad," he told me. "And wizards don't be *walking* anywhere."

CHAPTER 25

We rode the buffalo back toward the inn so Elmac could get the experience points from fighting Grimhalt. As soon as we crossed the imaginary line that ran through the outer wall (the Game boundary), Elmac blinked and smiled.

"Fireworks?" I asked.

He nodded. "Says I be second level. All from the one fight?"

"Yeah," I said. "A first-level wizard defeating a ninth-level cleric?" I whistled. "Pretty impressive."

It actually sounded *impossible*.

"How many points?" Morgana asked.

"Oh..." he told her and squinted at the invisible numbers. "Still a good way to go 'till third."

An achievement icon appeared on his placard. Within a circle was a silver silhouette of a tiny figure, fist raised in victory, and one boot set on the head of a slain giant.

I looked it up.

The "Underdog" achievement was awarded for fighting another player more than *five times* your level. And *winning*.

Obviously, your best chance to get this achievement would be at first level. Still, no minor feat. Any player seeing it would think long and hard about challenging Elmac.

Oh, and if you're curious, I received zero experience for the beating I took.

We turned the buffalo around and rode away.

"So, Elmac," I said. "These buffalo...?"

"Aye, summoned them with the spell, *Call Creature*. The description says, 'compels the nearest non-hostile animal to come to you. Said beast *might* perform a small task and then depart, but there is no guarantee.'" He looked up from his interface. "It be lasting an hour. We best part ways with them, though, well before that."

"Hold up a tick," Morgana told us. Without any visible command, her buffalo halted, as did the rest. "Let me have a word with them."

We dismounted and Morgana shooed us off.

The buffalo gathered about her and Morgana "spoke" to them in grunts and spits and stomps. They grumbled and replied in kind.

After a minute of this, Morgana came over to us. "Okay, chatted up these nice ladies," she said. "Just like you described those barbarians with the gold threads in their beards, Hektor, they know where that tribe makes camp this time of year. Two days' ride north. They'll take us in exchange for" —she lowered her voice to a whisper— "it's a bit of a delicate subject with them." She glanced over to the buffalo to make sure they weren't listening.

"I've got this little *Destroy Parasite* ritual these poor things are in dire need of."

Morgana did the ritual (the details of which I shall omit here for everyone's benefit), and we had a ride.

I'd been impressed when I'd first seen the buffalo of this world at a distance. Up close? They were demigods among lesser herd animals. They were *BIG*—ten feet tall at the shoulder. I'd had to climb up by grabbing handfuls of their thick mane (which had the texture of 14 gauge wire).

They were all muscle that felt more like seasoned hickory than flesh and blood. At a slow trot, they tore up the sod like a mechanized rototiller. I'd guess they weighed in at three tons.

Oh... and the horns.

Those on the side were five feet long each and had sturdy points. Judging by the scratches and scuffs, they'd seen a lot of use. The center horn was a foot in diameter at the base and gleamed like blackened steel. It followed the downward curve of the buffalo's skull. I imagined with their head lowered in a charge, that horn would be at the perfect angle to skewer whatever was dumb enough to be in their way.

I was never more grateful to be in the company of a druid who could make nice with the natives.

Nor did I regret my earlier investment of points in the *Ride* skill.

What a forbidding mount to take into combat...

Out of curiosity, I re-read the *Ride* skill's description to see how many non-combat skill points it would take to do such a thing. From what I could gather from the text—lots. Well, probably for the best I wasn't seriously tempted, considering how much it had to cost to keep such a large creature well fed, cared for, and happy.

These buffalo did leave a *little* to be desired in the odor department, but hey, I'd known Marines who'd smelled worse.

I turned to Elmac. "Thanks again for back there."

"'Tis what any true Hero of Thera would have done, coming to the rescue of the weak and oppressed."

I winced. I had that coming.

Compared to Grimhalt, I *was* weak. I'd been arrogant as well to have accepted his challenge. Maybe my luck wasn't so bad after all, considering I'd lived to regret it.

I noticed the clan name in Elmac's placard read "Heroes of Thera," not "Hero of Thera." That lifted my spirits a bit. I was no longer alone. We were a very tiny army of two.

Morgana maneuvered her buffalo between us. "Time to fess up," she said to Elmac. "I was bloody going out of my mind with worry. Tell us about the Free Trial. And your arm."

"The Free Trial—*that* be a funny story," he said. "Best save it, though, for when we all have a good long stretch 'o time and a few ales to be telling it right." He smirked as if he was keeping a dirty joke to himself. "Now me character creation, gods! Good thing you helped me plan most 'o that, Morgana."

"Yeah," she said, "go on."

"Course there be only one choice for race." He thumped his chest. "Prime dwarven flesh. Spent far too long fiddling with my features." Elmac smoothed his only hand over his face. "Decided to look like I was when I was a lad. Hard to improve on perfection, you know. I did fix a few 'o my old nose breaks and such."

"I thought your broken nose was adorable," Morgana said.

Now that he mentioned it, his nose was straighter. His brow a tad higher. And his eyes were no longer dark, but rather amethyst, a mix of quartz grey and royal purple.

Dwarven beauty. Who was I to judge? He still looked like Elmac to me... or maybe his grandson.

"Got a wee complicated when it came to the sub-racial choices," Elmac went on. "Did I stick with mountain dwarf? Or get a bit fancy with mithril dwarf nobility? Settled on half and half. Apparently, my birth 'twas quite the scandal."

"And the arm?" Morgana asked once more, not letting him sidetrack her.

"Oh, uh... that." He looked away. "That be in character creation too."

The color drained from her face. "Thought so. You did it on purpose, didn't you?"

I felt the heat of her words, and steered my buffalo a foot or two away, expecting incoming fire.

Elmac held up his one hand, thought better of *that* particular gesture, and dropped it. "I hadn't set out to be doing it. Not exactly." He glanced my way as if to say—*help!* "Maybe we best take a rest here, so I can get all my bits together?"

Morgana growled something that might have been agreement. We halted and dismounted.

Morgana pointedly ignored us and marched off a few paces. She retrieved a handful of seeds from a pouch, planted them, and spoke a few magic words.

Stalks sprouted, grew eight feet, and became laden with corn.

The buffalo gathered about this snack and grunted their appreciation as they ate.

"You have the stuff I gave you to hold?" Elmac asked me as he snuck a look at Morgana.

"In the clan inventory. Tap the icon of clasped hands in your interface. You'll see it."

He poked the air a few times and his gear appeared on the ground.

Elmac shucked out of the top of his robe and knelt next to his prosthetic metal arm. "Would you mind? A bit 'o help?"

I moved to him... but he hadn't been talking to me.

Morgana came over, briskly wound the straps of the arm around his torso and shoulder. The rest of the apparatus laced together and magically snugged tight.

She then grabbed him and kissed him, angrily at first, but it softened as they wrapped arms about each other.

I looked away.

How fascinating... the noble grazing buffalo... the endless sky... hey, clouds... and the vast, lonely grasslands.

I finally had to clear my throat.

The two of them detached.

"Oh..." Elmac breathed. He curled his now-animated left metal limb, but he never took his eyes off Morgana. "That be *much* better."

Morgana pushed him away. "Hope you enjoyed that," she muttered. "Because I'm not so much as shaking your hand until you're done explaining."

"Elmac?" I said. "What exactly does that arm do for you? I tried to read its description, but was blocked."

Elmac test-waggled the fingers. Apart from the pale gold color, the metal looked and moved just like a real arm.

"'O course it be blocked. 'Tis a dwarven relic, keyed to my soul and all. It does a smitch 'o this and a few things 'o that but has two main powers. First, it be a perfect match for my real arm. Can't tell you how hard 'tis to be casting spells one-handedly. And second, it gives my strength a little boost."

He plucked up his battle axe, *Dreadful Cleave*—gave it a playful spin, and said to it, "Oh, I missed you, you magnificent bastard."

A *little* boost?

That axe needed a *16 STRENGTH* to wield.

Elmac changed into gray linen pants, sturdy boots, his gladiator belt and daggers, and a black shirt that showed off his impressive chest hair. He slid the axe into a harness on his back and dusted off his hands.

I had a feeling Elmac was not going to be your standard run-of-the-mill Gandalf type wizard.

"There be a few things I still need to sort," he told us. "In the meantime, I bet you have questions 'bout Grimhalt? Take a gander at this beastie."

He stabbed at the air.

Grimhalt's mace dropped to the ground with a *thump*.

Morgana and I concentrated on the thing.

Bludgeon of the Red Rider
Flanged Mace (One-Handed Mace Class)
(Tier-VII magical weapon, unique)
DESCRIPTION: Ground from a single piece of meteoric nickel-cobalt iron, this dull black weapon is balanced for one-handed use even though it weighs 57 pounds. The flanges have been blunted flat from use.
SPECIAL ABILITIES: +8 to the wielder's STRENGTH. Greatly enchanted to increase hit and damage potentials. Always strikes *first* in any given melee exchange regardless of opponent's speed, abilities, or distance (within a quarter mile). The first hit in any combat is *always* critical.

Holy smokes. First strike. And a guaranteed critical hit.

That explained how Grimhalt had creamed me before I'd blinked.

I kept reading.

REQUIREMENTS: Minimum of 12 STRENGTH. Keyed only for worshipers of War in all its incarnations.

"Worshippers of War? So how was he using this?" I asked Morgana. "The Wild Hunt are gods like Diana, Orion, and Artemis, right?"

"Not by a good piece, Hektor," she said and slowly shook her head. "The Wild Hunt are a bunch of *warmongering* deities. They come to battles—feed off the carnage and death." Her lips curled in revulsion. "The bloodier, the more casualties, the more gratuitous the violence and innocents killed, the better that lot like it."

Once more, I'd made assumptions. No wonder Morgana had been so against any kind of duel with Grimhalt. And no wonder she'd looked at me like I'd been out of my mind.

I had to be more careful.

Being a little more humble and asking when I wasn't sure about something might be a good idea too.

There was a last bit to the mace's description.

WARNING: Once used in battle, the wielder is CURSED to one day be KILLED by this weapon.

Oh. Now Grimhalt's remark about melting the thing down made sense. What I didn't get was why had he used it in the first place? He had to have known about the curse.

Or maybe I could understand.

I still had the *Ebon Hands of Soul Death* rattling around in my inventory. I'd used them knowing the potential consequences... which were a lot worse than this mace.

I'd have to deal with those things once and for all before they accidentally destroyed the multiverse. I needed to put together a new to-do list.

The buffalo finished off the corn, so we mounted and continued our journey.

Morgana turned to Elmac. "You were saying about your arm and character creation?"

"Aye, my arm," he said. He sucked his lips, then admitted, "There be this section in character creation—Disabilities and Perks?"

"You didn't..." Morgana whispered.

Elmac dropped his gaze. "I had no arm before. And I had my backup stashed with Hektor..."

"Wait," I said. "I got rushed through character creation. What's this disability and perks thing?"

"You can gimp your character," Morgana told me, her voice ice-chilled, "if you're barmy enough. Minor insanity, bad vision, *lowered IQ*—things like that. In exchange, you acquire perks that you can't get in the Game. The Great Pooka warned me away from them." She stiffened and tilted her chin up. "So, let's hear it then. What'd you trade your one and only left arm for?"

CHAPTER 26

"I traded my arm..." Elmac took a breath. "There be this one perk I *couldn't* pass on, '*Old Soul*'?" He hesitated, but Morgana drummed her fingers, so he continued. "You were a biology teacher before the Game?"

She nodded.

"And you be remembering it all?"

"Of course." She nodded at our mounts. "Scientific name: *Bison bison,* or that's the closest classification to this world's variant. And their order is... Artiodactyla?" Her forehead crinkled. "Blimey. I'm not sure. It had something to do with the number of toes. I was positive I knew."

"And you, Hektor," Elmac said. "You were a soldier before I'm guessing, or something close to one, because a few days ago you were asking 'bout gunpowder and firearms and all?"

"Yeah..."

"But have you tried to shoot a gun in your new body?" he asked.

"No," I admitted, "but I'm sure..."

I looked at my six-fingered hands. Maybe not.

I *did* remember how to aim and shoot. But would *this* body remember? Muscle memory was a thing hard won, and Hektor the gypsy elf hadn't even gone through basic training. In fact, he had an entirely different set of neuromuscular pathways from decades of instruction at the Domicile of the Sleeping Dragon.

"I'm not sure I could anymore," I told him. "At least not like I could before."

"Exactly," he said. "That's where the *Old Soul* ability comes in. It be letting you remember and *do* one thing from your previous incarnation. Think it was meant for skills like gem-cutting or billiards and the like, but I typed in 'fighting' and it took."

My mouth fell open.

If he was implying what I think he was, it *had* been a genius trade.

I figured Elmac would have picked a fighter-type class for his reincarnated self. After all, he'd been the Grand General of all the Armies of High Hill. Why not stick with what you knew?

But with this *Old Soul* ability, he had most of that *for free*... maybe much more because his prior expertise far outclassed *any* first-level warrior.

"To get *Old Soul*, though, I had to be picking a disability and a fairly serious one at that." He glanced at Morgana. "So, 'twas born with a congenital defect... no left arm."

She stared at the horizon. "And you started out fighting like a bloody twentieth-level warrior?" she whispered. Her gaze found him once more. She pursed her lips. "Yeah, I guess that *was* a right good trade."

Which is how he'd beaten Grimhalt to a pulp with one hand. In effect, Elmac had something like eleven levels on the guy. Grimhalt had never stood a chance.

And I thought *I* was a min-maxer.

Had the Game Master bent the rules for Elmac? Seemed like a heck of a loophole in that perk to let slide. But since Elmac was a Hero of Thera, I wasn't about to complain.

"We might want to keep your fighting ability a secret," I said. "Save it so it's a surprise when we need it."

And so none of the other clans would go out of their way to target the new competition (any more than the Lords of the Abyss no doubt already were).

"Aye," Elmac said. "Thought Grimhalt killing you, though, qualified as us 'needing it.'"

I sighed. "Yeah... Good point."

Before I forgot, now that Elmac was a player, I could share the Drunken Monkey quest out to him.

I did, he accepted, and this alert appeared:

You have grouped with
Morgana Nox,
Druid (Mischief Maker) LEVEL 4 / Thief LEVEL 3
and
Melmak Argenté-Wolfram,
Wizard LEVEL 2

NOTE: Due to the level difference among party members, experience will be split 40%, 40%, and 20% for the two highest and the lowest-level players respectively.

"Don't worry," I told Elmac. "Once we find Karkanal's tribe and I learn that new martial art technique, I'm sure you'll make at least third level."

Elmac stared into empty space, probably trying to figure out from the limited descriptions of his current spells and abilities what his options might be when he leveled up.

I'd need to have a sit down with him and tell him everything I'd learned about the character progression process... after, that is, I figured out how to tell Elmac about me being a Mage of the Line. That seemed like something a fellow clan member should know.

As we rode through the evening, I told Elmac I'd deciphered the assassin's note and of our meals and misadventures at the Inn.

He paid particular attention to the part where Harlix, Cassie, and Grimhalt had been looking for the Red Knight.

I then messaged him a copy of the assassin's note, written out in plain Tradespeak.

Like Morgana and I, he puzzled over who might be targeting Duke Opinicus... and was none too happy to see Pendric, Colonel Delacroix, and the three of us on their hit list.

Around midnight the flat grasslands sloped into gently rolling hills, and farther, dipped to make moon-shadowed valleys.

We found a good spot to camp by a tiny grove of fruit trees near a stream. The trees were mature apricot and apple species with thirty-foot canopies. Their fruit littered the ground and looked very squishy—just this side of rotting.

Morgana spoke to the buffalo. She then went with them to the stream, where the beasts lingered for a long drink.

Meanwhile, Elmac and I cleared an area on the lee side of a low hill and set up his magical heat rock.

Morgana returned and rubbed her hands over the stone. She and Elmac made eye contact—then both quickly looked away. It was dark, but wearing Azramath's headband, I saw they were both blushing.

"Our ladies said we shouldn't worry about predators," she told us. "The local Sabertooth tigers are higher in the mountains this time of year." She paused, considered, then added, "Might be smart, though, to set up a few alarm wards."

I doubted even a Sabertooth would be a real threat to *these* buffalo... unless the tigers of this world hunted in packs.

"Wards sound like a great idea," I said.

She nodded and left us.

Elmac took his tent and pitched it forty feet distant under the trees, closer to the gurgling stream. Definitely a romantic spot.

I set my bedroll by the heat stone.

Elmac returned and offered me a half-liter mithril flask. "I be needing a favor, Hektor."

I accepted the flask. "You want me to take first watch?"

"Aye..." He nonchalantly examined the laces on his boot.

"And the second?" I asked.

"If you wouldn't mind, lad."

"Kind of figured that out. You kids take all the time you need."

He patted me on the shoulder. "Never had a truer friend."

Elmac hurried off, but was so preoccupied, he actually forgot his flask.

Well, couldn't let it go to waste. I took a sip.

A wave of fire crashed against the shores of my brain. Whoa. Red Dragon Whiskey. Sadly, it might be the last of it from the Bloody Rooster.

I'd better go easy on this stuff. It had been a very long day, and I needed to stay sharp tonight.

We hadn't seen any sign of the Silent Syndicate since High Hill. We also were in another world, had set up decoys, and were a long way from the gate and the Wayfar Waypoint Inn… so the odds of any assassin tracking us, were what?

Didn't matter. I'd made too many assumptions lately.

I scooted closer to the heat stone and warmed my hands.

I was glad for Morgana and Elmac. If ever two souls deserved a second chance at love and life, well—I raised the flask to toast my companions and their happiness.

I leaned back and gazed at the stars and the one lonely moon who'd be keeping me company tonight. Among the many worlds out there, was *my* soulmate waiting?

Come on. The Game was my priority, not dating.

That *didn't* mean I had to play like a monk who'd taken a vow of chastity.

Wait.

I riffled through my patchwork memories. No—gypsy elf Hektor had taken no such vows at the Domicile of the Sleeping Dragon. Whew.

With that cleared up, I then indulged in the time-honored and highly theoretical thought experiment of "who's your ideal mate."

There were the usual things that everyone looks for... a preferred set of physical attributes, sense of humor, kindness. There was, however, one extra thing I'd want: to share that most important facet of my life, i.e. the Game.

That seemed to narrow the field to other players.

Ideally, I'd also like to share the *big* secret I carried, the top-secret secret that our clan's sponsor was the Game Master of Thera... which I supposed further limited my choice... to other members of the Heroes of Thera clan?

Ugh. So I'd pick future clan members based on their dating potential? No way. Putting my love life over the fate of everyone in the multiverse would have easily made my *top ten worst ideas ever* list.

Man, I didn't even *have* a girlfriend, and it was *already* "complicated."

I raised Elmac's flask once more and toasted my starry companions.

You understand the bumpy road to true love, don't you, ladies?

Hektor, the gypsy elf and thespian, knew that Hamlet had said it better:

> *Doubt thou the stars are fire;*
> *Doubt that the sun doth move;*
> *Doubt truth to be a liar;*
> *But never doubt I love.*

Okay, that was enough of *that* tonight—both in the liquor *and* the theatrical self-pity departments. I screwed the cap back on the flask, tucked it away, and silently chuckled at my foolishness.

Until—I heard movement in the grass and stopped breathing.

Again, a slight rustling.

I eased from the glow of the heat stone and into the shadows. I squinted and focused my enhanced vision in the direction I'd heard the noise.

Thirty paces away.

I was thinking ninja or at the very least one of those three-headed vipers Elmac had mentioned before. Didn't he say their venom dissolved flesh? That sounded about right.

It was just a monkey though.

I exhaled. False alarm.

He had a tufted tail and fluffy mane. Cute little guy. I knew what it was: a lion-tailed macaque. There'd been a picture of one on the packages of banana-soy concentrate served at San Quentin. Funny, of all the things I could have remembered from two lifetimes—*that* had stuck.

He limped along and fell over.

Was it wounded?

No. He got up, belched, and then staggered merrily along, carrying an armful of that overly ripe fruit.

If I wasn't mistaken, *that* was a *drunken* monkey.

CHAPTER 27

The macaque scratched his crotch, and in doing so, dropped his armful of fruit.

He retrieved the fruit and stuffed half the rotten apples and mushy apricots into his cheek pouches. Juice and *things* dribbled and wriggled down his chin.

Scratch "cute." This little guy was disgusting.

He wandered in a circle, trying to figure out which way he'd been headed... then shrugged, and wobbled off the way he'd come.

Did I follow this simian? Was he part of the "Drunken Monkey" quest? Had to be.

The real question was: Did I leave my guard post to do it?

The most sensible option was to get Elmac and Morgana and *then* follow the monkey. They were, however, in the middle of... I didn't want to think *what* they were in the middle of, but I was sure they were in the middle of *something*, and whatever it was, my interruption would be cruel and unusual punishment for everyone involved. So in this case, "most sensible" didn't seem like the "best" option.

On the other hand, running off on my own broke the one rule in every horror movie that should never be broken: Do *not* go by yourself to investigate the strange noise in the haunted basement, attic, cabin by the lake, or woods.

And it could be that *this* drunken monkey was simply *a* drunken monkey.

I really missed the popup quest alerts with their convenient clues confirming one was on the right track. Outside the Game boundary, though, I was out of luck.

He sure didn't look like a kung fu master. The only thing he might be able to teach me was a decided lack of manners.

The monkey trudged up a hill away from our camp.

My mystical headband did not confer X-ray vision, so once on the other side, I'd lose him.

A compromise then: I'd go to the hilltop and get a general idea where he was headed—back toward the grasslands, along the stream one way or the other, or into the forest. This would at least give us a head start in the morning finding his trail.

From that hilltop vantage, I'd also be able to see or hear any trouble in our camp. I'd be able to sprint back in twenty seconds flat—less if I used *Perfect Motion*.

I leapt up and ran atop the stalks of grass as if I were a gentle breeze. Nice. Thank you, *Wire Work*.

At the top of the hill, I halted, hunkered down, and hid.

The monkey meandered toward the stream. So did another creature, cutting silently through the grass on an intercept course. If not for my headband, I would've missed the wolf because its silver and black stripes were perfect camouflage in the moonlight.

Its body heat, though, was a dead giveaway in the infrared spectrum.

The wolf charged at the monkey as fast as a crossbow bolt.

I was too far away to do anything. Sorry, little guy.

The wolf opened its jaws to snap up a well-marinated dinner, but the monkey stumbled.

And the wolf bit the dirt.

It snuffled and sputtered and shook its head.

That was the luckiest monkey ever... or had he lost his balance *on purpose?*

The wolf spun, snarled, and pounced.

There was no way it could miss.

The monkey, seemingly oblivious to the danger and still recovering from his stumble, pinwheeled his arms—flung his fruit, and the stuff nailed the wolf square in its snout.

The projectiles spattered across the wolf's eyes and went up its nostrils. It squeaked—sneezed, once, twice, thrice, and tried to paw bits of the nasty substance out of its nose.

The macaque howled with laughter and threw more fruit at the beast.

The wolf ran off.

The monkey kept laughing and fell over. After a few seconds, he got up and gathered his tossed fruit (most of it dripping with wolf snot). He cocked his head, stared at it, looked around, then sampled some. He nodded and shoved as much as he could into his mouth. Then, plodding along a zig-zag path toward the stream, he crossed and disappeared into the woods beyond.

The macaque had moves.

But was it martial arts or just a smart monkey and improvised weapons?

Yeah, it had all *looked* accidental, but his aim had been dead on. Kung fu moves or not, I no longer had any doubt the monkey *was* connected to our quest.

I was tempted to follow him farther but decided to stick to my plan. I'd spent my allotment of stupid today dueling Grimhalt.

With a hearty pat on the back for making a wise choice, I went back to camp.

All was well. The heat stone glowed merrily. The half dozen buffalo had peacefully settled in the grass. And there were no signs of carnage in the two minutes I'd abandoned my post.

I sat on my bedroll to meditate, or failing that, sort through everything that had happened in the last few days.

This was nice. Cool night air. The chirp of crickets. The unadrenalized steady beat of my heart.

I could see why some players might slow down, perhaps buy a tavern with some stolen dragon hoard, and spend their days and nights sipping a few ales, listening and telling tall tales to their patrons. I bet the other clans would be more than happy to leave such a "retired" player alone since it could only benefit them.

I snapped out of my fantasy.

It was too quiet. Apart from the subtle sounds of nature, I didn't hear what I'd thought I'd be hearing.

Look, I'm not a pervert or anything, but I did have *elven* ears. I'd expected to be actively ignoring, um, *sounds* coming from Elmac's tent yonder. Not to put too fine a point on the matter, but it'd only been ten minutes.

I wasn't even picking up hushed pillow talk.

Or Elmac snoring.

Of course, maybe they hadn't even started. I suspected Elmac was a hopeless romantic and a star-lit walk might be more his speed.

...away from camp?

...without telling the person on guard about it?

That didn't sound right either.

I got up and crept toward the tent. As I did so, I seriously considered picking up thief as my third character class for the stealth skill alone. Morgana would murder me if she found me lurking nearby.

There were no heat sources within the tent.

I jogged over.

The flap was open. Elmac's and Morgana's boots were inside... as were a bunch of slimy apricot pits that had been scraped clean.

Had they actually eaten...? No way.

I did a quick search of the area. No signs of a battle.

There were, however, two sets of bare footprints in the dewy grass heading toward the stream.

I relaxed. See? Just an innocent barefoot stroll.

I wandered over to the buffalo to check on them. I wasn't surprised that two were awake and tracked me as I approached.

The one I'd ridden today grunted a soft greeting. I scratched her head.

It *was* a bit surprising, though, that a bunch of that fruit lay nearby in the grass. Untouched. I'd have thought our beast friends would have snuffled it all up—half fermented and rotten or not.

On a weird impulse, I picked up a flabby fragment of apple and sniffed.

Yow—it reeked of that too-sweet, rubbing alcohol, decaying scent. Definitely *not* the subtle hundred-and-eleven-year-old whiskey I'd had the pleasure of sampling tonight.

...And yet, for some reason, I had an overwhelming urge to taste it.

What *was* I thinking?

I tossed it, but then caught myself bringing my juice-covered fingers to my mouth.

Alarm bells clanged.

I didn't need a quest alert or magically boosted super senses to know that something was definitely off with this fruit—other than it being "off."

I could only think of two reasons for those pits to be in Elmac's tent. Either a bunch of plastered apes had come, kidnapped my friends, and left their trash behind, or Elmac and Morgana had gorged themselves on the stuff and wandered off on their own.

The two sets of footprints seemed to imply the latter, disgusting explanation.

Or could it have been assassins? Those pits and tracks planted by them? Seemed unlikely—but I was not making any more assumptions tonight.

I double-timed it down to the stream.

Morgana and Elmac's trail was easy to follow through the grass.

The two of them weren't anywhere in sight, so I checked the opposite bank and discovered their muddy footprints stumbling deeper into the woods.

The same direction I'd seen the monkey go.

Ten yards into the trees, the ground dried and I lost their trail.

I considered calling out to them, but I was in unfamiliar territory and didn't know if hostiles were near.

Ah, wait. I was an idiot.

I opened my interface and tabbed to the Message Center—only to find the keyboard, fields, and buttons grayed out.

Of course, because we were beyond the Game boundary, there was no instant messaging.

What about the SKILLS & ABILITIES interface? If that still functioned, I was pretty sure I could find my friends.

I opened it, and *yes*! The buttons gleamed and every text field was crystal clear.

I flicked down the listings and found what I needed.

Track: Find tracks and other signs to follow an animal or person. May learn direction traveled, number of creatures, time passed, the physical state of the quarry, and other information. The skill is enhanced by user's PERCEPTION and INTELLECT. Higher skill levels allow the tracker to follow trails in increasingly difficult terrain as well as quarry with exotic abilities.

NOTE: A skilled tracker may attempt to *conceal* their tracks. At skill levels of ten or more, a tracker may counter a target's STEALTH abilities.

This seemed like a handy skill to have, especially with assassins looking for us.

The ten points needed to counter stealth abilities, though... that was about a third of the non-combat skill points I had banked. Was it worth it?

I'd take it one step at a time. If Morgana wasn't actively trying to conceal her tracks, three points ought to do the trick. If that didn't work, I'd consider spending more.

I assigned the points and new memories imprinted upon my brain. My older gypsy elf brother, Adam, taught me how to hunt deer... which started with first learning how to follow them. I never had the guts to actually kill a deer, but I had made a game of shadowing them.

And then I remembered Adam being slaughtered with the rest of my family.

It wasn't the same ice-pick-slammed-into-my-forehead feeling I'd had before, but it felt, if anything, worse. Without the immediate and overwhelming pain to distract me, I had time to grieve all over again for the deaths of my fictional loved ones.

I was beginning to resent the Game's backstory fill-in-the-blank intrusion into my... my self.

Compartmentalize, Marine. Focus.

Morgana and Elmac's footprints and other signs of their passage *popped* in stark relief—there, a twig broke—here, a patch of moss shifted—and the edge of a toe print.

It was all so obvious now.

I made out other recent trails as well: monkeys, some large, some small, crossing this way and that, back and forth—all with a swaggering stagger. Dozens of simians had come and gone over the last few days. Fruit seeds and pits and parts had been strewn about the forest floor. What a bunch of litterbugs.

I moved along, taking care to look and listen for danger.

The trails all converged and headed into the hills.

I crept along.

The trees thinned and I started, finding myself face to face with a giant monkey. Only the head, though... that had been carved into a granite outcropping like a statue from Angkor Wat.

I steadied my racing heart.

The monkey's mouth was frozen open in a teeth-baring grimace, and right down its gullet, curved a paved tunnel.

CHAPTER 28

A dungeon.

Well, not exactly a "dungeon" dungeon, but "dungeon" in the general gaming sense of the word, i.e. a scenario that occurs usually, but not always, underground.

Besides actual torture chambers and medieval prisons, there was the good-old bandit's secret hideout cave; the lich's crypt filled with deadly traps and priceless treasures; or what I suspected this might be, a long-forgotten and submerged temple that needed the evil scrubbed out of it.

Unless you were a noob, you went into dungeons armed with three things: background information so you knew what you were up against; a plan to act on said information; and a team who could watch out for each other, because once you entered there was a good chance you weren't leaving until you fulfilled your objective.

My background information?

My quest log was one of the Game systems offline. Uh... so let's see. I was looking for an old barbarian to teach me secret martial art techniques, and from the quest's title, I knew there might be drinking and monkeys involved. Sketchy data at best.

My plan? Seat of the pants.

My team? That'd be me.

I considered the stone monkey face: a crazed chimpanzee posed in an aggression display that subtly communicated: "Intruders welcome—*for dinner.*" Farther down its throat, torchlight flickered. And yes, I looked, no huge gemstones in the statue's eye sockets.

I checked my ninja chain, subcutaneous demon bone knuckles, and tightened the laces of my troll-skin boots... but this was just procrastination.

I was scared.

The last time I'd gone it alone, I'd faced my brother and his demonic army. I'd lived to tell the tale but still felt the scars on my soul from embracing ultimate evil, aka the *Ebon Hands of Soul Death*.

More than any danger *I* might face, however, I was afraid I'd let Elmac and Morgana down. I had a growing suspicion that whatever had stopped the Far Field tribes from coming to Thera wasn't just the Chaos Knight guarding the gate.

And whatever it was, it might be happening to my friends.

Okay, when all else failed, fall back on your training.

I couldn't figure out a grand strategy, because I didn't know my enemy, their numbers, strengths, or goals. But I *could* break the situation into bite-sized chunks and come up with a few tactical options and operational rules.

Right. Start with the easy stuff.

RULE ONE: Do *not* eat the fruit.

Since I'd come to Thera, I'd developed a habit of drinking and eating just about anything stuck under my nose. Since the fruit here seemed to be drugged and/or ensorcelled, I better stick to the rations in my inventory.

I suspected (and hoped) that the secret martial art techniques I was here to learn were along the lines of drunken boxing. If you're not familiar with the style, I suggest my favorite movie covering these techniques, the 1994 Jackie Chan masterpiece *The Legend of Drunken Master*, wherein he did all his own stunts (I bow in respect to you, Mr. Chan).

Learning those techniques *would* involve drinking. Lots of it.

That would come later, though, so I had to play it safe, because of my next rule.

RULE TWO: My *only* priority was retrieving Elmac and Morgana.

Until I knew they were safe, nothing else mattered.

Last and most important, RULE THREE: Do not get caught or killed.

A given, but worth repeating.

I had to assume Elmac and Morgana were out of commission... imprisoned, unconscious, or perhaps already dead. No—they were *not* dead. I couldn't, wouldn't, go there. For all I knew, they'd become pals with that little macaque and were having one big party.

The point was that I had no backup. If I failed, that might be it for us all.

I steadied myself.

Three operational rules. I could handle that.

My tactical priorities were similarly simple: "be cautious, cunning, and stealthy."

I took a deep breath and entered the tunnel.

Five steps in, the stone walls became mud-brick and the floor was covered with irregular slate tiles. I halted, noting that only some tiles were worn... as if the monkeys had specifically avoided the others.

Trapped? Sure, weren't all dungeons?

I spotted a sliver of wood on the ground. It was tipped with a sticky substance.

There might be pressure plates here that triggered spring-loaded darts.

I picked the splinter up, careful not to touch the tip, and sniffed, detecting the faint scents of blood and apricot brandy.

Please refer to RULE ONE (do not eat the fruit).

I decided against the torturous staggered path made by drunken simians. Instead, I bounded up one wall—leapt to the other—and back, parkouring my way down the passage.

I ended this feat, landing on a well-scuffed tile in a four-way intersection.

I listened. Nothing but the beating of my own heart.

Cautious, cunning, stealthy. Check, check, and check.

So far, so good.

The passage to my left was scaled for creatures the size of that lion-tailed macaque. Straight ahead stairs were built for legs slightly larger than mine and they descended into the dark. They were also covered in dust. The tunnel to my right, however, had plenty of tracks, and ah, there—wide dwarven-sized scuffs and Morgana's tiny footprints.

Something seemed different about my friends' tracks. I squinted, but couldn't quite figure out what (even though I could see them perfectly with Azramath's headband).

Maybe it was a trick of the flickering torchlight.

I heard snoring from the end of this passage.

I once more bounded off the walls down that corridor, making no more noise than a shadow.

The passage led to a vaulted chamber. At the far end, sitting Buddha-like was a fifty-foot tall orangutan statue, the granite darkened with wine stains. His cheek flaps were so fat and prominent they nearly covered his eyes. On his face was a ridiculous crooked grin, parted to receive a raised bathtub-sized sipping saucer.

Before this idol were what could only be described as "self" sacrifices: passed out in sprawling poses were dozens of lemurs, chimpanzees, and orangutans. From the scattered cups, broken bottles, spilled wine, and a few splotches of vomit... it looked like quite a shindig had raged.

No Elmac or Morgana, though.

Across the room, a shaft of moonlight filtered through an open iron door.

Okay, short "dungeon," but fine by me.

Unless I had to explore those other two passages...

Getting swarmed in a tunnel by dozens of tipsy, but I assumed nimble, monkeys was not a combat situation I wanted to try, though.

So I'd explore outside a bit first.

I started toward the door but paused because I saw the chubby orangutan statue *did* indeed have gemstones for eyes: basketball-sized purple-red orbs. Garnets? Rubies maybe?

But then I remembered RULE TWO (my only priority was retrieving Elmac and Morgana).

I turned my back on temptation and kept laser-focused on finding my friends, gingerly stepped between the snoring, farting, tossing and turning monkeys—and then slipped through the open door unnoticed.

Odd. This door had thick bars on *both* sides. Why would you want to be able to secure it either way?

Didn't matter. I had one job, and puzzling out architectural details wasn't it.

Outside was a wide valley nestled among steep erosion-cut hills similar to China's scenic river gorges. Neat rows of fruit trees stretched as far as I could see. The moon's soft glow shadowed the trees and made them look like skeletal hands. There were ladders propped along the trunks and on the ground lay half-filled baskets. It was apparently harvest time.

One of these tree shadows, however, took a step toward me.

Ah, not a tree.

A silverback gorilla, nine feet tall and close to nine feet wide at his shoulders, paused mid-sip with a bottle at his lips. His glassy eyes narrowed at me.

Me being cautious, cunning, and stealthy? Yeah, not so much anymore.

He charged using fists and feet, snorting like a locomotive—and was on me before his bottle hit the ground.

I fired off my *Perfect Motion* buff.

The ape made a grab for my throat with impressively long and well-muscled arms.

I ducked, slid through his legs, rolled to my feet, and punched him in the back.

A good solid hit. The demon bone knuckles added extra mass and a tingling of magic that gave my right-handed strike greater impact.

I'd nailed him so hard, the gorilla stumbled, fell—but managed to tumble back to his feet.

He rubbed his spine and snarled, "Ow!"

I was no biologist like Morgana, but I was fairly sure gorillas didn't talk. Also, when I'd been up close, I'd seen fine gold wires woven into the fur on his chin—just like Karkanal's men had worn in their beards.

My suspicions of what had caused the Far Field tribes to stop coming to Thera and the odd fruit here clicked together.

If I was right, this gorilla might not be *entirely* a gorilla. I might be able to reason with him.

"Hey, big guy. I'm Hek—"

He pounded the earth and charged again. This time it didn't look like he'd overshoot.

I slapped aside one of his meaty limbs, then ducked a massive fist that *whooshed* over my head.

This ape had power and good technique. He'd dish out some serious pain if he connected. I had to finish him before he got ahold of me.

I stepped closer and let loose a sequence of chain punches—to his temple—nose—chin—throat—blocked one of his punches—then planted a knee in his gut.

That should have taken the wind out of his sails.

But he only *roared* in outrage—right into my face.

The overwhelming reek of digesting banana and fermented peaches made my eyes water. It took me a second to blink away tears and regain my senses—time enough, though, for him to grab me and draw me to his chest.

And squeeze.

My *Spirit Armor* held, for a heartbeat or two, as I struggled and kicked and did my best to wriggle free.

His muscles were unbreakable iron bands, though, tightening with every breath I took.

My eyes bulged. Bones popped.

Damn.

I entered the aether and stopped my subjective time.

If I could have sighed in my astral form, I would have.

All my strikes *had* connected. And hard. But it had been like slugging a heavy punching bag filled with lead shot.

This guy might be able to take that kind of punishment all night.

In martial arts movies, drunken boxers were usually so intoxicated and numbed, they felt no pain. You practically had to drop a mountain on one to bring them down... and none of those boxers had been drunken *gorillas*.

This could actually be a problem.

So far I'd used non-lethal strikes on this ape, because if it was as I thought, and he was one of the Far Field barbarians transformed—I couldn't kill him. He could be Karkanal's son for all I knew. Besides, murdering the natives wasn't likely to make them share their secret martial art techniques.

But... back to RULE TWO. Elmac and Morgana came first.

Sorry, big guy. One way or another, you were going down.

So, what did I have at my disposal here?

There was the usual weave of golden spatial lines, a few threads of blazing crimson fire, more distant filaments of cold, one I hadn't seen before of smoking green... and ah, there, just beyond arm's length, a twisting sinew of cracking, sparking lightning, hazy with ozone, and the buzz of high voltage. That looked useful.

I reached for it and felt the magic of *Blackwell's Band* swell and stretch my astral form. If Lordren had known how useful an item that tripled one's range in the aether was, he would have increased its price a hundredfold.

My elongated hand caught the ley line. I winced from the initial shock, drew it to me, and wrapped it around my body.

When I'd used this trick on Grimhalt, the stun effect hadn't lasted long. That time, however, the power arced from my fist to his metal armor before we even touched. This time, I had more body contact than on my last date five years ago. Sad but true.

All I needed was the ape to let go—just for a second. I'd be ready to move fast.

I phased back into normal space and time.

A hundred blinding arcs strobed. Thunder rolled outward in peals.

The gorilla convulsed and dropped me.

I backflipped away before he fell on me, whistled, and my semi-sentient ninja chain jumped to my hand. I whirled the bladed end and whipped it around my neck once to increase its velocity.

The gorilla shook off the taser stun and got up. He stared at my weapon as it painted the air with smears of moonlit razor.

We circled each other.

I wasn't going to wear this guy out. A knockout was equally unlikely. And at all costs, I couldn't let him close on me again.

There were other ways, however, to win a fight.

"You're not afraid of a few little cuts, are you?" I said.

He squinted at the mesmerizing pattern of *Shé liàn*'s blade and went slightly cross-eyed.

"Or are you the type that faints at the sight of blood?"

He snorted.

Oh yeah. He'd charge me.

And why not? He knew he could take whatever I dished out.

Just as predicted—he sprinted, arms outstretched to grab and crush whatever piece of elf he might catch.

I whipped the weighted end of *Shé liàn* at him and nailed him in the gut.

He instinctively grabbed the chain.

Like I hoped he would.

I mentally whispered to *Shé liàn*, *Wrap him up like a birthday gift,* and then sidearmed the bladed end.

Shé liàn obliged—spiraled around and around—snaking about his knees—his midsection—and his elbows. Then it tightened.

The gorilla toppled like a giant sequoia. Face first.

He thrashed and flexed against the binding chain.

The links pinged and groaned... but held.

I jumped onto his back and squatted there.

Loosen up just a bit, I suggested.

The ninja chain did so, rendering the ape's great strength less effective.

I let him struggle for a few seconds.

"So, care to talk this over?" I asked him. "Or should I let you eat dirt all evening?"

The gorilla gave one last titanic flex and released a huge sigh.

"M'hhhurrph?" the gorilla inquired.

"Oh sorry." I rolled him over.

He spat out a chunk of sod. "You," he replied in a rumbling growl, "are walking dead meat."

I sat on his chest. "You'll have to explain how *I'm* walking dead meat. From where I'm sitting, banana breath, *you're* the one in a tight spot."

He tried a chuckle, but *Shé liàn* gave him a vindictive squeeze on my behalf.

Good girl.

"This is the Valley of the great drunken god, Dà Xiào Hóu and his many, many disciples."

"Yeah, I saw them. Passed out in the temple. Not that impressed."

"The priests?" he scoffed. "Useless. I meant the *rest of us*."

Rest of them?

I looked up.

From every tree in the orchard, monkeys dropped from the branches like it was raining simians. There were spider monkeys, macaques, baboons, chimpanzees, howlers, lemurs, and a few more gorillas. They lit torches. More of their kind stirred from the dew-drenched grass. They grabbed tools and makeshift clubs.

And there weren't a dozen.

Not even a *mere* hundred.

It was like that scene in the 1932 flick, *Island of Lost Souls*. The entire half-human, half-animal population of the island had Dr. Moreau cornered in his House of Pain, intent on dissecting him alive.

And likewise... what looked like a *thousand* drunken monkeys surrounded me with murder gleaming in their eyes.

CHAPTER 29

They swept over me like a hurricane took a drowning man.

And I choked.

It wasn't fear... not *exactly*.

It was the shock and awe of seeing *so many* creatures intent on ripping me to pieces—each hairy face contorted with an exaggerated outrage that only the truly drunk can manage. Just imagine all those long arms reaching for *you*, those gnashing teeth, and the screams—my God, they sounded like a stadium full of inebriated soccer fans protesting a referee's call.

I came to my senses and punched and punted the first half dozen of the smaller ones—but there were too many, too fast. A pack of them got on my back and started gnawing at my *Spirit Armor*. Little punks.

Chimpanzees dove for my legs and I went down. More grabbed my arms. They knew how to apply a proper armbar, too.

An orangutan jumped on my face, and headband of mystical sight or not, I couldn't see anything but... well, you figure it out.

And finally, a gorilla bellyflopped on me. At least that's what I assumed happened because of the sudden weight crushing me (and from the squishing squeals of lemurs and macaques caught under him as well).

Very effective squadron tactics.

I wasn't able to draw a breath.

Enough was enough. I executed a tactical retreat to the aether.

I'd just grab as much electrical energy as I could and—

Hang on. The ley line I'd used a minute ago was glass clear. Not a spark of energy pulsed inside. Had I drained it? I didn't even know that was possible. How long did these things take to recharge?

My questions had to wait.

That boiling green ley line I'd seen before *was* within reach. Just looking at it made my fingers itch and burn, filled my nostrils with the smells of sulfur, and my esophagus clenched as I suddenly recalled the time I'd mixed peppermint schnapps and Southern Comfort and hurled the resultant mixture.

This was the essence of elemental acid.

Not much choice, so I snagged it, and

—phased back.

There came the sizzling sound of water on a hot griddle and the stench of burning hair.

The gorilla jumped off me and rolled in the dirt. The mob of monkeys leapt off as well, all screeching and scraping their blistering parts over the grass.

I flipped onto my feet.

Thankfully, as before, I was immune to the forces I channeled from the aether. Also good, the ten points of damage I'd done had been distributed among many, so the little guys were scared, some might be scarred, but they'd live.

The gorilla rounded on me, his left shoulder smoking, and he snarled.

I'd have to deal with him... along with the other nine hundred monkeys who hadn't yet gotten their turn. They looked, if possible, even *more* pissed.

Time to follow RULE THREE (do not get caught or killed) and use the ancient martial art technique known as *A Hundred Footsteps*... executed as rapidly as possible.

I reached out to my ninja chain.

It unwound from the other, bound gorilla and leapt to my hand.

I jumped for the nearest tree and landed in its topmost branches.

Monkeys scampered up after me, all grasping hands and howls of fury.

I vaulted to another treetop.

Flying through the air, I took a look around.

Beyond this orchard, the valley was surrounded by cliff walls. Next to a mighty waterfall, the adjacent stone had been carved into a three-hundred-foot column comprised of titan monkeys of various species. These statue simians stood on their hands, their heads, or were in other improbable gymnastic poses. A few drank from the adjacent waterfall (actually diverting water down their throats), and lower in the stack other monkeys then *discharged* that water in graceful arcs.

Mist from the waterfall made a moon-lit rainbow, and beneath a silver ribbon fed a mirror-placid lake. On the shore sat a mill with paddlewheel and grain silos.

Still farther I spied stairs chiseled into a cliff at an absurdly precarious angle. They led up to a pagoda with sweeping beams and white-tiled roofs. Past that—I got just a glimpse at the apex of my trajectory—a trail that snaked higher into the hills.

That was my way out of here.

I fell toward my target tree.

Four orangutans with double sticks waited for me in its branches.

I slung the weighted end of my ninja chain at one, knocked him off, and landed in the spot he'd so graciously vacated. I dodged a few of the remaining monkeys' strikes, kicked two of the creatures off, but the last one jabbed me hard enough to penetrate my *Spirit Armor* and cracked a rib. Someone had definitely trained these guys.

I glanced at my health and mana bars.

Health was at 98/180, due to various scratches and bites and being crushed nearly flat. Spiritual mana at 70/90. And reflexive mana down to 73/120 from the blast of lightning and acid and lingering in the aether.

Not bad, but at this rate, I wouldn't last long in a prolonged fight.

Smaller, faster monkeys started to swarm up the tree.

I kicked my last orangutan sparring partner in the face—he fell back, grasping at air—and I used the borrowed momentum to launch myself to the next tree.

Rather than land there, however, I threw my ninja chain ahead, snagged a branch—yanked myself forward, and aimed at a large apple tree at the orchard's edge... a hundred feet away.

This did indeed bend the laws of physics, but as promised, my upgraded *Wire Work* ability let me fudge the boundaries of Newtonian mechanics with *"maneuvers limited by your imagination and only sometimes the force of gravity."*

I glanced over my shoulder.

I *had* put a bit of distance between myself and the ape mob.

Who was I kidding, though? They had to see I was heading for the stairs. I just had to get there faster than them.

I alighted in the tree. A perfect landing. The branch under my feet, however, snapped—as did every other limb and twig I tried to grab as I tumbled to the earth.

Only slightly dazed (my pride took most of the damage), I got up.

My pursuers had closed my lead by half.

I ran out of the orchard, ignored the path, and cut through a garden of Japanese maples, arched moon bridges, and gracefully arranged bonsais—leapt from stone to stone over koi ponds—and dashed *over* a lake inlet covered with lily pads and lotuses, my feet leaving only feather-touch ripples in my wake.

Dozens of pursuers attempted to follow me over the water, only to splash through the surface, squawking their confusion and displeasure after me.

I next plodded through a Zen rock garden, losing time and ground over a large patch of soft groomed gravel.

Finally at the stairs, I paused to take in what I was up against. I estimated the cliff face was between sixty and seventy degrees, and the stairs mirrored that angle—so steep that one stumble and I'd bounce down the entire half-mile length.

The stairs were narrow. Two people (maybe) could squeeze by one another.

Past a low wall on either side of the steps, the adjacent cliff was covered in slimy moss.

One more thing: stacked next to the base of these stairs were hundreds of wine barrels. What poor monkey got saddled with the job of carrying them up and down?

Projectiles splattered the cliff over my head.

Oh, shit.

I spun around.

My monkey friends had closed to thrown-weapons range.

I bounded up the stairs.

I had to focus on climbing, for even with my 5 STRENGTH and 17 BODY, this was a grind, and soon my legs burned with fatigue and I sucked wind.

After a minute, though, my pursuers' war screams and calls for my entrails weakened, and ceased... replaced by exasperated, exhausted cries.

These monkeys, while decent fighters, were apparently in *lousy* shape. They faltered a quarter way up the steps, panting, slumped upon one another and wheezing. The result, no doubt, from too much fruit and liquor and not enough exercise.

With a sizable lead and halfway up, I might just get out of here in one piece. Then I'd circle back and—

A shadow appeared at the top of the stairs.

I squinted and recognized the shape: hunched, quadruped, an unmistakable high-domed, no-neck head.

Gorilla.

He charged down the stairs. His long arms gripped the low walls on either side so he wouldn't go ass over teakettle on the precarious grade.

Did I face one five-hundred-pound gorilla, or be nibbled to pieces by fifty ten-pound lemurs?

It was no contest. I ran up to meet him, pumping my shaky legs to build speed.

The gorilla thundered toward me, black eyes glinting with the anticipation of extreme violence. He took his hands off the side walls to grab for me.

The instant before he could—I stopped, planted, braced, grabbed his wrists, and yanked.

I rolled onto my back, kicked him in the stomach, and judo flipped him.

His momentum did the heavy lifting and he sailed over me.

I slapped with one arm and used *Shé liàn*'s blade to catch the edge of a stair to keep from following him.

The ape soared fifty feet—all that muscle flailing uselessly—hit, bounced, and tumbled wild and uncontrolled—crashed into the exhausted mass of monkeys and steamrolled them. It was a wonderful landslide of simian flesh.

I turned to resume my dash.

Now, however, *two* gorillas stood at the top... and rolled wine barrels down the stairs.

Uh-oh.

The barrels together filled the width of the stairway, rolling, sloshing, and picking up speed.

I jumped over one, and ducked under the other as it went over my head.

From the thick rumbling sound, I knew they were full.

Getting hit would flatten me and certainly knock me down the steps... or off them.

I tried to resume my ascent, but two *more* barrels were incoming. These hadn't been rolled. They'd been *tossed* and arced through the air toward me.

My dad (the human one) had played a primitive video game when I was a kid. He'd showed it to me and my brother on an antique console. A little plumber in red overalls had to jump over barrels rolling down a series of catwalks sent by, you guessed it, a psychotic gorilla. When I'd tried the game, my plumber got squished over and over.

The airborne barrels overshot my position by thirty feet.

They impacted, shattered to kindling, and the contents washed down the stairs, momentarily transforming steps into rapids.

The downstream monkeys ran back or hugged the sides to avoid the tumbling debris and flash flood. Some of the smaller ones were swept away.

Looking farther back, I saw the monkeys of the valley all clamoring at the base of the stairs, pushing and shoving their fellows—all trying to continue the chase, but getting bottlenecked.

This mob stretched back to the gravel gardens, hundreds and hundreds of them all brandishing sticks and torches and shrieking for my head.

It was like a video I'd seen online of army ants swarming through the Amazon. They killed and disassembled any creature caught in their path—even cattle.

This army, however, only wanted to take apart one thing tonight.

Splintering crashes startled me—as three barrels stuck ten feet ahead.

They broke and dark amber brandy washed about my ankles, nearly cresting my troll-skin boots.

Those gorillas were dialing in their aim.

I had to—

Whoa. The smell of this stuff... a smooth blend of apricot, apple cider, mango, banana, notes of caramel and mellowed oak, and a hint of bubblegum? Something else too: an exotic scent, thick, mysterious, enticing. Mmm.

I wobbled.

Then I blinked and snapped out of the contact high.

Move. Go—go—GO!

I followed the screaming drill sergeant voice ground into my subconscious for just such occasions (incoming fire with no cover was the same stupid tactical position in *any* reality).

I sloshed through the brandy to get upwind.

Even as I cleared the liquor, though, I had an irresistible urge to sample it. Just a sip wouldn't hurt, right?

I quashed that impulse.

One taste and I was sure there'd be one more disciple in the valley of the great drunken monkey god, Dà Xiào Hóu. Would I become a chimpanzee or orangutan, I wondered?

The apes at the top now hefted barrels in *each* hand and chucked them like Olympic shot putters.

Far below, the gathered monkey crowd had stopped trying to come up, and just watched and cheered.

The projectiles looked dead on target this time. I might be able to duck and dodge all four... but that would simply give those gorillas time to reload and try again.

I had to outthink these primitives. Morgana and Elmac were counting on me.

Okay. Engaging an army on open ground with incoming artillery fire? That wasn't going to end well.

If only my *Small Pass* ability had the range for a longer teleport—say, to the top of the stairs. Not particularly useful, though, at its present power level. If only I'd picked the illusion variant of *Small Pass*, I could make myself vanish like a rabbit into a stage magician's top hat.

I glanced at the barrels tumbling toward me—down at the legions of monkeys.

Three seconds to figure this out.

...Vanish, huh?

Yeah, I think I could pull that off.

CHAPTER 30

Now, pay close attention. There's nothing up my sleeve. I'm going to explain this technique but once, and if I'm *very* lucky actually show you... and survive.

Any stage magician worth his or her salt can make something vanish. A coin. A card. Sometimes, even themselves.

When I'd picked Mage of the Line as a second class, I got a freebie skill, Sleight of Hand. My father had taught me bits of prestidigitation so I could help with his performances.

The steps to making a thing vanish are as follows. First, the magician requires a means to conceal the object to be vanished—a closed hand, box, velvet curtain, or top hat. Next, some showmanship is applied to distract the audience while the mechanics of the trick occur. Such distractions are often a lovely assistant or a handful of flash powder. Finally, there must be a way to remove the object: a handy sleeve, hidden compartment or trapdoor for example.

I had all the ingredients right here.

One minor snag, though. For this evening's performance, the concealment, distraction, *and* the means to remove myself offstage all happened at the same time.

The positioning and timing had to be *perfect*.

My eyes locked onto the leading barrel among the four falling toward me.

I crouched and cocked my right fist.

...Waited one more heartbeat—and leapt, just a bit to one side of the projectile.

Then I hit the pause button.

Floating motionless in the aether, it dawned on me how much I was loving this class. So many practical applications in battle. I knew there'd be hell to pay for being a Mage of the Line later, but in the meantime, I'd use it to my advantage and enjoy doing so.

But back to the matter at hand.

I gave my impromptu vanishing act maybe a one-in-three chance of working, a two-in-three chance of... well, making me disappear permanently.

Okay, what did I have to work with here? My reflexive mana was at 72/120 and steadily bleeding away. Still, plenty in the tank to attempt what I had in mind.

There were a dozen ley lines within reach.

The filament of electrical power I'd tapped earlier, though, was still dark and inert. No more of their kind were within sight either. Had I drained the entire region of that type of energy? I'd moved more than a mile from where I'd used it, but "space" in the aether didn't necessarily translate one-to-one outside the odd dimension.

There was so much I didn't know about this magic.

67 mana and ticking...

My scientific curiosity was going to get me killed.

I squinted and found the essential ingredient for my plan: A crimson thread that smoldered like a vein of molten metal.

I wrapped it about my fist. I tasted hot copper in my throat, smelled burning marshmallows, and my hand prickled with tiny blisters.

That'd do.

And back to normal space-time I went.

My fist sparked then blazed with white-hot flames.

I continued along the arc of my original jump—twisted so my back was angled toward the cliff face (this was a crucial part of my act)—then slammed my fist into the barrel.

Three things happened at once.

First, the barrel disintegrated into matchsticks.

Second, my strike altered my trajectory, sending me on a line directly away from the barrel.

And third, a blast of elemental fire shot through pulverized oak and mingled with the brandy inside—ignited it with a tremendous *whooosh* and transformed it all into a brilliant boiling ball of blue flame.

Distraction *and* concealment *and* the removal of the object (yours truly) all in one maneuver.

I hoped the ghost of Balaster Saint was watching.

But now the *truly* dangerous part of this vanishing trick.

I knew the elemental fire I'd channeled wouldn't harm me. I was, however, at ground zero of a sizable detonation, and the expanding heat and pressure and wooden shrapnel from *that* did indeed shred and char my tender flesh.

Most of the red pixels in my indicator bar sparked and smoldered and went dark with little *hisses*. Two-thirds of my health just went up in smoke.

I resisted the instinct to ball up. Doing so would mean certain death.

I soared off the stairs—into empty space.

Wire Work or not, it was a fatal fall.

Meanwhile, the scarlet and sapphire flaming brandy cascaded down the stairs, just as the second barrel crash landed.

That barrel did *not* break.

It did, however, splash in the liquor and catch fire… as it rolled… and bounced… and picked up speed, which fanned the flames enveloping it hotter and brighter.

Barrels three and four landed a moment later and did the same.

It looked as if a portal to hell had opened and a giant fire serpent slithered forth, racing headlong down the stairs.

Every monkey crowding the base now stared at Armageddon boiling straight toward them.

No need to pay attention to the hairless ape flying through the darkness, my good audience. I assure you he's been blown to smithereens. You clearly saw it with your own eyes.

I twisted like a cat, turning my body.

And smacked into the cliff.

I clutched for any purchase.

Slid.

Scrambling, grabbing, then—

three fingers caught a minuscule ledge.

I jerked to a stop.

The mob of monkeys below scattered, running for their lives—as the first barrel, and the next, and then the last collided into the *hundreds* of barrels stacked at the bottom.

It was like the finale of Burning Man and the biggest dumpster fire of all time rolled into one spectacular display of fireworks.

I felt the wave of pressure and heat even up here.

Not bad, Hektor. Take a bow... uh, when you can.

The monkeys screamed as they retreated to the safety of the orchard. A few of the larger apes took out their fear and frustration by attacking the smaller guys along the way.

I clung to the ledge and started shaking.

I didn't dare move, unsure if the stone under my fingertips would give way.

My *Perfect Motion* and adrenaline had run their course, and the pain and exhaustion hit me in waves. I held on with all my strength. My fingers cramped.

I used a few *Spiritual Regenerations*. The magic dealt with the second- and third-degree burns but did nothing for the mental and physical fatigue.

And... I had a thousand-foot climb ahead of me.

I didn't have to be stupid about it, though.

I went into my game interface and dropped three skill points into this:

Climb: **The ability to traverse walls, cliffs et al. by means of hand- and footholds and/or with ropes and other equipment. At higher skill levels more difficult surfaces may be safely ascended—those with tiny holds, covered with ice or slime, or even across inverted or horizontal "ceiling-like" surfaces. With a skill greater than ten, you may impart one-third of your ability to party members you equip and coach. Total expertise depends on this skill and to a lesser degree, your STRENGTH, PERCEPTION, and INTELLECT stats.**

Great.

I quickly found another handhold, and there, a lovely crack for my left foot, and then one for the right. I arched my body out to apply tension and move my center of mass so it wasn't working against me.

Only then did I start breathing easier.

With my new expertise, enhanced sight, and *Shé liàn* doubling as climbing axe, I knew I could handle this ascent.

I still went slow and careful, though, checking and double checking each hold. I'd stretched my luck too far tonight.

I reached the top and pulled myself over the edge.

I lay there and savored the *flatness* of the granite.

That white pagoda I'd seen earlier was to my left. It was ten stories tall, and up close looked more fortress than temple with a thick stone base and shutters about the numerous windows. Blooming cherry trees were skillfully arranged about the entrance to look natural. It was a nice touch.

More important however, I spotted that path winding farther into the hills.

I'd be able to sneak out of here, rest, then figure out how to find Morgana and Elmac.

Only, there was one last thing to deal with.

A chimpanzee sat on a rock. His fur was golden but tipped silver with age. With a shaky hand he clutched a crooked walking stick, and in his other hand, he cradled half a coconut.

He toasted me, grinned, and took a long sip.

For some reason, the old guy's smile reminded me of Karkanal.

I doubted he was a serious threat... unless he raised an alarm. Well, one little tap on his chin and he'd go to sleep.

The old guy stood and staggered toward me. He was so sloshed all I'd have to do was push him over, if that is, he even got to me.

I stood.

The chimp was right in front of me.

I took a step back but somehow tripped over his walking stick.

I tumbled and was back on my feet.

And once more the guy was right in front of me, smiling his gummy grin, and taking another sip from his cup.

What the heck?

Sorry, senior, but you're between me and a clean getaway.

I kicked him hard enough to knock him silly.

And I *missed*?

He simply hadn't been there.

A furry foot planted in my groin—then he hit my stomach, chest, and chin with that half coconut.

I tried to block.

His strikes flowed around my arms like water. Each left my body stinging as if I'd been pricked by a hundred pins and needles.

I fired off *Perfect Motion*, and—

his gnarled fist introduced itself to my nose.

How strange...

the night was so bright...

full of streaking black comets.

A bit of awareness then bubbled up through my brain to the conscious level.

I was on my back, staring up at the stars while the world under me spun. I coughed blood from my nose and mouth.

A simian face appeared in the center of my tunneling vision.

"At last," the old chimpanzee murmured, "a worthy challenger. More or less."

The end of his cane blurred toward me.

And then I saw no more.

CHAPTER 31

I awoke, opened my eyes, but the light blazed so bright I had to squint my lids nearly shut.

Was Colonel Delacroix here? Turning monkeys into smoldering charcoal with her solar magic? That didn't make sense. Of all my stalwart companions, she sort of hated me.

Oh... it was coming back now. I'd taken this nap because that geriatric chimp had knocked me out.

That couldn't be right.

I sat up.

The motion made my head feel like it was being twisted into a balloon animal.

On the other hand, maybe what happened last night made *perfect* sense. In martial art movies, didn't the most frail village elder *always* turn out to be the kung fu master of masters? I should have known.

I used *Spiritual Regeneration* and it eased my discomfort. A bit.

At least my eyes focused.

I found myself on a pile of silk pillows in a room with screened windows (the source of the offending sunlight). Overhead was a mosaic of sky and cranes and clouds; the walls had scenes of jungle flora; the floor a picture of swirling waters, koi, and floating lotuses. Instead of tiles, though, these mosaics were made from coins: tarnished black ones, others mint green with verdigris, a few gold Krugerrands, buffalo nickels, ones with holes in their centers, triangular brass slugs—mementos perhaps from a hundred different worlds.

With my incredibly keen perception, I then noticed the two chimpanzees sitting on either side of me.

One made a soothing murmur and handed me a folded cloth.

I took it, nodded my thanks, and held it to my temple. It was cold and helped quiet the hammers performing Verdi's *Anvil Chorus* on my head.

The other chimpanzee poured a half coconut of wine and offered it to me.

"No thanks," I said.

Yeah, drug the guy who wasn't quite lucid. I'd been at that party before.

Something other than my concussion felt wrong, though.

Wait—I patted my waist and brow.

I went cold. It was what every player feared as much as death. Apart from my clothes, my gear was *gone*. Oh man, even my troll-skin boots?

Even...? I flexed my right hand and examined the back where there were now dozens of fine scars. They'd taken my demon bone knuckles too. At least they'd done me the courtesy of performing surgery and not *ripping* them out or amputating the hand.

But why? Last night every monkey in this valley had been screaming for my head.

I better start from square one.

Was I a captive? I gave that a ninety-nine percent chance of "oh hell, yes."

Apparently, however, I was a well-treated captive.

I'd return the favor and be similarly civilized while I puzzled the rest of this out; namely, *why* I was alive, *where* my stuff was, *what* happened to Elmac and Morgana, and *how* the three of us could escape.

I got to my feet, wobbled, but made it to an open window.

A breeze cooled my face. Beyond I saw the valley I'd run through, the waterfall, the lake, and orchards. It was gorgeous with greenery and flowers and sparkling water. Sixty feet down were those nightmarishly steep stairs.

I had to be in the pagoda.

On the curved beam architecture outside the window, six gorilla guards balanced and/or hung about and glared at me.

Of course: One could not be a captive without jailers.

I backed away.

A screen on the other side of the room slid aside and a chimpanzee with silver-fringed fur hobbled in. He shut it behind him, and bowed to me, leaning as he did so on a crooked walking stick.

It was the old guy who'd bested me like I'd been a novice.

I showed him respect and returned his bow (but didn't take my eyes off him).

He gestured to the pillows and then waved away the chimpanzee attendants.

"Sit. Please," he said.

It hadn't registered on me last night, but he had a British accent. Unlike Morgana's more colloquial dialect, he sounded as eloquent as Peter O' Toole in the 1962 Academy Award-winning *Lawrence of Arabia.*

I did as he suggested.

The monkey similarly sank to the floor on his heels.

"I am Master Cho."

"Hektor Saint-Savage," I said, doing my best to sound like a gracious guest.

"A pleasure to make your acquaintance." The chimpanzee set a hand over his heart. "Accept my apologies for taking advantage of you last evening. Hardly sporting of me, considering your wounds and state of exhaustion."

My face burned.

"I assume you came to our valley seeking our secret techniques?"

He said "seeking" like he meant "steal."

I'd give just about anything for a handy pop-up quest alert to confirm I was on the right track... or better yet, give me a clue what to do, like:

QUEST ALERT!
You have met Master Cho.
Present him with a legendary bottle of
liquor to become his friend.
Rewards: The freedom of your companions, the return
of your gear, and Master Cho will teach you as
many martial art techniques as you desire!

Wishful thinking. No such help since I was outside the bounds of the Game.

"I have come to *learn* your Drunken Monkey style," I admitted, "but I am also looking for my friends who might have accidentally wandered into this valley. And if possible, could I collect my belongings, which you have so thoughtfully stored for me?" I set my hands together in a prayer gesture and gave him another bow.

"Ah." He smoothed the long white whiskers on his chin.

The partition slid aside and a troupe of lemurs entered. They carried a small table, kettle, and cups, and set the afternoon tea service between us.

Master Cho poured. "Tea?" He offered me a ceramic cup so delicate it was translucent.

I accepted and inhaled the scent. Green tea.

He sipped and narrowed his eyes with satisfaction.

I brought the cup to my mouth, tilted it, but didn't let the contents touch my lips.

Master Cho shooed the lemurs away.

"It has been many years since such a skilled aspirant has come to challenge me." He gestured to my arm and the golden dragon tattoo that glistened in the sunlight. "From the Domicile of the Sleeping Dragon, no less. I am honored."

I tensed. "I am not here to challenge you, sir."

He drained his cup and set it down. "So you say. You want your belongings. And your friends. I understand. But this may not be so simple. You see, you made quite a show of defeating my top students. It is expected that you will now challenge the master of the temple." He hesitated, looking slightly embarrassed. "If we do not fight, my students may think me afraid and that I declined your challenge."

I felt the urge to jump up and punch my way out of here... which I sensibly put back into its box.

I wouldn't get one step closer to Cho before the gorillas outside swung in and pummeled me to paste. This was assuming, of course, Cho didn't flatten me first.

"I sense you are modest." The old ape stared into the distance. "What is the human expression? I have forgotten so many of them. Ah, yes... let us 'strike a bargain.'"

He had forgotten so many *human* expressions? Implying he'd *been* human? I didn't need any more convincing that the wine here made monkeys of men. Dwarves and elves for that matter too.

"Go ahead," I whispered, deadpan. "Strike away."

"If you prevail in the challenge, I shall gladly return your safely secured possessions and—" Cho snapped his fingers.

The partition slid aside and a gorilla entered. In one meaty hand he carried a bamboo cage that he set next to Master Cho. He then bowed to Cho and withdrew.

Two creatures cowered in the far corner of the cage, a young orangutan and one of those little lion-maned macaques.

The orangutan's hair was a bright orange and shot with gold. It was thick about his face... like a beard. And he had only one arm. The macaque was sleek and cute with needle-sharp claws. Its fur was black with tufts of blood red, the same colors a certain druid-thief trickster favored.

If not for years of training and meditation, I would have attempted a number of stupid things. I kept my cool, though, and managed to restrain my pulse from becoming a drumroll.

The two monkeys stared at me with something approximating recognition in their wild panicked eyes.

The orangutan then touched the side of his nose, the unmistakable gesture I had seen Elmac make so many times.

My friends, what have they done to you?

Monkey Elmac and Morgana dipped their paws into a tiny bowl and licked wine-stained fingers. Whatever dark magic was in that wine, it looked to be highly addictive as well. Could it even be reversed?

Cho snapped his fingers once more.

The gorilla outside returned and picked up the cage.

As he removed my friends from the room, Morgana raised a tiny imploring paw to me.

The gorilla left and slammed the partition shut behind him with a *bang*.

I took a slow, careful breath in, and just as slowly released it.

"You were saying, Master Cho? If I prevail...?"

A smile rippled over his thick lips. "If you prevail, you regain your possessions *and* friends, who I believe still have a fair chance at reverting to their prior, albeit lesser, forms."

I said nothing, knowing if I spoke any of the replies boiling in my brain, I'd make the situation worse.

He must have taken my silence for acceptance for he went on. "Good. We fight until one of us yields or is rendered unconscious. Nonlethal combat, naturally."

I had a flashback to my duel with that cheater, Grimhalt. Cho sounded like he was setting the terms of a PvP duel. Or was I just imagining that?

"Additionally, if you win, I shall gift you with scrolls instructive in the basic techniques of drunken boxing as a token of my respect. In fact" —he paused to feign surprise as if he had just thought of this— "please, you would do me a great honor if you examined some of those materials beforehand. You will find them illuminating. The library is just down the hall."

Why the heck would he give me a chance to evaluate his style's strengths and weakness *before* we fought?

"Thank you, Master Cho. Most generous terms. But, uh... if I lose?"

"Then you remain, as will your friends. I shall train you myself. I am sure you will be my best student."

As a monkey.

"It will be an incredible privilege," I lied, "to test my humble skills against yours, Master Cho."

He tilted his head.

"However... might I get my gear back *before* the challenge?"

"Oh, I have no wish to take advantage." He shook a hairy finger at me. "If you had your weapons, I would be obliged to use mine. I think bare fists will be to your benefit. Besides, my fellows have had enough of your summoning fire and lightning with your magical objects."

They thought those elemental effects had come from my gear? Why not? No one would have guessed I was a dual-classed Spirit Warrior/Mage of the Line. I might be able to use that.

"Still, it is hardly a fair match," I said.

"You are too modest," Master Cho replied. "And even if true, the game *you* play is hardly fair."

I froze.

Had that been an innocent coincidental expression?

Or could Cho know about *the* Game?

He wasn't a player. There was no placard over his head. The only thing floating over his liver-spotted scalp were gnats.

I stared into my cup of tea and focused on the surface reflection.

I had no name tag over my head. Come to think of it, I hadn't seen them over monkey Elmac or Morgana either.

We were obviously so far outside the Game they no longer displayed... so, Master Cho *could be* a player.

This made little sense, though. Why would a player be hanging out here, teaching kung fu to monkeys?

Cho made a show of struggling to his feet as if he had arthritis. "I shall leave you to your meditations then. Until tonight." He paused at the screen and gave a tiny bow. "And please, feel free to review the scrolls in my library."

I stood but didn't return the bow. There was only so much hypocrisy I could swallow.

"We fight at dusk." Master Cho left and slid the screen shut.

I'd meditate all right—meditate on just how screwed I was. Why had the Game Master given me *this* quest at first level? A test of my worthiness? Or had he simply wanted me out of the picture? It would have been a surefire way to get my first-level butt and the *Ebon Hands of Soul Death* outside the Game's boundary where no one would find them, or me, for a long, long time. If ever.

Hmm. Something was fishy here.

The fact was, however, I *was* on this quest and had only a few hours to find a way to beat Master Cho or escape with Elmac and Morgana. I had to stay focused on that.

Did I have any advantages?

A surprise attack with magic? The elemental effects and extra damage were nice, but it was unlikely to sufficiently tip the scales in my favor.

My Spirit Warrior skills and abilities? Well, Cho had identified me as from the Sleeping Dragon school, so it followed he'd be familiar with their techniques.

Ah, maybe I still had *some* gear.

I opened my inventory. Thankfully *that* system still worked this far from the Game's boundary.

There were the two vials of *Karl's Guaranteed De-toxinifier* I had bought to counter the Syndicate's poisoned weapons, the nub of the candle I had used to talk to the Game Master (that I was pretty sure wouldn't work outside the Game), the comped 1762 bottle of *Gautier Cognac de Âme* courtesy of Hiltmyer & Co., that half liter of Red Dragon Whiskey I hadn't had the chance to return to Elmac, a bunch of other miscellaneous non-magical gear... and last and least, the black-scaled *Ebon Hands of Soul Death*.

I could simply don the scaled gloves...

No. No. And *definitely* NO.

Wearing them would guarantee victory. It would also guarantee me killing every living thing in the valley, including my friends. They were an evil beyond evil, and I was keeping the wretched things only until I found the equivalent of Thera's Mount Doom to dropkick them into.

Worrisome, though, that I'd considered it even for a second.

I was about to shut the window but spied one last item: the penny that had been my father's final gift.

My heart swelled with sorrow and nostalgia. How far I had wandered from the painted wagons that had once been home. I'd have given anything to be back there now.

I sighed and waved the window away.

None of that stuff would help in a straight-up fight against Master Cho, or a more improbable escape while under the watchful eyes of his gorillas.

That exhausted *my* options.

What about my surroundings? Some advantageous terrain? A handy magical spear on display? Heck, I'd settle for a local chapter of Alcoholics Anonymous.

Or... those scrolls in Cho's library?

What if, as unlikely as this sounded, that while Master Cho had to fight me to maintain his position of authority, he might also be taking pity on me and throwing me a lifeline of sorts?

I didn't really buy that—but okay, I'd play along.

I slid open the partition.

A short hall led to another silk screen. Four gorillas loitered in the corridor.

They didn't immediately attack, so I took a chance and quickly averted my gaze (which the apes might have taken as a challenge) and took a few slow steps forward.

With mutterings and sub-vocal growls, they shuffled out of my way.

I crossed the hall, opened the partition, entered, then shut the screen.

This room had a low table in the center and floor-to-ceiling shelves holding hundreds of scrolls. On the table was a bowl of smoldering incense and three scroll tubes.

I sat on the floor and tucked under the table. It was walnut and about its edges were carved skulls, frigates, pirate flags, and stormy seas.

I shook out a roll of parchment, smoothed it flat, and read.

Whoever had inked this had been three sheets to the wind, but if I understood the shaky calligraphy and illustrations, this scroll was a primer of Drunken Monkey style. The basic techniques allowed the practitioner to flow around defenses, and take advantage of openings with constant forward pressure. All standard stuff.

That, however, is where the similarity to the human-based kung fu ended, and something else started. Something more... how to describe it? "Random" might be close, but that still missed the mark.

A Drunken Monkey boxer had counters for every strike and block in *my* Sleeping Dragon-style arsenal. And they could use them effortlessly. Unthinkingly. In fact, the *less* they thought, the *drunker* they were, the *better* this worked. Or so claimed the text.

I swallowed and read the next scroll.

This one was on special techniques.

Little was legible. Many passages careened off the rice paper and never wandered back to finish the sentence they started. I could make out a few of the titles, though, like: *Stinging Scorpion Slap*; *Broken Back Forward Kick*, *Chasing Swarm of Moths*; *Sticky Face Sticky Hands*; and *Dance of Endless Firecrackers*.

And I swore there were a few lines of non-linear differential equations. That, or a spattering of old browned banana. Hard to tell.

The parts toward the end covered *advanced* special techniques. These were more complicated and correspondingly harder for me to puzzle out. I managed, though, to decipher the titles and a portion of the text for two.

The first was called *Wings of Butterfly*. It began with delicate, almost poetic hand motions—this was followed by a part where ink had been spilled and completely obliterated most of the remaining instructions. One could, however, clearly make out the move's finale where a monkey boxer inserted his fist *through* the midsection of an armored opponent. Yikes.

The other was the technique of the *Strangest Attractor*. It had dizzying foot placement charts along with stick-figure contortionist instructions. Using a weave of chaotic motions, the practitioner trapped their victim with increasingly smaller, more refined locks and joint compressions, and then with an accelerating spiral of momentum finished with an elbow strike between the eyes. A surprisingly clear anatomical illustration showed the result of that last blow—the force blasting both eyes and optical nerves into the brain where they bounced about the skull, smashed the brainstem, and severed the spinal cord.

This stuff *had to* be made up.

And yet, in what I could read I found no flaw in the physics or martial arts.

Then, only with the greatest trepidation, I dared unroll the last scroll.

It was covered by smeared monkey paw prints. Totally useless.

I'd seen enough, though, to know that if this was real, without training to counter Drunken Monkey boxing, I couldn't win against my equal in this style, let alone defeat a *master*.

Cho had wanted me to see these... so I'd know I was going to lose.

CHAPTER 32

It was an hour after dusk (when Cho had set the start of our match), and he hadn't yet shown. Apparently, the Master was entitled to be late.

I stood waiting in an open-air arena surrounded by concentric rings of stone bleachers. About the sandy floor tiki torches stood blazing.

Of course, there were spectators: the monkeys I'd beaten, bruised, electrocuted, or partially blown up. They hooted and jumped up and down, eager to see the nasty elf who'd wreaked havoc on their valley get slaughtered.

They might get their wish.

I'd spent the day reading scrolls in Cho's library. My assessment of my odds hadn't changed.

Master Cho finally waltzed into the arena.

The crowd applauded and cheered and threw flowers at him.

The elder chimpanzee sat on a stool on the far side of the arena and proceeded to "prepare" for our match. This entailed his troupe of attending lemurs handing him sloshing gourd after gourd, and him guzzling more booze than Elmac could on his worst night of debauchery.

I was actually a little impressed.

Until that is, he staggered to the edge of the ring and relieved himself.

What a class act.

Nonetheless, Cho would be hard to hit, harder to damage, and his strikes would be difficult, if not impossible, to block.

What *wasn't* he good at? Well, in his current blitzed state, he wouldn't have the concentration to use mystical powers like *Spiritual Regeneration*. He'd also thought my elemental powers had come from my magic items, so he wouldn't be expecting any more such attacks.

I better check what I had to work with in that department.

I phased into the aether.

The red and blue ley lines of fire and electricity I'd used yesterday *were* here, but feeble, thin strings, flickering like shorting-out neon. An improvement, however, from being *completely* drained. Still useless for my purposes.

My best option would be to tap one of the two fuming white threads of elemental cold.

The freezing effect hadn't slowed Grimhalt much. Would Cho even feel it? I couldn't afford *not* to try, but I better not count on it either.

The icy ley lines were just out of reach. Without *Blackwell's Band*, I'd have to watch my position.

I then noticed something wrong with my health and mana bars. My maximum health was 160, not 180. My reflexive mana was 110, instead of its normal 120.

Oh... of course, the demon bone knuckles that Cho had removed had given me +1 to my STRENGTH and REFLEX.

I had a feeling I was going to sorely miss those points.

I returned into normal space-time and then did the only reasonable thing under the circumstances. I sat on the sandy floor and meditated to top off my mana... and hoped inspiration struck.

Besides, I wanted to at least *appear* cool and collected, like I faced drunken boxing masters all the time.

Master Cho meanwhile performed a backflip and landed on his monkey ass—confirmation that he was blasted out of his mind.

He got up, pointed at me, and slurred, "Youssh an meez gooona fite nooow." He teetered and fell over. So much for his Lawrence of Arabia impersonation.

The gorilla I'd chained before limped to the center of the arena. He smiled maliciously at me, narrowed his eyes, then turned to the audience and raised his long arms.

The crowd grew slightly less rowdy.

He yelled, "The challenge match is about to begin!"

Yeah, this was happening—whether I wanted it to or not.

The gorilla went on, "The rules of this challenge? *There are no rules!*"

The crowd screamed and pounded on one another as their anticipation of seeing my blood grew.

My adrenaline kicked in.

I forced my pulse to slow.

Easy. Save it for the fight.

"And the stakes?" the gorilla yelled. "If, or rather *when*, the challenger suffers a humiliating defeat, and *if* he is not killed, he will join our ranks. Another in a long line of recruited adepts and priests and *slaves!*"

Howls of ape laughter and rude gestures bubbled through the spectators.

"In the very, very unlikely event that the challenger wins—"

Boos and hisses and feces were lobbed into the arena.

"—he wins his freedom, his belongings, and—"

The spectators drowned the announcer out, and tossed rotten fruit and coconut husks at him.

He roared and bared his teeth.

That settled them down.

"And," he continued, "he will also win freedom for his companions, who will rejoin him in their boring, sober, sad lives."

He turned to Cho and then to me.

"Are the combatants ready?"

I made a show of rising to my feet with great dignity and nodded.

Master Cho drained his gourd and in the process spilled half the amber liquor down his chest. His attendants rushed to him and slung a bandolier over his shoulder with three similar containers attached.

Hey, hadn't he said no equipment?

Cho gave the announcer a thumbs up.

We approached the center of the arena.

Cho started to wander off in the wrong direction, but his crew of lemurs steered him back toward the ring.

We halted four paces from one another.

What kind of drunk was Cho? The happy-go-lucky karaoke signer? The emotional I'll-always-be-your-best-friend type? Or a "mean" drunk?

I'd go out on a limb and guess "mean," which meant if he got me on the ropes, he might not stop beating me if I passed out. Or if I was dead.

"Let's have an entertaining fight," the gorilla whispered to Master Cho. "You wanted me to remind you, sifu, to not *instantly* kill the challenger like you have many times before."

Master Cho grinned.

The gorilla turned to me, considered, and said, "Die well, stranger."

Thanks, buddy.

The gorilla backed off and barked: "FIGHT!"

I fired off *Perfect Motion* and gave Cho a quick bow.

Master Cho bowed as well, but kept curling over, and remained that way... snoring.

Oh, for a ranged weapon right now.

Of course, this was a trick.

And of course, I still had to give it a shot.

I circled around and crept up.

The monkey audience hissed at me and called warnings to Master Cho.

He snored louder.

I jumped and used a spinning hook kick for its power, speed, and *distance.*

The instant before I made contact, however, Cho's head rolled out of the way in the wooziest of motions.

He grabbed my foot and wrenched my leg straight. He then vaulted up, somersaulted, and upside down in the air planted his foot in my face...

I woke a moment later—slamming onto the ground.

He rolled to his feet and chuckled.

The spectators gushed a tidal wave of cheers.

He'd knocked off an impressive quarter of my health.

I got up and worked my jaw. Cracked, but still in one piece. "You little drunken excuse for a furry."

I checked my anger. I couldn't afford to lose my cool.

"Yoush gohanna loohk-hup mush bettur wid no teehesh," he said.

Lovely. He might have the *Taunting Tenor* ability too.

I used a *Spiritual Regeneration* to top off my health, then made a snap call.

I closed on Cho and loosened a series of probing strikes—not overcommitting like I had last time. I needed to see if he'd counter them as I'd seen in the scrolls.

He did, lazily swatting my punches aside as if he were playing with a toddler. He yawned and I got a strike through his guard.

I took him open-palmed under the chin—snapped his head back.

That should have broken his C-5 vertebra.

Cho's head, however, came right back like it was made of rubber, apparently no worse for the wear because he was *still* grinning.

Had *he* just tested *me*?

His smile faded. He launched a barrage of weaving snake strikes that cracked ribs, and jabbed me in the armpit, sending lightning strikes of pain down the side of my body. One sliced at my throat.

I backpedaled to avoid the windpipe-crushing blow. Barely.

Ouch.

And wow.

His attacks had been nearly impossible to predict. They didn't follow the laws of physics—never going where I thought.

How to penetrate such a flawless defense? And how hard did I have to hit to get through his feeling-no-pain state?

There was no such thing as a *perfect* martial art. There had to be weaknesses.

He staggered back. This had nothing to do with any attack of mine. He'd simply lost his balance.

Master Cho pulled a fresh gourd off his bandolier and helped himself to a snootful, closing his eyes in bliss.

The crowd chanted: "Chug—chug—chug!"

He obliged.

If anything might distract him, it would be savoring the taste of his brandy.

I took the chance, moved to his side—lunged, going for his neck.

He dropped his chin and caught my wrist, pulled the arm straight, and rolled forward, using the *same* damn maneuver he'd just used on me!

And once more, I slammed onto the sandy arena floor.

This jolted my memory and I recalled this move from one of Cho's scrolls. It was the *Sticky Face Sticky Hands* technique.

So that stuff wasn't just propaganda to scare off the competition. Not good. At all.

In my half-dazed condition and while my thoughts had wandered elsewhere, it hadn't registered that Cho still had my arm.

Big mistake.

He snapped the elbow.

It felt like razor wire whipsawed through the joint—so intense every muscle in my body clenched.

He twisted about me, further torturing the joint, and his free arm and legs entangled about mine.

Agony haloed my vision with pulsing red.

If I didn't get out of this soon, I'd pass out from the pain.

I shifted, balled up, and kicked out my legs.

Normally this would have broken his hold, but his ground fighting style was beyond "soft." It was like trying to wrestle hairy Jell-O.

He got his calves about my throat and scissored them together. A textbook-perfect chokehold.

Now I was passing out.

I withdrew...

and floated in the aether.

Too close.

I had to admit, Master Cho's Drunken Monkey boxing was astonishingly effective.

So what was my next move?

I had one surprise. I had to use it.

I coiled a smoldering blue-white ley line about the length of my body. Oh man, it was c-c-cold. My nose burned with menthol; my skin crinkled so tight I thought it might split.

I took one more second to center myself then reluctantly returned to the fight.

The cold flowed to Cho with the sharp *crack* of water flash freezing.

He squawked, jumped off me, and danced about swatting ice from his upper thighs.

I lay in the dirt, panting, fuming from the extreme chill.

Well, that worked. Yay?

My health was at 13 points.

Loathing what I had to do, but having no choice, I pulled my arm straight (hoping this action didn't do enough damage to finish me off). I clamped down hard to hold my screams inside. Then while Cho was otherwise occupied, I spammed *Spiritual Regeneration* until I was back to good... although I didn't think that elbow would ever feel the same again.

I'd be able to fight, though.

With my spiritual mana at 20/90, however, I wasn't going to last much longer.

My usual strategies of using the terrain to my advantage, and/or outwitting my opponent wouldn't work here.

Surrounded by hundreds of bloodthirsty spectators in a simple sandy arena offered me few options (although kicking sand into Cho's face seemed like my best, albeit, desperate tactic).

And outwitting Cho? How? He seemed to be both frighteningly cunning and so sauced I wondered if he even understood what he was doing. There was nothing there to outwit—just a happy idiot savant.

Cho staggered closer, stopped, and swayed back and forth like he was trying to pick a direction to fall. "Yeep..." he gargled. "I booord. Lezt end dus aaa mak youz monkey, hookay?"

CHAPTER 33

"Now I shooo youz how stron arrr eyhhe..."

Cho waved his hands, kicked right and then left—flopped and tumbled on the ground, looking... like a three-year-old imitating kung fu after watching *Enter the Dragon*.

Was he *too* drunk now to fight? Or was he messing with me again?

This time I wasn't taking the bait.

Cho's capering shifted gears and he launched into a display of flawless acrobatic kicks, standing double and triple backflips, going faster, still faster until he blurred into a continuous sinew of motion.

No drunken dance was this.

It was the *Strangest Attractor* technique.

There was no way I could engage Cho and *not* get caught in that web of death.

He ended with the best spinning kick I'd ever seen—a full three-hundred-sixty-degree sweep in midair.

His adoring audience clapped and called for more.

He bowed and waved, lingering and smiling at some of the lady chimps.

Regardless of his intoxicated condition, Master Cho was just too skilled.

I faced a simple choice: yield or die.

Or wait... what if his murderously effective moves *depended* on him being drunk? Could I change that condition?

Maybe.

I could get him *so* drunk he'd pass out.

Highly unlikely given his supernatural capacity.

Okay, how about *me* getting sloshed and using his own Drunken Monkey techniques against him? That might work, *if* I knew Drunken Monkey boxing.

One last possibility. Yes. This was it.

I had to sober the monkey up.

Somehow.

Cho turned and looked me over. He made a fist, cracking his hairy knuckles. "Wee finnish dis, so Iz getz hon wid moar-hor drinkin."

He took a full gourd from his bandolier, popped the cork, and tilted it to his mouth.

How the heck, though, was I going to dry him out when he was *still* drinking? Given his body mass, and how much he'd already guzzled, I was astonished he hadn't keeled over from alcohol poisoning.

...*Poisoning*, huh?

I opened my inventory and focused on one of the potions I'd picked up at Hiltmyer & Co.

KARL'S GUARANTEED DE-TOXINIFIER
(Tier-IV alchemical, rare)
DESCRIPTION: Colorless oil with a burning cinnamon aftertaste.
SPECIAL ABILITIES: Scours the imbiber's blood, lungs, bones, and other organs of all organic toxins, poisons, venoms, radioactive elements, and heavy metals.
WARNING: This elixir will not counter magically-cursed poisons or the effects of psi-program viruses.
Toxins/poisons et al. are excreted via the most expeditious means and may induce immediate vomiting, sweating, and/or excretion.
VALUE: 2,500 golden quins.

As much as I hated to admit it, ethyl alcohol *was* a poison... so the anti-toxin just *might* purge it from Cho's blood.

No alcohol, no drunken monkey, no special techniques.

The problem was *how* to get him to drink this?

I had to figure that out. Fast.

I phased into the aether.

How about a little fast talk to trick him into downing it? Doubtful that would work. Why would Master Cho drink anything I offered him when he was in the process of knocking back that full gourd of brandy in his...

Ah, that was how: The gourd of brandy in his hand, conveniently tilted into his open mouth.

I wouldn't *have to* convince him to drink anything, because he'd *already* be drinking it.

I just had to use my *Small Pass* ability and teleport the potion's contents *into* Cho's gourd. It would mix with the brandy, which he'd then imbibe as soon as I phased back from the aether.

I reached for one of the gold ley lines that corresponded to position and space. The glittering filament met my grasp halfway and made its usual solid-connection in the palm of my hand.

I couldn't just tie the line to the potion in my inventory. That was a mere virtual projection. I'd need the actual object. So, I tapped the icon of the vial to summon it.

It remained in my inventory.

I tapped it once more. Nothing.

...And I thought I understood why.

The description of my Mage of the Line abilities had stated they appeared "almost instantaneous" from the perspective of those in normal space-time.

Almost instantaneous.

I could only think of two reasons for this "almost instantaneous" effect. Either no time passed in the aether and any perceived delay was from the split-second it took to transition here—or, and I hoped this was the case, time just moved very slowly in this dimension.

So, if the game interface was like other computer interfaces, it had a time-delayed response—a microsecond while the system processed a finger tap and executed the command triggered by that input.

That microsecond delay would either take infinitely long here (if time was truly stopped)... or something less than that (if time crawled along at a snail's pace).

I waited...

for the span of twenty non-existent heartbeats...

and watched my reflexive mana tick down...

and kept waiting.

Come on come on come on.

A blue crystal vial popped into my hand. Yes!

I had to be quick—just 35/110 reflexive mana left.

I made a loop of the gold ley line and pushed it into the vial—just past the inner surface, so it encircled the liquid contents. I then made another loop, and with a flick of the thread and a mental push, directed it toward Cho and made it halt *inside* his upraised gourd.

I finished the *Small Pass*.

The potion within the vial shrank and vanished.

Had it worked? Did this count as teleporting one object into another? The description of *Small Pass* had warned of a lower chance of success.

Only one way to find out.

I phased back to normal space-time.

Cho's gourd dipped slightly from the added weight.

He kept drinking as if nothing had happened.

I watched and prayed to all the gods of alchemy.

"Ahhh." Cho dropped the drained gourd, raised his fists, and took a step toward me.

He halted.

His face went blank.

The monkey's stomach rumbled... flexed, clenched.

Karl's De-toxinifier then performed as advertised: Master Cho took two steps back—and power-vomited in a wide arc.

I successfully dodged.

The audience fell silent.

Cho groaned, held his gut, blinked, and his glazed eyes cleared. He shook his head and looked about as if he'd been soundly asleep and slapped awake, which I imagined was what it must have felt like going from fully ripped to completely sober in three seconds flat.

Master Cho may have not known the reason for what just happened, but the effect was clear enough even for his simian brain.

He glanced at the discarded gourd. "How—?"

His eyes widened as it dawned on him what this meant.

He grasped for the last gourd on his bandolier.

Oh no, you don't.

I raced to Cho, stepped into the aether, grabbed a fuming filament of frost, then back—and dove for the chimp.

My fingers stretched for the gourd.

Cho tipped it.

An amber stream poured into his opened mouth.

I touched.

The booze froze. Instantly.

The gourd exploded.

Shards of ice bounced off my chi armor and lacerated Cho's hand and face.

Solid chunks of brandy hit the dirt.

Cho's face contorted with surprise—panic—rage.

"No!" he spat out through clenched teeth.

He attacked.

I deflected his strikes, redirecting his force, and landed a counter kick.

He got in a spear strike to my abdomen.

I punched him in the throat.

I fell backward—my breath hitching in my chest.

Cho clutched at his throat and coughed.

"Life's harder when you're sober, huh?" I asked.

"One is... hardly alive... sober," he wheezed.

Cho had a few levels on me. That was obvious. But I'd just short-circuited his special abilities.

That's all I needed.

This called for a new, *ugly* strategy.

I moved in, threw punches and kicks, not bothering to deflect, block, or dodge.

I simply had to slug it out.

I scored a half-dozen quick strikes to his chest and two to his face.

Cho ignored his defense as well, and hit back: a kick to my groin, two in my gut, and he bit my knee so hard his teeth sunk into the bone.

I landed a hammer blow on his skull.

He spun away and rubbed his head.

I jumped back, hopping to keep the weight off my savaged knee, and used *Spiritual Regeneration* to heal the damage.

Cho stood there panting wet wheezes, one eye swelling shut, as he watched my wounds fade.

Hair then dropped from his body in clumps, his arms shortened, and his skin smoothed. He looked... more human? Perhaps the drunken monkey god's curse only worked as long as there was alcohol in the blood. That was good news for my friends, but for Master Cho? I couldn't imagine what the hangover was like after, what? Decades of inebriation? Decades of being a chimp?

So, I offered him an easy way out.

"Do you yield?" I said quietly and with respect.

He stood straighter. "Never."

"I don't want to do this," I said, "but I will. Just give—"

He rushed me, screeching like an ape, but really just sounding like an old man imitating one.

Did he *want* me to humiliate him in front of his followers?

Maybe. Then the monkey mob would avenge his honor and tear me limb from limb.

Sorry, Cho, but you *have to* cry uncle. No matter what it took.

He tried a simple straight punch at my throat. The old guy was still fast.

I let the strike pass millimeters to one side, stepped inside his reach, twisted around and trapped the crook of his arm. I then grabbed his wrist and tumbled forward, throwing him to the ground in the process.

This was a but pale imitation of the far more elegant *Sticky Face Sticky Hands* technique Master Cho had used on me. I still couldn't figure out how he'd trapped my arm just with his chin.

This wasn't a lesson, though. I just had to finish him.

I planted my foot in his armpit, stretched, and twisted his arm.

In a perfect yin-yang symmetry of poetic justice—I snapped *his* elbow.

Bits of broken bone ground into cartilage and there were more pops as something else came loose.

Cho didn't make a peep.

"Give—it—up," I grunted.

He thrashed about trying to escape.

Well, I'd given him a chance...

I rolled on top of him and pressed my knee *hard* into the mangled joint. I felt more bones and cartilage crush.

Then he screamed.

The audience gasped.

I rolled off.

Cho whimpered, in so much pain, he couldn't move.

Did I feel sorry for him? Yes. But he'd kidnapped my friends and almost made a monkey of me, so good sportsmanship and sympathy only covered so much.

"You have more bones to break," I whispered. "Please, Master Cho, yield."

Cho grew quiet.

"Tell your followers I used 'evil magic' to remove the blessing of the valley's wine," I said. "That's not far from the truth. They'll call you a hero for holding out so long... uh, dry."

He sniffed, nodded, then said, "Yes. That would be" —he hesitated, searching for the right word— "equitable."

I helped him sit.

Six gorillas charged into the arena.

Cho shot them a look that stopped them in their tracks.

"I am grateful," he murmured, "for allowing me to save face. I suppose there is a bit of self-preservation in your offer too? Heh. You would have made an excellent student, Hektor Saint-Savage of the Sleeping Dragon."

I looked him in the eye. "I do not approve of your recruitment methods, Master Cho, but your Drunken Monkey boxing is the most formidable style I have ever encountered. I am honored you think I would be good at it."

He managed a smile of cracked teeth.

The assembled monkeys began to chitter in agitation. A few climbed higher to see why the two guys who'd been trying to kill each other a minute ago were sitting in the middle of the arena having a nice chat.

While I had Cho's full attention, however, I had a few other things to ask him.

I opened my inventory and pulled out a four-inch stick of ash wood. Carved upon it were three primitive faces.

"Are there any from the Far Field barbarian tribes here?" I offered him Karkanal's counting stick. "I was supposed to show them this."

Cho took the stick and ran his finger over its carvings. Sorrow contorted his face.

He didn't answer, so I went on, "A comrade gave me this for helping him break his death curse. He told me that one of his tribe was a martial artist and might be able to teach me a thing or two. That wouldn't be you, would it?"

Cho's features smoothed. He stared far away and nodded. "Yes. I gave this to Karkanal Kayestral."

"You are from the Far Field tribes?"

"Was. As I was once Karkanal's father." His voice hitched with soft sobs. "So he is dead." He turned to me and I was surprised to see hope, not grief, shining in his eyes. "Tell me how."

The monkeys now called out to Master Cho. Worried. Angry.

He held up a hand to silence them.

"It was the best of deaths," I told him. "He defeated a cabal of Black Hand wizards and saved many innocent souls. After, the Valkyries came for him. Queen Kára-Prima herself escorted Karkanal to Valhalla. This I saw with my own eyes."

He blinked away tears of joy. "You have my most profound thanks then for fighting by his side."

It was good to know that Karkanal's story had a proper closing chapter and that his people would know he died a hero.

I had a feeling, though, I'd missed something important, as if many things that had no business connecting—just did.

"One more thing," I said and leaned closer. "You said before, '*the game you play is hardly fair.*'"

All emotion faded from Cho's features.

"Are you a player?" I whispered. I looked around to see if any apes were within earshot, then added, "In the Game? The capital-G Game?"

He stroked the whiskers on his chin.

"I *was*," Cho whispered back, "but left when I found the gods I served played *other* games. They traded and sacrificed players in side bets, for favors, perhaps alliances? I was never certain. But I was sure that the Game is more than what I was told it was—trickery within lies inside layers of scheming. In the end, I wasn't sure who, or what, I fought for anymore."

I let this sink in.

It made sense that there was more going on than I'd been told. No surprise either that the powerful entities playing the Game wouldn't play by anyone's rules—even ones they themselves created.

So they'd found ways to cheat? By teaming up? Or extorting less powerful clans to join them... but all off the books? How did this figure into the Game Master's secret plan to keep anyone from ever winning?

I suddenly felt insignificant and ignorant—like I understood but the smallest, simplest part of what was going on in Thera.

"I escaped the boundaries of the Game," Cho went on, "came to the Far Fields, grew a family, and then a tribe. I was happy. When my oldest son, my beloved Karkanal, became a man, he left to seek adventure and glory. I was so proud. But as years passed, he never returned, and divinations told neither of his death or his life. He was just... gone. When all my hopes faded, I wandered off, searching for a quiet place to sit and simply pass. Instead, I found this valley..." He spread his hands in a gesture that said *you know the rest.*

And you found a bit of solace in the wine? Yes, Cho, I understand too well your grief.

So players could really just pack up and leave the Game? The gods and other various owners of the clans had so little sway over them? No wonder they had sought other ways to influence the Game.

The audience crept closer, the less brave among them shoving others ahead.

We couldn't stall any longer.

I stood, taking Master Cho's good arm and helped him up.

He raised my hand, showing all that I had won.

Catcalls and jeers boiled from the crowds.

Yeah, I'd won.

So how come it felt like I was way behind in the larger game within the Game? The *real* game. One I hadn't even known was being played.

CHAPTER 34

That night we rode across the Ojawbi Far Fields. I wanted to put as many miles between us and the Valley of the Drunken Monkey God as possible.

Before we departed, Master Cho had graciously offered to throw a party in my honor. I declined (I'd thought the sneaky simian might spike my drink). As promised, however, Cho returned my gear, Elmac and Morgana, as well as their items.

I even considered a return trip to discuss martial art techniques.

One day.

Much later.

Maybe.

But that was all behind us now.

Here on the grasslands the only conversation was the grunts and snorts among our buffalo friends, and the dream murmurs of Elmac and Morgana as they held onto one another.

They were sleeping off their monkey curse, half transformed back from their previous orangutan and macaque states. I'd made a little bed for them out of a few branches, Elmac's tent, and our bedrolls, all strapped atop the most gentle of our mounts (who I'd nicknamed "Mother").

Cho had suggested I let them sleep as long as possible to avoid the worst of the withdrawals from the valley's wine.

So I did.

And we rode.

And I enjoyed a few hours without having to run, or fight, for my life.

It's the little things you take for granted, you know?

I realized, though, that we'd soon part company from our buffalo. I was going to miss them. The beasts had the strength of two elephants and horns that could have tossed a car aside, but they could also be gentle, even friendly when you got to know them.

I knew it wasn't so, but I felt like they'd adopted us into their herd.

I patted the neck of my mount, now accustomed to her wire-coarse fur. This one I called "Auntie Brown." Silly, I know.

The sun rose.

I stopped for breakfast.

My friends had mostly reverted back to their old selves, so they fit into their clothes and gear... save for Elmac's prosthetic arm (it still rejected him because he wasn't "dwarf" enough to meet its standards). But apart from that, and a few whiskers clinging to Morgana's chin, they were as good as new.

"'Cepting the dragon-sized hangover," Elmac complained. "It be the worst skull splitter ever." He buried his face in his hand. "Oughhh."

"And," Morgana croaked, "no hair of the ruddy dog to help, either. Downright uncivilized."

"I be a wee tempted to test Hektor's theory 'bout that," Elmac whispered to her.

"I wouldn't," I told him. "Alcohol is a catalyst for the metamorphosis. Let's see... it takes about an hour to burn off one good belt... but more to completely purge all traces from your body. I figure you two better stay sober for three or four days just to be sure."

They groaned.

I made breakfast (that neither Elmac or Morgana wanted). They did, however, drink most of the water we had, which I took as a good sign of their recovery.

We broke camp, and once underway, Morgana said, "Oi, when we get back to Thera, can you blokes help a lady wrap up a quest or two of her own?"

Elmac looked a bit seasick but nonetheless grunted his assent.

"Seems fair," I told her. "I certainly owe you—not that I'd *have to* owe you to lend a hand. I think, though, we need to first deal with the Silent Syndicate."

"Right." Morgana furrowed her brow. "Forgot about them. Probably 'cause my bloody head still feels like... like monkey."

"What was it like?" I asked. "Being changed?"

Elmac perked up. "'Twas pleasant at first. A slippery slope, though, from 'oh that be a tasty bit 'o fermented fruit'—to tipsy—to drunk—to... be having all the talk in my head go quiet. If that makes sense."

"More of an instinctual existence," Morgana added for clarification. "I've brushed against such primal feelings when I shift shape. Under the monkey curse my thoughts transformed too. Radically." She sighed. "It's hard to put into exact words, because exact words was what got removed."

"Did you *know* you were turning into monkeys?"

"I *think* so," Elmac said. "'Tis hazy. If I knew I be changing, I didna care."

Morgana turned to him and said, "So more of an existential nihilism versus Platonic ideal argument, yeah?"

Elmac cocked his head. "I was thinking it be more a draining 'o one's stoic viewpoint as *rationalized* by Platonic universal truths..."

Ah, philosophy. The one class I almost had to drop in college. With a marathon session of cramming, I'd scraped by with a C- and then promptly forgot it all.

I let them talk and took the opportunity to unpack all the thoughts I'd put away last night.

First, I think our Drunken Monkey quest had been completed. No handy pop-up alert to confirm that, but we'd be back in the Game proper soon enough and find out.

Regardless, *I* was done with that quest.

Next to consider: the Silent Syndicate.

I smoothed over my hand, feeling the outline of the demon bone knuckles back under my skin where they belonged.

Had we thrown the assassins off our scent?

If so, would Elmac let the matter drop? I doubted it. He'd have his revenge for the burning of the Bloody Rooster and for the injuries and deaths of those who had been inside. I couldn't fault him for that.

Likewise, I didn't think because we'd yet to accept or decline the "Something Rotten in the Duchy of Sendon" quest, that we were off the hook.

Avoiding the Syndicate, temporarily or not, however, had had its upsides.

Elmac had become a player in the Game, and a "Hero of Thera" no less. It felt good to have a co-conspirator (not to mention one with the fighting expertise of a twentieth-level warrior). I bet he'd ding third level when we crossed the Game boundary too. All good.

I'd also had a chance to play with my new Mage of the Line abilities—just scratching the surface of what might be possible, but a decent test run nonetheless.

Furthermore, we'd deciphered the assassin's hit list—an essential clue. But what did it mean? What did the people on that list have in common? Sister Rada? My comrade-in-arms, Sir Pendric Ragnivald? Colonel Delacroix? Not to mention Duke Opinicus?

I still believed the Lords of the Abyss were behind this sanction... yet I couldn't make sense of that since there was a Game rule preventing clan owners from interfering with (let alone murdering) other players, or even ordering their players to do so.

We were all supposed to be on our own.

Big questions for which I had only big question marks.

The Wayfar Waypoint Inn was near, though. Why not stay there a few days, maybe a week or two? We could recharge, unravel these mental knots, and plan our next moves.

For a moment, I imagined my brother with us at the inn, laughing and talking game strategies like the old days.

Oh yeah, Bill. I'd almost forgotten about my incarcerated anti-paladin brother.

I opened my Message Center.

The systems that sent and received messages remained offline, but I could still read the missives he'd previously dispatched to me, messages that I'd so far ignored.

These were longer than the usual short, back-and-forth in-game texts. These were whole letters with subject lines like: "Need to talk to you"—"Where are you?"—"Getting bad, respond"—"Talk NOW"—and then the latest one, "I wish you were DEAD."

Wow. Good to know Bill still had all his social graces.

I skimmed them, but apart from more of the same increasingly belligerent and urgent requests for me to talk to him, even to come visit him in the Duke's dungeon (if you could believe that)—there was no real content in them.

I wonder what he wanted to tell me? Or was he trying to lure me into... what?

Well, I couldn't message him back, even if I had wanted to.

For now dear brother, I'm afraid you'll have to take a number.

Family troubles, harder to figure out than saving the multiverse, yes?

I turned back to Morgana and Elmac for a bit of easier-to-digest small talk.

"Ironically universal truths," Morgana went on, "might find their best, most *stoic* representation in the Catholic Bible. New Testament, of course."

Elmac made a face. "Might as well be hauling out the Vedas and talk 'bout the nature 'o Dharma."

They laughed.

"Hey Elmac," I said, not letting on that I'd ignored them this whole time, and even if I hadn't I'd still be clueless about their discussion. "How is it you know so much philosophy? No offense, but Morgana was a teacher. You" —there was no delicate way to put it— "you were a…"

"A drunk?" He gave me a half smile. "A washed-up general? Aye." He leaned forward and patted his buffalo. "Those conditions do not preclude me also being a barkeep, lad. What'da think I be talking to my customers 'bout in the wee hours 'o the morning? 'Twas hard not to be picking up a few bits on the fundamental nature 'o knowledge, reality, and existence along the way."

I guess. Or had Elmac, now Melmak the reincarnated wizard, dumped several stat points into his INTELLECT?

Whichever, I felt a little inadequate.

"Well," he said, "'tis all just words, and we be out here in the real world, eh? And to that, I say 'all's well that ends well.' Just… I be a mite irritated 'bout one thing."

"Oh?" I asked.

"I'm not saying it be your fault, Hektor. We did our part eating the fruit to get in that mess in the first place—and thank you greatly, by the way, for saving us—but the whole thing 'twas for nothing, wasn't it?"

Morgana sighed in agreement to whatever Elmac was driving at.

"You mean the Drunken Monkey quest?" I asked.

"Aye. The point was to be learning some monkey fighting techniques."

Morgana shrugged. "And that went sideways. Just one of those things, I guess."

"Maybe not," I told them. Before I could explain, though, my magically enhanced eyes spotted something ahead. I stretched taller to see farther. "Hang on…"

Yes. There. The crenelated top of a tower. A wall extending to either side. It had to be the compound of the Wayfar Waypoint Inn. I swore I also caught a whiff of fresh-out-of-the-oven cinnamon rolls.

"Salvation and food just yonder," I told my friends. "And, I think, a pleasant surprise about our quest."

Morgana arched an eyebrow. "That so? In that case—" She touched her buffalo and snorted a word in their beast language.

They sprinted off and left Elmac and me in a cloud of dust.

She called back, "It's a race, you twonks. Loser buys dinner."

Elmac and I looked at each other.

I had no idea how to "spur" a mount this size into action, especially one with so thick a hide, and me technically not having "spurs" on my troll-skin boots.

Our buffalo, however, seemed to understand what was going on because they started to trot, then run after Morgana.

The rest of the tiny herd caught the spirit of the thing and they ran with us.

I had to hold on with both hands or get jostled off.

Morgana had a big head start.

I didn't mind. I'd settle racing Elmac for second place.

We ran side-by-side, neck and neck.

Elmac laughed and whooped.

Our small stampede of six thundered over the grassland and birds took flight before us.

I shouted encouragements to Auntie Brown. She doubled her efforts and we pulled a body length ahead of Elmac.

Elmac then gave some ancient dwarven battle cry and his buffalo leapt forward, caught—then passed me by a nose.

We ran by where Morgana waited.

And crossed the Game boundary.

Alerts chimed and windows popped open, so many I could barely see ahead.

These were all the Drunken Monkey quest parts we'd unlocked, then cleared, in the last two days. It was neat to see the whole thing unrolled at once.

QUEST ALERT!

"A THOUSAND DRUNKEN MONKEYS"—PART I

COMPLETED

You have found Master Cho among

the Far Field barbarian tribes.

Reward(s): Bonus Experience.

Special Hidden Reward: You have impressed Master Cho with your abilities and cunning and have unlocked the prerequisite to earn new abilities.

and

QUEST UNLOCKED:
A THOUSAND DRUNKEN MONKEYS"—PART II
("WRITE DRUNK, EDIT SOBER")
Gain insights into Drunken Monkey Boxing and obtain the means for further study of this martial art.
Reward(s): Bonus Experience and a new skill for martial artists in the party.
Suggested Party: N/A

and

QUEST ALERT!
"A THOUSAND DRUNKEN MONKEYS"—PART II
("WRITE DRUNK, EDIT SOBER")
COMPLETED
You have gained insights into Drunken Monkey Boxing and obtained the means for further study of this martial art.
Reward(s): Bonus Experience and martial artists in the party acquire Drunken Monkey Boxing (Tier 1; Rank: Pilsner Sash).

and, still more...

> **QUEST UNLOCKED:**
> **A THOUSAND DRUNKEN MONKEYS" – PART III**
> **("SOBRIETY SMACKDOWN")**
> Defeat or otherwise beat Master Cho in a challenge bout (and do so in a way that does not end in your death).
> Reward(s): Bonus Experience and the party's freedom.

and

> **QUEST ALERT!**
> **"A THOUSAND DRUNKEN MONKEYS" – PART III**
> **("SOBRIETY SMACKDOWN")**
> **COMPLETED**
> You have defeated Master Cho in a challenge bout and lived!
> Reward(s): Bonus Experience.

and then finally

> **ALERT!**
> **EXTRA HIDDEN BONUSES**
> For completing the Drunken Monkey quest line without killing any inhabitant of the Valley of the Drunken Monkey God, Dà Xiào Hóu has blessed you with the boon "First Round's On Me."
> All martial artists have their Drunken Monkey Boxing skill upgraded to the next tier, Rank: Mojito Sash.

***All party members* receive a new passive ability: Drunken Resistance (tier 2).**

There were *special hidden rewards?* Interesting. Compensation for playing outside the boundaries of the Game perhaps? Not having hints from the quest text certainly upped the difficulty. More risk, more reward.

I checked out the new skills and abilities.

Drunken Monkey Boxing (tier 2; Rank: Mojito Sash)
Proportional to your level of inebriation, you become harder to hit and grapple, have increased damage resistance, and may sporadically use a *random* basic special technique, including, but not limited to: *Chasing Swarm of Moths, Chair with Two Legs, Dance of Endless Firecrackers, No Personal Space,* and *Sticky Face Sticky Hands.*

NOTE: Your effectiveness *rapidly* declines when you are *too* drunk to stand.

and

Drunken Resistance (tier 2)
While you still are subject to the state of inebriation appropriate for your stats, race, and degree of liver degradation—your ability to drink *more*, remain conscious longer, and hangover recovery time are improved by 40%.

Nice.

I checked my experience bar. It was 80% filled with sterling silver pips, although I also noticed the ghost of a second, longer indicator superimposed over the first.

I went to the CHARACTER section of my interface.

Yes—I was close to becoming a fifth-level Spirit Warrior, but if I spent the same experience on my Mage of the Line class, I'd only be about halfway to the next level. An expensive class, but maybe justifiably so, given the power of even its beginning abilities.

Elmac jumped off his buffalo and danced a little jig.

I couldn't tell if this was due to the new *Drunken Resistance* ability or because his placard now read:

Melmak Argenté-Wolfram
WIZARD / LEVEL 3
Heroes of Thera

Cool. I wonder if he'd pick a new second class, start down a wizard specialization path, or like me build up his core abilities first?

Morgana slid off her buffalo. "I think it's time we let our lady friends go about their business, yeah?"

Elmac and I likewise dismounted.

Elmac bowed to his wooly steed. "Fare thee well, grand beastie."

She lowered her head. Elmac scratched under her chin.

"I'll just leave them with a bit of supper then," Morgana said. "Come on, girls. Corn and honeysuckle's on the menu." She clucked her tongue and marched toward a sandy patch among the tall grass.

The buffalo were so excited they followed her with the bison equivalent of the flashy tall-gaited "park trot" common among show horses.

Auntie Brown, however, remained and nudged my shoulder.

I turned and stared into her bottomless brown eyes.

I patted her neck one last time and gave her a hug.

"Thank you," I whispered.

She snorted, and maybe it was my imagination, but it looked like she wanted to say, "*You're very welcome, my adopted elf-calf.*" She then joined the rest of her kind.

I was going to miss these majestic, gentle, and *terrifying* creatures.

Morgana left the sandy spot. Behind her, corn stalks sprouted and honeysuckle vines twined about them.

"I'm confused," she said to me. "How'd we complete the quest? The objective was to *learn*, or I guess more accurately find the means to learn, Drunken Monkey techniques. You couldn't have learned anything in the day we were there."

"Oh," I said and sighed. "Yeah, Master Cho did promise to make a gift of a few of his instructional scrolls if I won our match. Funny thing, he conveniently forgot about that little detail afterward, and to tell you the truth, I just wanted to get out of there, so I didn't press the issue."

"...And?" Morgana said.

"And, I'm not especially proud of this, but..." I opened my inventory and removed a scroll, then another, and then six more.

"I *borrowed* a few select topics from Master Cho's library before the match."

"Well, well, well," Morgana murmured and looked me over appreciatively. "Might make a decent thief of you yet."

"Maybe," I replied, then changed the subject. "So, dinner?" I nodded toward the Waypoint Inn.

"Brilliant," she said and started marching.

Elmac fell in line with her and muttered, "Aye, dinner be fine, but what be the point without a few Silvercrest Ales to wash it all down?"

She gave him a fake pout and ruffled his hair. "But you made a cute little orangutan. *Pongo tapanuliensis*, if I'm not mistaken. Don't worry, though, love. You fall off the wagon, I'll keep you as my pet."

CHAPTER 35

We grabbed a few menus and seated ourselves in the far corner booth. It was a good spot as no one was within earshot and we had a commanding view of the entire room.

The place wasn't as crowded as it had been last time. I counted eight customers eating, no one at the trade tables, and only two waitstaff.

Elmac had just gotten his prosthetic arm back on. He gave it one more shoulder roll and hand flex and then seemed to be satisfied with the fit.

"This place has the best food," I told him.

"As long as there be lots 'o it," he replied and looked at his menu. He flipped to the drink selections at the end, sighed, and flipped back.

A crowd of travelers then entered wearing heavy pewter-colored cloaks with silver-star clasps. They were an odd collection: a few humans; I spotted a dark elf in sunglasses; a hobbit or two; and three individuals that looked over seven feet tall, but I couldn't tell *what* they were as they kept their hoods up.

Elmac followed my gaze.

"Guild 'o the Empyrean," he murmured. "Elite merchants. Best steer clear 'o that lot."

"Dangerous?" Morgana asked.

"To your money pouch," he said. "The Empyreans have routes between a few well-hidden gates. They be known for procuring rare and exotic fare, but only for equally rare and exotic prices."

Morgana studied them as they sat at a long table on the trade side of the room. "Think I ought to give my upgraded pickpocket skill a whirl?"

I tapped the table to get her attention. "Really?"

She turned back, all dimples. "Just kidding, mate. Don't get your new 'Mojito'-colored sash in a bind."

I snorted.

But I wasn't convinced she *had been* entirely kidding.

I wondered if her player and real personas were mixing too? Morgana, the ex-high school teacher, might be part light-fingered trickster now as well.

"Let's look at the assassin's note," I whispered. "The people on that hit list have to have *something* in common."

Elmac and Morgana nodded, and from their subsequent stares at nothing, I figured they'd opened their interfaces and were reading the text I'd previously deciphered.

> *Yamina,*
> *As prescribed by shadow and blade, herein are thine orders, not to be circumvented by blood nor bane nor broken heart: terminate these unfortunate walking dead*

with extreme prejudice. With regards to the last six, use Summa protocols, and even then additional precautions may be warranted.
Good hunting.

"When I looked at this before using Azramath's headband" —I tapped the silver silk tied about my forehead— "I got a lot more than the translation. I also learned the note was written by the blind master assassin, Gashton Grex, and given to one first lieutenant, Yamina Sussara, aka the Serene Knife, aka The Whispering Blade, and a bunch of other *noms de guerre*. Heard of them?"

They shook their heads.

"Maybe you should be taking another gander with that headband," Elmac said.

"I don't think so. I got all I could—just before the magic overloaded my optic nerves and blew my brains out."

This fell under the category of *even your magic items could kill you in Thera*.

"Right," Morgana said. "Then back to these names on the hit list."

My gaze lingered upon the people I knew among those marked for death:

>   Duke Reginald Opinicus
>   Sister Rada Borovkova
>   Colonel Sabella Delacroix
>   General (retired) Elmac Arguson

Captain (?) Pendric Ragnivald
Hektor Saint-Savage
Morgana Nox

"Elmac," I said, "you told me you knew some of these others... uh, Padre John Adam-Smith, Dame Rose Beckonsail, Niblen Chatters?"

"Sure," he replied. "John be a padre; Rose a captain in the Duchy's Gryphon Cavalry, and that last fellow be a court scribe or some such."

"Besides the cleric," Morgana asked, "they're all connected to the Duke, yeah?"

"That be a fair assumption." Elmac frowned at the list. "But he employs hundreds 'o folk, so that's not giving us much."

"Are any of these other names familiar?" I asked.

Elmac rubbed his temple. "Well, this fellow be a guard, I think. This one, ugh... 'twould be much easier with a tankard or two to grease my thinking."

"Let's simplify this," Morgana said. "Don't try to connect *all* the dots on the list. Can we connect *any* dots? Start with Pendric and Delacroix. We fought with them to save High Hill. Is anyone else on this list connected to us five?"

"The Duke," Elmac remarked. "He sent us to you after he interrogated us 'bout connections between the ghosts in the deserted part 'o High Hill and that zombie invasion..." His words trailed off.

"Sister Rada was in on that discussion," I said. "In the Duke's high-security meeting chamber."

"So was Padre John, Captain Beckonsail, and the scribe," Elmac said, tugging on his beard as he thought. "Pendric, me and Hektor, Colonel Delacroix, and 'o course the Duke were all there too."

"Where the others on the list there?" Morgana asked.

"Maybe," Elmac whispered. "'Twas a tad hungover, but they all *could have* been there. 'Cept you, Mor—" He looked up.

The waitress who'd served us last time walked up to our table. Sadie, if I was not mistaken. Her caramel hair was pinned up and she wore perfume—a whisper of lilac, citrus, and something wondrously unidentifiable.

"Why it's the dueling gypsy elf," she cooed and beamed at me. "I didn't get your name last time."

This was... uh, strange. Why was she so happy to see *me*? I looked and smelled like you'd expect after wrestling several dozen monkeys and riding a buffalo all day.

But of course, this obviously *wasn't* about me. Hair up? Perfume? Most likely she had a date after her shift. Lucky guy. Or girl. Or whatever.

"I'm Hektor Saint-Savage."

"Nice to meet you," she said, "again. Are you folks ready to order?"

"I'll take the *coniglio pasto completo*," Morgana said before I could jump in and ask for a few more minutes. I hadn't even cracked the menu.

"Of course, ma'am." She turned to Elmac. "Sir?"

"I be having the Donn Cúailnge porterhouse. Rare. And a ruddy cup 'o coffee."

"And you, Mister Saint-Savage?"

"Does the house have a specialty this evening, *mademoiselle*?"

"*Trois choix fantastiques, monsieur*," she replied.

Her French was flawless but had an accent I couldn't place. Vietnamese? No, that wasn't quite right. Odd.

"*Très bon*," I said. "Would you mind picking the best of the lot for me?"

One of her eyebrows arched, and she nodded as she scribbled on her notepad.

The waitstaff usually knew what was good (although I was taking a *bit* of a gamble that Sadie would pick the *best* dish, not necessarily the most expensive one).

I almost asked her to add a frosty Silvercrest Ale to my order but had pity on Elmac. "And a small pot of green tea," I added. "Thanks."

"I'll have everything ready as soon as possible," she told us, then took our menus, and flounced off.

Once Sadie had gone into the kitchen, I said, "So, the people on this hit list, minus you, Morgana, were at that meeting. At the time, we suspected there was a plot against High Hill. Our clues pointed us to the druids at the Grove of the Thirteen Ancients. We found you there, battled that shadow demigod, and picked up the last part of the quest to save the city."

"So what be the reason to kill those on this list?" Elmac asked.

"Revenge for the demon army we stopped?" I suggested.

"Then why the *rest* 'o these people?" Elmac said. "Why not just us, Pendric, and Delacroix? We be the ones that stopped them."

"Hang on a tick," Morgana said, leaned forward, and furrowed her brow at me. "You're not still on about the Lords of the bloody Abyss arranging this sanction? If they *could* have done that, wouldn't they have done it *before* they invaded? Off the city's leaders all in one go? Would have made things ten times easier for them, yeah?"

"Makes sense," I muttered, irritated that my theory had another hole in it beside the Abyssal Lords being forbidden from direct involvement in the Game.

We pondered this for a few minutes.

No new insights... or hunches... or even wild guesses came.

Sadie returned, wheeling a cart, and proceeded to unpack our feast.

Elmac's steak barely fit on its three-foot platter. The slab of sizzling meat had to be four pounds and was blackened and crusted with spices and seasonings. A sprig of parsley had been arranged next to it, the only greenery on the plate. I assume put there for irony.

Sadie set Morgana's dishes out. "Your *coniglio pasto completo*" —she pointed to each plate— "rabbit cacciatore, caprice salad, and rolls just out of the oven, smothered with buffalo butter and crushed elephant garlic. Your tiramisu will be ready soon, ma'am."

Morgana cut into the rabbit and stuffed her face like a starving panther (which may have not been far from the truth), and made a ravenous growl of approval.

Elmac ignored the silver steak knife and pulled one of his ivory-handled daggers from his belt. He cut into the meat and grinned at the bloody interior. "'Tis perfection," he said.

"And for you." Sadie placed a platter before me and removed the cover. "*Salmon en Cruote del Rey.*"

A croissant the size of a loaf of bread sat steaming on a slab of obsidian. Green pesto sauce had been drizzled hither and yon. Smells of salmon and rosemary and sage made my mouth water.

Elmac pointed at my meal with his dagger. "And what be that?" he asked with a full mouth.

"This," Sadie said with a flourish of her hands, "is the triple-gill salmon black-plate special. It was caught this afternoon, seared, brushed with a delicate teriyaki glaze, and then wrapped in blankets of *sept beurre* pastry dough with baby purple asparagus, saffron and other special spices."

It was something I would have never picked on my own... but as I inhaled its delicate scents, my doubt melted away, and I felt like a bear just awakened from hibernation—famished.

Sadie served our beverages with the precision and grace of a tea ceremony master.

Elmac scowled at his un-whiskeyed coffee.

Morgana had ice water.

"If there's nothing else, I'll be back in a moment with dessert." Sadie wheeled the cart off.

I took a bite.

The creation was salty and honey-sweet and so fresh I could practically taste the mountain lake the fish had splashed in hours ago. God only knows what it was seasoned with, but every bite sent chills cascading through my insides.

Food should *always* be this good.

We ate.

I got through half of my meal but then *had to* stop or burst.

Morgana and Elmac had finished their plates and wiped up the last bits with crusts of bread.

Sadie returned with Morgana's dessert: layers of cake and mascarpone cheese, drenched in espresso, and sprinkled with cocoa.

Morgana took a bite. She shut her eyes in obvious pleasure.

"Anyone else for something sweet?" Sadie asked.

Elmac shook his head and patted his distended stomach.

"I'm good," I told her.

Sadie's eyes locked with mine for a fleeting moment. Some odd micro-expression flashed across her features... or it could have been just the light shimmering off the golden sea elf scales on her cheeks and brow.

"Can we get two rooms?" Morgana asked. "One for us." She indicated herself and Elmac. "And one for this disreputable character here." She nodded at me. "Although, I think the stable might do for him."

Sadie produced a tiny menu from her apron and handed it to Morgana.

I spied various rooms listed there and their corresponding ludicrous prices.

Morgana pointed at two.

"Let me check if those are available, ma'am." She hurried to the front station and riffled through a ledger.

"For a night in a *real* bed," Morgana whispered and closed her eyes. "Just ten hours of totally reasonable overindulgence before we have to deal with assassins, other players, or more monkey curses. And a bath! Bubbles are *bloody* mandatory."

"Aye, me too," Elmac said, his cheeks flushing.

"In full agreement," I said. "At least about the bed part. But what's our next move? Head back to High Hill? Contact Duke Opinicus first?"

"No, Colonel Delacroix," Elmac said. "If I be knowing her, and assuming she got our note through Lordren, she'll already be dealing with the Syndicate."

A waiter came by with the check for dinner and our room keys.

Funny that Sadie had forgotten about the Inn's pay-*before*-you-eat policy. She must have been preoccupied with her plans for later this evening.

Elmac dropped a small sack of gold quins on the table. "My treat."

"But *I* lost our race," I told him.

"Consider it partial payment for saving us from making monkeys 'o ourselves."

"Thanks, Elmac. I appreciate that."

Truth be told, I hadn't been sure I had the quins to cover the food, let alone the rooms.

Elmac stood. "I've got nothing left, lad. My head be feeling like solid granite."

Morgana got up and stretched. "We should pick this up in the morning. I'm knackered, too."

So we went upstairs, bid our good nights, and my two friends continued down the hall holding hands.

Good night, indeed, you two.

I got to my room, unlocked the door, and found inside a feather bed, a small table with two chairs, a bathroom with instructions on how to ring for hot water to fill the large copper bathtub, and even a small larder filled with snacks (although the prices on these things were ridiculous).

I scrubbed a few layers of grime off my body, changed, and was just about to fall into bed...

But there was a soft knock on the door.

Elmac? Morgana? I thought they had better things to do.

Or, if my luck ran true, it was an assassin from the Silent Syndicate.

But an assassin knocking? Unlikely.

Just in case, though, I readied my ninja chain and adjusted my stance.

I opened the door.

Sadie stood there with a bottle of wine and two glasses.

"Nightcap?" she said.

CHAPTER 36

My luck had *never* been this good—in any incarnation. Why then, did it feel like I'd stumbled into a James Bond movie?

No. Something was wrong with this picture.

Or it might be me just not thinking straight after going without sleep for—this couldn't be right—two, two and a half days?

Sadie must have read the confused emotions on my face. "Oh, no." She took a step back. "I'm not here to—" She glanced down the hall. Her throat and cheeks reddened.

"Offer me a nightcap?"

I hadn't meant that to sound creepy, but it did. I felt like a jerk for it.

Sadie's gaze dropped to the floor. "I... I didn't think this through. It's not a *nightcap*, nightcap. It's wine, and *only* wine. Really."

Her head had dropped so low I could no longer see her face, but I *could* practically feel the pulses of red-hot humiliation roiling off it.

"Can I come in?" she whispered. "I don't want anyone to see me, and you, together, and get the wrong idea…"

Without a second thought, I waved her in.

Then I had that second thought.

I wasn't sure what this *was*, but I was sure it *was not* some harem anime or Bond movie with dangerous and exotic women, complete with bottles of chilled *Dom Perignon*, flinging themselves at me.

Although, there could be a grain of truth to that. The "dangerous" part, I mean. Could Sadie be an assassin?

No, that didn't track. Sadie was here before Morgana and I got to the Inn. If she was an assassin from High Hill she would have had to defeat Oswald or the Chaos Knight to get the Ojawbi Far Fields… which obviously hadn't happened.

"Mr. Saint-Savage?"

I was still standing at the open door like a half-wit.

I made to shut it, but instead left the door open a crack.

"So what's this about?" I said.

Sadie sat at the small table.

To be polite, I took the other chair but scooted it away a bit to give her space.

Her fingers fidgeted. "I'm sorry," she said in a quavering voice. "This was a mistake." She tried on a fake smile. "But here." She slid the wine bottle toward me. "An Empyrean merchant ordered this and left it in his room after he checked out. Take it. Please. Compliments of the house for the interruption this evening."

She stood, took a step, then halted.

Worry lines creased her brow. She licked her lips. Swallowed.

She was terrified... but not, I thought, of me.

"Don't go. Tell me how I can help."

She sank back into the chair and clasped her hands together to stop their shaking. "Well, I saw you fight the other day."

"You mean fight that idiot with the mace?"

The beginning of a laugh twitched over her mouth, then died. "That fight was no draw," she whispered and leaned forward. "*You* won. I saw you and your friend both at the end. He couldn't even get to his feet."

Of course, she couldn't have seen the actual fight—just the part where Grimhalt had knocked me over the center field wall, and the last bit with him clearly beaten to within an inch of his disreputable life.

"How did you do it?" she asked. "I didn't see you draw a weapon. Or use spells." Her eyes widened. "Did you defeat him with *your hands*?"

I tilted my head to indicate "yes," so I wouldn't have to outright lie about my true role in that fight (i.e. target dummy).

"Are you—what do you call them?" She made a fist and shadowboxed. "A pugilist? Or a marshall-something?"

"A martial artist." I gave a half bow. "Master of the Dance of Death, and formerly of the Domicile of the Sleeping Dragon."

She stared at the golden dragon tattoo on my arm. "Oh... then you *can* help me." She took a breath, held it a moment, then continued quickly, like if she didn't get the words out, she'd never have the courage to say them again. "I need a lesson how to fight." Her gaze met mine. "I can pay. I have quins."

Well, that made more sense than what I had originally *thought* this was. But lovely damsels or not, quins or not, I was exhausted. In the morning, Elmac, Morgana, and I had to come up with a plan to stop the Syndicate from murdering us and the others on that hit list. I suspected there would be another long walk ahead of us too.

Just thinking about it made my eyelids feel like lead, my body stuffed with cotton, and my thoughts kept drifting over to that lovely bed just two paces away.

"My friends and I are leaving in the morning," I whispered. "But next time I'm here, I'd be happy to teach you a—"

"I see." Sadie sagged, then pushed away from the table to stand.

As she did so, her dress sleeves pulled back.

There were bruises on her wrists and forearms.

Finger-shaped bruises.

She caught me looking, pulled down her sleeves, and became very still.

I wanted to ask who had done this, find the guy, and convince him that such ungentlemanly behavior might not be in his best interests... and do so *with my fists*.

But Sadie hadn't asked for a protector. She had asked to be taught how to defend herself, and not owe anyone for it, either.

I respected that.

"I'll show you what I can tonight," I told her. "Basic principles. Some escapes. No charge. And no strings. Okay?"

Yeah, I'd be a little tired in the morning. So what? This was more important.

She studied my face, blinked rapidly as she teared up, and nodded. "Thank you."

I heard a considerable amount of iron, and pride, in her voice. Good.

So I taught her.

We started with a few wrist-grab escapes. If she got nothing else out of tonight, I wanted to make sure no one could hurt her like that again. One especially nasty technique left the aggressor with a choice: let go or have his thumb and wrist broken. An even nastier variant I showed her didn't give said aggressor a choice about it. Sadie *liked* that one.

We then covered basic stances and moved on to discussing overall defensive strategies: Use simple moves, not fancy ones; faster is better than stronger (especially for her body type); be prepared; train; be aware of your surroundings and *who* is around you.

That last one Sadie already seemed to know. No surprise. Waitresses typically had a good eye for cads and a few points in the *Evasion* skill.

This took a few hours.

I was beat, but had a little left in me to cover a few specific tactics I thought would work for her: keep a barrier, if you could, between you and your opponent; control your opponent's hips and hands; and most important, fight as dirty as hell.

This included instruction and a few slow demonstrations of eye gouges, face rakes, punches to the throat, and the classic knee to the groin (seven variations on that one).

I started to show her elbow strikes but stopped. My mind was fogged over. If I didn't teach her these strikes well, she could end up hurting herself along with her opponent.

As someone who had his elbow recently snapped, I was a tad sensitive about this.

By this time, Sadie had worked up a decent sweat, so she washed up in the bathroom.

I used the few minutes alone to sit and meditate (and maybe I dozed).

Sadie came back glowing and sat at the table across from me. She produced a corkscrew from her apron, grabbed the wine bottle, and opened it. She brushed the dust off its label. "A thirty-year-old dwarven vintage, Cabernet Ferico Alberto," she said. "Cost that merchant a fortune. If you're not going to drink it…"

She smiled, a sly curling thing upon her lips.

I thought that might be her real smile, one never shown to mere customers. Maybe good friends, though.

She poured a glass for herself, and then since I wasn't objecting, she poured one for me as well.

For one second, I considered letting whatever was about to happen, happen. That is, whatever Sadie wanted to happen; as always, it's the lady's choice.

I then remembered, given my unique circumstances, all the reasons why I wasn't dating. One might sum it up as, bad for me, probably lethal for my partner.

So, whatever might have happened tonight, wasn't going to.

Also, this: Some lone neuron in my brain still awake enough to care, continued to bring up the notion that Sadie could be with the

Silent Syndicate, and this wine could be, well it's such a cliché... poisoned.

She plucked up her glass. "What shall we toast to?"

I took my glass and held it lightly, examining its garnet-colored contents. "May you know peace in your soul," I said, "and failing that, may you live to hear the lamentations of your enemies."

"And their silence forever thereafter." She clinked her glass to mine. "*Kanpai!*"

Okay... a little bloodthirsty, but like I said, there was iron in her. I wouldn't want to be the person who had given her those bruises after tonight.

Sadie leaned over the table and quickly kissed me.

It wasn't one of those kisses that drew one in and invited more, but it sure as heck wasn't a demure little peck, either. Her lips were hot and velvet soft.

She detached and sat back down.

"That's for being a complete gentleman," she whispered.

I thought I detected... what? Disappointment? No. But some odd melancholy nonetheless that I didn't understand.

Sadie took a large gulp of her wine.

My lips still burned from her kiss and I wanted more.

With a slightly shaking hand, I lifted my glass.

As much as I could have used a drink just then, I'm not *always* a complete idiot.

Like I had done with the tea Master Cho had offered me, I tilted the glass to my mouth, but didn't quite let the liquid touch my lips... just in case this wine was poisoned.

Too bad. Its bouquet was magnificent.

I set the glass on the table.

Sadie's sly smile was gone. "I *am* sorry, Mister Saint-Savage." There was an edge to her voice that hadn't been there before, cold and jagged and cruel.

I was going to ask what she meant, but I no longer felt, or could move, my lips—nor my hands... along with the rest of my body.

WARNING!!!
You have been poisoned...

CHAPTER 37

The entire in-game alert before me read:

WARNING!!!
You have been poisoned with:
Venom of the "Glory of Onoskelis" cone snail
(*Conus Cor Subsisto*). **Causes immediate**
voluntary muscle paralysis, followed by
***in*voluntary muscle paralysis and death.**
Seek *immediate* assistance.

Thank you, faithful game alert. I would have never figured that out on my own.

I blinked. Or tried to. I couldn't move my eyelids. Or my eyes.

Adrenaline made my heart race, pumping the venom deeper into my tissues. My heart fluttered—*seized* for a beat—then resumed its thumping.

The red pixels in my health bar soured to sickly green. Pips started vanishing at an alarming rate.

Sadie walked to the door, shut, and locked it.

"If not for my assignment," she said, and her sweet voice was now all business, "I would have very much enjoyed your company this evening." Sadie looked me over and sighed. "I must stay until the sting of Onoskelis's Glory finishes her work. I have my orders. There will be details to be seen to... after. You will, at least, not spend your last moments alone."

Thanks a bunch.

"Mister Saint-Savage—may I call you Hektor?" she asked. "My thanks for not taking advantage of Sadie tonight. I find seduction effective, but it is a common gutter tactic that I disdain. Fortunately, your weakness finally revealed itself." She placed a hand over her heart. "Chivalry is not dead after all."

If she was here to murder me, why hadn't she just slit my throat already?

I struggled to move one finger... just a millimeter...

No dice.

Every voluntary muscle in my body had locked tight.

How long until my heart and diaphragm did the same?

Right. I'd use *Spiritual Regeneration*. I needed only one second free from the paralysis to drink the vial of Karl's Detoxinifier in my inventory.

I fired it off.

ALERT!

The Venom of the "Glory of Onoskelis"

Is not affected by magical healing.

"I felt that," Sadie whispered and smiled. "The Spirit Warrior's famous chi-regeneration ability, yes?"

She moved the other chair in front of me and sat.

"Mystical healing will not work on this venom. It was quite difficult to obtain, but you destroyed four Syndicate squads and escaped the basement of the Bloody Rooster without detection." She shook her head. "So I can see why they insisted on this exact species of Cone Snail venom. Your fourth-level Spirit Warrior status indeed does not represent your true threat level."

She *knew* I was a Spirit Warrior? A player?

But *she* wasn't a player. Or at least, there was no placard over her head.

Although, the assassin player class must have a way to hide their placard, something like my *Obscura Totata* ability. Otherwise, every player would see them coming.

"Oh hello, Madam Assassin. Nice shiny placard you have there. I'll just slowly back away."

She cocked her head as if she heard something, got up, and blew out the candles. She slinked to the only window on the far side of the room and peered out.

I had to find out who and what I was dealing with.

Dreading the side effects, I nonetheless activated the "absolute truth" ability of *Azramath's Headband of Grim and Fateful Insights*.

In a flash, I saw it all.

Sadie's caramel skin was really the color of ocean fog speckled with different colors. Those specks were tiny scales, round and smooth with the surface of her skin, and capable of shifting the tone and patterns of the surrounding cells.

She was a devangari (a reptile humanoid choice for player race). They had a natural chameleonic ability that, with training, could be used to mimic others' appearances.

A scar traced from her left ear, down, and across her throat. This she had received from a broken bottle of Shirixian absinthe in a duel to advance to the rank of lieutenant in the Syndicate.

More data screamed along my shredding optical nerve—she manicured her nails every day—under her simple linen dress she wore a bodysuit made from the silk of the dreaded and never-seen tesseract spider whose weave was as tough as Kevlar and, with subtle psychic commands, the wearer could alter its texture from diamond-grit abrasive to a near-zero coefficient of friction—there were seven daggers (six poisoned, one not) hidden on her person— her left pinkie had been severed three years ago and she wore a non-magical prosthetic of living wood that was hollow and had recently contained the crystalline venom of the "Glory of Onoskelis" cone snail (*Conus Cor Subsisto*), named after the murderous fallen angel, which only requires brief contact with a victim's eyes, mouth, lips, nasal membranes, open wounds or other orifices to...

Still more truth forced its way into my mind: She was originally Yumi Ishida, who at fourteen joined the Yakuza. She stole, killed, and was a good soldier until she lost two kilograms of heroin. For that, the Yazuka cut off her legs and left her to die in a dumpster. That is when the spirits of death, the Phonoi, came to her. They wanted her to play the Game for them, not only because Yumi was a nationally ranked champion gamer—but because she had been *both* victimizer *and* victim. With every ounce of her being, she believed that life was a choice between these two roles. The Phonoi approved and knew she would do *anything* to avoid being a victim ever again.

My brain boiled with this overload of information.

As if striding through hardening concrete, I willed my perspective back before I became lost in this spiral of ever-increasing data.

My enhanced focus shrunk to a pinpoint, but before it faded entirely, I caught a glimpse of Kirlian lines of force about her: a magnetic field of shadow draining color and power from the nearby ley lines.

Not magic in and of itself... more like its *opposite*. Perhaps an anti-magic field?

Silver smears then appeared over her head and sharpened into:

Yamina Sussara
ASSASSIN (Soul Stealer) / LEVEL 8
The Phonoi

That's all I needed.

And that's all I could handle.

I turned off the power of Azramath's headband.

Blood trickled out my nose from a hundred bursting micro-aneurysms.

I fired off a *Spiritual Regeneration*, which saved me from stroking out and dying... for a little time anyway.

Yamina turned from the window and stared at me wide-eyed. "You *are* full of surprises. The headband of Azramath the Trembling? I thought it a mere legend."

She returned to me, drew a dagger, and slipped its tip under the silk band.

"I was instructed not to take any items from your corpse or inventory, but you are not dead yet, true?"

She dragged the headband off.

And in the process, nicked me with the dagger.

WARNING:

Player versus Player rules, systems, and prohibitions have been NULLIFIED.

The Neutral Ground status of this region has been NULLIFIED.

The alert was only there for a flicker of a moment before it vanished.

Another handy assassin ability?

Did it matter? Drugged—stabbed—dead was dead.

She knelt, tapped her dagger tip against my jugular, and murmured. "I apologize for the venom taking so long. There are many that are faster, but this poisons the soul along with one's flesh. Whoever has paid for your death went to great expense to assure it would be irreversible even by the strongest of divine magics."

Great. The Lords of the Abyss were going to make sure I'd be enjoying their hospitality—forever.

My heart and diaphragm seized.

My health bar was at the halfway mark—poisoned green pips now popping faster and faster.

"I believe it might matter to you," she said, "so let me assure you, this" —she pointed to herself— "is merely borrowed. Just enough to pass for the real Sadie. She is safe and alive with a few others that we drugged and have secured."

Borrowed... I wonder if her assassin specialization, this Soul Stealer, gave her the ability to clone the appearance, mannerisms, and maybe even more from another person?

Gods! She was really good at keeping me distracted.

Wait. Had she said *"We* drugged and secured"?

We?

Yamina was not alone.

I had to message Morgana and Elmac. They were in danger (and if I'd been smarter, I would have done this the instant I became paralyzed).

>_Hektor Saint-Savage: Assassins HERE. RUN!

There was no reply. Not even a Privacy Block Alert.

There could be many reasons they weren't answering, most of them bad.

It now felt as if iron hands gripped my throat, inexorably tightening.

Yamina drew closer, not quite touching, but so near I felt her pulse on my skin.

Her eyes were still blue, but not the real Sadie's shade of tropical waters. These were the color of a guttering coal fire. The same eyes I'd seen glowing behind her veil the night we had both watched the Bloody Rooster burn.

"I picked up your trail at the city dump and might have done this sooner, but when I saw your five cohorts at the Inn, I took no chances and sent for reinforcements."

Five cohorts? Along with Elmac and Morgana, she must have mistaken Grimhalt, Harlix, and Cassie as members of our party... and chalked off my duel with Grimhalt as a friendly match? Well, he had left more or less intact, so maybe.

I guess after that fight, Yamina replaced Sadie and set her trap. She knew that we'd have to use the nearby gate to eventually return to Thera, and the inn was the logical place for us to visit on our way back.

"And your decoy was brilliant," she continued, nodding with admiration. "The fairy with his illusions. That is why my scouts lost you. Do you know the little fey wouldn't give you up? Even after we tortured him for twenty hours straight. How he squealed when I tore off his wings."

Molten rage flashed through my thoughts—and intensified because I couldn't move, couldn't even *try to* strangle this cold-blooded murderess.

Oswald, I misjudged you. I swear if you're alive...

I'd do what? *I* was almost out of time.

And I had gotten sucked into her monologue *again*.

She was good.

"In another life," she whispered, "you and I might have made a formidable team."

She moved even closer as if she were going to kiss me again, but halted. "No," she breathed, swallowed, and then added, "that would just confuse matters... more."

Yamina pulled away. "And you deserve, at least, my respect."

If I could have, I would have thrown up.

She strode to the door and seemed to stare at her interface, then set her ear to the wall.

I couldn't believe I'd almost fallen for her (or rather, her version of Sadie).

I entered the aether.

My reflexive mana was full, so I had about two minutes, give or take, to pull a herd of rabbits from my collective hats and wriggle out of this. Wishful thinking, if there ever was.

Okay, *Spiritual Regeneration* didn't work on this venom, but I *did* have something worth a shot: the last dose of anti-toxin in my inventory. One mental tap and it would be in my hand... and be useless, of course, because I couldn't *move* my hand.

Almost funny. Ha ha.

I had been in a similar situation, though, hadn't I?

I'd used the same anti-toxin to neutralize the alcohol in Master Cho. Only that time, he hadn't drunk the potion directly; I'd used my *Small Pass* ability to teleport it into his gourd of brandy, and *then* he'd drunk it.

Could I do the same for myself? Not teleport it into a gourd, but inside *me*?

My insides, however, didn't have a well-defined empty space to trans-locate the potion into. Hmm. There had been a warning about that...

I tabbed to my SKILLS & ABILITIES.

Small Pass (Physical): **Teleport an object less than five pounds.**
Range: 10 yards.
Cost: 10 mana.
NOTE: Attempts to move one object inside another *significantly* decreases the chance of success and may have dire effects on the object *and* spellcaster.

A significantly decreased chance? Happy to take the long odds as long as they weren't zero.

Dire effects on object and spellcaster? Well, what was the worst that could happen? Die in excruciating pain... as opposed to just dying? Worth it.

I snagged a golden spatial ley line and felt the familiar *clicking* into my astral grasp.

I tapped the potion in my inventory.

I'd learned my lesson from trying this last time, though. I couldn't afford to wait and burn through reflexive mana, so I flashed into normal space-time—a quarter of a second ticked by, the game interface responded, and I felt the vial of anti-toxin in hand—then I phased back to the aether.

I looped the gold filament inside the bottle and made another loop that I pushed into my center. It gave me an odd rollercoaster free-fall sensation.

I then performed the *Small Pass*.

The potion fought back. It was like trying to push an ocean wave headed one way—in another direction. It just slipped around and through my fingers.

I tried again, and with excruciating care and focus, tightened the loop, and forced the contents ever so slowly into my body.

My inner plumbing distorted and distended and stretched as the teleported matter tried to fit into the same space as... well, me. The titanic over-pressure felt as if I were swallowing a pound of nails and they poked my tender insides, punctured organs, and ruptured cells.

And this was in the super slowed time of the aether. When I phased back, it would be a lot worse.

My health bar, however, hadn't fallen one pip.

Good?

No. The damage was coming. The game interface just hadn't caught up yet.

The question was: how many points of health? Let's see... internal rupturing of several vital organs? Maybe nitrogen narcosis bubbles in my blood? Safe bet to say all of them.

I spammed *Spiritual Regeneration* four times. That would get me from zero to full health, *if* I didn't explode first.

And again, my health bar didn't change.

I checked my reflexive mana: 36/120. Yikes. That had taken longer than I'd realized.

I phased back—

into a new dimension of pain.

My viscera ruptured, blood squirted through my insides, third-degree burns made my intestines sizzle, and bubbling acid excoriated every blood vessel.

The damage just as fast regenerated.

Tissues and organs knit together, burns cooled, but it was just as painful going the reverse way. I also wasn't sure everything got *exactly* back into the right spot.

I would have screamed but was still paralyzed.

That was actually a lucky break. If Yamina had heard, she'd have taken care of me before I could fully recover.

I watched my health bar drop to zero—I blacked out for... an instant?—then was back. The indicator climbed to half, ticked down to 57/180... and halted.

I quietly took in a shaky breath. The fresh air felt so good.

I tried to wiggle my fingers. They moved. A bit. Good.

I felt prickly sensation spread up my arms and legs.

Yamina froze by the door. "One *more* surprise?" she said without turning. "Why Hektor, you *do* know how to show a lady a good time."

"Yeah?" I panted. "Well. Worst. Kiss. Ever."

CHAPTER 38

It was dark in the room, but even without Azramath's headband, I could see well enough from the moonlight filtering in through the window.

I used another two *Spiritual Regenerations*. Pins and needles crawled over the rest of my body. The last of the paralysis burning off, I hoped.

I stretched my back, flexed my calves.

And that was all the time I had because Yamina leapt at me.

The blur of a spinning kick scythed toward my face.

I slapped it, sidestepped—but her speed and power nearly knocked me over.

I willed *Shé liàn* to my hand.

The ninja chain, however, remained wrapped about my waist.

So I *had* seen correctly; Yamina did have some sort of anti-magic field about her.

I made a fist. The demon bone knuckles bulged under my skin. No magic, no explosive power, but I'd take the added weight to my right-handed strikes.

Yamina slashed with daggers and wove ribbons of steel in the air.

I rolled over the table where we'd toasted one another. Glasses bounced and skittered over the floor. I managed to grab the wine bottle—broke its neck.

Considering how she'd gotten the scar on her throat, this improvised weapon might give her pause.

Two steel streaks cut the air before me.

I spun a quarter turn.

Daggers whispered past my Adam's apple and the back of my head—

and *thunked* into oak wall planks. To their hilts.

I hadn't even seen her throw those.

I dove under the table—came up on the other side. *Keep a barrier, if you could, between you and your opponent.*

She appeared on the opposite side and used a hammer strike to reduce the furniture to kindling.

I brandished my pathetic broken bottle her way... as if it might do anything other than amuse her at this point.

The bottle's contents slopped onto the floor and filled the air with the fragrant bouquet of thirty-year-old Cabernet Ferico Alberto.

Ah—inspiration! I give thanks for your blessings, wisdom, and teachings, oh drunken monkey god, *Dà Xiào Hóu!*

I leapt back to the door, opened my inventory, and in a flash had Elmac's flask of Red Dragon Whiskey in hand—and guzzled. All of it.

My *Drunken Resistance* helped me down the entire thing without gagging. Liquid plasma scorched my lacerated organs, but also warmed my blood, lubricated muscles, loosened tendons, and soothed my jagged nerves... and wavering wobbling dots then lined up in my fuzzy thinking.

Hello, drunken boxing.

I laughed and dropped the emptied flask. This might be fun.

Yamina stared confused... then a glimmer of understanding crossed her features.

Oh, look! In my still-open inventory, that *1762 Gautier Cognac de Âme* compliments of Miss Lillian Carat-Bringer. I'd been saving that for Elmac, but he wouldn't deny a comrade a drink or three in a pinch. A fine friend, that Elmac.

I tapped it. The bottle appeared in my hand.

Yamina was on me in a blink.

Double cobra-style strikes sliced at my eyes and throat, smashing through the door where I'd stood a split second earlier.

Fortunately, I had tripped and made a teetering-tottering recovery, the so-called *Broken Stairs* defense.

I toasted my good fortune, upended the cognac, and drank.

Yamina grabbed for it.

I twisted out of her way.

She missed.

With one hand.

Her *other* hand, though, landed an open palm to my gut.

I reeled back, arms pinwheeling.

It didn't hurt as much as I thought it might. Actually, I wasn't feeling much of *anything*. Hurray!

That strike did regrettably expel the contents of my mouth and throat—shot them out my nose, blasting alcohol straight through the blood-brain barrier of my sinuses.

This was the dreaded *Salamander Breath* technique (not recommended for novices). Usually one used it in conjunction with a firebrand to produce a gout of flame. Without fire... the results were slightly less than spectacular.

I wiped lines of snot from my face.

Two new daggers were in Yamina's hands. She did a double feint and stabbed.

I danced, back and forth, this way, that—a cross between a dwarven jig and a Cossack's kicking-jumping display of manly acrobatics.

She missed.

Missed again.

And screamed in outrage as she missed once more.

I then zigged when I should have not.

She sliced me open to the rib bones.

It felt like a swarm of wasps stung along that unzipped line of flesh, but the pain quickly faded.

Had her blade been poisoned? I hadn't seen any pop-up alert. On the other hand, I could have missed it in my *moderately* sloshed state. Well, I was numb—so either way, I really didn't care.

My swimming vision then centered upon Yamina perfectly poised in Tiger Stance.

And I remembered... *she* had burned down the Bloody Rooster, chased me and my friends across two worlds, murdered who knew how many along the way... and Oswald. My poor friend, Oswald.

Oh yes, Miss Yamina Sussara, we did indeed have accounts to settle this evening.

I stopped messing around and fought.

Together we stepped and counter stepped, blocked and riposted, kicked and threw knees at vital locations—locked in a precise, lethal tango.

Her blades flicked and probed my defenses; I slapped aside the razor edges, grabbed her wrists; she twisted away.

I couldn't tell where my body ended and hers began, that's how evenly were we matched, so intertwined were our limbs. It was a seduction of sorts, the courting of two praying mantises (perhaps not the best metaphor here, considering how that ended for the male).

Then... with what I thought were my unpredictable staggering steps, she began to stagger as well.

Mirroring my motions.

Improvising her own.

Was she learning *my* moves? Some ability of her Soul Stealer class?

Foul I say! Where was the referee?

I had to up my game, so I focused (or whatever the equivalent was in my current condition) on my new Drunken Boxing skill—calling upon the part that let me *"sporadically use a random basic special technique."*

I then employed the slopping *Toast to Heaven* and she blocked the uppercut with the *Two Broken Gates* defense.

I tried the *Stinging Scorpion Slap;* she nullified it with *Fumbling Fists*.

I started *Chair with Two Legs*; she planted her foot between mine and stopped it with the *No Personal Space* technique.

What a cheater!

I grabbed her sleeve, twisted, and locked her arm in place.

Yamina's eyes narrowed.

With the flexibility of a contortionist, standing less than a handspan from me, her foot lashed straight up—and caught me under the chin.

As I flew off my feet, Yamina transformed her leg's upward momentum into a full cartwheel and a backflip *out of her dress*. This could only be because of the bodysuit of tesseract spider silk she wore and its slippery properties—but *still* a magnificently executed maneuver.

She landed in the corner of the room, a feat worthy of a master ninja with high levels of *Wire Work*.

I, meanwhile, executed a not-as-perfect backflip, and landed with the grace of a bag of cement, breaking the nightstand and bed.

I caught a glimpse as she pulled up the hood and mask of her bodysuit... and faded from view.

I got up (sort of), braced against the wall, and slid to the corner opposite where she'd been.

What's worse than being in a locked room with an eighth-level assassin trying to kill you? Why, being in a locked room with an *invisible* eighth-level assassin trying to kill you.

Another problem: I wasn't plastered anymore, merely well-oiled. Those drunken special techniques burned through alcohol like mana. No wonder Cho had been guzzling non-stop. He'd had to.

I sighed. Well, as far as first dates went, I'd had worse.

"Goo kish," I slurred, trying to say "good kick."

No reply. Too bad. It would have been nice to get a fix on her location.

Was I outside her anti-magic radius, though?

Shé liàn? You there?

The weapon awoke and pinged confusion along our mental connection.

Good. When *Shé liàn* went inert, I'd know she was close.

And while I *could* use my magic, I *should*.

I had 20/90 Spiritual Mana, enough for either two *Spiritual Regenerations* or one *Perfect Motion* buff—but not both. So healing or an increased defense? Uh... too complicated for my half-sober neurons to figure that one out.

Mage of the Line tricks? Not enough reflexive mana for anything effective.

Ebon Hands of Soul Death? Phht! Don't be silly.

That left the demon bone knuckles. Which were useless. To use its blasting power I'd have to be close to her... *inside* her anti-magic field, where it wouldn't work.

No. That wasn't quite right.

I could use them right here—pull the same trick I'd used on the Grand Imperial Champion of Disorder and blast the floor out from under her feet.

There was no way, though, I'd catch Yamina off guard with that maneuver.

She must be similarly sizing me up, planning some surefire final attack (with the added advantage of having her full wits). I'd probably never see it coming. Probably wouldn't even feel it.

Although in this particular situation I had one option I hadn't when I'd faced the Chaos Knight and Master Cho.

So simple, so stupid, only the simple and stupid would think of it.

I could run like hell.

I triggered the explosive power of my demon bone knuckles, turned, and punched the wall.

The side of the building blasted into a cloud of splinters, pulverized plaster, and smoke.

I dove through the still-smoldering six-foot hole, glided from the second story to the ground, and sprinted—*back* toward the inn.

Let's see how Yamina fared against me; an irate dwarven wizard (and secret high-level warrior); *and* a druid-thief, shape-shifting trickster, ex-high school teacher. The three of us together punched well above our weight class.

The guards that had been posted outside the inn's front door were missing. Likely dead.

I tried to push through the door—bounced off.

It was barred from the inside.

I kicked it.

The door flew off its hinges; the four-inch oak brace snapped neatly in half.

I stepped inside.

And froze.

...As did the two dozen Empyrean Guild merchants I'd seen at dinner (no doubt the reinforcements Yamina had called for).

They'd draped their pewter-colored cloaks over their shoulders... the better to move as they wielded swords, barbed chains, weighted nets, and aimed hand crossbows—at two people wedged back-to-back in the far corner.

Elmac and Morgana.

CHAPTER 39

Elmac gripped his flaming battle axe; Morgana held curved daggers. Both had cuts and bruises. Elmac's front teeth were missing. Morgana was out of breath.

Four warriors with iron-shod spears had them pinned in the corner so Elmac couldn't close and swipe out knees or lop off legs.

My friends locked eyes with one another as if they were saying goodbye.

Not if I could help it.

I fired off my *Perfect Motion* buff and leapt, flipped, and my foot touched upon the shoulder of the nearest combatant—and *I ran*.

This maneuver could only be attempted with *Wire Work* (and I suspected only while half drunk). I took five miraculous steps upon shoulders and heads before the stunned warriors could react.

I dodged upthrust blades and ankle grabs—tripped, kicked, stumbled forward, pushed off a snarling orc face—then bounded onto the brawny shoulders of a stout hobgoblin holding a trident and net. I launched off him with all my strength and sent him sprawling onto his butt—and I crashed into the corner, sliding to the floor behind Elmac and Morgana.

The hacking and stabbing resumed.

I got up, pulled Morgana back, and took her place on the front line.

Elmac and I shuffled forward a step to give her room to cast spells.

I dodged one—two—three spear thrusts.

These warriors weren't bad; if not for my *Wobbling Floor* drunken boxing defense, at least two of those would have landed.

Morgana chanted, "*Nastrotium et excoquam ad sanandum.*"

She set one hand on Elmac's shoulder, the other on mine.

Warmth poured into my body.

I noticed the pips of my health bar were a sickly green. So Yamina *had* poisoned me when she'd sliced me open. Thanks to Morgana's healing spell, however, the color returned to its normal arterial red and filled to 109/180.

Unfortunately along with the removal of one poison, so went the other flowing through my veins. I was sober. No more drunken boxing.

Elmac's wounds sealed and new teeth pushed back to fill his homicidal grimace.

Shé liàn leapt into my waiting hands.

I tangled a spear thrust with the chain and cast the bladed end of my weapon at the holder of the spear.

It caught his exposed wrist and coiled about the appendage. The chain links sharpened to razors and cut. Deep.

I tore it free—and left my assailant screaming and clutching a stump.

I dodged another thrust, slapped aside a crossbow bolt that would have impaled my right eye, grabbed a spear and yanked. That caught the snarling werewolf warrior holding it unaware and he lost the weapon to me.

I tossed the spear into the air with a bit of spin—and while I had my hands free, I slashed in twain another bolt aimed at Morgana.

My appropriated spear fell, flipped so the sharp end was in the preferred orientation; that is, *not* pointed at me. I chucked it back to its original owner—who caught it with his sternum.

"Sent you messages—" Morgana yelled and made an arcane gesture in the air.

"Didn't get them," I said between blocks and stabs.

Elmac parried a spear shoved at his face, held out a hand, and shouted, "*Scintillam!*"

At the same time, a warrior with a morning star charged up to replace the guy without a hand.

An arc of electricity flashed from Elmac's palm and crackled across the charging warrior's mail shirt. The guy dropped, convulsing.

"It be a good time for a brilliant idea," Elmac suggested.

I shook my head. The only idea I had was: *fight for our lives*.

"You gents buy me a few ticks," Morgana whispered in a trance. "Doing an *invocare animus*."

I didn't get what she meant, but if the lady asked, I'd do my best to oblige.

Seven paces away, I spotted a group of gray-cloaks as they waved their hands and chanted.

We weren't the only ones with spell power.

I nodded in that direction. "Trouble."

Elmac stood on his tiptoes. "Make an opening for me, lad."

I glanced into the aether.

Glowing crimson lines thrummed about the spell casting assassins. I didn't think they were summoning a friendly campfire to roast hot dogs. One well-placed pillar of flame and Morgana could be cooked.

And there was *another* group behind those wizards.

Coalescing about *them* were threads of shuddering ultraviolet filled with ghostly screams. Bad news: Necromancy.

I phased back.

"And another group behind those," I told Elmac.

He grunted.

I swung my ninja chain and then whipped it about my forearm to increase the momentum. Showy... but that's what I wanted.

The spearmen facing me closed into a defensive hedge.

I commanded *Shé liàn* to snake about their tight formation of spears.

She wrapped around the shafts, and with a *shiiiinck*, constricted, pulling them together.

I sidestepped the cumulative pointy ends, grabbed the spears, and lunged forward.

I caught all three off guard.

They staggered, dug in—shoved back, and rammed me into the corner.

I almost squished Morgana.

But Elmac had his opening.

He rushed forward through the legs of the spearmen, taking swipes, back and forth, severed two Achilles tendons—then he was in the thick of the fire casters, hacking with wild abandon... laughing.

Their chanted words, "*Ignis nent conburite*" became, "Wha?? My foot! There he is!"

The floor was tangled with cloaks and limbs, arcs of sparking steel, and sprays of blood.

"One more tick," Morgana murmured. Her hands traced swirls of vivid green magic in the air.

I pushed back against the spearmen. It was easier now as two were on their knees, and I had a wall to brace against.

The wounded ones slipped in their own blood. The one standing dropped his spear, drew a scimitar, and closed.

I commanded *Shé liàn* to return to my hand, hooked the hilt of his sword, disarmed him, then planted a machine-gun sequence of punches into his chest that crushed his ribcage.

"Next row," I shouted to Elmac. "Clerics!"

Elmac was there, chopping and slashing, and doing a fine job of distracting the priests with a few precision amputations and mortal wounds to their soft centers.

They weren't going down without a fight, however. They drew serpentine daggers and strangulation cords and moved to surround Elmac... as did others with spears and nets.

I lost track of him as a tide of melee closed about me.

More of the Syndicate's people rushed into the room—gray cloaks fluttered in confusing waves, blades flashed, nets were thrown, and crossbow bolts *zinged* through the air in all directions. Skulking shadow shapes flickered in and out of view, stealthy maneuverings undoubtedly to line up a backstab.

Farther back where Elmac had been, I caught a glimpse of spell energies twisting along the floor and solidifying into ink-black tentacles.

This was going to get messy. Fast.

Morgana once more had her daggers in hand, and between parries, feints, and thrusts—she glanced about, obviously searching for Elmac.

She found me instead and nodded to the far side of the inn.

Morgana then slashed the throat of the elf in front of her... as her body thinned and she transformed into a twenty-foot-long cobra that went slithering among unsuspecting enemies.

One, two, three assassins cried out, went rigid, and fell frothing.

Nice. Two could play with poison.

I'd understood her unspoken message. *Over there—fast!*

But how? Easy to do when you were a—

Whoa!

Shé liàn jumped out of my hand and tripped a swordsman. He'd been about to cleave me with an overhand chop. He toppled to the floor.

A kick to the back of his head kept him down permanently.

A half-troll leapt at me.

I punched him in the nose. The demon bone knuckles did a superb job of smashing his face into the back of his skull.

I lashed out with a scissors kick and caught a pair of hobbits about to clothesline me with a net.

A blade slit open my side—a strike from behind that just missed my kidney.

WARNING!!!
You have been poisoned with:
Sanguine Hellebore (*Helleborus album sanguis*).
Causes necrotizing blisters for additional damage.
Has a small, but cumulative, chance to auto-catalyze
and rapidly consume the entire body.

I grabbed the offending blade—slippery in my chi-armored fists of steel—yanked it forward, and caught the backstabber's arm. I snapped the limb and planted an elbow in his face for good measure.

Burning boils bubbled along the wound.

I dropped to one knee and threw my limp assailant at two crossbowmen aiming at me.

They shot—pincushioning their comrade.

I then caught a glimpse of Elmac.

His opponents had him surrounded, spears and shields holding him at bay, nets at the ready to tangle him.

I crashed into their ranks, took a spear in the shoulder, wrapped my ninja chain about one warrior's neck and dragged him down with me.

This gave Elmac enough wiggle room to rush their line and start hacking anew.

I hoped whatever spell Morgana had cast was a doozy, something like *Slay All Enemies* or *Teleport Party to Safe Location*.

I fought on, but my strikes were weaker. I was slowing down.

They had numbers on us... and Yamina had yet to join the fray.

My thoughts turned to Sir Pendric Ragnivald and how my friend would have given anything to be in this mess. What better way for a half-Valkyrie knight to die but fighting alongside his comrades, slaying evil before a valiant end?

It was what poets wrote heroic odes about.

I grinned.

How could I do any less?

I sucked it up and fought. I'd do Pendric proud, and if need be, go down swinging and kicking and biting to the very end.

The floor and walls rumbled.

Dust rained from the ceiling.

Earthquake? A spell unleashed by the Silent Syndicate?

No, the assassins looked just as confused as I was.

Plaster cracked, and outside the inn a continuous drumroll of thunder grew.

Windows shattered and the eastern wall crashed inward—demolished by charging buffalo.

The beasts' eyes were dark with rage as they trampled and gored astonished assassins.

The few who had the wits to fight back faced a room full of three-ton creatures who slashed their ten-foot horns to and fro, kicked and crushed and caved in heads and launched bodies across the room.

These were *our* buffalo, and it looked like they'd brought a few friends, rounding out the tiny herd to an even dozen.

Morgana, you beautiful brilliant druid. That spell you cast was a distress call.

The assassins, however, regrouped and tangled one buffalo's legs with nets.

The beast went down—crushing a few of her attackers. They stabbed her over and over. She screamed and kicked until she moved no more.

All thoughts of my pathetic self-absorbed noble death vanished.

This was *my* herd they were messing with!

I plucked up a spear, looked about, and found Auntie Brown. I leapt onto her back.

She tensed as if to buck, but I whispered, "It's me, Hektor."

Auntie Brown snorted. It sounded to me like an expression of relief that she'd found her little hairless calf alive.

The mob rushed us.

I had 12/120 reflexive mana left, so I had to make this quick.

I shifted into the aether.

As fast as I could, I tabbed to my SKILLS & ABILITIES interface, and selected:

Ride (Animal): Master animals as a means of conveyance by friendship, cajoling, or domination. Total expertise is the combination of this skill, and your REFLEX and EGO stats. At

higher skill levels, riding in difficult terrain and combat are permitted, as well as mastering exotic animals. Only at the highest levels of skill are flying mounts ridable.

I spammed the UP ARROW to spend my non-combat skill points.

How many... I wasn't sure.

I just went until my reflexive mana got to 2/120 and—

snapped back to the thick of combat.

Windows popped around me. The first one read:

Congratulations!
You may now effectively use tier-1 mounts *in combat*.

and then

Congratulations!
You have mastered tier-2 mounts:
warhorses and similar equine quadrupeds.

and more of the same until I got

Congratulations!
You have mastered tier-4 mounts:
light reptile types and heavy mammals such as rhinoceros.

—and finally,

Congratulations!

You may now effectively use tier-4 mounts *in combat*.

Bingo!

I clutched the spear tighter and tapped the butt end to Auntie Brown's flank

"Flatten 'em," I yelled to her. "Flatten them all!"

CHAPTER 40

Auntie Brown gruffed and stomped, seeming to understand, if not my actual words, then at least my bloodthirsty tone.

The herd shook their heads and snorted agreements—then kicked and slashed their horns back-and-forth with new abandon.

The assassins backed off.

As if hearing a silent starting gun, the buffalo collectively scrabbled and sprang into motion: more than thirty tons of lean muscle that tore up the floorboards.

The acceleration whiplashed my head back.

Wait. Where was Morgana? And Elmac? They'd be stomped into paste.

None of the beasts would be looking out for one snake or dwarf among the wreckage and piles of broken furniture and bodies. Even with my improved *Ride* expertise, I wouldn't be able to stop their combat run now. We were committed.

The eleven buffalo plowed a swath through our enemies. Nothing stopped them.

I spotted Elmac smack in our path.

His eyes widened as death raced toward him. He stepped left, right—unsure *which* way, or if there *was* a way, to escape.

I squeezed Auntie Brown's flank with one knee, urging her a bit to the left.

She obliged.

I tossed my spear at an assassin near Elmac.

The assassin dodged—directly in front of the buffalo on my flank—and fell under her hooves with a brief succession of snaps and pops.

I clutched Auntie Brown's ruff with one hand, leaned over, and reached for Elmac.

He jumped.

I caught him and swung him up.

He landed behind me (albeit facing backward).

"Morgana be outside," he yelled.

Had she known the scale of carnage she'd unleash when she'd cast her druidical call-for-help spell?

I looked up—just in time to see the western wall dead ahead.

The buffalo didn't blink or miss a step as they plunged straight at it.

I ducked.

Correction: they didn't plunge *at* the wall. They went *through* it.

They might as well have passed through layers of cardboard—timbers and boards and stucco blasted out—and we were then galloping into the night.

I signaled my mount to halt, but unlike the stampede's sudden start, hitting the brakes took a good hundred and fifty feet.

The herd followed my lead, though, slowed to a trot, and we wheeled about.

The Waypoint Inn creaked, listed to one side... then the other.

Two of the building's walls had been smashed to smithereens.

I spotted some of the Silent Syndicate assassins inside. A few helped their wounded comrades; others made a hasty exit into the grasslands; but most of them stood, dazed... not quite grasping what had just hit them.

Apparently, even die-hard professional killers hadn't trained to fight a herd of charging buffalo *inside* a bar.

The second and third floors of the inn were partially collapsed and shifted as I watched. I swore I spotted a figure there, a silhouette of ebon black against the ordinary dark of the night.

Yamina? Or my imagination?

I caught a glimpse of two indigo eyes that narrowed at me with smoldering hatred.

I returned the sentiment... but she was already gone.

I heard rustling in the tall grass.

I tensed, readied *Shé liàn*, and nudged Elmac.

Auntie Brown took note of the sound, ears flicking forward, but she merely sighed.

The rustling ceased. The shadows in the grass compressed... stood... and Morgana vaulted onto the back of Mother next to me.

"Brilliant," she said, straightening the collar of her leather armor. She patted Mother's neck and murmured reassuring noises to the beast. "Glad you made it out all right."

Elmac cleared his throat. "What 'bout the other folk, the staff, cooks and such?"

"I looked," she whispered. "The Syndicate, what they did to all of them..." Morgana couldn't finish and shook her head.

"Maybe not all of them," I said.

Yamina had told me she'd kept Sadie and a few others alive. I wasn't sure I believed that, though.

Professional assassins. They were nothing more than butchers.

The adrenaline raging in my blood cooled and distilled to a refined desire to show these murderers exactly what killing was all about.

I nudged Auntie Brown to head back toward the inn.

She tossed her head—maybe thinking the same thing I was: When you wounded a pack of hyenas, you finished the job so they couldn't come back.

Auntie started to trot.

The other buffalo snorted and pawed the earth, and then followed her, building speed, heads and horns lowered.

Elmac gripped me with one hand, and in the other appeared his battle axe. "Aye, let's be sending these devils to hell."

Morgana atop Mother galloped alongside me.

I leaned forward.

Auntie Brown went faster still, tearing up yards of sod with each stride, leading the herd in a wide arc... as we lined up and charged toward the inn's intact northern wall.

Elmac screamed directly into my ear: "*Waaaaghhh!*"

I flattened.

Held tight.

And we hit.

The wall didn't stand a chance.

Board and beam shattered into toothpicks—exploding inwards, sending wood shrapnel into what was left of the Silent Syndicate assassins.

I heard but a split-second of screaming—but that was then drowned out by the crashing of hooves and rolling destruction that washed over the villains.

To their credit, some of the assassins *did* react in time and raised weapons, but it made no difference as the First Grassland Cavalry slammed into them.

It took less than two jackhammer heartbeats to crash and churn through the wreckage and then we faced the last untouched wall.

Once more came the gunshot retort of demolished wood, the grinding rumble of hearthstones and chimney—and we were running once more in the cool night air.

The buffalo bellowed with bloodlust and rage and grief for their fallen comrade.

I managed to slow Auntie Brown, and then turned to behold our violent handiwork.

The Wayfar Waypoint Inn stood still, its four corners intact... but the remainder of the first floor had been leveled. Not a single window of the three stories was unbroken.

The staircase and half the second floor collapsed.

The whole building then swayed

...and in slow motion twisted.

Cries arose inside from the few assassins who had miraculously survived.

The inn collapsed and crushed them all.

Huh. That was more satisfying than I thought it'd be. Apparently revenge, regardless of how it played out in the movies, was highly underrated.

It was, however, far from enough to balance the evil done this evening.

I was sure Yamina had gotten away. The smartest rats were the first to leave a sinking ship.

And who else was to blame for this? Who had led these killers to the Waypoint Inn in the first place?

Yours truly.

I'd been so cavalier to think I could lose the pack of assassins tracking us and just ignore the sanction on my head as if it were *only* a game quest.

We trotted back, wary for any enemy who dared to try their luck again.

Nothing.

Where the kitchen had been, lumber smoldered, caught fire and flames tinged the night with the color of blood.

Déjà vu all over again. How many bars were we going to destroy before this was over?

"This was my fault," I whispered to no one in particular.

Morgana maneuvered Mother next to Auntie Brown. "That may very well be, Hektor," she said, "but don't you *dare* wallow. Not until we've snuffed every one of the blighters." Her tone was cutting. "We've got to keep our heads on *one thing*, the extermination of the bloody Syndicate."

I blinked at her words.

Then the magnitude of what she was saying sunk in. We weren't up against just this bunch of assassins and Yamina. If they weren't before, the entire Silent Syndicate would be coming for us now.

The only way to survive would be to wipe them *all* out, the whole Assassins Guild... before they could do the same to us.

CHAPTER 41

I wanted to say something appropriately heroic, like *"We shouldn't be afraid, Morgana, they should,"* but a blast of French horns and shower of sparks left me speechless.

Congratulations!
ACHIEVEMENT UNLOCKED!
"KILLER OF KILLERS"
You have killed more than ten assassins
in under ten seconds.

NOTE: New Party HIGH SCORE for this achievement. This badge, therefore, will be displayed in PURE GOLD.

Hovering near the alert window was the achievement icon. In it, a silhouetted figure crouched in the classic sneaky "backstab" pose. Behind this assassin, stood a guy with a huge smile—

stabbing the backstabber. As promised, the whole thing was gold surrounded by a halo of spattered blood.

Cute. In a universal-symbol-for-carnage sort of way.

I thought, however, the buffalo deserved this more than we did.

"Be putting this in my title," Elmac declared. "Let 'em see what they be dealing with." He swiped the icon onto his placard.

I was going to tell Elmac it might not be smart to advertise that we were "Killers of Killers," but then again, why not? It wasn't like we could hide our placards. Any player in the Silent Syndicate would see our names and know who we were anyway.

So, I displayed the achievement as well. Felt a little better for it, too.

Come at us villains, blaggards, and scoundrels. We Heroes of Thera *fear you not.*

Pendric would have been able to say those words with the proper bravado. I hoped wherever he was, he was safe.

Morgana nodded at the now half-burning wreckage of the inn. "Oi, let's take a quick look-see while we can. I might have missed someone in there." She shifted into her wolf form and started sniffing.

We each took a different section, moving timbers, listening, searching as quickly and efficiently as we could as the fire spread. Alas, the only civilians I discovered were murdered, their features frozen in rictus grins from poison. As for the assassins I found, all were dead from combat wounds or cyanide capsules.

I'd seen carnage like this after suicide bombings, artillery barrages hitting villages... I'd never gotten used to it.

I turned and looked across the compound. I saw no movement. The front gates had been battered down, likely from our buffalo charging to the rescue.

Wait. There was one more place there might be survivors: the tower by the front gate.

I sprinted there and broke down the iron-bound door.

Inside were many guards. All dead.

To my relief, though, seven people, including Sadie, were there, bound and gagged, terrified out of their wits, but alive.

Elmac caught up to me and together we freed them, explained as best we could that the inn had been attacked and destroyed... and they were the only survivors.

They staggered outside and stood stunned at the sight of the burning inn. Some wept, others held each other, most collapsed onto the grass.

Sadie sat and cried and hugged herself. I wanted to go and try and comfort her but didn't dare. Just being near me could put her life in danger.

The best way to help her... was to leave.

Elmac whispered, "We need to be getting back to look for any... you know, before the whole thing be one big bonfire."

I nodded and we returned to the scene of the crime.

Morgana was searching *inside* the fire and dragged out more corpses. She must have cast *Endure Flames* on herself because she had not a single singed hair.

"No mana to cast another spell," she told us, out of breath. "Going back in before this one wears off. You two take a look." She gestured at the smoking bodies.

I focused on one.

Priest of the Phonoi, LEVEL 3

Not the first or second-level flunkies we'd fought in High Hill. And just who were these death-spirt Phonoi they worshipped? I had some homework to do.

In his loot window were a few coins, weapons, vials of poison, and such. No notes or other obvious clues.

Morgana pulled four more bodies from the wreckage.

She sat next to us, exhausted. "Guess we know if we can ignore a quest and hope it goes away," she remarked.

I bristled. I wasn't sure if she'd meant that as a dig at me, but it sure did feel like it. "Would we have done anything different if we'd known?"

She exhaled. "Suppose not, mate. Sorry."

"Aye," Elmac said. "If you could game the Game that way, 'twould be cheating. And that be wrong."

One had to admire Elmac's simplistic moral take on this.

But everyone *was* cheating.

The Game Master had admitted he did. Master Cho suspected the gods cheated too. Heck, I suppose even players took advantage wherever and whenever possible.

Cheating was, in my opinion, a bad long-term strategy. It caught up to you. I'd found it better to win by skill and *honest* cunning in the games I'd played rather than to fake it.

In a universe of cheaters, though... was cheating *back* the only way to win?

I wasn't sure.

And where exactly did *my* actions fall? Not cheating per se. Something between "creative innovation" and a *slight* bending of the rules?

"We might as well take that assassin quest now," I said. "Must have already completed at least one part."

"Right." Morgana then stared at nothing as she accessed her interface. "Might get a pointer on what to do next too."

The original quest we had never accepted nor declined appeared before me, still waiting for a response.

ALERT!
Morgana Nox would like to share
the following quest with you:

"*SOMETHING ROTTEN IN THE DUCHY OF SENDON*"
The Silent Syndicate has sanctioned innocent people for elimination. Investigate and get out of High Hill before you too are *murdered*.
Rewards: Tier-IV (or better) treasure, political secrets.
Suggested Level: You and anyone else you can convince to help.

Accept? YES / NO

I accepted and this appeared:

> **QUEST ALERT!**
> **"SOMETHING ROTTEN IN THE DUCHY OF SENDON"— PART I**
> *COMPLETED*
> **You have escaped the Silent Syndicate assassins of High Hill (for now).**
> **Reward(s): Tier-IV treasure (or better).**

Odd. I hadn't seen any "Tier-IV or better treasure." Or did our shopping spree at Lordren's count? That didn't seem fair, having to buy our own rewards.

Before I could ponder this further, two new alerts popped:

> **QUEST UNLOCKED:**
> **"SOMETHING ROTTEN IN THE DUCHY OF SENDON"—PART II**
> **(*"MURDER MOST FOUL"*)**
> **Within the next 24 hours, solve 1-3 of these mysteries:**
> **WHO has been targeted for murder,**
> **WHY they have been targeted, and**
> **WHO ordered the hit.**
> **Reward(s): Bonus Experience, extra time to avoid the Silent Syndicate.**

and

QUEST ALERT!
"SOMETHING ROTTEN IN THE DUCHY OF SENDON" — PART II
("*MURDER MOST FOUL*")
COMPLETED

ONE mystery solved: You have decoded the Syndicate's hit list and discovered WHO has been targeted for murder. Reward(s): Bonus Experience.

"*One* 'o three clues?" Elmac tugged on his beard. "Suppose there still be a bit 'o brain sweat to work up."

"Apparently," I murmured, "we missed a lot."

"More skullduggery or not," Morgana said and chewed her lower lip, "I'll take the ruddy experience points. Just a smidgen away from leveling my thief class."

Ah yes, leveling. No fireworks, though, heralded me making another level. I'd been 80% of the way there before this evening.

I checked. Just a few points to go.

I better start thinking now how I was going to advance.

I still had to deal with the same problem I'd had before, however. Adding new skills and abilities meant more memories shoved into my brain... memories that were becoming as vivid and familiar as my real ones... while my Hector-of-Earth memories were fading, at times seeming made up.

Would it be such a bad thing to leave my old existence behind? No.

Yes—I had to keep the things that made me, me. Didn't I? Shouldn't I?

I had better put serious thought into this and come up with some guidelines. *If* that is, there *was* anything I could do about it. All players might be fated to eventually become their fictional characters.

Before I could indulge in more of this psychological analysis, this appeared:

QUEST UNLOCKED:
"SOMETHING ROTTEN IN THE
DUCHY OF SENDON"—PART III
(*"THE NIGHT OF BLOOD"*)
Avoid Syndicate assassins and/or survive
the evening in the Grasslands.
Optional: Solve these remaining mysteries:
WHO ordered the murders, and
WHY it was ordered.
Reward: Bonus Experience.

"Would have rather taken the 'or survive the evening in the Grasslands' option," Elmac muttered.

I stared at the pile of blazing timbers. No argument there.

Morgana scratched her head. "You still think your Lords of the Abyss are behind this?"

"They're not *my* Lords of the Abyss," I told her. "But yes, they're the only group I can think of that'd want all the people on that list erased."

Elmac dug in his pocket and got his pipe. "That be a wee bit odd, since the Lords cannot be getting involved directly with the Game, or be giving orders to their players." He turned to Morgana. "You ever be hearing such orders from on high?"

"I was told my choices are mine to make in the Game," Morgana replied. "Past the initial meet and greet, you're never supposed to hear from your clan's sponsors again. Except of course us druid and cleric types." One corner of her mouth curled into a smirk. "The gods give inspirations and visions, and we do rituals and pray, but all Game references are filtered out. We can't ask. They can't tell."

Morgana glanced at the remaining unsearched corpses. She knelt next to them and tapped open loot windows. "And speaking of inspirations..." From thin air, she plucked out a scroll tube.

She gave it a few prods with her dental picks. "No traps" —she tossed it to me— "that I can find."

The case was ivory with scrimshawed whaling ships and plesiosaurs. I popped the cap off. Inside was a parchment that I took out and unrolled.

"That be another clue?" Elmac asked and inched closer.

"No such luck," I told him. "Just our friend the Red Knight."

I held out the now-familiar WANTED poster.

Elmac took a glance at it. "That fellow gets around."

Morgana snatched the parchment from me. "This is the same bloke Harlix and his gang was looking for, yeah? Blimey, he's worth 50,000 quins dead now. Why would an assassin have *this*? Elmac, you've seen this before? Where?"

"In Low District," he told her. "And the Bloody Rooster. In fact, went up all over High Hill the day before" —he gestured around— "this all be starting."

Morgana looked like she had something more to say, but remained silent as she stared at the sketch of the Red Knight.

I would have pressed her, but what Elmac had said a moment ago still rattled around in my skull. The gods didn't, couldn't, give their players direct orders or information.

So that meant the person who'd put the hit on us had done so on their own initiative. They'd have to hate us enough to warrant such an exorbitant revenge. Furthermore, if the reason for that hatred was as I'd guess—stopping the demonic invasion of High Hill—then they'd also have to know who had been responsible for that.

Only one person fit that description.

William Savage.

Okay, technically he knew it was only me, Elmac, Pendric, Morgana, and Colonel Delacroix. It wasn't too much of a stretch, though, to think he'd have a contact in Duke Opinicus's organization to get the rest of the details.

Plus, he had extra motivation to want us dead—to get back into the good graces of his demon prince masters.

I opened my Message Center.

There were no new correspondences from my brother.

I tapped out a quick message to him:

>_Hektor Saint-Savage: We DO need to talk. RIGHT NOW.

ALERT:

William Savage has BLOCKED all messages from Hektor Saint-Savage.

He was blocking *me* now?

"So guys…" Morgana whispered, "about those Red Knights?"

"Hang on a sec," I told her. "And it's not '*knights.*' There's just the one."

"Think you're wrong about that, Hektor."

I turned to her.

Morgana faced the broken gates. In a smooth silent motion she unsheathed her daggers.

A fog had rolled in and wavered at the edges of the compound. By the flickering firelight, the mist looked as if it were boiling.

Figures emerged from the mist—odd creatures with two heads and many limbs.

No, there were knights on horseback… and on bison… one rode a bear?… and another on a gigantic gray wolf. There were twenty of them, with lances pointed in a most unfriendly direction.

They wore angular slabs of plate mail that looked so heavy I doubted they could have stood without assistance. …And I counted five among them whose armor was *red* (almost cherry red, actually, in the ruddy light of the fire).

With a jolt of recognition, I then spotted three familiar non-knights in their ranks: the stylish swashbuckler, Cassie

Longstrider riding the monster wolf; on foot was the slate blue, nail-crowned Harlix Hadri; and wearing his curved-horn helmet and sitting astride that huge obsidian-black bear, was Grimhalt.

Cassie waved to me and smiled.

I got chills as I recalled the text from our latest quest: "*Avoid Syndicate assassins and/or survive the evening in the Grasslands.*"

This had to be the "AND" option.

We were on foot against mounted opponents, and I'd seen just how effectively cavalry could destroy infantry.

We needed to get on our...

I cast about. Our bison were nowhere to be seen.

"Do we fight or run?" Morgana asked, trying to look everywhere at once.

Elmac and I stepped to her side.

"Run," I whispered. "And when they chase us down—we fight."

CHAPTER 42

We sprinted for the nearest corner of the compound. If we could get there, the walls would protect our flanks and keep the knights from running us down. With a little luck, we'd be able to boost over the wall and escape.

A good tactic, *if* Elmac had been a sprinter. He wasn't even an especially good runner, though, and after six strides Morgana and I were far ahead of him.

So we ran back to Elmac, stood our ground... and the knights easily overtook and surrounded us.

Harlix walked up and stood with the knights. His hands were open and spread apart in a gesture of peace. "Please lower your weapons and come with us," he said.

I might have actually heard the guy out if Grimhalt hadn't piped up.

"Or fight if you want," Grimhalt said, his words dripping sarcasm. "You'll still be coming, just more... tenderized." He smacked his mace into his gauntleted hand in case we missed the subtlety of his argument.

Charming fellow. I wished Elmac hadn't talked us out of murdering him when we'd had the chance.

Morgana had heard enough. With a snarl, she shifted to her panther form.

Or at least *started* the transformation.

Cassie Longstrider held up a heart-shaped charm. It shed a pink light that forced Morgana's metamorphosis to shift gears... and instead of becoming a fearsome two-hundred-pound cat, she shrank to a mouse.

Mouse Morgana's growl turned into a squeak of surprised outrage and she scampered for the grass.

Cassie whistled.

A white eagle plummeted from the dark and pounced upon the mouse. The raptor returned to Cassie, who took the proffered prize (thankfully alive and in one piece) and popped Morgana into a tiny cage.

Elmac cried havoc and charged.

Harlix flexed his hands.

From nowhere came a rattling and clattering of metal. Chains materialized about my dwarven companion, wrapped tight, and seemed to anesthetize the poor guy because he toppled over... snoring.

Neat spell, that.

And what did *I* do? I'd like to say that I fought to the very end and pounded a dozen knights flat.

Not *quite* how I played it.

Clearly, the neutral ground of the Waypoint Inn that prevented PvP combat was no longer in effect... probably because there *was* no more Waypoint Inn. It also looked as if Harlix had a way around the game rule that prevented players more than five levels apart from fighting one another—as he was twelfth level, and Elmac merely third.

I was outgunned, outnumbered, and with Harlix on the scene, I suspected outsmarted as well. I was low on health and mana and exhausted from the previous battle. If I fought, I'd lose.

So... I surrendered.

I don't know how the Marines work on your Earth, but on mine, they never surrender (the actions of the Pacific 4th Marine Regiment in WWII being debatable).

I was not, however, giving up my weapons (since *I* was a weapon), and I had every intention of resisting the enemy (by staying conscious long enough to find a way to rescue Morgana and Elmac).

At least, that's how I justified it. I nonetheless burned with shame and heard the howls of every Marine who had given their lives rather than do what I just had.

I was hooded, bound, and tossed over the hindquarters of a horse.

For hours I bounced along and then got dropped onto the ground like a sack of stones.

A few additional restraints were then added to my person. Chains hobbled my feet. Behind my back, manacles secured my wrists. As an extra special measure, an iron bar between those manacles spread my arms apart, wide enough to be just this side of medieval torture.

I was flattered they thought me so dangerous.

Some jerk yanked the hood off my head.

My vision was blurry from the long stretch of sensory deprivation. It was dark and wherever I was smelled like old concrete, water, dust. A cave?

The half-melted features of Grimhalt resolved as my eyes adjusted.

"Oh, so sorry," he said. "Was that too rough?"

"I'm sure you can't help it," I croaked, "having been spanked every night by your mother before bed. Childhood issues are the worst, aren't they?"

His left eye twitched. Must have hit close to the mark.

Grimhalt hauled back his gauntleted fist.

Cassie caught Grimhalt's bicep, checking his motion.

Too bad. Apparently, Grimhalt had forgotten he'd sworn an oath to his Wild Hunt gods never to harm a Hero of Thera. I would have liked to have seen what they would have done to him.

"Don't," Cassie told him and glanced over her shoulder. "Not until *you know who* has his say."

Grimhalt grumbled, dropped his arm, and skulked off like a moody teenager.

"You seem like a reasonable fellow, Saint-Savage," Cassie said. "Play nice with Grimhalt. He has issues socializing with other children his age."

"Let me loose," I whispered, "and I can show you how reasonable I can be."

Cassie took off her ostrich-plumed pirate hat and stared into my eyes. "Tempting, but no. You're too smart and charming for your own good. Mine too." She then held a flask of water to my mouth.

I drank the whole thing. "Thanks."

She patted my cheek. "Make life easier and behave, okay?" She strode off.

I watched her go and wondered what her story was. She didn't seem as maniacal as Grimhalt, as frightening as Harlix, or as evil as Yamina. Then again, it could be an act. She could be part of the Silent Syndicate for all I knew.

But they'd taken us alive, which ran counter to the whole assassination thing.

An escort of six knights marched me through the dark (at a snail's pace due to my restraints).

There was light ahead—magically glowing rocks set every ten paces. I could see now that we were in a limestone passage with dripping stalactites.

Could we be in the hills west of the Grasslands? Or had we backtracked through the gate to Thera? No telling.

We emerged into a grand cavern the size of a stadium. There was a strong breeze and cooking fires spiced the air with alder wood smoke and percolating coffee.

More knights camped here. They stopped talking and mending their armor and stared at me.

I counted fifty, then stopped.

Okay, not assassins—not with all the heavy plate armor lying about being meticulously repaired and oiled. I also didn't get that "bandit" vibe from them. Too neat and organized. No, this had the feel of a *military* camp.

I noticed that one in ten of them had the red-brown colored armor that had been sketched on the WANTED poster.

If they were doing what I thought they were doing... it was ingenious.

The poster had shown only *the* Red Knight and mentioned his "band of cutthroats." The Red Knight could have been anyone when they wore that armor. He could pop up in several places at once and be impossible to kill, for if one Red Knight fell in battle, another would simply step up to claim the title.

My knight escorts pushed me ahead.

Before me upon a dais of rippled limestone was a throne. It was stout enough for an ogre to sit upon and made entirely of skulls, most from large animals, but yes, there were a few artfully placed humanoid skulls that stared down at me.

Cassie hauled Elmac's snoring carcass next to me.

She unlocked a padlock securing his magical chains. They fell away and faded to nothing.

Elmac started, coughed, and sat bolt upright. "Did we win?"

He reached for a battle axe that wasn't there—with an arm he no longer had. His prosthetic had been removed on our journey.

"Oh, suppose not then," he whispered.

"It was close," I lied.

Cassie then set a tiny cage on the ground and opened it.

Lightning quick—a mouse darted out.

Cassie pinned her tail. "Not so fast, sister rat," she said. "Run off and we'll be obliged to kill your friends. It's not a good time to test anyone's patience."

The mouse ceased struggling and gave a tiny exhale of defeat.

Cassie took out the charm she'd used before and waved it over the mouse.

Morgana became Morgana once more.

"Bloody *rudest* thing ever." Morgana stabbed a glare filled with daggers at Cassie.

Cassie merely tilted her head in reply and then proceeded to relieve Morgana of twenty assorted weapons and various lock picks and tools secreted on her person. Cassie allowed Morgana to keep her leather armor on, though, so there was a *modicum* of professional courtesy.

The knights in the cavern gathered about us. With lit torches and unwavering, unfriendly gazes, it set the scene for a nice cozy lynching.

"So," I asked Cassie, "how do you execute prisoners here? Drowning in wine, I hope?"

She gave a soft laugh. "I always thought the Duke of Clarence got off easy for his treachery. But for *you*, I'll be happy to put in a good word."

I was surprised she got the reference. Cassie must come from a version of Earth similar enough to mine to have had a War of the Roses, and a King Edward who executed his brother by such an imaginative means.

Harlix made his way through the crowd.

The knights parted for him. Of course, they did, he was a powerful high-level wizard (not to mention his eerie skin and creepy crown of nails). Who *wouldn't* get out of his way? The way they looked at him, though, it was more grudging tolerance than the respect I'd have expected if he led this bunch.

Harlix halted next to the throne of bones. He smoothed his star-filled robe, and said, "My apologies for the extreme methods used to bring you here."

"Easy enough to make amends," Morgana said. "Let us go and all's forgiven."

He gave her a weak smile. "I will, but I require the answers to a few simple questions first."

Yeah, I trusted this guy as much as Yamina, Mr. Null, or my brother, William "the Bloody" Savage.

"If you be asking questions," Elmac said, fidgeting, "be asking them and get it over with. I'm hungry and hungover and want my arm back."

Grimhalt shoved his way to Harlix's side and pointed at Elmac. "That's the one I told you about," he whispered.

Harlix nodded, then to Elmac said, "Mr. Argenté-Wolfram, you are from Thera, yes?"

Elmac frowned, seeming to take a second to recognize his new name. "Aye, I be the nephew to Count Augustus Wolfram of the Grand House 'o Seven Hammers. Eighty-fifth in line to the Peacock Throne. 'O course I be from ruddy Thera."

Elmac had mentioned his new incarnation was half mountain dwarf and half mithril dwarf, and that he'd been "quite the scandal." Bastard royalty?

Gasps of astonishment rippled among the knights.

Curious reaction. But maybe it was the response any knight would give after realizing they'd just manhandled a true royal. Wasn't there a code or something? Until now, I'd thought the "knight" title I'd been calling these jokers was a euphemism, part of their act. Maybe not.

"And you are new to our…" Harlix waved about his head, a gesture anyone but a player would dismiss as swatting at a gnat. "…*endeavor*?"

"As you can plainly see," Elmac replied.

Harlix could literally see Elmac's name, level, and clan affiliation on his placard. So why ask?

"And you three were in High Hill a few days ago?" Harlix went on.

"Sure," I said. "So were you. We saw you outside the Rooster as it burned to the ground. What's your point?"

"A moment more of your indulgence please." He closed his eyes and held out his fingertips as if touching, feeling, searching for something I couldn't see. The nails embedded about his forehead sank deeper into his skull.

"He's got some blinking truth magic, I bet," Morgana murmured to me. "Careful with your words, mate."

Okay, in that light, this made more sense. He might be testing our responses to questions he knew the answers to, to get a baseline.

Well, question-and-answer sessions could work both ways.

"You three were looking for *the* Red Knight before," I asked and waved to the assembled warriors. "So you found—what? His band of not-so-merry outlaws?"

"Not outlaws, you idiot," Grimhalt spat. "Anyone with eyes can see they're the finest legion of—"

Harlix turned to him and black flames crackled in his eyes.

If that was an illusion, it was a good one. I felt the heat from those tiny fires five paces away.

Grimhalt shut his trap and took a step back.

A legion, huh? That fit with the whole military look and feel of the camp, and their reaction to Elmac's royal status. I was now convinced they were true "Sirs" and "Dames." But that begged the question: why were real knights roaming the countryside as wanted bandits?

Harlix regained his composure and nodded at me and Morgana. "You two came to Thera a month ago, yes?"

Morgana and I exchanged a look. It was an odd question to ask, even if he was getting a baseline for his lie-detecting magic.

"Shy a few days of that," Morgana told him, "but yeah."

"About a week here," I said.

"That is... correct." Harlix nodded and his eyes stared far away as if in deep thought or accessing his interface. His focus then returned to me. "Just one more question."

Something was very off here.

I mean, it was *all* off, but suddenly alarm bells jangled in my head—those annoying intuitive warnings that had saved my hide more than once. I had the feeling if I answered Harlix's question, I might be doing so with my final words.

"I'm not telling you anything more," I said. "Unless whoever is *really* in charge here asks me themselves. Unless they're too *craven* to face three prisoners."

All the gathered knights shifted as I tossed this verbal gauntlet at their feet.

"Please," Harlix said, his smile back, but now through gritted teeth. "Are you truly Hektor Saint-Savage of the Domicile of the Sleeping Dragon? The Hero of Thera who saved High Hill from demonic invasion?"

I pretended to ponder this as if it were a problem in quantum mechanics, my brow furrowed, lips pursed, then I told him, "Go fish."

Wait. How many people knew I'd been in the Game for one week?

Damn few.

All the partially connected and misaligned dots then clicked into a neat row in my continually concussed mind.

It was so obvious.

What if the leader of these Red Knights was my brother, Bill?

An anti-paladin of his stature could rally and command a bunch of black-listed knights. And it sounded just megalomaniac enough to suit his sense of self-grandeur.

As a sixteenth-level character, he'd have the clout and resources in the underworld to arrange a hit with the Silent Syndicate. He was also cunning enough to gain leverage or otherwise pay off these three players.

Furthermore, the poster had said the Red Knight was wanted for "murder, theft, and crimes too numerous and heinous to fully list herein." That sounded like Bill.

True, he'd been thrown into Duke Opinicus's dungeon, but what player *hadn't* escaped from at least one prison in their favorite fantasy game?

And the last piece of this puzzle: why was Harlix going way out of his way to know with absolute certainty I was who I claimed to be? Because Bill would have insisted on a positive ID before they sent for him. I imagined he was on *very* thin ice with the Abyssal Lords after his previous failure. He couldn't afford another mistake.

How I wished I *was* truly Hektor Saint-Savage, gypsy elf. *His* brothers might be dead, but at least they had lived their lives with honor.

My one real brother?

Bill was pure trash.

A wrenching squeal of un-oiled metal bought my attention back to the cavern. The earsplitting noise came from the assembled knights.

The knights all turned toward the sound.

A figure rose from their ranks. He must have been sitting there all this time, because standing he was a head taller than any here and I wouldn't have missed him.

His armor was covered with bloody handprints and spatters. The plates comprising this armor were ludicrously thick, made from different suits welded together, overlapping three layers in some spots.

The guy had to be close to seven feet tall, and weigh... what? That armor alone had to tip the scales at two hundred pounds. Bill had bulked out since I'd last seen him. Some enlarging magic? Or perhaps the armor had simply been built to appear bigger than its normal-sized occupant.

My heart beat faster. I might have made a *slight* tactical error in calling out my serial-killer brother.

The Red Knight clanked toward us.

The full helmet covering his head had bolts securing it at the neck, slanted slits for eyes, and the breath holes made the shape of a fanged mouth.

Harlix stepped away from the throne as the Red Knight sat there.

The Red Knight pointed at me, and in a booming voice that echoed out from that helmet, he demanded, "ANSWER..."

I gave it an eight out of ten for its theatrically evil effect.

And yeah, it worked.

I'd only rarely won when I played against Bill. And the last time I'd defeated him, well, let's face it, that'd been a fluke. I'd been lucky to come out of that battle with my soul and sanity intact.

Funny how my big concerns before the Bloody Rooster had burned down were if I could ditch the Silent Syndicate by simply turning down a quest, and which of my STATs to increase.

I inwardly cringed at the guesses, decisions, and many mistakes I'd made since then.

But I took heart as well, because if my bad choices affected the Game and thereby the whole of Creation... that meant an idiot was messing with the gods, demon princes, and super-entities of power in the multiverse.

I found the irony somehow comforting.

Trying to understand the true nature of the universe and one's role and purpose in it, though, was all the sound of one hand clapping as far as I was concerned. I could only play this out like I would have in any game—with a bit of honor, grace, and style.

Even if it was the last thing I did.

Especially if it was the last thing I did.

But first thing first: the chains and manacles had to go.

I phased into the aether, wrapped ley lines of elemental cold in tight coils about my wrists and ankles—then returned.

The iron restraints rimed with ice and groaned from thermal stress.

I gave them a good jolt.

They shattered.

Knights drew swords and maces and crossbows; magic sparked about Harlix.

The Red Knight, however, remained calm and held up his hand to forestall my murder.

I stared into the slits where his eyes had to be staring back at me.

"I *am* Hektor Saint-Savage, adept of the Domicile of the Sleeping Dragon, and if my modesty is pressed, I suppose the Hero of Thera you seek."

The Red Knight leaned back and sighed.

Have I disappointed you, Bill? Sorry, my brother, but I will never bend my knee before the likes of you.

The Red Knight unscrewed the bolts securing his helmet.

Hang on a second. If this was Bill, then where was his player placard?

The knight removed his helmet with a flourish and shook out a mane of golden hair. He swept it from his face with a graceful gesture.

He beamed at us.

His sparkling smile, framed by blonde and exquisitely waxed mustaches, was unmistakable.

Elmac, Morgana, and I stared dumbfounded, mouths agape... and together we cried, "*Pendric*?!"

The end.

To be continued in the next *Hero of Thera* novel: *Fallen Phoenix Rising*.

Thanks for reading *A Thousand Drunken Monkeys*.
If you enjoyed it, please take a moment to leave a review on Amazon USA, Amazon UK, Amazon CANADA, or Goodreads.
If you *loved* it, please tell a friend. Your good word of mouth is the *best* thanks any author could ask for.
See you again in Thera *soon*.

Until then go forth and play *your* game—live, die, fight, love, and conquer all! May your dice roll critical hits, may your aim be pixel perfect, and may you always level up.

Made in the USA
San Bernardino, CA
24 February 2019